FALLEN LIGHT

"There are elves and sorcerers in *Fallen Light* but the real magic, the thing that keeps you turning the page, is the underlying humanity of the characters."

—Herb Terns, author of *Iron Sharpens Iron*

"...Once you get into the heart of the book, you soon realize you are completely lost in the story and do not want to leave or have it end."

—Missi's Book Reviews

Fallen Light

FALLEN LIGHT

BOOK ONE OF THE
FALLEN LIGHT SAGA

WRITTEN BY

Z. R. Coffin

For Emily,
Thank you for always pushing me to pursue my dream,
and for reading the book almost as many times as I have.
Forever yours.

CONTENTS

Acknowledgements

There are a few people in particular who have listened to me rant and ramble about the story, and have read almost every single iteration of the story that I've written. I want to thank Tyler, Andy, and Alistair for providing me invaluable feedback on the book, and for entertaining my conversations for hours on end. You saw a much rougher version of this story, and have helped me mold it into what it is today. I couldn't have done it without you. I also want to thank the friends and family who agreed to read the story and share their thoughts with me.

I'd like to thank the wonderful people at the Troy Book Makers for helping me through the self-publishing process. It has been an absolute pleasure working with you.

Finally, I want to thank my family and my wife for their unwavering support.

Eutrox
Neu Ocean
Okrein
Rutna
Tu
Orde
Dwarven Empire
Ytrant
Vyuticon
Alric
Klantra
Grey Manor
Behaldur
Sakreed
7 Kingdoms
Luthrine
Efona
Cahn Oc

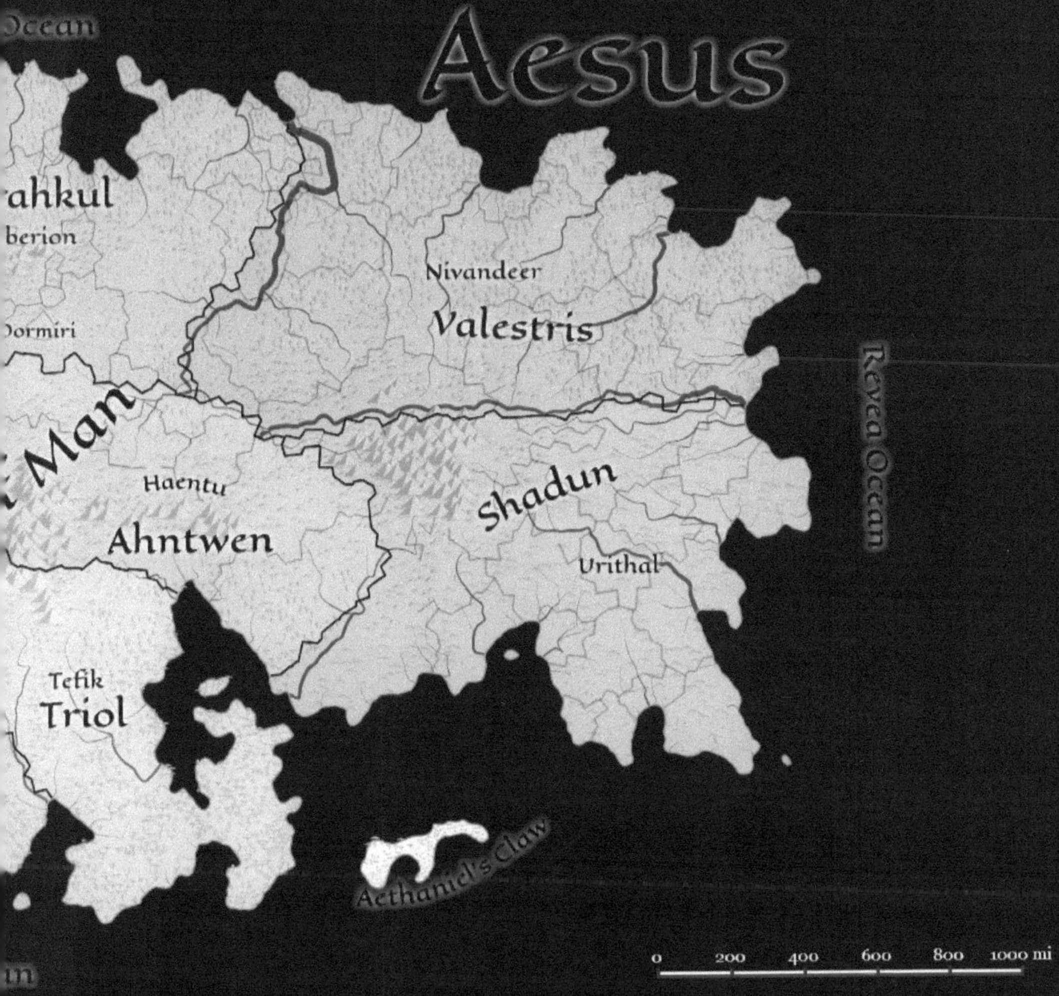

Ocean
Aesus
ahkul
berion
Nivandeer
Dormiri
Valestris
Man
Haentu
Shadun
Ahntwen
Urithal
Revea Ocean
Tefik
Triol
Aethaniel's Claw
0   200   400   600   800   1000 mi

PART 1

SHADOWS OF THE PAST

CHAPTER ONE

THERE WAS SOMETHING IN THE AIR THAT DAY.

Something that made their mother, a woman Isaac was used to seeing so carefree—so happy—now nervously eye every shadow she passed; her once warm expression reduced to a twisted amalgamation of unease and worry.

It was evening, just barely dark, when he heard an explosion come from their front door, followed by the sound of debris clattering onto the dirt floor. Their mother jolted up from her bed, almost tripping over Isaac who lay on the floor next to her. She had moved them into her room, out of fear of them being too far away.

She peeked out of her bedroom door before quickly slamming it shut.

"Devlin, take your brother and run!" she said urgently, her unkempt, curly black hair whipping around her face as she turned toward them. Her wild brown eyes were devoid of any warmth they once held.

That night, she looked like a cornered animal.

Feral.

Afraid.

Devlin threw one of his toys through the bedroom window, shattering the glass, as their mother dashed toward the front door. He grabbed Isaac under the arms and gently tossed him through the window, being careful to avoid the shards of glass. Devlin wasn't far behind, grabbing Isaac's trembling hand as soon as he was outside.

"C'mon," Devlin said, trying to sound comforting.

The sound of metal clashing rang out like a harpy's screech from their home; the sharp smell of fresh blood stung the back of Isaac's throat.

What's happening? He tried to look behind them. Their mother should have come out by now.

"We have to go!" Devlin urged, pulling hard on Isaac's hand as a gut-wrenching scream filled the air.

That scream chilled him and left him feeling numb, as if winter itself had found a new home in his veins.

It came from their mom. He knew it did.

He wanted to stop.

He *needed* to stop.

He needed to turn around and see if she was okay.

But Devlin told him they couldn't. They had to keep going.

They ran until they couldn't see the house anymore, and the echoes of their mother's screams were a distant macabre song.

Isaac stumbled forward as Devlin came to an abrupt stop, frozen in place as if caught in an invisible web. Devlin cursed as he struggled to release his grip on Isaac's hand.

"Run," Devlin whispered, his hand shaking as he slowly inched it open enough to allow Isaac to slip free.

Isaac hesitated. He didn't want to leave his brother. What was he supposed to do without him?

"Go!" Devlin cried. "Go! I'll find you!"

Isaac hesitated again before turning and running through the woods, his pulse pounding deafeningly in his ears.

Where was he supposed to go?

What was he supposed to do?

Dad, where are you...?

Isaac's foot caught on a gnarled tree root, sending him tumbling face-first into the dirt. A long shadow loomed over him as he pushed himself up. He looked up at the figure, its appearance shrouded in the blackness of its hood. It held a single, bloodied knife loosely in one hand.

Isaac shut his eyes tight and braced himself.

Dad!

* * * * *

Isaac shot up, gasping for air as his heart threatened to punch through his chest. His sweat-soaked body felt cold in the cool morning breeze.

Another nightmare...

"Isaac, are you alright?" Alison asked, her hand resting comfortingly on his shoulder. Isaac squinted, his eyes slowly adjusting to the sunlight streaming into the cave they had rested in for the night. He met her mesmerizing yellow eyes and smiled. Alison was as beautiful as the sunrise, with her wavy, waist-long dirty-blond hair, and the rich, light caramel skin of an Eutroxian. Just looking at her was enough to wash the dread he felt away.

"Yeah, I'm fine, Alison. Sorry if I woke you." Isaac ran his hands through his messy, long black hair, doing his best to push it out of his eyes.

She shook her head. "Don't worry about it. I'm more concerned that these dreams seem to be happening more often. Can you remember this one?"

He shook his head as the fuzzy images in his mind faded into darkness. He was never able to remember his dreams. Trying to was like trying to catch the wind: it always slipped through his fingers.

But, given the panic and trepidation that he felt when he woke up, perhaps it was for the best that he *didn't* remember anything.

He stretched and looked around, letting his eyes continue to adjust to the light.

The remnants of a fire crackled close to him. The once roaring fire from the night before had long since gone out, leaving nothing but the smoldering embers and the rich smell of smoke behind. Alison's bedroll was beside his; her belongings, unlike Isaac's, were neatly put away and organized, while Isaac's gear was tossed haphazardly against the wall closest to him.

Sigmund didn't throw my things outside this time? How nice of him. Speaking of which...

"Where's Sigmund?" Isaac asked, noticing that Sigmund's gear was gone. Sigmund liked to get up early, often even before the sun. By the looks of it, the sun had just barely crested the horizon. Meaning Sigmund had probably been up for at least an hour.

No sooner had Isaac spoken than Sigmund's tall form blocked the entrance of the cave. For someone pushing into his mid-sixties, he was still a formidable sight. He wore his usual steel armor, which was decorated with lazy, golden swirls that spiraled against the silvery canvas. His claymore, which was almost the length of his body, was in its usual place strapped across his back. He had the fair skin of a Northerner, with white hair and a long beard that gave his face a grandfatherly appearance that didn't seem to match the rest of him.

"About time you two woke up," Sigmund grumbled. His thick Northern accent made it sound like he was growling every time he spoke.

It fit Sigmund perfectly.

"Good morning!" Isaac greeted cheerfully. "What have you been up to so early?"

Sigmund crossed his arms impatiently. "Scouting ahead and waiting for you."

"I'm flattered you waited for me this time," Isaac said, putting a hand on his chest. "Last time, you left me at that inn in Beignknost."

Sigmund shrugged. "At least I left you somewhere with a roof."

He had him there.

"So, how close are we to the Temple?" Alison interjected.

Sigmund reached into the small pack tied around his belt and pulled out a large, tattered map. He unfurled it and held up the map of Eutrox for them to see.

His finger cut through the Seven Kingdoms of Man before resting on the border between Klantra and Sakreed. He pointed at a jagged drawing of his design of the small mountain where they were currently holed up.

"We're here." Sigmund tapped the map, then slid slightly to the right, his finger falling on the crude drawing of small trees. "Our reports indicate our target is somewhere in the center of this forest. It's another six hours walk at least. Pack your things and get ready. I don't want to waste any more daylight."

Isaac quickly threw his belongings into his pack. Despite how untidy he generally was, it didn't take Isaac very long to get ready. Unlike Alison, who wore leather armor, adorned herself with a ridiculous number of knives, and carried a short sword, he didn't wear any armor. Just his usual black shirt and pants.

He *hated* wearing something so restricting and uncomfortable, much to Alison and Sigmund's chagrin. Sigmund especially *constantly* pestered him about wearing something proper, but the old man's words fell on deaf ears. Isaac just wasn't a fan. Besides, if the leader of their family, Jack, never wore any armor, then why should he? If Isaac ever hoped to catch up to him and become as powerful a Mage as he was, he'd have to take some risks.

Unlike Jack, however, Isaac chose to carry two short swords, one on each side. Though he preferred to use magic—again, like Jack—it was never a bad idea to have an additional method of protection.

Finally, the last piece of his attire, and the one he took the most pride in, was the Grey family cloak. He swung it around himself and affixed the latch at his neck, the brass clip clicking satisfactorily into place. The Grey symbol depicting a large, proud tree in full bloom with the rising sun on the right and two descending crescent moons on the left was embroidered above his heart. He smiled as he ran his fingers over the stitching, feeling the grooves in the fabric.

"Are you both ready now?" Sigmund grumbled impatiently.

"Always," Isaac responded.

Alison nodded curtly.

"Then let's go. Mind your footing," Sigmund muttered as he shuffled down the narrow path they had made the day prior. Isaac followed after him, each careful step sending rocks scattering down the steep decline and into the forest below. Their pace was slow and agonizing but, after a few minutes, they found themselves at the foot of the mountain and facing an endless expanse of trees.

The forest was almost impossibly dense. The thick underbrush was a tangled mess of roots and branches twisting around each other, reaching for the sky as they fought for sunlight. The trees were monstrously tall, almost half as tall as the mountain behind them. Their massive canopies blocked out much of the light, making the forest floor dark and sun-speckled.

Sigmund scratched at his beard contemplatively. "We'll have to cut through this to forge a path…" Sigmund began, pushing through some of the brush with his hands. "You two, clear the way."

My time to shine. Isaac rubbed his hands eagerly together.

As an Arcanist, Isaac was blessed—or cursed, depending on who you asked—with the rare ability to manipulate mana, the same primordial energy that, according to Jack, the Creator Himself used when He shaped the world. Being able to tap into that same source of power made Isaac giddy with excitement. He was always looking for an excuse to use magic. A fondness of Jack's that had definitely rubbed off on him.

Alison stepped in front of him and swept her hand forward, the air around her picking up and whipping at the trees. With another flick of her wrist, the wind cut through the underbrush, chopping apart branches and opening a small path for them to walk down.

Isaac's jaw dropped. She'd gotten stronger since the last time he'd seen her use magic. She was really coming into her own as an Air Arcanist.

"Hey! No fair! At least give me a chance."

"If I waited for you, we'd be standing there 'til sundown," Alison winked. She stepped through the underbrush with her hand extended, the air beating back the tangled mess of a forest.

Isaac grumbled his annoyance and caught up with her.

"At least let me help you. Don't want to exhaust yourself unnecessarily," Isaac offered.

"I'll be fine," she replied confidently. Alison was strong; Isaac could not deny that. She had kicked his ass more times than he cared to remember growing up. His ribs ached just thinking about it.

"Well, you're getting my help anyway," Isaac flashed her a cheeky grin.

"How generous of you," Alison teased.

Isaac extended his hand out, mimicking Alison's motion. He felt a cold, familiar tingle run down his spine as he reached out with his mind to the mana in the air around him. He projected his will into it, commanding the wind to become a sharp, focused blade. The wind around them grew stronger as it buffeted the plants in front of them, cutting smaller trees and plants in half. Isaac winced, noting the damage he was causing, and reigned in his intensity to match Alison's. Together, they trudged forward, beating back the forest as they went.

* * * * *

What felt like hours had passed, and it didn't seem like they had made any real progress. Isaac looked worriedly over at Alison, the strength of her wind had died a bit, and she was sweating heavily.

"Why don't we take a break?" Isaac offered, letting his hand fall to his side. He couldn't help but feel a bit frustrated. They had been cutting back branches and trees for hours, and it felt like they weren't anywhere closer to their target. What's more, the underbrush seemed to get thicker as they went, as if the forest itself was trying to keep them out.

"If I can't get through this forest, how the hell can I expect to be invited to the Trials this year?" Alison panted, leaning against a tree, her face twisted in irritation. "How long have we been at it?"

Sigmund gazed up at what little sky could be seen through the forest canopy.

"Roughly six hours, I'd say."

"So, we're close then," Alison said hopefully.

Sigmund nodded.

"Alright, let's keep going." Alison took in another deep breath and a shaky step forward. Sigmund grabbed her shoulder, stopping her.

"You're no good to anyone exhausted; rest for a few minutes until your stamina comes back to you."

"But—" She began to protest, but stopped when Sigmund shot her an unquestioning look.

"Fine," she said, plopping down on the ground and sprawling out.

"I don't think I need to stress how important this mission is for you two. Jack has entrusted us with retrieving an artifact. A task not given out lightly. If we were to fail and allow just *one* of the Ancient One's artifacts to fall into the wrong hands, it could bring catastrophic consequences to the people of Eutrox. It is our mission as Greys to prevent that from happening. We have no clue what traps or dangers we may face once inside, and I need you both on high alert. Understood?"

Isaac and Alison nodded. The gravity of this mission certainly wasn't lost on Isaac. This is what they had been trained to do, after all. Years of preparation had all culminated in this mission. For Jack to trust them with this now meant he was confident in their ability to succeed. He wouldn't let Jack down.

They'd do the Grey family proud.

"You lot rested enough?" Sigmund asked, breaking the long silence.

Isaac and Alison nodded.

"Forward march then."

Alison and Isaac returned to their work of clearing a path through the forest. It didn't take long for them to make out a break in the tree line, and a colossal red structure came into view. Before them stood a grand pyramid-shaped temple with a flat top that seemed to go upwards into the air forever. If the trees hadn't been so tall, they might have seen it from the mountain.

"Woah…" Isaac said, entering the clearing and shielding his eyes with a hand as he looked toward the top.

Alison whistled. "So, this is it."

Sigmund pushed past them, positioning himself at the head of the group. "Stay close to me. Don't go wandering, and don't touch anything. We're only here for the artifact. Understood?"

Isaac and Alison locked eyes briefly before nodding.

"Let's go."

CHAPTER TWO

Isaac, Alison, and Sigmund carefully climbed the ancient, crumbling steps of the Temple. Each footfall turned a piece of the stairs into powder, the small rocky dust tumbling down the side carelessly in the wind.

A large gate-like opening stood before them at the top. Its gaping maw allowed nothing but shadows to exist, swallowing up sunlight and leaving nothing but blackness a few feet from the threshold.

"No door?" Isaac asked. "Must not want this thing to be protected too badly."

"The Ancient One's probably figured no one would be stupid enough to go after it," Alison offered.

Sigmund nodded his agreement. "No door doesn't mean no security."

Isaac held his hand up before him as thoughts of light flooded his mind. Three small balls of white light dazzled into existence as the mana responded to his will. The balls separated, each one taking a place beside them.

"Good thinking," Alison complimented.

Sigmund nodded his approval, a rare sight that made Isaac grin.

"Stop smiling like that, your face will get stuck," Sigmund grumbled and started forward into the Temple with Alison and a slightly deflated Isaac following closely behind.

The balls of light scattered shadows across the walls, illuminating old paintings of long-forgotten tales of heroism and tragedy. Isaac pinched his nose as a strong scent suddenly assaulted him, making his eyes water.

"What's wrong?" Alison asked.

"You don't *smell* that? It smells like... rotten eggs and old meat!"

Alison chuckled. "Well, yeah, did you expect the couple-thousand-year-old Temple to smell like fresh bread?"

"No, but I didn't expect it to smell like Sigmund after a long day."

Sigmund shot him a glare.

"Stay focused," Sigmund grumbled.

* * * * *

Hours passed as they navigated through the winding corridors of the Temple. With no branching paths, they were forced forward until they finally came upon a completely empty room. Like the rest of the Temple so far, there were no doors, no hallways, nothing. Even the paintings were gone.

"Did we miss something?" Alison peered around the room, perplexed.

"I don't like this…" Sigmund's voice trailed off as he readied himself, his hand against the hilt of his sword.

Suddenly, the ground beneath the three of them opened, swallowing them before they had a chance to react.

The wind buffeted Isaac as he fell, his cloak flapping violently around him. He projected his will onto the air, commanding it to slow his plummet into the abyss. His fall slowed to a gentle descent just as he dropped into another barren room, with a single, long hallway with a torch shining brightly at the end of it.

This looks promising.

He glanced around himself and cursed. Alison and Sigmund were no longer with him. He was about to call out their names but stopped. He wasn't sure what creatures could be lurking in the Temple, and calling out to them could bring unwanted attention to him.

He was on his own, for now, until he could find a way to reunite with them. He just hoped that they wouldn't find themselves in any serious danger.

Well… no way to go but forward.

Trying to be as stealthy as possible, Isaac dimmed his light, masking his approach as he crept to the next room. Isaac raised an eyebrow as he peered in. This room, again, was barren, except for the floor, which was covered in dirt and red sand. Across the room was another hallway and another torch.

"What the hell...?" Isaac said aloud as he stepped into the room. He knew it wasn't smart to walk haphazardly across... whatever this was. He picked at the stone doorway, taking a sizable chunk off, and threw it into the dirt as hard as he could.

The stone hit the ground hard, sending some of the sand flying upwards and lodging the rock into the dirt.

He eyed it carefully for a few moments, yet still nothing happened.

Isaac took tentative steps across the dirt; the rock hadn't alleviated many of his concerns. Something still felt off. But he had no choice but to move forward.

As he approached the center of the room, his feet began to sink slowly into the dirt. Isaac yanked his feet away reflexively, but the ground chased after him, grabbing at his legs and forcing him back down. He lost his balance and caught himself against the floor. The sand sucked his hands down and clamped around his forearms with an iron grip. The more he struggled, the harder it pulled him down.

Isaac reached out with his will to the dirt, commanding it to release him.

The sand ignored him.

Isaac took a deep breath as the sand rose over his head.

He tried manipulating the air around him to shove the dirt away from him.

Again, the quicksand didn't move. It seemed to ignore all magic directed towards it.

Isaac thrashed inside the sandy prison, feeling himself sink lower beneath the surface.

Am I really going to die here? Isaac clawed helplessly as panic flooded into him. His mind raced, desperately trying to formulate some plan to get out, but each strategy was quickly abandoned as the quicksand continued to ignore his commands.

Abjuration. The thought cut through the noise of his mind, instantly silencing the chattering panic that gripped him.

There was no guarantee that it would work, and it would tax his stamina greatly, but he didn't have much choice.

Isaac reached out to the mana around him, visualizing a thin barrier forming over his body like a bubble. Isaac felt the familiar tingle of the warding surrounding him in a protective cocoon, the quicksand slowly falling away from him.

He slowly clawed his way upward, his pulse thundering in his skull from the combination of crawling and holding up the warding. Isaac felt his chest spasm as it yearned to draw in air.

Almost there...

Isaac broke through the dirt, spluttering and gasping for air. He panted and wheezed as he crawled across the floor to the other side of the room. Isaac collapsed at the entrance of the next hallway, drenched in sweat. He lay there for a moment, catching his breath, his magelight bobbing slowly over to him from where it had waited for him above ground.

That was close... Isaac glanced at the quicksand and shuddered, feeling momentarily like he was back in its grasp.

Isaac stood shakily, cautiously eyeing the corridor in front of him. The Abjuration magic had drained him more than he thought. He felt sluggish and heavy, as if he were still moving through the quicksand. Even with Jack's warning of the strain that sustained use of warding magic can put on the user, he hadn't expected it to tire him out like this. With more traps certainly up ahead, could he really handle another one like the quicksand?

Isaac shook his head. He didn't have a choice. He had to keep moving. He'd just have to be more careful.

Isaac shuffled at a slow, hesitant pace down the hallway, his magelight bobbing dimly over his shoulder. The new hallway was oddly wide—wide enough to fit two carriages side by side—with intricate swirls and geometric shapes littering the walls, painted in a variety of now-faded colors.

The hallway seemed endless, with no turns or branches in sight. At this rate, it would take him hours to meet up with Alison and Sigmund.

Isaac paused as he felt a floor tile sink under his foot. He carefully shifted his weight to the side to reveal an old rune carved into the tile, glowing a bright, ethereal blue.

Isaac stood completely frozen.

What was he supposed to do now? He couldn't stand there forever, but he knew that if he moved, he would trigger something undoubtedly unpleasant and potentially deadly.

Don't have much of a choice.

Isaac dove forward and rolled across the ground before turning to face where he had once stood.

Isaac felt the ground shake as a swirling, black and red substance oozed out from the rune and formed into a sphere that floated a few feet off the floor.

Isaac eyed it carefully, waiting for the blob to move.

The sphere suddenly ignited into a ball of blue flame and came screaming toward him. Isaac ducked reflexively and quickly threw up a barrier as the ball redirected itself back toward him.

The molten fireball blew right through the barrier, shattering it like glass.

Isaac cursed as pain shot through his body, dropping him to his knees. For this ball of fire to shatter his warding so easily, he must be more exhausted than he thought.

Isaac threw himself to one side as the fiery orb scorched past him, slamming into the wall where his head used to be.

How the hell am I supposed to stop this thing? He was fairly confident that, like the first trap, his magic would not be enough to slow it down.

The fireball came close to obliterating Isaac on its next pass as it rocketed toward his stomach. The fire lashed at Isaac's clothing as he dove out of the way at the last second, the ball smashing once more into the stone wall, leaving a small fist-sized hole behind.

Isaac felt a faint breeze come from the hole, along with the high-pitched screech of metal sliding against metal.

He stared at the ball as it hovered motionless before him and weighed his options. He knew he couldn't stay in this hallway and try to outsmart the ball. Given its tenacity, even if he tried to run away, he wasn't confident that it would stop following him.

His only other choice was to gamble with whatever was on the other side of the wall that the fireball had just blown a hole in. Judging by the sounds coming from the adjacent room, it didn't look very promising.

However, if he was lucky and played his cards right, he might be able to get the fireball to accidentally attack whatever creature was lurking beyond that hole.

So, does he stay here and try to outrun the trap, or does he chance it on whatever could be waiting for him in the next room?

I'll take my chances in the next room. Isaac thought as he dove toward the hole and simultaneously reached out to the stone wall, willing it to give way and explode inward.

He rolled into the next room in a shower of small rocks, and came nose-to-nose with a short, ugly creature with sickly green skin. Its cat-like eyes glowered at him as the tip of its long nose poked into Isaac's, its pointed ears flattening against its skull as it snarled at him.

And behind him were hundreds of his friends.

Fuckin' goblins.

Isaac jumped to the side and knocked into something taller than a normal goblin. Isaac turned, catching the dumbstruck gaze of Alison, who was covered in orange goblin blood and looking rather unhappy about it.

The goblins didn't let them have their reunion for long, charging at them with their spears and rusty blades held high.

The dimly lit room filled with light as the fireball took out a weakened section of the stone wall; the fiery orb hovered patiently, as if waiting for Isaac to move.

"I'll handle the annoying candle," Isaac answered in response to Alison's worried look.

"Better you than me," she said, turning her attention back to the goblins.

Isaac threw his hands down at his sides and grabbed his short swords, unsheathing them for the first time in a while. He couldn't afford to exhaust himself any further by continuing to use magic. Isaac and Alison had dealt with goblins before, so he was confident that they'd be able to handle them here if they were careful. Magic would be his last resort.

They came onto him and Alison in a frenzy. Isaac side-stepped attacks he could and parried others, careful not to let their weapons cut him. Goblins were known for dipping their blades in a paralytic poison. Just one small cut and a couple of seconds would render one completely immobile.

Isaac tried to keep his eye on the fireball while fighting, but it had made no move to follow him. Which hopefully meant that it was confined to that hallway and couldn't follow him indefinitely.

Isaac cut down swaths of goblins, killing enough of them that he feared his swords might be permanently dyed orange. But they just kept coming. For every one he killed, another two took its place. He glanced over at Alison and saw her practically dancing across the room. Each stroke of her blade and twist of her body was clean and precise.

"Where are they all coming from?!" Isaac shouted above the chaos, shearing the head off yet another goblin.

"I'm not sure!" Alison called back. "As soon as I stepped in, they all came flooding in from behind me."

She must've triggered a trap like Isaac had, most likely a portal of some kind. Unfortunately for them, neither had the power nor the skill to close a gateway.

They had to find a way out of here quickly; more goblins were streaming in, and they would soon be overrun. After a few more seconds of scouring every inch of the room between sword clashes, he spotted a narrow corridor tucked into the far corner. He wasn't confident the goblins had the same constraints as the mobile inferno, but they had no other choice.

"Alison! Follow me!" Isaac charged forward, slicing through the endless horde.

Alison bounded after him, cutting her way through the growing mass of bodies.

They fought their way to the other side and squeezed into the narrow hallway. Alison went in first, with Isaac bringing up the rear, and the goblins not too far behind him.

Luckily for them, the narrow entrance created a sort of funnel, so only a few could get in at a time. Still, if they wanted to escape, they were going to have to separate themselves from the goblins somehow.

"Take the front for a second," Isaac said, pushing past Alison.

"What the hell for?!" she cried out, barely deflecting a slash across her stomach.

"Just give me a second!"

Isaac sheathed his weapons and reached out to the mana in the stones above them, commanding them to crumble and fall from their perch. Chunks of rock began falling, crashing onto the heads of the goblins.

Alison's body shook as a small rock smacked her on top of the head.

"Hey!" she protested. "Watch what you're doing!"

"Sorry!" Isaac yelled. "Now, get back!"

Alison leapt backwards just as the ceiling above where she had been standing collapsed. They coughed as dust and debris filled their lungs. They could still hear the goblins on the other side, angrily shouting and clawing at the fallen rocks.

"That will hold them for a while." Isaac sighed, slumping against the wall, but mindful of any runes that might be etched into the walls.

"Great..." Alison said, barely above a whisper.

Isaac looked up as she turned around and saw that her hand was wrapped around one half of a spear that was lodged in her side, poking out from under her armor. Alison let forth a loud, wet cough, blood splattering her palm. She crumpled to her knees and fell face-first to the floor.

CHAPTER THREE

"Alison...?" His heart jumped up into his throat as he rushed over to her.

He gathered her in his arms and sat back against the wall, supporting her while he tended to the injury. The jagged spearhead was lodged a few inches deep. Blood was beginning to pool where the wooden shaft met skin, and already her flesh was turning blue-black from the poison.

Did I do this...?

It's possible a goblin could've snuck in an attack when she was hit by that rock...

Isaac shook his head, trying to clear his mind of his worries. His fault or not, he had to act quickly before she either bled out or the poison set in completely.

Slowly, Isaac pulled the head of the spear out of Alison's side. It reluctantly relinquished itself from her flesh with an unsettling squelching sound as blood poured out of the open wound. Even coated in blood, he could still see the vibrant purple coating on the blade.

The paralytic poison. Isaac tossed the broken spear onto the pile of rubble beside them.

He slipped his pack off his shoulders and set it down next to him. He rummaged through the small compartments, hunting for the antidote, stopping when his fingers brushed against a small, rectangular vial.

He removed the vial from the pocket and popped the cork off with his teeth. Isaac angled the lip of the vial just above the wound and let the contents pour into it. Alison's unconscious body squirmed as her wound bubbled and spasmed.

"I know it hurts. I'm sorry," Isaac whispered as he stashed the vial back into his pack. The antidote would work quickly once it was exposed to the wound. He had almost left it behind, but Sigmund had insisted on bringing some 'just in case.'

Isaac often ignored Sigmund's constant nagging, but this time, he was glad he had listened.

Isaac placed his hand over the gash on Alison's side, wincing as his hand became uncomfortably warm as her blood ran down his fingers. He connected to the mana in her body, directing it to mend her wound. Isaac watched his will take shape, as Alison's flesh slowly stitched itself back together in a sort of macabre sewing.

Isaac's hand began to tremble under the strain of healing Alison. Healing magic was a complicated, careful process that required a lot of focus. You couldn't be exhausted and expect to mend any serious wounds. He was still recovering from using Abjuration, and now he was paying the price for trying to use another complicated type of magic.

Isaac gritted his teeth as his eyes slowly began to close. The bleeding had stopped a few moments ago, and her wound was almost completely healed...

But his exhaustion was catching up with him.

No. Not yet. I'm almost done...

He felt his head roll backwards and hit the wall behind him, his vision going black.

* * * * *

Alison groaned as her eyes fluttered open. Her entire body ached, but her left side felt almost completely numb. Isaac's sleeping—no, unconscious—face was dangling a few inches above hers, his body slouched forward. His gray cloak was almost black from the grime and blood collected on it.

He won't be happy about that. She thought. He loved that cloak. Every time he put it on, it was like the first time Jack had ever given him one.

It was cute.

She reached to her side, remembering the goblin's last desperate attack before Isaac had brought the ceiling down on them. To her surprise, the spear shaft was gone. Only cold, drying blood and a rough patch of skin remained.

He must've healed me... and given me the antidote as well. Thank the Creator he actually listened to Sigmund this time.

"Thanks," she croaked out, her throat dry and caked in dust.

Isaac groaned and moved stiffly, pulling her closer to him.

She smiled weakly. Even unconscious, he tried his best to comfort her.

Her mind drifted as she lay there, warmth coming back into her limbs, to when she and Isaac had first met. Alison's parents had always been supportive of her using magic, despite being Vaccars—those who can't use magic—themselves, but they had died from a plague that tore through their village when she was a child. In a desperate effort to both save her from the disease and to give her the chance at a better life, they spent whatever coin they had for her passage to the Order of Dormiri to learn how to use magic. Most other Vaccars would've had their children killed as soon as they discovered their child was an Arcanist.

But not hers.

They thought her birth was a blessing and encouraged her to grow and become strong.

Unbeknownst to her parents, however, the Order had a strict policy regarding the age of the students they would accept, and Alison was too young by several years.

They wouldn't take her out of fear for her own safety, or so they said.

"Teaching children younger than ten can be extremely hazardous... Your abilities are too volatile with your growing body. We're sorry."

In that instant, she felt the world crumble around her. This was her only hope. Without the Order, she had nothing.

She had no one and nowhere to go.

But that's when Jack Grey came for her.

The Order quickly arranged for Jack to take her in. Jack Grey was the only Arcanist that the Order allowed to train Arcanists, of any age, outside of their walls.

She had heard of him before in rumors and whispers around town. Stories of an Arcanist befriending and helping Vaccars, and the Vaccars actually trusting an Arcanist for the first time since the fall of the Ancient Ones thousands of years ago.

When she first met him, she expected him to be quiet and imposing. Instead, he was warm, inviting, and smiling ear-to-ear, doing his best to assure her that everything was going to be fine. To her continued surprise, everyone in the Grey family was just as nice and friendly. They were all like her: Arcanists without a home looking for a place where they belonged and where they felt safe. Jack gave them that and more. He gave them a purpose. Everyone in the family dedicated themselves to Jack's mission of healing the relationship between the Vaccars and the Arcanists, and to collect and guard the Ancient One's artifacts.

Soon after arriving at the Grey Manor, she received word of her parents' passing. The weeks that followed were difficult, and Jack and the rest of the family allowed her space to grieve.

A day or so later, she had heard that someone new had joined the Greys—a young boy about her age. From what she heard, he had also lost his family, but the circumstances remained unclear.

He couldn't remember anything that had happened to him. The only thing he could remember was his name: Isaac.

The day they met started off particularly somber. Alison was hiding in the garden, between the rose bushes, wishing to be alone. She heard the soft swish of grass moving around her as she caught a glimpse of small, explorative feet through the bush.

"Are you okay?" Isaac asked.

Alison turned around and was shocked by how close he was. He was kneeling beside her, his big gray eyes full of concern, and his messy black hair flopping around lazily in the wind.

This must be the new boy. She thought bitterly, glaring back at him.

"Go away," she replied solemnly and turned away from him.

"What's wrong?" he asked curiously, inching closer to her.

"I said go away!" she shrieked, turning and pushing him as hard as she could. Isaac landed on the ground with a soft thud. Alison waited for him to look angry and storm off, hoping she had done enough to make him leave.

But instead, he just looked perplexed, stood up, and moved back closer to her.

"It's okay," he said, smiling. "I don't have parents either."

His brazenness shocked her. And how did he know about her parents already?

Her confusion must've been noticeable. "Jack told me," Isaac said. "He also told me not to bother you, but... I heard you crying, and I couldn't help it."

"I just want to be left alone," Alison said quietly.

"Then we'll be alone together." Isaac nodded, as if his word was final. He brushed a tear off her cheek with his thumb and wrapped one arm tightly around her shoulders. "It'll all be okay. No worries!"

He sat with her all day that day, never leaving her side.

They've been inseparable ever since.

Isaac finally began to stir, his eyes straining open.

"Look who decided to wake up," Alison teased.

Isaac shook his head back and forth, trying to regain some sense of alertness. "How long were we out for?"

"Long enough for Sigmund to be worried sick, I'd imagine."

"A few seconds is enough for him to worry. He's probably a slobbering mess right now." Isaac cracked a tired smile. "How are you feeling?"

"Better than you look, I think." Alison smiled back. "Just can't feel much on my left side yet, but it's coming back."

Isaac nodded, his expression turning serious and stonelike. "I'm sorry... if I had been more careful..."

Alison placed a hand against his cheek. "It's alright. It was an accident. Let's just make an agreement to *not* hit me on the head anymore. Deal?"

"I suppose I can live with that arrangement." Isaac winked, his usual half-smile returning.

Isaac helped Alison up and let her lean against him for support. While she was feeling stronger, her legs were still a bit shaky.

"So... where to next?"

"That way," Isaac nodded down the hallway. "The rubble behind us *should* keep the goblins at bay. The only thing we can do is continue on and find the artifact. Hopefully, Sigmund is already there."

"Agreed. Let's get moving."

CHAPTER FOUR

Their progress was slow at first, with Alison trailing just behind Isaac, her hand on his back to stabilize herself as she walked. Gradually, the rest of her strength returned, and she could walk without assistance. Isaac was on high alert as they walked, eyeing the ground where they stepped, being exceedingly careful not to trigger another rune. If he activated another trap in a space as small as this, they'd be done for.

Eventually, the two found themselves in a large, expansive room adorned with obsidian walls lined with torches burning a green flame and sleek, white floors. An empty granite pedestal with another rune etched into its top sat in the middle of the room. A yellow liquid pooled out from the rune, dripping silently down to the pale floor below.

"I'm guessing this would be the artifact room," Isaac said, examining the rune.

Alison nodded her agreement. "Certainly appears that way. But where is it? It looks like there might've been something on top of that pedestal."

"Alison! Isaac!"

They both turned and saw Sigmund walking toward them, a black sphere tucked under his arm. What looked like a thick, dark mist twisted and swirled in the orb.

"Is that it?" Isaac stared, mesmerized by the sphere.

Sigmund nodded. "Indeed. Interesting, isn't it?"

"Thanks for waiting for us," Isaac said.

"And for taking care of whatever made that mess." Alison pointed at the strange yellow pool forming around the base of the pedestal.

"Of course. I knew it was only a matter of time before you two showed up. The trap I triggered posed no difficulty at all."

Isaac raised an eyebrow. Something was off. Sigmund was *never* this nice or conversational with anyone. Ever. He was convinced it was a sacred rule of Sigmund's to be as short and curt as possible.

Alison flashed him a worried glance. She noticed the same thing.

"So, how do we get out of here?" Isaac asked. They would have to be careful and not let on they were suspicious. If they were right, and this was some kind of imposter, they wouldn't want fake Sigmund to know that they were onto him.

Sigmund pointed to the wall opposite him. "Probably through there. I came through the corridor behind me, and you two popped out of that one. So, it can't hurt to try."

Sigmund motioned forward. "After you two."

They both nodded and led the way toward what they hoped was the exit. If Isaac was suspicious before, now he was downright convinced that something was wrong with Sigmund. He would never allow Isaac and Alison to walk in front of him. He was way too overprotective for that, always taking the lead with them trailing behind. But what could they do against who, or what, was behind them? Should they try to attack? If this thing got the real Sigmund, what hope did they have?

Behind him, Isaac heard the soft crackle of leather being squeezed tightly.

Guess he decided for us.

Isaac tackled Alison to the ground as Sigmund's claymore screamed through the air where their heads used to be.

Isaac and Alison rolled quickly to their feet and turned to face their attacker.

Sigmund's face was like a stone mask, his eyes glaring straight through them. He held his claymore lazily in one hand, the other clenched into a tight fist. Isaac gulped. The fake Sigmund also seemed to have the real Sigmund's strength. He had always been impressed by Sigmund's ability to swing around such an enormous weapon with one hand while re-maining in complete control over it.

Now, that amazement turned to fear.

What's more, if this fake Sigmund inherited Sigmund's strength, Isaac wondered, could it have inherited Sigmund's magic as well?

"Sigmund, what's gotten into you?" Alison asked.

They dodged another swipe from Sigmund, again narrowly escaping being cut in two.

Is he getting faster?

"Alison..." Isaac drew one of his short swords. "That's not him."

"Even so, we can't kill him!" Alison yelled. "We couldn't even if we tried."

"No, but if we don't do something, we'll be dead for sure."

Alison nodded and drew her sword in one hand and readied a knife in the other.

Sigmund came after them with a fury. His strikes were heavy and precise. Isaac stupidly tried blocking a downward slash, and the impact brought him to his knees. Alison quickly pounced at the not-Sigmund, hoping to sever the tendons in his arm and render his sword hand useless, but he was too quick. He kicked Isaac away, hard, and deflected Alison's blow before punching her in the jaw. Isaac and Alison tumbled across the floor away from each other.

Isaac scrambled to his feet as Sigmund lunged after him, his clay-more poised to strike. A powerful gust of wind slammed into Sigmund from the side, sending him flying across the room.

Alison rushed over to Isaac and helped him to his feet.

"Thanks," Isaac smiled sheepishly.

Sigmund was back up in a matter of seconds. Isaac felt the blood drain from his face as water started to swirl in a vortex around Sigmund.

Shit. He had really hoped he was wrong about the fake Sigmund also having his magic.

What are we supposed to do now?

Sigmund darted forward, the water curling around him in a defen-sive cocoon.

Fire flared to life in Isaac's hands as he sent a stream of it at Sigmund. The fire lapped harmlessly against the water shield; the flames extinguished almost immediately after making contact.

Sigmund's sword leveled at Isaac's waist, aiming to cleave him in two. Isaac attempted to throw himself out of the way, but he was too slow. He felt fresh panic shoot through him at the realization that he was about to be cut in half.

The claymore stopped just before it reached him, a strong current of air holding the blade in place. Isaac turned his head to see Alison struggling to hold back the sword. Air currents slapped at the steel, the wind howling around it as it increased in intensity. Isaac jumped backwards and commanded the earth around them to rise on either side of Sigmund. Two stone walls shot up through the ground and then came quickly together, smashing Sigmund between them.

The earthen wall exploded as it was ripped to shreds by Sigmund's water vortex. A long tendril of water shot out from the mobile whirlpool surrounding Sigmund and smacked into Alison, sending her careening across the room. Another similar tendril sped after Isaac, slamming into his stomach like an iron rod and sending him pinwheeling into the wall behind him.

Isaac felt the wind leave his lungs as he crashed to the ground, his body exploding with a deep, throbbing pain. He took several short, raspy gasps of air as he clawed his way to his feet. With blurry vision, Isaac could just make out Sigmund rushing after a still-recovering Alison, his claymore bearing down on her. Isaac reached out to the wind around Alison, manipulating the air currents as she had, stopping Sigmund's attack mid-air. The claymore quickly ground to a halt as Sigmund pressed downward hard, trying to get his blade to complete its stroke.

Alison rolled out of the way, summoning her air magic to push hard back against Sigmund's sword until it was almost wrenched free from his hands. Sigmund growled and let go of his weapon, the claymore pinwheeling through the air before lodging itself into the wall several feet away.

The water vortex suddenly expanded, catching Alison by surprise, crashing into her, and throwing her backwards. Alison's head cracked against the obsidian wall, her eyes rolled back, and her body slumped limply to the ground.

"Alison!" Isaac darted forward uneasily, his head still swimming. He wasn't sure what he was going to do against Sigmund. So far, he had only learned elemental-based magic and some introductory Abjuration magic. His fire wasn't hot enough to evaporate the water; his earth magic would be torn to shreds; he definitely couldn't try to overpower the water Sigmund was controlling; air magic seemed to be deadened against Sigmund's vortex; and he for damn sure couldn't take Sigmund in hand-to-hand combat.

He was, unequivocally, screwed.

I have to do something...

Isaac gritted his teeth as he weighed his options. His best option was to counter Sigmund with Lightning magic. But, Lightning magic was the most difficult of the elemental magics to use because of the raw, unbridled energy that was generated to use it. It was for that reason that it was the last elemental magic that an Omnis Arcanist like Isaac had to learn. Next to Abjuration, he was the least familiar with Lightning magic. Given his current state, it was quite likely that he could end up electrocuting himself if he wasn't careful.

But he had no other option. He had to try.

As he sprinted forward, he reached out to the mana around him and ordered it to become conductive; his mind flooded with thoughts of lightning. He felt the mana hum and crackle around him in response as the air became charged with electricity.

Isaac reached out toward Sigmund, who had begun running to meet Isaac, and let a small barrage of lightning fly from his fingertips. Sigmund's eyes widened in surprise, the lightning chaining around the vortex as it arced its way toward the center. The lightning raced into Sigmund's body, driving him to his knees as he spasmed uncontrollably. The smell of ozone and scorched flesh slammed into Isaac's nostrils, making his eyes water as the boom of thunder echoed around the chamber with each crack of lightning. Water spilled across the ground like a burst dam as the vortex surrounding Sigmund shuddered for a moment and then died.

Isaac eyed Sigmund cautiously as he slowly approached his kneeling, smoking body. Sigmund appeared to be completely unresponsive.

Isaac cradled his hand against his chest, dropping to one knee, as pain exploded in his hand. Blisters were already beginning to form on his fingertips from the current flowing through them. If he continued to use Lightning magic, he could seriously hurt, if not kill, himself. But he didn't have any other options. He had to make sure this not-Sigmund was dead. He'd worry about the consequences later. Isaac extended his hand out toward Sigmund, lightning crackling between his blistered fingertips.

Isaac felt his body jolt, followed by a sudden pain in his side. When he looked down, he saw a large ice spike digging into him, his blood already staining the ice a bright crimson.

Isaac staggered backwards as another spike slammed into him from the other side. He felt all the strength leave his body as he crumpled to the floor.

Isaac cursed through labored breaths. He had been so focused on dealing with Sigmund that he hadn't noticed that the water on the ground was slowly circling around him, out of his sight. He had been careless.

Sigmund stood uneasily, ripped his claymore free from the wall, and dragged it over to where Isaac lay. As Sigmund hefted his weapon high above him, aiming to sever Isaac's head from his body, the sudden screech of metal grinding against metal reverberated throughout the room. Another claymore protruded from not-Sigmund's chest. The real Sigmund stood behind the imposter with a white-knuckled, angry grip on the hilt of his sword. With one great heave, Sigmund twisted around and cut straight upward through the doppelgänger's body, splitting him in half from the chest up.

The clone staggered forward a moment, its body beginning to smoke. As it fell to the floor, it disappeared into a thick haze, leaving the orb to roll carelessly along the floor, the rune on the pedestal no longer glowing.

Sigmund knelt over Isaac, inspecting his wounds.

Isaac smiled weakly up at him, happy to see his grumpy face.

"You look like shit, but you'll live," Sigmund said, as he plopped his pack down on the ground beside him to retrieve the bandages he had brought.

Yup, this was the real one.

Sigmund made quick work dressing Isaac's injuries and carefully removing the spikes that were lodged in his sides. Isaac winced and cried out as Sigmund poured a strong alcohol solution over his wounds.

"Quit your squirming," Sigmund grumbled.

"There," Sigmund said a few moments later. "Heal yourself if you can, but that'll hold you until we get back home. Stay here while I help her."

Isaac nodded and sucked in a sharp breath as he tried to heal his wounds, pausing as the world began to spin slowly around him, followed quickly by intense nausea.

Easy, no need to push myself anymore.

Isaac watched as Sigmund made his way to Alison. He stopped briefly to pick up the black orb. He squinted hard at it for a moment before wrapping it in a white cloth and stuffing it away in his pack. Sigmund knelt over Alison and quickly began bandaging her head, which had a trickle of blood coming down the back of her neck. Alison was awake now, thankfully, though she was clearly in a bit of a daze. She looked over at him and offered a tired smile and waved.

Isaac smiled back, returning her wave.

They were lucky the real Sigmund showed up when he did. If he had just been a few moments later...

Well, things would have been very bad.

Isaac stared at the ceiling, his entire body throbbing and aching. He had expected that this would be difficult, but he couldn't have imagined it would be like this. There had been a lot of close calls since they got into the Temple, each of which could have easily resulted in any of them dying.

They'd been very lucky with how things had worked out. Now that the orb was in their possession, he would like to start the trek back home before their luck ran out.

I could use a week-long nap... nothing crazy.

Sigmund's hulking figure loomed in his vision, and an exhausted Alison clung to him as he held her in his arms like a child. He gently set her down next to Isaac, handling her delicately as if she were made of glass.

"Rest," Sigmund commanded.

They both began to protest, but Sigmund's glare quickly silenced them.

"You're not good to anyone if you're dead. I'll keep watch for a bit. Now, rest. I'll wake you."

CHAPTER FIVE

"TIME TO WAKE UP," Sigmund's voice rang in Isaac's head like a church bell. He could feel Sigmund shaking him awake. Not gently either. Sigmund was all but slamming him against the floor.

Isaac groaned and struggled to open his eyes. To say he felt exhausted would be a gross understatement. All he wanted to do was sleep.

He blinked groggily awake and came nose-to-nose with Sigmund. Alison giggled as Isaac's face twisted in horror.

"Ever heard of personal space?"

Sigmund smacked Isaac's forehead as gently as Isaac thought Sigmund could manage, and he sat back away from him.

"Sorry it took me so long."

Isaac gaped. Sigmund? Apologizing?

Did Isaac die in his sleep? Was he still dreaming?

The pain he felt coursing through him felt real enough for him to be awake.

Alison smacked Isaac's arm, quietly telling him to drop the look. She looked like she had been awake for some time.

"What happened to you?" Alison asked, rubbing the back of her head.

Sigmund pointed at the pedestal. "Even though I was careful, when I grabbed the orb, the enchantment on that rune was activated. I had hoped to deal with whatever came out before you two showed up. However, seconds after the rune began to glow, I woke up in a sealed room with no recollection of how I got there. I could hear fighting off somewhere in the distance. After I broke out of the room, I made my way toward the sound and found you two."

"Did you encounter any other traps on your way here?" Alison asked.

"Nothing I couldn't handle," Sigmund shrugged. "How did you two fare?"

Isaac and Alison described their encounters with their respective traps, and Sigmund only nodded in acknowledgement, without betraying the slightest bit of concern.

"Good thing we were prepared," Sigmund said matter-of-factly. "We need to get going. We've wasted too much time here."

Sigmund stood, waiting for the two of them to join him.

"Not going to help us up?" Isaac asked pleadingly.

Sigmund didn't budge.

"Alright, alright, you hardass. I'll get up myself." Isaac slowly pushed himself off the ground, shimmying his way up a nearby wall and leaning against it so he could stand. Once he was up, he helped Alison to her feet too. Isaac felt alright standing, but Alison looked worse once she got to her feet. She wobbled back and forth and held her head in her hands.

"Are you alright?" Isaac asked.

She nodded. "Yeah, just can't get my balance."

"Help her," Sigmund said. "And stay behind me; you two are in no position to fight."

Isaac did as he was told. He certainly didn't feel like he could go another round with anything, and Alison didn't look like she could either.

No need to press my luck.

Isaac took one of Alison's arms, wrapped it around his neck and wrapped his arm around her waist to steady her.

"How're we getting out of here?" Isaac asked.

Sigmund pointed toward the pedestal. "Hallway opened up behind it after you passed out, probably because we took care of the trap."

Slowly, they shuffled down the new corridor. Like the room the orb was in, the hallway was decorated beautifully. The entire passage was constructed using a deep, ocean blue stone with specks of silver and gold splashed throughout that twinkled like stars reflecting off a still lake. Isaac's nose crinkled as the faint smell of salt water peppered his nose, and the soft sound of waves crashing against the shore filled his ears.

"These Ancient Ones were something else," Isaac whispered.

Sigmund held his hand up, signaling them to stop. Before them was another large, open room with a shimmering, silky-white portal on the other side. Through the gateway, they could vaguely make out the outside of the Temple. It was nighttime now, and the moon was casting devilishly twisted shadows through the dense canopy of the forest.

"Is that our way out?" Alison asked desperately.

Sigmund carefully scanned every inch of the room, careful not to set off another trap.

After a few more rounds of scouring the area, he stepped forward and waited.

Nothing.

He continued the slow process of stopping and waiting until he stood right in front of the portal.

Still nothing.

He motioned them forward. "Step only where I did."

They nodded and carefully followed his path.

"So... are we going through?" Isaac asked once he and Alison were next to Sigmund again.

"Don't have a choice," Sigmund said warily, then stepped through the portal.

Isaac and Alison paused for a moment and then followed him. In the blink of an eye, they were outside the Temple, on the other side from where they had entered. Isaac closed his eyes as the cool night air washed over him. He smiled at the chilly hug the wind gave him. It was quite refreshing after being stuck in the muggy, stale air of the Temple for Creator knows how long.

It's good to be out.

Isaac opened his eyes and saw an unmoving Sigmund, who was standing unnaturally rigid, his gaze locked ahead of him.

"What's going on? Forget something inside?" Isaac peered around him and spotted two figures roughly a hundred feet away. One was a woman, about Isaac's height, with long blonde hair and pointed ears that stuck out from under her locks. She wore leather armor, like Alison's, and had a long sword at her side.

Next to her was a mountain of a man who managed to make Sigmund look small. He wore a black mask across the bottom half of his face and had a bow and a quiver slung across his back, with a short sword stuffed inside his quiver. Isaac caught the glint of chainmail from under the black cloak that engulfed his hulking frame.

"Ah, there you are," the woman said with a thick Elvish accent. Her voice was light and elegant, as if her words were art. "We knew we'd run into you eventually. Couldn't figure out how to get in, you see. The only entrance we could find was closed. You wouldn't have happened to recover a round object from the Temple, would you?"

"None of your business," Sigmund snarled.

She chuckled. "I'll take that as a yes. If you would be so kind as to hand it over, I can promise that you will die quickly. Otherwise..." The large man swung his equally massive bow from his shoulders and notched an arrow in one smooth motion, aiming directly at Sigmund's head.

"We can always take it by force," she smiled politely.

"You two stay put. Hide near the Temple," Sigmund ordered as he stepped forward, his hand hovering near the hilt of his sword.

The elf clapped her hands together in delight. "Force it is then!"

Isaac helped Alison hobble over to a corner of the Temple and crouched down behind it, his heart racing. This wasn't good. Sigmund was at a huge disadvantage. Not only did he have to fight two of them, but he also had to protect Isaac and Alison.

Are we really supposed to just sit here and watch?

The thought sent pulses of rage down his spine. It infuriated him to no end to feel so useless. But he knew that if he and Alison tried to help in their current conditions, they would only get in Sigmund's way and most likely get themselves all killed.

All he could do right now was look after Alison and hope Sigmund could take the two of them by himself.

"Djaro. Whenever you're ready," the woman commanded.

"Always ready, Azrael," the man's voice was a low, bellowing rumble like a vocal earthquake.

Djaro let his arrow fly. Sigmund swung his sword in response, cleaving the shaft of the arrow in two before it could hit its mark.

Djaro continued his glare, seemingly unimpressed, and readied another arrow. Sigmund charged them, his claymore parallel to the ground. Azrael unsheathed her blade and jumped at Sigmund from the side. Sigmund stopped mid-sprint and spun around her. His sword cut through the air as he twisted, hoping to catch her on the way down to the ground.

Azrael smiled as a pillar of earth shot up from under her. Sigmund's sword crashed through the tower and became lodged firmly in place as Azrael landed deftly atop the stone column. Djaro let another arrow fly, aiming once again for Sigmund's head. Sigmund let go of his weapon and spun back around the earthen column, Djaro's arrow grazing the right side of his head, drawing blood as it passed.

Azrael jumped down from her perch and rushed to meet him, swinging her sword hard at his neck. Sigmund nimbly ducked out of the way of Azrael's strike, ice coating his fist as he delivered a hard punch to her stomach. Azrael stumbled backwards, a stone spike shooting out of the pillar beside Sigmund. Sigmund darted backwards, narrowly missing being impaled as the rock pounded a shallow hole in the left side of his breastplate.

Azrael leapt back up to the top of the stone column and rubbed her stomach.

"That kind of hurt," she said, frowning. "Guess our source was right; he is a Water Arcanist."

A flash of blue lit up Isaac's vision, along with the twang of Djaro's bow and the smell of the air being scorched. His eyes went immediately to Sigmund, and he felt all the color drain from his face.

Sigmund's left hand was impaled by the arrow; the arrowhead stopped just inches away from Sigmund's skull.

He must've brought his hand up at the last second...

Isaac couldn't help but be in awe of his mentor. He wasn't even able to see what had happened; meanwhile, Sigmund could react to it without any trouble.

Isaac cast a worried glance over at Sigmund. Djaro being a Lightning Arcanist was a problem. If the little bit of lightning that Isaac could produce had brought the Sigmund doppelgänger to its knees, what would lightning magic from an experienced Lightning Arcanist do?

Isaac shivered at the thought. Alison squeezed his hand, clearly sensing his worry.

"He'll be alright, Isaac. Don't worry. Sigmund can take them both."

Isaac nodded. Her confidence in Sigmund was well placed. Jack wouldn't have put him in charge of them if he didn't think Sigmund was up for the job. Sigmund had saved his and Alison's asses plenty of times, always swooping in at the last minute like a hero from the folktales.

The arrow froze and broke in two before silently falling to the ground. A chunk of ice formed like a cork in the hole left by the arrowhead.

Sigmund side-stepped another arrow as Azrael leapt down at Sigmund, slashing furiously at him. Blocks of ice formed in the air in front of Sigmund's hands as he batted away her blows. Sigmund dodged a downward slash from Azrael and maneuvered behind her, ice forming around his fist once more as he punched her in the back of the head. Azrael shuddered, her knees caving under her, as she fell to the ground.

Sigmund turned just in time to meet Djaro's advance. His bow was slung over his shoulder now, his sword in hand. Djaro's first slash caught Sigmund just below the eye. Sigmund dove to the stone pillar that his sword was planted into and, with a great heave, ripped his claymore free from the column's grasp.

Sigmund spun around and deflected Djaro's strikes, the metal of their swords screaming as they ground against each other. Sigmund parried one of Djaro's blows and kicked him hard in the chest, sending the giant tumbling backwards.

Azrael, now reunited with Djaro and still reeling from Sigmund's attack, eyed Sigmund carefully as she silently planned her next move. Not waiting for them, Sigmund took in a deep, controlled breath and forcefully exhaled. A thick, heavy fog began to roll off his body, quickly cloaking him in a misty haze. Within seconds, the entire area around the Temple was covered in an impenetrable mist.

Isaac pushed his body closer to the wall and motioned for Alison to do the same. The thick fog that Sigmund had made was a double-edged sword: while the enemy couldn't see them, it was also quite difficult for them to see anything.

Isaac squinted, straining his eyes to peer through the mist. He could just barely make out Djaro and Azrael. But he had lost sight of Sigmund.

"Find his companions. He might be trying to escape. If we find them, we lock him here too until we're through with him. I'll find him," Azrael commanded, her voice dripping with venom.

No sooner had her words left her mouth, Azrael was face-to-face with the sharp end of an icy spear cutting through the mist. Djaro's sword cleaved the spear in two, seconds before it could hit its mark.

"Stay focused," Djaro growled; the leather hilt of his sword groaned as his grip tightened in frustration.

Another spear came soaring through the mist, this time at Djaro, who again blocked the strike.

Another spear shot toward Djaro

And another one.

And they kept coming in a never-ending volley. The assault pummeled Djaro, forcing him backwards, and cutting any exposed part of his body. Djaro dove into the forest, ducking behind trees trying to avoid the onslaught. Just as Azrael was about to help her comrade, a gigantic wall of ice erupted in front of her, separating them from each other.

Azrael didn't even have time to try to suppress her shock as Sigmund came furiously after her with ice magic and masterful sword strokes. She backpedaled, desperately trying to put distance between her and Sigmund as she became riddled with deep cuts. Azrael shrieked like an enraged harpy as she attempted to fight back against Sigmund, who deftly blocked and dodged her strikes.

Azrael side-stepped one of Sigmund's large, sweeping slashes and, before Sigmund could launch another ice-based attack, she opened the ground under him, trapping him up to his waist in the dirt. Sigmund leaned backwards as far as he could as Azrael slashed downwards, her sword cutting a wide hole through his armor. Sigmund sucked in air sharply as Azrael's blade cut into him. Sigmund slashed at Azrael's legs, forcing her to jump backwards away from him.

Ice erupted from under the ground around Sigmund, shattering the dirt prison into millions of icicle shards, freeing him from the earth. He stepped out of the pit and eyed Azrael, who was covered in cuts and drenched in her own blood.

Isaac watched with bated breath as Sigmund fought with Azrael. Isaac had hoped that, after Sigmund separated Azrael from Djaro, Sigmund would be able to take care of them quickly in single combat. However, even with them being separated, Sigmund still seemed to be struggling to finish Azrael off. And he still had Djaro to worry about.

Speaking of which...

Isaac glanced around. He had been so focused on watching Sigmund that he had neglected to watch for Djaro.

Where did he go?

"Isaac!" Alison's panicked voice slammed into his ears.

Isaac turned just in time to see Djaro's hand crash into Alison's skull, knocking her to the ground. Before he could react, Isaac felt a sharp pain erupt from his stomach as an arrow lodged in his gut. Djaro cracked Isaac across the face with his bow, knocking Isaac to the ground next to Alison.

Djaro placed the heel of his boot on Isaac's skull, notched another arrow, and aimed it at Alison.

"No!" Isaac growled. He clawed at Djaro's boot, and the pressure on his head increased in response.

He looked over at a dazed Alison; the blow had reopened her head wound. She looked back at him, her eyes cloudy and unfocused.

Fear rushed through Isaac's body, gripping him so tightly it made it hard for him to breathe. Now, as blood slowly ran down Alison's neck and with Isaac's head feeling like it was about to pop like a squashed grape, he knew he had been right before: they had just been lucky getting through the Temple.

His mind went quiet as the realization slowly sank in.

He was going to die here.

They were going to die.

Helpless.

Defenseless.

"Drop the fog and give us the orb, or we kill your companions," Djaro roared. "Do it now."

A long silence followed until, slowly, the fog began to lift. Isaac could just barely make out Sigmund's form. He was more battered than he had been able to make out through the fog. He looked exhausted and was cut and bleeding in several places. The ice wall that Sigmund had created dropped, revealing an even more battered Azrael. She looked like she'd been through hell.

Good.

"Let them go," Sigmund said, his voice low and serious.

Azrael limped over to Sigmund with an arrogant smugness in her steps.

"The artifact," Azrael held out her hand. "Hand it over, and they go free."

"Don't move!" Djaro boomed. Isaac strained his eyes to catch a glimpse of Alison trying to get to her feet.

She's still fighting?

Even now, with Djaro's arrow fluttering with electricity, she glared at him as if he were a wall she was about to crush to dust.

Alison flashed a defiant glance at Isaac, her eyes pleading with him to do something. Isaac nodded weakly in response.

They couldn't give up now. It was their duty to protect the artifact, and to keep people like Azrael and Djaro from taking it. They still had a job to do.

Isaac pushed down the chattering panic in his mind and, against his fear's reasoning, he slowly reached for one of his swords. Isaac caught Sigmund's cautioning gaze, but Sigmund seemed to understand immediately what he and Alison were trying to do.

"Alright," Sigmund grumbled. "It's in my pack. On top."

Azrael strode over confidently and began to rummage through Sigmund's bag. Isaac quickly unsheathed his blade and slashed as hard as he could at Djaro's achilles, severing the tendon in a single smooth motion. Djaro howled and fell backwards as Isaac and Alison raised their hands toward Djaro, buffeting him with gusts of wind using every ounce of strength they had left, tossing Djaro several feet away.

Sigmund spun around, ripping Azrael's hand out of his bag, and swinging his claymore around in a sweeping slash. A stone column shot up from the earth under Azrael, launching her backwards away from Sigmund's attack.

We have to help him. Isaac thought, and Alison seemed to agree as they both struggled to their feet. A flash of blue lit up Isaac's vision, blinding him for a moment as an arrow sank deep into his right shoulder. The impact of the arrow threw Isaac backwards, slamming him into the Temple wall as his body spasmed violently. He felt all his strength leave his body at once, like one big exhale, feeling too weak to even move a finger. Djaro notched another arrow and aimed it directly at Alison, lightning magic hissing ferociously.

Everything around Isaac seemed to slow to a crawl as he watched the string of Djaro's bow slide forward, the arrow crackling as a blue streak through the air.

Move. He told his body.

He remained motionless.

The arrow drew closer.

Move.

Again, nothing. He felt drained... powerless.

He couldn't help Sigmund, and he couldn't protect Alison.

MOVE. He screamed.

Everything around Isaac went black until he felt the piercing tip of an arrow sink behind his shoulder blade. As Isaac's vision slowly returned to him, he saw Alison looking up at him with worry and anger in her eyes. His blood dripped slowly down onto her in soft plops.

They were both on the ground now, with Isaac's body covering hers almost completely. He must've tackled her to the ground but couldn't remember when he had moved.

Isaac heard the drawstring of Djaro's bow being pulled taught.

"You first, then," Djaro said.

Alison sat upright, pushing Isaac out of the way, throwing knives in hand. She hurled them at Djaro as hard as she could, the first one catching him by surprise, finding its mark in his left hand, severing his fingers. Djaro roared and dropped his bow, blood spurting out from where his fingers used to be.

Several ice spears shot through the air toward Djaro, cutting through his chainmail. Djaro rolled as quickly as he could, his armor coming off in chunks as he went.

Isaac glanced over at where Azrael and Sigmund were fighting a moment before and saw a bloodied and broken Azrael on her knees, panting heavily and missing her left hand.

Sigmund closed the distance between him and Djaro, releasing an unrelenting barrage of ice spears. A flicker of Lightning magic ignited around Djaro and struck Sigmund, who shuddered momentarily, but his assault kept coming. Another flash of lightning illuminated the night as Sigmund and Djaro clashed.

The ground shook beneath Sigmund as a stone spike shot out of the ground and pierced his side while Djaro's lightning threw Sigmund backwards.

Isaac watched as Azrael desperately crawled over to Djaro. Djaro had collapsed and was now struggling to sit up, his breathing coming in short, raspy gasps, his body littered with holes where Sigmund's spears had punctured him.

Sigmund shoved his claymore into the dirt, steadying himself as he fell to his knees. Isaac winced at the sight of him. One of his eyes was almost completely swollen shut, and blood was beginning to flood out from his hand where the arrow had struck him earlier. He was panting hard and shaking from overexertion.

"We're leaving," Azrael croaked out, wrapping her arm across Djaro's body. "We've failed."

Djaro slowly nodded.

Azrael chuckled and coughed up blood. "We *will* get the artifact, one way or another. Mark my words."

The earth enveloped them, shielding them in a sort of cocoon. The ground rumbled once more; the cocoon disappearing deep into the earth.

Sigmund let out a hard, throaty cough and fell backwards onto the ground.

"Shit," Alison cursed, dragging Isaac's limp body over to Sigmund, quickly grabbing the bandages they had stuffed in their packs. Sigmund grabbed weakly at her arms as she tended to his wounds.

"Him first," he grumbled.

Alison glanced at Isaac, who shook his head defiantly.

"I'm okay," Isaac wheezed. The arrows were, at the very least, holding all of Isaac's blood in. If Sigmund didn't get help quickly, he'd bleed out faster than Isaac would.

"No, you need attention first. Let us help you," Alison insisted.

Sigmund hesitated before nodding and resting his head in the dirt.

Isaac watched nervously as Alison tried to dress Sigmund's wounds. Each bandage she used was instantly saturated with crimson. No matter how many gashes or punctures she wrapped or packed, the bleeding didn't seem to stop. Alison was doing her best, but it was a lot for one person to do. He had to help somehow.

Maybe if I try to heal him...

Isaac shook his head lightly. It would be foolish of him even to try. In his current condition, he could barely speak, let alone use magic to heal Sigmund. If he puts any more strain on his body, he might end up killing himself.

Isaac went cold as his desperation-turned-panic gripped him by the throat. Once again, he couldn't help.

He couldn't heal Sigmund.

He couldn't heal Sigmund, and the bandages weren't working.

He watched as Sigmund's blood ran lazily down his side.

Sigmund was going to die.

He was going to die, and there was absolutely nothing Isaac could do about it.

Isaac jumped as Alison gently touched his arm. He slowly turned toward her, then looked at Sigmund. His breathing had stabilized, and his bleeding had slowed.

"Sigmund will be okay," Alison reassured calmly. "I know you want to help, but I can handle it. Trust me."

Isaac nodded stiffly and took a deep, steadying breath, pushing down the chattering panic that was growing in the depths of his mind. Isaac gently rested his hand on Sigmund's forearm and closed his eyes as Alison tended to his wounds.

CHAPTER SIX

Isaac groaned as he shuffled along the dirt path, slowly making his way up the steep hill. They had spent the better part of the day walking through the peaks of the Valley of Dyanspar, which served as the natural highway from Sakreed to Klantra. It was a long, winding trek with some of the best views in Eutrox.

The Valley of Dyanspar was named after the late Queen Dyanspar of Klantra some seven hundred years ago. Queen Dyanspar loved leaving the castle and riding up and down the valley hills and peering out at the scenery. It wasn't hard to see what she had liked about it: the way the sun shone in the valley made everything glow; the trees were a rich earthy color with beautiful orange leaves; a large lake sat in the middle of the valley that was so clear one could see the bottom and the fish below the surface; the grass was a tall, vibrant green that danced lazily in the wind, the sound of the rustling blades made a sort of soft hum around the valley.

But walking it *again* was not making Isaac particularly happy, especially considering how much his body ached and throbbed. The three of them had started their way back to the Grey Manor a day ago, and they had been making good progress despite how injured they were. Isaac had tried again to heal what injuries of theirs he could but, without having much time to recover, he wasn't able to mend anything serious.

They were all looking forward to a day or two of rest. They needed it.

But they would have business to take care of first when they got back. They'd have to report everything that happened at the Temple, and he knew Jack would have a plethora of questions about who attacked them.

Alison caught Isaac as he stumbled forward, casting him a worried glance.

"I'm fine," Isaac smiled, trying to reassure her.

She scoffed. "You need rest. Hey, Sigmund, can we stop for a second?"

Isaac shook his head as Sigmund stopped and turned around. "No, I'm fine. I just want to get back. No sense in taking any more time than necessary."

Isaac eyed Sigmund's weary state; the old man was limping, and his hand absently clutched at his side where he had been stabbed.

If Sigmund can keep going, so can I… I don't want to keep him from getting the rest he deserves either.

Isaac slowly pushed off Alison and steadied himself. "We can keep going."

Sigmund nodded, and Isaac saw what he thought was appreciation glinting in his eyes.

*   *   *   *

As the sun was retiring over the horizon, they finally broke through the tree line surrounding the Grey Manor estate. The Grey Manor sat in the middle of a large plot of land that stretched several acres across. The Manor was made of warm, light gray stone and burgundy shingles that burned a deep red in the setting sun. A tall watchtower-like structure sat in the middle of the Manor, towering above the rest of the house. Roses and lilac bushes—Jack's favorite—in front of the manor splashed red and vibrant blue against the gray stone. The scent of the flowers wafted down from the Manor as the wind picked up around him, passing through the trees and making leaves and flowers dance.

Isaac's pace quickened as he limped down the path to the manor.

Home. He thought excitedly.

Alison clearly shared his sentiments as she raced him to the door. A sense of calm washed over him as he felt the light tug of the barrier as he passed through it. With Jack's barrier in place, no one uninvited could enter the Manor grounds.

They were safe at last.

The large front door, with the Grey family crest burned into it, swung open as they approached. A man with the same build as Sigmund, but much younger, stepped through the threshold. He had soft, caramel Eutroxian skin, and short, spiky earthy-brown hair. His bright green eyes seemed to glow, shining light everywhere they looked. A gray cloak hung off his shoulders, almost completely covering the cotton-white shirt and the dark brown pants he wore. Isaac could just barely make out the tattoo of a kitsune—a fox with nine tails—on his forearm, a mark that served as a symbol of his mastery of magic and a display of his title within the Order: Mage.

A large, welcoming smile spread across his face, an act that his whole body appeared to mimic as warmth and joy seemed to roll off him, his arms stretched out wide.

"Welcome home!" His voice, light and full of infectious mirth, carried across the estate.

"Jack!" Isaac yelled, pushing past Alison and embracing his adopted father. Alison quickly joined him, and the two of them hugged Jack together, who was more than happy to return the favor.

Sigmund caught up a moment later and stood a few feet away.

"I see your quest didn't go without problems." Jack pulled away from them and eyed each of them seriously. "What happened, Sig?"

"Long story," Sigmund said curtly. "Put the kids to bed and we'll discuss in detail. They need their rest."

Jack nodded. "First things first, then."

Jack's eyes passed back and forth between Isaac and Alison, pausing for a few moments between each glance. He stopped after a few seconds and nodded. "Done."

Isaac raised an eyebrow in confusion. He started to ask what Jack meant when he realized that the aches and pains he had were completely *gone.* Isaac pulled at the collar of his shirt to look at his shoulder and gasped in surprise. No marks remained, not even a scar. Isaac was so caught up in the excitement of being home that he hadn't even noticed Jack's magic working on him. Alison and Sigmund appeared to be better too. Sigmund was no longer holding his side, and Alison was testing her balance, jumping around on one foot.

Isaac looked up at Jack in awe. He had seen Jack use magic a few times before, but the feats he accomplished never ceased to amaze him. If Isaac had tried to heal everyone back up to tip-top shape, it would've taken him a few days. But Jack did it in a few *seconds*.

Someday... Isaac thought dreamily.

"Thanks," Sigmund grumbled.

"Now, you two," Jack stared at Isaac and Alison, his voice breaking Isaac from his dream-like trance. "Go get some rest. Magic won't take care of your exhaustion, only your physical ailments. I'll talk to you two about what happened later. But for now, take it easy. You earned it."

The two of them nodded. They both could still feel the toll that the Temple had taken on them. They said their good evenings to Jack and Sigmund before retiring inside.

Stepping inside the Grey Manor would never get old to Isaac. The foyer walls had the same light gray color as the exterior, but inside they swirled and twisted as if a river were trapped inside them. The floors were an icy marble white. Orbs of light floated lazily in the air close to the high ceiling, illuminating every inch of the Manor. A grand staircase welcomed them a few feet from the door, rising high up toward the second floor before splitting off in opposite directions. The Manor was an ever-expanding spider web of hallways and doors that one could easily get lost in if they didn't know where they were going. Jack had created this house entirely through magic and continued to add to it or change it as he saw fit.

Isaac and Alison shuffled quietly to their rooms. Alison's room was first in a hallway of similar pine doors, marked by a rose burned into the center.

Isaac paused as he passed by her door, lost in thought.

"Is everything okay?" Alison asked, her hand pausing on her door-knob.

Isaac smiled sleepily and nodded. "Yeah, we can talk about it later. It's no big deal."

He wrapped his arms tightly around her, as if he were afraid that something would pull her away from him. She returned the embrace, nuzzling into his chest.

"I'm glad everything worked out," he whispered, kissing the top of her head.

"Me too." Alison smiled, pulling back from him so she could look at his face. "Are you sure everything is okay?"

Isaac nodded again. "Yeah, everything is fine. We'll talk another time. Okay? We both need some rest."

"If you're sure."

"Positive." Isaac flashed a grin at her. "Good night."

Isaac waved and turned from her and shambled zombie-like down the hallway toward his room.

* * * *

Jack leaned back in his large, dark leather armchair opposite Sigmund, who sat in a matching seat. The room was mostly dark, except for the fireplace that crackled brightly in the middle of the wall. The space was enormous, with rows upon rows of bookshelves littering the room, each filled with old tomes and texts. Beyond the shelves, toward the entrance of the room, sat a desk, messy with parchment paper and a quill with the ink still drying on it. The walls were a dark, flat stone, and the floor was an equally dark obsidian stone with specks of white flashing through them like lightning streaking across the night sky.

"So, that's everything then?" Jack held the orb in his hand, the odd swirling black surface insidious in its attempts at pulling his attention away from Sigmund.

Sigmund nodded, staring into the fire, the light glinting in his eyes.

From what Sigmund had told him, it appeared that someone had been sent to intercept them on their way out of the Temple.

"What do you make of it?" Jack inquired.

"Doesn't sit right with me," Sigmund snorted before continuing. "They knew we were going to be there and were waiting for us when we got outside. They also knew I was a Water Arcanist. Few people would know both where we were going and what kind of Arcanist I am. Someone from the family sent them."

Jack nodded. "That was my unfortunate conclusion. Everyone here knew that you three would be taking this mission, so our pool of suspects isn't exactly small."

Sigmund shook his head.

"I have been hearing... whispers. Rumors, mostly, from my correspondents in the Seven Kingdoms of Man. There has been talk about someone gathering Arcanists for something. I'm not sure if this is related to what happened at the Temple, but..."

"Can't rule out the possibility," Sigmund grumbled.

Jack nodded. "Correct. We'll sit down and discuss it further once Adara returns from her trip to Drahkul. Kenna had asked for her assistance with a little group of miscreant Arcanists."

Sigmund made a sound that could have been interpreted as a chuckle in his throat. "The Queen of Scorched Earth needs help with a bandit group?"

Jack smiled. "She's a queen now. She doesn't have time to deal with something so small personally."

Sigmund shrugged. "What would you like me to do?"

"Stay on standby until Adara gets back. Unless I need you to accompany Isaac and Alison again, that is. But you and Adara will be at the forefront with me in finding out who's behind this."

Sigmund nodded. "Understood."

While Sigmund on the surface appeared rather calm, his eyes betrayed his impatience. It was clear that Sigmund was eager to figure out who was responsible for betraying the Grey family, if their assumptions were correct, and Jack was too. Jack couldn't deny Sigmund the opportunity to help, especially since he was at the center of it all.

"May I ask you something?" Jack asked, breaking the ensuing silence.

Sigmund nodded.

"From what you've told me, both Isaac and Alison held their own at the Temple, showing tremendous strength and courage."

"Yes, they were both helpful," Sigmund said.

"Do you think they're both ready for the Trials? The Order of Dormiri is holding them within the next few days. Normally, it'd be too late to submit their names. But all I have to do is reach out and let them know..."

Sigmund scratched absent-mindedly at his beard, lost in thought, before nodding. "I think they're both ready. Seventeen is a fine age, and they've gotten enough experience. However... I would say to not have those two test together. Isaac, I think, is a bit ahead of Alison currently."

Jack beamed. "I had the same thought. So, next cycle for her then."

"Next cycle."

The two sat in silence for some time before Sigmund stood and walked out of the room. Jack smiled lightly. Sigmund never was one for pleasantries. He had known Sigmund for several years, adopting him into the Grey family when Sigmund was in his early twenties. He had watched the man age before his very eyes, and it was an honor to see him grow.

Jack's fingers danced along the orb in his palm. This artifact had been more troublesome to acquire than he had anticipated. The tales surrounding it said that it could wipe out entire armies in an instant, so it should come as no surprise that someone else would seek to claim it. However, the number of people with both a means to retrieve artifacts and knowledge of their existence was small. The Vaccars ignored magic artifacts left behind by the Ancient Ones because they still feared the power and the malice of the Ancient Ones, and rightly so.

The Ancient Ones were rather genius with their creations. They channeled the magic power of multiple Arcanists into an object so that any one person could power it and unleash magic that would usually require several Mages.

Jack had collected several artifacts over the years, studying them and trying to figure out how they worked and what their purpose was. From what he could tell, the Ancient Ones created these artifacts to help subjugate the Vaccars and their progeny—who they referred to as the Luminares—into slavery. Even going so far as to kill any Luminares children that were discovered as being an Arcanist to prevent their slaves from rising against them. A practice the Vaccars adopted after the Ancient One's rule, though for a different reason.

Before their downfall toward the end of the Divine Civil War, it is thought that the Ancient Ones locked away their creations to ensure that their slaves could never obtain the power of their former masters. However, the artifacts being sealed away behind a litany of traps, or some artifacts being traps themselves, did not stop some people from trying to find them and use them anyway.

The assailants at the Temple were a prime example.

Jack watched the reflection of the fire dance in the orb. He would have to investigate every member of his family to find out who could've betrayed them. The hardest part was that he didn't know where to begin. He trusted and adored everyone in his family. He didn't think any of them were capable of such a thing.

For now, though, until Adara's return, he had an artifact to research.

CHAPTER SEVEN

Alison groaned loudly as she slowly recovered from her deep slumber. She stretched across her spacious bed, taking joy in the comfort of the expansive mattress that enveloped her.

So much better than my bedroll. She thought happily.

She looked out the window across from her bed and stared out at the rich blue sky. She had slept away a better part of the day, which she normally hated, but, given everything they had gone through at the Temple, she was willing to let herself rest more than usual.

It had been a couple of days since their return from the Temple, and Jack had allowed her and Isaac to recover as much as they needed. She hadn't seen Isaac much recently, only at lunch and supper, where he always seemed a little distracted.

She frowned, thinking about how little time they had spent together in the past few days, and quickly shook the thoughts out of her mind.

He's just recovering in his own way. Alison reassured herself.

Her stomach growling startled her.

Guess it's time to eat.

She threw the heavy covers off herself and got dressed. Her hair was a tangled mess, as if it had a fight with itself while she slept. After a few minutes of fussing with it, trying to untangle it the best she could, she decided it was good enough for now. She would fix it later after she got some breakfast.

As she was making her way down the corridor toward the dining hall, she heard the faint echoes of metal clashing.

Sounds like someone is sparring.

The noise grew louder as she approached a door with two swords etched into the wood. She cracked the door open and peeked inside.

The training room was massive and mostly bare except for a few different weapons mounted on the wall. The floor was a solid slab of gray stone, and the walls were a rich, dark red wood.

Alison was unsurprised to find Isaac inside, training like his life depended on it, with Margaret and Jane. Margaret was a tall woman with curly, fiery-red hair and an equally fiery personality. Her dull blue eyes were like small puddles of water amidst the raging inferno of hair that engulfed the rest of her head. Jane, on the other hand, was a short, grandmotherly old woman whose snow-white hair framed her aged face beautifully. She walked with a slight hunch in her back and used an enchanted cane to help her move around.

Isaac squared off against Jane, who was keeping him on his toes with her cane-turned-whip. Jane moved the serrated whip around her gracefully, showing her years of practice at honing her craft. Margaret was supporting her with Teleportation magic to switch up where the whip would strike next. Isaac was doing his best trying to keep up with the barrage of attacks Jane and Margaret were sending his way. He was using one short sword, with his other hand free to use magic.

Isaac's training clothes were in tatters from the whip striking him, but Jane knew enough to pull away before her weapon cut him too deeply. Isaac lunged at Jane, but was teleported several feet away by Margaret. The ground opened underneath Margaret as Isaac reached his hand out toward her. Jane's whip wrapped around Margaret, pulling her quickly to safety. Jane and Margaret's teamwork was incredible; their skills perfectly balanced each other.

Alison smiled as she watched him. He was always so focused and driven to improve himself, devoting hours of his "rest" days to tireless training to the point of exhaustion just to get up the next day and do it all over again. He was crazy, no doubt about that.

But she admired his tenacity.

He had always wanted to grow up to be strong, always chasing after Jack, but, since they returned from the Temple, he seemed to be training a little harder than normal.

Alison frowned slightly.

If only he could see how far he's come already.

Jane's whip smacked into Isaac's abdomen and sent him careening into the far wall, cracking the wood as Isaac slid to the ground.

"I think that's enough for today." Jane's light voice called out, her whip returning to its normal, unassuming cane form. The room was littered with scratches, dents and holes from their session. Alison could see Jack's enchantments working as the blemishes in the room began to fade, as if someone were slowly rewinding time.

Isaac groaned as he struggled to stand, slouching against the wall for support.

"You going to just stand there with your mouth open, or are you going to come in?" Margaret shot at Alison, her eyes pinning her in place.

"Margaret, don't embarrass the poor girl." Jane cast a sideways glare at Margaret. "Alison, you can come in!"

Alison slowly slunk her way into the room, closing the door gently behind her.

Isaac's dead-tired expression turned to a wide grin when he saw her enter, an expression that made Alison's heart flutter.

"Well, good morning! What brings you here? Come to train?" Isaac asked.

"No, not this time. I got hungry and heard a lot of noise coming from here. Should've figured it'd be you."

Isaac kept smiling as he moved his hands over his cuts, mending them.

"Any time you want to join in, just let us know," Margaret offered, a little too enthusiastically for Alison's liking.

"Yeah… I'll do that."

Alison jumped in surprise as three loud knocks came from behind her. She opened the door and found Sigmund standing in the doorway, looking as grumpy and irritated as ever.

"Figured I'd find you here." Sigmund nodded toward Isaac. "Jack wants to see you in his study."

Isaac raised his eyebrows. "What about?"

Alison exchanged a curious glance with Jane and Margaret, who both shrugged.

"It's time."

"... Be any more specific?" Isaac asked, exasperated.

"He wants to discuss taking the Order of Dormiri's Magician's Trial. Coming or not?"

Isaac's jaw hit the floor as shock and excitement lit up his face. He sheathed his short sword, shouted his thanks to Margaret and Jane, and sprinted out of the room. Sigmund let out a long, annoyed sigh and followed him.

Alison couldn't believe it. Isaac was going to test for the rank of Magician.

Normally, only students of the Order of Dormiri could participate in their Trials. The Grey family being the only exception to that rule. The Trials were designed as a way for the Order to measure their student's progress, and the awarded ranks for each Trial a way for Arcanists to denote their strength to each other.

Information about the Trials was kept a secret, and no two Trials were ever the same to prevent students from preparing specifically for the Trial. The only thing that Alison knew for sure was that the passing rate was extremely slim. She's heard of hundreds of students participating in the Magician's Trial, and perhaps only a handful will succeed at a time. Even fewer have claimed the three higher titles.

For an Omnis Arcanist like Isaac to be eligible for the Trials, he'd have to have both a recommendation from a high-ranking Arcanist that's recognized by the Order; *and* show a strong proficiency in the foundational schools of magic for Omnis Arcanists—the elemental magics.

Alison beamed. She was so overwhelmed with joy for him. With Jack's recommendation, she hoped that this would ease whatever tension he had been feeling since the Temple. He worked hard and should celebrate that his hard work is paying off and being recognized.

He deserved this.

"Yoo-hoo, Alison!" Margaret stood in front of her, waving her hands crazily back and forth. "You in there?"

Alison stepped back in surprise. "Yeah, sorry, my mind was somewhere else."

"That's an understatement." Margaret frowned. "Thinking about Isaac?"

Alison felt heat rise in her face. Margaret roared with laughter at the sight of Alison's flustered expression.

Jane smacked Margaret in the back of the head with her cane. "Leave the girl alone." Jane eyed Margaret, who put her hands up in defeat.

"Good." Jane smiled at Alison. "It's very impressive that Jack thinks he's ready. I'm sure he'll do a fine job in the Trials. Come. Why don't we get something to eat?"

Alison's stomach growled again at the mention of food, and she followed Margaret and Jane out of the room.

* * * * *

Isaac knocked hurriedly at the door of Jack's study with quick, enthusiastic intensity.

"Come in!" Jack called out from inside.

Isaac entered, barely able to contain himself. He rushed over to Jack's large desk, where he was jotting something down.

"Just finishing up now," Jack reassured, smiling like always. "Had to get this letter sent out to King and Queen Edefin."

Isaac raised an eyebrow. "Why them? They've been quite clear that they don't like Arcanists. Do you remember the last time one was found in their capital, Luthrine?"

Jack nodded solemnly. "I do. And that's why I have been communicating with them. We've made good progress, I think, in repairing the damage the Ancient Ones have done. Unfortunately, there are some Vaccars who remain skeptical, and sometimes hostile, toward us. I can't blame them for it given our history, but that doesn't mean we can't try, does it?"

Isaac shook his head, and Jack smiled as he finished his note.

"I'll send that out once we're done." Jack waved his hand over the parchment; a gentle breeze rolled off his hands, drying the ink. "Where's Sigmund?"

"He's catching up." Isaac smiled sheepishly.

"Next time I need something done, I'll say that Jack asked for your help. At least then I know it'll get done quickly." Sigmund grumbled, entering the room a moment later.

Jack laughed as he stood from his chair, carefully rolling up the parchment before placing it in his drawer. He walked around his desk and leaned against the front of it, standing in front of Isaac.

"I'm sure Sigmund must've already told you what was going on, given your current excitable state."

Isaac nodded rapidly; his enthusiastic grin permanently painted on his face.

"I visited The Order earlier today and presented your name. The deadline for submitting students to attempt the Magician's Trial was today. Based on our recommendation, you were accepted to take the Trial immediately."

Isaac's excitement was almost too much for him to bear. But a word choice of Jack's had perplexed him.

"*'Our'* recommendation?" Isaac asked.

Jack nodded. "Yes. Mine and Sigmund's."

Isaac cast a shocked glance at Sigmund, who glared at him in return. "Aw, Sigmund! You *do* think I'm worth something!"

"Don't get carried away," Sigmund growled.

"But wait..." Isaac began, still confused. "Sigmund doesn't have a rank, *and* he's not associated with the Order, so how does his vote matter? I thought only recognized people have any say in who tests?"

"Normally that is true, yes. But the Order knows Sigmund, and they trust his judgment as they do mine. The Order wanted two recommendations to eliminate bias. Sigmund was the perfect fit, since he has watched you grow the most."

"Thank you." Isaac directed to Sigmund, who nodded his head in response.

That was the closest to a "You're welcome" that Isaac thought he was ever going to get.

He would cherish the memory of it forever.

"So, when do we leave for the Trials?"

"Two days," Jack said.

Seeing Isaac's shocked expression prompted Jack to continue.

"But the Trial doesn't start until three days from now. The Order requires all of those going through the Trials to report the day prior. You'll meet others testing with you, and even have time to explore The Order's keep."

Wow... just two days...

"Any training allowed while I'm at The Order's castle?"

Jack chuckled. "That wouldn't be advised. Rest as much as you can. You're going to need all the energy you can muster."

Isaac squinted his eyes at Jack. "What's the Trial entail?"

Sigmund slapped Isaac on the back of the head, eliciting a loud groan from Isaac.

"What was that for?!" Isaac asked, speechless.

"Like he'd tell you what the Trial has in store for you. Think for once."

"Now, now, it is hardly an unexpected question. But Sigmund is right. I can't tell you what the Trial is going to be. It changes every year. Just make sure to leave your weapons here; you won't be needing them at the Trial."

Isaac nodded his understanding. He figured Jack probably wasn't going to be able to tell him anything about the Trial, but it was worth a shot anyway.

"So! Enjoy your day today and tomorrow at home. Try to keep the training to a minimum to avoid hurting yourself unnecessarily. Brush up on your magic skills. We'll be leaving the day after tomorrow early in the morning."

Isaac nodded excitedly again; his growling stomach echoed throughout the study. Isaac felt his face flush red in embarrassment.

"Guess I worked up quite the appetite," Isaac said.

"Enjoy your meal. From what I've been hearing about your training, you deserve it." Jack cast his usual warm smile at Isaac, eliciting a grin from him in return.

Isaac darted off toward the dining hall, his stomach rumbling as he sprinted down the hallway.

Isaac had been so determined in getting as much training in as possible that he found himself skipping meals more than he'd like to admit. It wasn't a good habit for him to form, but he was about to rectify his forgetting breakfast with a heaping plate of whatever was available.

Isaac burst through the grand double-doors of the dining hall with hunger-fueled glee. The dining hall was ridiculously large, capable of easily seating a small town. The floor was lightly carpeted with black and white stripes intertwining and zigzagging across it. Giant one-way magical mirrors lined the stone walls, each showing different scenery. One showed a lush forest where you could hear the different songbirds singing, and another displayed silent wintery mountains with the rumbling hum of the wind swirling around its peaks. Tables lined the walls beneath each mirror, with the center of the room left open for people to stand and chat.

He saw Alison out of the corner of his eye, waving and smiling at him with a mouth full of food, sitting with Margaret and Jane beneath a spring theme mirror showing a garden of flowers in full bloom.

Isaac smiled. Of course she would sit there. Spring was her favorite season.

Isaac felt his stomach growl ferociously as he caught sight of the piles of warm meat, fresh bread, vegetables, and a cooled mug of ale waiting for him. Isaac licked his lips as he watched a small bead of moisture slide down the mug.

He hurried toward them, plopped himself down beside Alison, and began piling food onto his plate.

"Little hungry?" Alison asked, amused, as Isaac ripped into a flank of beef, his hands his only utensils.

Isaac smiled sheepishly as he tore off another chunk of meat like a feral dog. "Very." He choked out between bites.

"This kid's testing for Magician...?" Margaret looked at Isaac with a combination of utter shock, bewilderment, and disgust. "I guess they're letting just anyone in now, eh?"

"If you question Isaac's admission, Margaret, then maybe reflect on how it was you got yours with that type of attitude," Jane said with a knowing smile as she quietly cut her food into bite-sized pieces.

Isaac and Alison laughed at Margaret's dumbfounded expression. Margaret never expects Jane to say something witty in response to her uncouth approach to things. But when Jane does respond, it always puts Margaret in her place.

"So, when are the trials?" Alison asked, taking a big swig of her ale.

Isaac wiped his mouth with his cloth napkin. "Two days."

Jane frowned. "That's not very long at all."

Isaac shrugged. "It was short notice since we were at the Temple, and it wasn't until after this mission that I guess Sigmund figured I was ready."

"Sigmund endorsed you?!" Alison gasped in disbelief.

"I know! I was surprised too! He was his usual miserable self when I thanked him, but knowing I have his vote of confidence is enough for me."

"I'm surprised they took the old man's recommendation." Margaret sat back in her chair, kicked her boots up on the edge of the table and shrugged. "Desperate times, I guess."

Isaac's eyes narrowed on Margaret. "Sigmund has done a lot for this family, and the Order. Ranked or not, I think he's earned some respect," he said bitingly.

Margaret smirked at him. "Relax, kid, I know Sigmund's plenty strong and he's done a whole bunch of stuff, blah blah blah." She twisted her hand in the air as she talked.

She pulled up the sleeve of her dark brown blouse to reveal her tattoo of a Qilin—a creature with a dragon's head and a horse's body covered in serpentine scales—denoting her rank as a Sorcerer, the next rank after Magician.

"I've been recommended to test up for Warlock for a while now..." Margaret continued, "And, I'll be honest, I just can't be arsed to go through with the Trial... But Sigmund is at least as strong, if not a little stronger, than me. Even at his age. So trust me, I know he's the real deal."

Isaac relaxed a bit. Despite her never-ending goading, at the very least Isaac knew she respected her family.

"Any advice then for the Trials?" Isaac asked between a sip of ale.

Margaret shrugged. "Don't fall asleep while Aephes is talking."

Jane chuckled at Isaac's confused expression.

"You'll meet Aephes there, and I'm sure the members of the Order will fill you in on his title," Jane explained. "He just loves to convey a sense of importance to what you're doing and the ranks the Order gives us. He has a bit of a flair for the dramatic."

"A bit?" Margaret rolled her eyes. "I listened to him drone on for an *hour* about how the Qilin 'represents an Arcanist becoming a leader' and how 'it's our duty to protect the weak.'"

Margaret scoffed and waved her hand flippantly. "Boring. That's why I said, kid, *don't* fall asleep no matter how hard it is to stay awake."

"I rather liked his speech for mine." Jane rolled up her sleeve, revealing a tattoo of a griffin on her forearm. "Though, for us Warlocks, our speech was *two* hours. Perhaps a little too long, but I thought it was sweet and sincere."

Margaret waved dismissively at Jane. "Like I said: boring."

They ate silently for a few more minutes. Eventually, Jane neatly folded her napkin onto her plate and stood with the help of her cane, the bottom of her old gray dress dragging slightly across the floor as she moved.

"Come, Margaret. Let's give these two some privacy. We have other members to train today besides. Mustn't keep them waiting."

Margaret let out a loud burp and slammed her feet onto the ground and stood with one swift motion. "Sounds good to me."

As Margaret walked by, she punched Isaac lightly in the arm. "Good luck, kid. You're going to need it."

"Gee, thanks."

Margaret cackled, trailing behind Jane as they left the hall, leaving Isaac and Alison alone at the table.

"So, only two days away, huh?" Alison asked.

Isaac nodded. "Yup... Kind of came at me faster than I was expecting."

"Do you think you're ready?"

Isaac shrugged and looked down at his food thoughtfully.

"If I'm being honest? I'm not sure. Before the Temple, I would've thought so. But now..." Isaac trailed off before he spoke again, "I'm still excited and honored to be going, don't get me wrong, but... something is different. There's a nagging at the back of my mind that's making me second-guess everything."

Alison frowned and placed a hand on his shoulder. "I thought something was bothering you. Why didn't you say something earlier?"

Isaac shrugged again. "I meant to, truly. I just lost myself in training. I thought that by training, I might be able to avoid that feeling of helplessness again, but it hasn't really gone away."

"Well," Alison took a sip of her drink, "Jack and Sigmund seem to have faith in you, even despite what happened at the Temple. Perhaps it is even because of what happened there that Sigmund thought you were ready. Did you consider that?"

Isaac gave a half-hearted smile. "No, I hadn't thought of it like that."

"Exactly." Alison sat back, clearly satisfied with herself. "Hell, even Margaret wished you good luck. If *she* didn't think you were ready, don't you think she would be the first, second, and third person to say something?"

Isaac's eyes widened at the thought. "Remember when Rouw was put in for the Sorcerer's Trials and Margaret charged into Jack's office and screamed for hours?" Isaac shuddered.

"See? At least you're not him!" Alison smiled reassuringly. "I think I know where you're coming from with the Temple. It was the first time I had felt vulnerable. Like Sigmund might not be able to swoop in and save us. It makes me feel uneasy every time I think about it, but I'm not going to let it stop me from doing what I want to do." Alison looked at him, her eyes steeled in determination. "We survived, and that's all I can ask for. And you can't let this define your next moves either. It's fine to be scared; I still am, but we can choose how to respond to that fear."

Isaac offered a soft half-smile. *She is so much stronger than me.*

It was a relief to know that she felt similarly about the Temple, that he wasn't alone in his fear. It amazed him that she could channel that fear into something motivating and not something that would hold her back.

However...

He couldn't yet find it in himself to overcome his own fear. The fear that he could die on their next mission. The fear that he wouldn't be strong enough to help the people he cared about. There was a pit growing inside of him, and he felt as if he were slowly falling into it, helpless to do anything about it.

Perhaps the Trials will help give me some control back. If he could prove to himself that he could take on the Trials and pass, maybe that would assuage some of his fears.

He hoped.

"Feeling any better?" Alison's face was suddenly in front of Isaac.

Isaac lurched backwards, startled. "Yes, a little. Thank you." He offered her a soft smile.

Alison smiled back. "I'm always here for you; remember that. Anyway, what're you going to do over the next two days?"

Isaac shrugged, the cloud in his mind retreating a bit. "I'm not really sure. Jack told me not to train, so there goes most of my plans..." Isaac trailed off into a series of irritated grumbling.

"Creator forbid you take a break," Alison teased.

Isaac stabbed a plate-size slab of meat with his knife, brought it to his mouth, and tore off a chunk, gnawing on the fat.

Alison's look of disgust made Isaac chuckle and choke between bites.

"I think best while I'm eating," Isaac choked out between mouthfuls of food. "Trying to figure out how to fill up the rest of my time..."

Isaac smiled as an idea took shape.

She would absolutely love that.

He wolfed down the last bit of his food and gulped down the last drops of his ale. "Are you busy later?"

Alison shook her head. "Not at the moment. Why?"

"Good! Keep it that way. I'll get you from your room around sunset, hopefully with a surprise for you." Isaac beamed. "See you then!"

Isaac dashed from the table, almost knocking into several other family members on the way out of the hall.

No time to waste!

* * * * *

Alison sat in the nook of the large window in her bedroom, watching the setting sun as the last remnants of its light peaked out from the treetops, waving the day a peaceful farewell. After Isaac's mad-dash out of the dining hall, Alison had done little with the rest of her day, allowing herself to relax and eagerly await Isaac's surprise.

She had taken a long bath, after which she was finally able to untangle the crazy knots in her hair from this morning, allowing it to return to the long, wavy flow it naturally had. She even put on some of her better clothing: a pair of tan pants, free of any stains or blemishes, and a blue, flowing shirt that enveloped her in a silky hug.

She glanced over at the mirror, where she could just make out her reflection in the corner of it, and smiled.

I look good today.

She picked at a loose string of fabric on her pants as she glanced restlessly at the door. He should be here any minute now...

A few quick knocks came from her door.

"Yes?" she called, eyeing the entrance hopefully.

The door creaked open, and Isaac peeked his head in through the doorway. Alison smiled at him and waved for him to come in.

Finally. She thought excitedly.

Isaac beamed and pushed his way into her room. "All set to go?" Isaac had changed into clothes not destroyed by training, but otherwise his attire was the same: black everything.

Alison leapt up from her nook. "Been ready for a bit, just had to wait on a certain someone," she teased. "Mind telling me where we're going?"

Isaac smiled bashfully. "Can't spoil the surprise. Come on!"

Isaac grabbed her hand and took off through the manor.

"Why are you in such a hurry?!" Alison exclaimed.

"I don't want to miss it!" Isaac said, stopping abruptly in front of a door, the name "MARGARET" scratched crudely into it with what Alison assumed was a knife.

Margaret...? Why her room?

"We're here!" Isaac called, knocking excitedly.

Margaret swung the door open so quickly that Alison swore she was going to take it clean off the hinges.

"Keep knocking like that, kid, and I'll teleport you somewhere you don't want to be. Got it?"

"Yeah, yeah," Isaac brushed off her threat with a smirk. "Are you still going to help me?"

Margaret let out a pained sigh. "Yes, yes, I already said I would."

Margaret lifted her hand to point behind Alison and Isaac and, in the blink of an eye, a swirling purple and black ethereal rift as wide and tall as a door crackled in the hallway.

Alison glanced over at Isaac and couldn't help but smile when she saw the big grin that was painted on his face, completely enchanted by the beauty of Margaret's magic.

"Another portal will open up for you in twenty minutes. That should give you plenty of time," Margaret said.

"Thank you, Margaret!" Isaac flashed his big grin at her.

Margaret shooed him away. "Don't get the wrong idea. If Alison wasn't going with you, I'd leave your ass there and have you figure out how to get back."

Isaac's expression turned to fake pain as he clutched at his heart. "Your words cut deep."

Margaret pinched the bridge of her nose. "Kid, I swear…"

"Let's go before she sends us somewhere unpleasant." Isaac winked at Alison and pulled her through the portal.

They stepped out onto the top of a large, grassy hill surrounded by maroon-colored trees with burnt-orange leaves. The surrounding hills sloped gently downward to meet the shimmering crystal blue lake at the bottom. The two moons were low in the sky; the larger one, Ieia, was ghostly pale with large, deep ravines across its surface. Its sister-moon, Aiei, was small and pink, trailing in the shadow of its big sister. The moons looked as if they were chasing the sun out of the sky.

Before them stood a tall, crudely made stone tower with short, narrow stairs that wound around to the top of the spire.

"Just a little further." Isaac motioned. He took slow, purposeful steps, carefully guiding her up the narrow stairs.

After a few moments, the two made it to the top of the tower, which afforded a grander view of the lake and the forest below. The crimson sunset made the tree leaves glow, making them all seem as if they were on fire.

"Wow…" Alison breathed. "Where are we…?"

"Where do you think?" Isaac grinned. "We're in Ahntwen. Or, more specifically, we're at Fairies' Rest."

Alison felt the breath catch in her throat. "No way…"

"Way."

Alison watched the reflection of the sun and moons dazzle across the lake in a sort of celestial dance. She had read the story of Fairies' Rest in a book when she was younger. It was a love story as old as time, about a Fairy Prince who fell in love with a silver-eyed Sprite, a relationship the Fairy King did not approve of. But, every night, the Prince and the Sprite would sneak out and meet at this lake to steal what time they could together. One day, the Sprite the Prince was so in love with no longer came to the lake. The Prince suspected the King in her disappearance, but could prove nothing. So the legend has it that the Prince comes down every night to turn the lake silver in memory of the love he lost, hoping she will one day return to him.

A sad smile spread across her face. She read that story until the pages began to fall out, and she had always wanted to come and see this place someday. But between training and their missions, someday felt like it'd never come.

"I know how much you've wanted to see Fairie's Rest," Isaac said. "And I know that we're always busy, so I figured we could take advantage of this rare time off."

Alison turned and wrapped her arms around him in a tight hug.

"Thank you," she whispered. "This means a lot to me."

She felt his arms wrap around her, and they stood like that for some time. Despite her having been with him for years, she was always surprised by how soft and warm he was. For someone who was normally rather boisterous, he was surprisingly gentle.

He patted her gently on the back. "Look, it's starting!"

Alison turned her head to look down at the lake. The crystal blue water slowly faded into pure silver. Hundreds of small beads of silver and gold light began floating upwards from the lake, shining like small suns as they ascended before fizzling out just above the trees. The fiery color of the leaves dimmed and took on an ember-like glow.

"Thank you," Alison said, breaking the long silence they'd been sitting in since the spectacle began. "This is everything I dreamed it would be."

"Anything for you." Isaac smiled again, though this time it wasn't his usual cheeky smirk.

It was sweet and sincere.

Alison felt her face flush, and she smiled back at him.

"So, what'd you have to do to get Margaret to do this?" Alison asked.

Isaac looked off into the distance dejectedly. "I have to clean her room for a month..." he grumbled.

Alison laughed. "That's all? I'm surprised."

"She also figured that if I do pass the Trial, I'd be getting sent out on more missions, so that means I won't be able to bug her for a while, a thought that she relished a bit too much, in my opinion."

That's right... Alison hadn't even thought of what would happen if Isaac passed. Jack normally starts giving people solo missions once they make Magician.

Which means that they could be split up for a while.

But, more importantly, Isaac would be alone.

"How do you feel about going on missions by yourself?"

Isaac shuddered. "I definitely don't want to think about it. Not right now, anyway. Maybe after I pass the Trial, and I prove to myself that I *can* handle things on my own, then ask me. Besides, not every mission will be solo."

That's true. Looking at him now, she could see a darkness forming in his eyes. It was slight, but it was fierce. It was clear from the look on his face that he was fighting with himself, going back and forth about what happened at the Temple and what it meant for him. She truly did understand where he was coming from, and could understand his fear. She wished she could help him more in some way.

"What's wrong?" Isaac asked, noticing Alison's frown.

"Nothing," Alison said, shaking her head. "Just thinking about how I'm going to make the Trials next year."

"Well..." Isaac began with a cheeky smirk, "You better get training. You're already so far behind me, I'm not sure how you'll be able to catch up!"

Alison scoffed. "Catch up to you? Please, I'm already ahead of you. They just didn't want me to outshine your ass this year. Don't worry, I'll be a Magician next year."

Isaac let out a hearty laugh. "I look forward to congratulating you then."

Alison smacked him lightly on the chest and turned her attention back to the lake, enjoying being close to Isaac and the mesmerizing scenery. They watched as the sun fell out of the sky and the lake quieted, the balls of light fading and the water returning to its usual blue. Below them, they heard the soft crackle of a portal opening.

"Guess it's time to head back." Isaac smiled sweetly.

"Guess so," Alison reluctantly agreed.

They made their way down the stairs and stopped before the portal. Isaac turned to dismantle the tower, but Alison stopped him.

"Leave it, in case anyone else wants a view."

Isaac smiled.

"Oh, and Isaac." Alison began, stopping him as they were about to step through. "Thank you again for this... and, good luck. Kick some ass."

Isaac grinned. "Thanks."

Alison smiled back at him and took one last glance at the lake before stepping through the portal.

CHAPTER EIGHT

J ACK CLOSED HIS EYES as he ran his hands over his face and leaned back in his chair. His desk was a mess of papers and scrolls, each written in a different language.

Still nothing. To say he was frustrated would be an understatement. He had poured over countless stories of the Ancient Ones, who were known as Primis during their time, and their use of their artifacts. He examined records from old human civilizations, Elven parliaments, Orx scribes, and even Dwarven wordsmiths, and *none* of them had any mention of how the orb worked, if it even mentioned its existence at all.

He held up a small piece of parchment, written in the flowy, elegant Elven script, that mentioned the existence of the orb and its supposed power. It was this half-destroyed note that sparked the mission in the first place. It was unusual for an artifact to be so ill-recorded, though, to be fair, most of the artifacts have very little information about them. But this one... this one appeared as if someone tried to erase any trace of its existence.

Perhaps for good reason... Jack thought. Primis were known to set traps on some artifacts they left behind, with no indication about which were true tools and which were meant to trick the user. So, for this artifact to be so shrouded in mystery meant that it was either incredibly powerful or a trap. Perhaps both. Only through more careful research and learning how the orb worked would tell Jack for sure.

He just had to not get himself or anyone else killed in the process, which sometimes, depending on the artifact, had been much easier said than done.

A sudden, hard knock came from his door.

Jack placed the paper down and sighed. "Come in."

Sigmund entered slowly. "Good time?"

Jack smiled and nodded. "Always."

"She's back," Sigmund said, pushing the door further open. A tall, Northern woman around Jack's height strode confidently into the room. Streaks of blue ran through her long, black hair, which bounced against her gray cloak as she walked. Her mesmerizing purple eyes looked like radiant gemstones on her doll-like face.

"Hello, Jack," Adara said with a soft smile.

"Adara!" Jack stood from his chair and hugged her tightly. "Welcome back! Tell me, how is Kenna doing these days?"

"Fiery-tempered as ever." Adara chuckled, "Happy that I took care of her problem."

"I can't wait to hear all about your journey, but, another time," Jack said, motioning for them to sit as he took his place at his desk. "If you two would be so kind, we have much to discuss."

"What is it?" Adara asked, a twinge of concern behind her voice.

Adara sat in stunned silence for a few moments after Jack and Sigmund had finished recounting the events of the Temple.

"So... there's a rat, eh?"

Jack nodded, his face a rare, serious mask. "Indeed. And I need your help in figuring out who it is. As I've already told Sigmund, I've heard rumors that someone is recruiting Arcanists. For what, I'm not sure, and I need to know if this is connected."

Adara's already pale expression turned paler.

"What is it?" Jack asked, leaning forward in his chair.

"Well, I uh..." She swallowed hard. "While I was up North, I also had heard rumors from my informants up there, and even Queen Hestia had heard about it, that indeed someone is recruiting Arcanists, and I heard they were going after artifacts."

A heavy silence hung over the room as Adara's words rang like an ominous bell.

"You sure?" Sigmund grumbled.

Adara nodded. "Yes, I planned on letting Jack know about someone going after artifacts as well. It's not unusual for bandits to seek powerful items, but for these two events to happen so closely together…"

"It's no coincidence," Jack said with a sigh. "Unfortunately, I will be away for a couple days, and I really need both of your help to get this investigation underway. Adara, I know you just returned, but I need you to head out again and gather more information. We need to try to understand more about what's going on. Talk to Sigmund, Isaac, and Alison too since they were the ones attacked."

"Understood," Adara said. "I will leave as soon as possible."

"And Sigmund, I want you and Alison to return to the Temple and see if there are any clues they might've left behind. I'm sorry to ask you to go back to that place, but we need to check."

"Fine with me." Sigmund stood from his chair. "The lass and I will be on our way by nightfall."

"Thank you both." Jack stood as well. "When I return, I expect a full update. If anything urgent happens, you know where to find me."

Adara and Sigmund nodded.

"We're here for the family, Jack. We'll figure out who did this," Adara said, placing a reassuring hand on Jack's arm.

"Thank you." Jack patted Adara's hand. "Now, if you'll excuse me, I have a protégé to retrieve."

Jack left his study and strode down the long hallway toward Isaac's room. His mind raced with excitement at the prospect of seeing how much Isaac had grown. He couldn't help but feel a bit guilty for being so preoccupied recently; normally, he tried to keep a close eye on Isaac's training. But Sigmund was more than willing to keep the pressure on him, and he knew that there was no way Sigmund would let Isaac slip even a little.

Jack stopped at the door with the polished gold plaque that read *Isaac* in flowing script and knocked. He heard a brief rustling inside and, a few moments later, Isaac had the door opened as wide as his eyes were with excitement.

An image of Isaac as a child flashed in Jack's mind.

Still has the same look on him. Jack remembered warmly.

But there was something more there this time. Faintly, as if Jack could see into Isaac's mind, he could see conflict in his eyes. Jack shoved down the nagging questions in his mind.

He'll tell me when he is ready.

Jack beamed at Isaac. "Ready to go?"

"Are you kidding? I've been ready for the past hour!" Isaac exclaimed.

Jack laughed and placed his hand on Isaac's shoulder. "Then, we're off!"

END OF PART 1

PART 2

A MAGICIAN'S TRIALS

CHAPTER NINE

Isaac felt his body tingle for a moment as he watched the world around him contort, disappear, and get replaced by a new landscape.

A colossal, ethereal white castle stood before him, its towers and battlements rising high into the clouds, making it almost impossible to see the top of them. A cobblestone pathway lined with trees with violet leaves that turned red when the sun hit them led up to and beyond the giant metal gate and the shimmering ward magic that guarded the keep.

Beyond the gates, Isaac could make out a busy courtyard paved with glowing rainbow-colored stones that circled a marble fountain that spat water high into the air, forming different intricate patterns each time. At the gate, two giant red flags flapped silently in the breeze, displaying four dragons whose necks were coiled around each other in a knot, each one breathing fire to one corner of the flag.

"They depict the Elder Mages that run the Order of Dormiri," Jack explained, pointing at the flag. "The dragon with twisted, demonic horns on its head represents Tor, the leader of the Elders. Ailith is the second Elder, depicted by the dragon with a cloth covering its eyes. The third with the missing left arm is Gideon. And finally, the fourth that is covered in fur is Alycca."

"Sounds like quite the group."

Jack laughed. "They are... something, that's for sure. Come, the inside is even more breathtaking."

Jack ushered Isaac forward, the gates opening on their own as they approached. As soon as they passed through the gates, everyone occupying the courtyard stopped what they were doing and stared directly at them.

More specifically, at Jack.

Jack smiled widely at all of them, greeting them all by name as he walked by. Everyone came out of their stupor and began following Jack, each practically begging for his attention, and all of them completely oblivious to Isaac's existence.

Isaac knew Jack was well-known, but he had no idea that he was *this* popular.

Jack slowly pushed through the growing crowd and guided Isaac to a large foyer that was packed with other Arcanists, each one wearing a different colored robe, and some with pendants that, as Jack had explained once, allowed Uhnius Arcanists to extend their lifespan like Omnis Arcanists naturally can. Everyone was gathered around one of the many tables of food, talking and laughing as they waited.

"This is where the examinees are meeting. As you might've guessed, most of the Arcanists here were trained within these castle walls, and have not had the life you've lived. It might be good for you to exchange stories with some of them and get to know them." Jack patted Isaac on the shoulder. "I must go meet with the other Mages, but I will see you later. Promise."

Isaac nodded and watched as Jack shuffled away, still politely greeting everyone who surrounded him.

What is with these people? Isaac wondered. *It's like they've never seen the man before.*

"Hey, what's your name?" a low, masculine voice rumbled behind him.

Isaac turned to see a tall, muscular man with an electric-blue robe flowing down around his wide shoulders. He wore his blonde hair pulled back in a tight knot behind his head. Despite his gruff appearance, his hard, green eyes were kind and warm. Another, identical man stood beside him: same blonde hair kept the same way, and the same eyes, but this man was skinny, with a long unruly beard, and a light cyan-colored robe.

Isaac raised an eyebrow.

What an interesting pair.

"Isaac. What's yours?"

"I'm Olfen," the larger one said. "As you might've guessed, this is my twin brother, Olyen."

Olyen waved a fragile-looking hand through the air.

"Sorry for the abrupt introduction, we saw your cloak and immediately wanted to speak with you," Olfen explained. "Not often that a Grey comes around."

"That easy to spot, eh?" Isaac chuckled.

"Well, gray in a sea of color tends to stick out like a sore thumb." Olfen smiled.

"Speaking of, what does the color of your robes mean?" Isaac asked. "Seems like most people have different ones."

Olfen raised a curious eyebrow. "Lot for you to catch up on, I see. It shows what type of Arcanist you are. For example, I am a Lightning Arcanist."

Isaac felt himself wince and unconsciously rubbed at his chest where he had been shot by Djaro's arrows, causing Olfen to pause.

"Not a fan of lightning?" Olfen asked teasingly.

Isaac shook his head and smiled. "Sorry, not that. Just a bad experience with one recently. Didn't mean to offend you."

"No offense taken." Olfen held up his hands in understanding. "Anyway, Olyen here has a unique disposition: he is a Pestilent Arcanist."

Isaac cocked his head to the side. "I've never met a Pestilent Arcanists before."

"We're quite rare, even among Arcanists," Olyen finally spoke, his voice barely above a whisper.

Isaac made a mental note to ask Jack about Pestilent Arcanists later, and what other types of magic are out there for Isaac to learn. Judging by the sea of colors around him, he had a long way to go before he could hope to become a Mage.

"And what're you, then?" Olfen asked, grabbing a pastry from the table next to them and taking a monstrously large bite.

"Omnis," Isaac responded.

Olfen and Olyen looked at each other and grinned. "Ah, special one you are. And here I am bragging about Olyen." Olfen laughed and slapped Isaac on the shoulder.

"So, you're the same as Jack, eh? Must make for interesting training."

"What's it like being Jack Grey's pupil?!" Isaac winced as Olyen's voice rose to a high shrill of excitement, causing the surrounding crowd to stop for a moment before returning to their conversation.

"It's awesome. He's encouraging and pushes you to do better, never puts you down, and is always constructive. He's a great guy to be around with unbelievable stories."

Olyen frowned, his voice returning to a whisper. "That's it?"

Isaac's brows furrowed. "What'd you mean, 'that's it'?"

"We just expected something more... dramatic," Olfen explained. "He's the talk of the town around here. The way it's talked up, we figured anyone who was with him would be leagues above everyone else with some crazy stories."

"All the teachers here use Jack as an example of greatness. He's what we're taught to look up to. His story of how an unremarkable peasant boy rose from the ashes of his desecrated town and became the strongest Arcanist that the world has ever seen? They find that to be rather inspiring," Olyen added.

It made sense now why everyone was behaving around Jack the way they were. With Jack being portrayed as this paragon that everyone should aspire to be, every time he visited it was akin to a king gracing his subjects with his presence. It made Isaac more appreciative of the time he got with Jack. Everyone here practically begged for his attention, and all Isaac had to do was walk into his office.

"But enough of that," Olfen said with a snort. "This is your first time here, yeah?"

Isaac nodded.

"Well, let us show you around then! What would you like to see first? The training grounds, enchanters' rooms, library—"

"Library?" Isaac cut Olfen off. Isaac had a penchant for old books, and this place had to be chock-full of them.

"Like to read, eh?" Olfen grinned. "Me too. Library it is then! There's plenty to see on the way there."

Olyen sighed exaggeratedly and waved one skinny hand flamboyantly in the air and left.

"Forgive my brother. He's much more of a hands-on guy. More of a doer than anything. Probably heading off to the training grounds already. Come!" Olfen's large paw clapped Isaac on the back, jolting him forward.

Olfen escorted Isaac away from the crowd and towards a large, winding staircase just off the entrance. The white stone of the spiral staircase sparkled like diamonds where the sunlight streamed in from the windows.

"When did you and Olyen find your way here?"

"We came at ten, right when the Order would take us. Our parents, bless them, weren't ashamed of us. The rest of our village? Not so nice, so the first chance our parents got, they put us on a wagon and off we went."

"I'm sorry to hear that your village distrusted you. Must have been hard growing up after your status as an Arcanist became known."

"I think it was harder on my parents than anything. Them not knowing quite how to defend us and everything, and not quite knowing how to keep Olyen from scrapping with the local boys." Olfen chuckled to himself. "Aye, he was a troublemaker..."

"Have you been back since?"

Olfen nodded again. "Aye. We've been back to see our Ma. Our father died two years ago; a flash flood swept him up and swallowed him. Nothing no one could do."

"I'm sorry."

Olfen patted Isaac's shoulder. "It's alright. We're past it. Anyway, let's not dwell on terrible events. What do you know of the Order's history, eh?"

Isaac scratched his chin thoughtfully. "I think I know enough. I know the Elder Mages were the first Luminares Arcanists to learn how to use magic, taught by their Primis teacher, Dormiri. After Primis was eliminated during the Divine Civil War, the Elders formed the Order to house and teach the next generation of Arcanists, and perhaps to protect them too from the malice that Arcanists garnered thanks to Primis."

Olfen nodded his head as Isaac spoke. "That's about the sum of it. Lots of little details in there, but they are not overly important right now. Ah! Here's our stop."

Olfen pushed Isaac into one of the hallways that branched off the stairs and saw three large, ornate portraits decorating the wall, hung against glowing emerald stone that replaced the white marble. Pairs of red and white banners framed each painting, with the Order's symbol emblazoned at the bottom where the banner's edges came to a point. A different dragon dominated the rest of the flag, depending on which picture you were looking at.

"What is this...?" Isaac asked, his gaze drifting across the portraits.

"This is the Hall of the Archmages," Olfen said proudly. "Where all previous Archmages are remembered forever."

Olfen strode past the paintings, naming each as he went.

"This is Bahtun." He pointed to the first picture, where a woman with fierce white eyes glared back at him. "The first Archmage and the first student of the Elders."

He pointed to the second picture of a man with a ring of metal wrapped around his head, covering his mouth. "This is Aultret the Silent, the Second. And this..." Olfen gestured to the third portrait of a woman with elf-like features and large, watchful eyes. "This is Virua the Wise, the Third."

There are so few... Isaac thought. It made sense, though, given their extended lifespan. But still, he thought there would've been a few more...

Isaac paused at a picture he had failed to notice when he first entered the hallway. There was only darkness in the frame, no carefully drawn portrait like the rest.

"What about this one?" Isaac asked, pointing.

"Ah, that one." Olfen walked up to the last frame and smiled. "That would be where Jack Grey's smiling face *would* be if he had accepted the title. Damn shame."

Isaac furrowed his eyebrows. *Jack? The Archmage?*

Isaac had never heard of him being offered Archmage.

"He *declined* the position? Why?"

Olfen's eyes widened in surprise. "I thought you would know more about that, to be honest. I had heard he declined because of personal reasons that Jack didn't elaborate on. However, many speculate it was because *he* was somehow involved in releasing the Primis Beast that killed Virua. There are many theories, but it seems all lost to legend and myth."

Jack caused the death of the third Archmage? Isaac thought. He had heard some stories of the Primis Beast from Jack, mainly to warn the Grey family of the danger that these artifacts pose if left out in the world. Jack had told them how the Beast had killed the Archmage at the time, dozens of Mages, and several more Warlocks that were called to help. Thinking back on it, he never mentioned Virua by name when he told the story. If Jack did cause her death, was it guilt that kept him from uttering her name? Isaac couldn't picture Jack causing anything like that, and certainly couldn't picture him letting anyone die. But, even after being at the Order for such a short time, it appeared that there was much that Isaac didn't know.

I'll have to ask Jack more about it later.

"Well, are you ready to see the library now?" Olfen asked, beginning to walk down the hallway. "It's just up ahead. There! You can see it from here. This entire floor is practically dedicated to it."

Further down the hallway, Isaac could see a giant open space packed with shelves and books. To say the library was massive would be an understatement; it made the great halls in castles look like a peasant's shed. Bookshelves lined the walls, with several more lined up on the floors. The library seemed to go up forever, with a giant staircase that spiraled upward seemingly forever, each floor lined with more books. A giant, rainbow-colored stained-glass window illuminated the library, painting the slate-gray stone of the library in shards of colorful light. Magelights bobbed around the room lazily, stopping near those who beckoned to them for additional light.

Olfen laughed at Isaac's slack-jawed expression. "It *is* quite the sight to behold, especially the first time. The thought that thousands of years of history are housed here... It's astounding."

"Well, don't just stand there! Go on. Explore! We have time to kill. I'll wait around for you." Olfen clapped Isaac on the back, half pushing him forward.

Isaac stumbled and nodded his thanks before he began his walk around the library, turning, and craning his head as he went. Isaac ran his fingers across the bindings of some of the old books, enjoying the feeling of the cool, cracked leather against his skin. Despite the age of the documents in here, the entire library smelled like fresh bits of parchment paper. It was almost completely silent in the library, save for the soothing sound of pages being quietly turned.

One binding made Isaac stop in his tracks. It was hard, smooth, and shining like a diamond. He pulled it off the shelf, almost dropping it because of its unexpected weight. There was a silver plate with decorative gold writing on the cover written in the language of the Divines that read *Divinous Civil Baellyum.*

The Divine Civil War. Isaac thought, his hand tracing down to the art etched into the diamonds below the plate. The picture showed clouds parting over an earth riddled with bodies, with a screaming demon-like figure shrieking below it.

Jack's library had many books on the Divine Civil War, but *nothing* looked like this. Isaac's interest in history meant he had read each of those books thoroughly.

Isaac began flipping excitedly through the text.

At first, the book discussed much of what Isaac already knew: Three thousand years ago, Ranatrael, the Archangel of Light, and the first Archangel, turned against the beings of the Eutrox and his allies in Heaven. Ranatrael sought the help of the Lord of Hell, Xyteres, and together they launched an attack against Heaven and Eutrox, hoping to conquer both. Ranatrael thought that, with the Creator gone, he was the rightful replacement to control and direct all of existence. In the end, five of the six remaining Archangels met with Ranatrael in battle to end the Divine Civil War. Realizing their brother was too strong for them to kill, they opted to sacrifice their lives to seal Ranatrael away until the end of time.

The heading on the next page caught Isaac's attention.

FORBIDDEN RACES AND THEIR ROLE IN THE WAR.

Forbidden races...?

According to the text, there are three races that are "Forbidden" by the Dogmata, the ruling council of Heaven: Nephilim, Hefaimon, and Xyar. Nephilim were half-angel and half-human, while the Hefaimons were half-demon and half-human. And the Xyars were an *'even more unnatural, despised combination possible only through the union of an angel and a demon...'*

An angel and a demon having a child? Is that even possible? Isaac thought.

From what Isaac could gather, the Dogmata was very concerned with the existence of these races. Despite the fact that a hybrid being born was extremely unlikely, the Dogmata adopted a malicious stance against them because of their ability to grow stronger than their Divine parents, and their resistance to weapons that would normally injure them.

Hefaimons were given a special mention, as the Dogmata feared them for their resistance to Smiting and weapons forged in the Holy Fires of Heaven.

The Xyars, though, seemed to catch the most ire, being highlighted as an affront not only to Heaven, but to existence itself, claiming it to be *'the unholiest of unions.'*

However, despite the Dogmata's hatred for these races, Nephilim fought on Heaven's side in the war against Hell and Ranatrael, just as Hefaimon fought for Hell. But there was no mention of any Xyar being present during the War.

The existence of these Forbidden Races gave Isaac pause. Why hadn't he ever heard of them before? How was it that there were no Xyars fighting in the Divine Civil War? Surely, beings as powerful as the Xyars wouldn't stand idly by, would they?

"Reading anything interesting?"

Isaac jumped at the sound of the gentle voice behind him. Jack leaned over Isaac's shoulder, smiling, and seemingly reading along with him.

"Always." Isaac smiled back, turning to face Jack.

"Do you mind?" Jack held out his hands.

Isaac shrugged, handing him the heavy book.

"Ah, the Divine Civil War." Jack tsked, examining the cover. "Certainly an interesting time in our history. However, what is *more* interesting, in my opinion, is the stuff that came before this."

Jack closed the book and placed it gently back on the shelf.

"What do you mean?"

"Well, for example, there are texts here that certain interested parties have gone to great lengths to destroy that depict Ranatrael in a much more... sympathetic light, prior to the War." Jack said, his eyes skimming across the bookshelves.

"Why would anyone do that?"

Jack smiled and leaned against the bookcase, propping an elbow on the shelf. "For the simple reason that it could've been true. Dozens of texts depict Ranatrael as a sort of great protector who loved all creation. Yet, after the War, most of that history was erased and replaced with tales of him being twisted from the beginning, eventually leading to the Dogmata crowning him the new King of Hell. The Demon King. The only good thing he did, perhaps inadvertently, that everyone can agree on is that his war killed Primis."

Isaac scratched his head. "If that were true, then why do the books after the War tell a different story? What made him turn against everything he supposedly loved? If history was altered, why was it changed, and by whom?"

"Ah, now *those* are the types of questions you should be asking." Jack nodded emphatically. "Why indeed did Ranatrael, supposedly, turn his back on creation, and what would someone gain from rewriting history?"

Isaac glanced at Jack suspiciously. "Do *you* know the answers to those questions?"

Jack laughed and patted Isaac's shoulder. "I know a lot of things, but even I do not know why a Divine being acts the way they do. Perhaps one day we'll find out together." He smiled. "The important thing is not to believe everything you hear. Be inquisitive! The answer, most of the time, is somewhere in the middle of it all."

Isaac nodded and smiled back. He had never thought to question what history had told him. Why would he? Up until now, he had never heard any alternative stories about Ranatrael, and that's perhaps exactly what whoever changed history wanted to happen. What Jack said did raise the question though: what really happened all those years ago?

"Now, if you are ready, let's go find your friend," Jack said, taking off toward the second floor.

How'd he know I made a friend here...?

Jack and Isaac met up with Olfen, who, not surprisingly, went slack-jawed at the sight of Jack walking over to strike up a conversation with him. Isaac swore Olfen was damn near swooning as Jack escorted them down to the reception at the training grounds.

If Olfen is like this, I can only imagine what Olyen would be like... Isaac thought.

Olfen assaulted Jack with a barrage of questions about the stories he had heard about him. Isaac was surprised Olfen could cram so many questions into one sentence. Jack, as usual, handled it with a smile, not seeming to care how overexcited Olfen was. Jack left them close to the training grounds to join the rest of the Mages, leaving Olfen and Isaac to find Olyen in the growing sea of bodies. The training grounds were packed with Arcanists ready to take on the Trial. The grounds were a stadium-like field of sparring pits, with archery-style lines littered throughout. For the Trials' commencement, a grand stage made of polished white and black stone sat directly in the middle of the field. The crowd huddled so tightly together started to make Isaac feel claustrophobic.

I didn't think there would be this many people.

"Oi, Olyen!" Olfen shouted across the crowd.

Isaac squinted where Olfen was looking and could just make out the skinny frame of Olyen, sitting on a fallen training dummy. Olyen looked up, somehow hearing Olfen over the throng, and trotted over to them.

"It's about time you two showed up," Olyen whispered, his voice barely audible.

"Sorry, we got caught up at the library." Isaac smiled apologetically.

"Guess who *I* met?!" Olfen yelled in excitement. "Jack *freaking* Grey! He walked us down to the grounds!"

Olyen's jaw dropped. "No way... And I *missed* talking to him?!" His voice rose to a high-pitched shrill.

Isaac laughed. "I'm sure he'll be around later too. Don't worry about it."

Seeing how excited Olfen and Olyen, and everyone else, got when they saw Jack made Isaac reflect more on the relationship he had with Jack. To him, he was just Jack, his friend, and teacher.

His father.

But to them, he was this legendary Arcanist who they would give anything to get a five-minute conversation with.

In that aspect, I am lucky.

A brilliant flash of light lit up the stage, and in the next moment, a line of Mages, including Jack, stood proudly before their students waiting eagerly on the field before them.

The crowd erupted into a cacophony of cheers and applause. Isaac couldn't help but smile. The excitement of the people around him was infectious. Isaac looked on in awe of the Mages on stage. Jack and Adara had been the only two Mages he had ever known, and they all seemed to exude the same air of power and confidence.

"Welcome, students!" One of the Mages stepped forward, his deep voice booming. He had a Northerner's accent, like Sigmund's. He was tall, broad, and dark-skinned. The sunlight reflected off his bald head, but cast a small shadow from his curly black beard. His smile was warm and welcoming, much like Jack's, and his years of experience and knowledge shone in his crystal-blue eyes. A long, colorful cloak hung off his shoulders, the colors lapping against each other like gentle waves on a beach.

"What's with the cloak?" Isaac leaned toward Olfen, noticing that the other Mages wore similar ones, except some only had one color slithering across their cloaks.

"Mage's cloak. Shows their mastery in their respective schools. Omnis Mage cloaks have all the colors of the different schools," Olfen explained.

"For those that may not know me, I am Aephes, the Warden and leader of the High Council of the Order. I have gathered with me today Mages many of you may be familiar with, to help oversee this Magicians' Trial. Two in particular will play vital roles in its execution. Pay attention, students, for their magic will give you a hint as to what you will be facing in the Trials to come! Now, allow me to introduce them. First, our Conjurer Mage, Kaitlin!"

Aephes pointed behind him to his left to a short, olive-skinned woman with sharp facial features and slightly pointed ears that protruded from her almost white-blonde hair. She wore a burnt-orange robe that flowed elegantly down to her legs.

"Quite a sad story with her," Olfen said. "When the High Lord of Nivandeer found out that her mother had conceived a child with a human, they were both tortured and killed. Her relatives had to hide her until she was old enough to come here."

"Damn Elves..." Olyen hissed.

"And secondly," Aephes voice boomed again. "The 'all-seeing-eye' of the Order of Dormiri: the Mage with the predilection for divination, Yvek!"

Aephes pointed to the dwarf on his right as Yvek stepped tentatively forward, his rainbow-colored cloak shimmering as he did. Yvek was a short, stocky, pale-skinned man with a full head of long red hair and a beard that hung down to his chest. His eyes were smoky and reflective, like glass.

"One of the few blind Arcanists we have here," Olyen whispered. "Don't let that fool you; most will destroy you before you have a chance to do anything."

"Oh, and I almost forgot to mention our special guest." Aephes winked at Jack. "He does not come around often, so please, learn from him while you can. Welcome, Jack Grey!"

The crowd erupted into cheers and whistles again as Jack stepped forward, smiling warmly at the crowd as if he were saying hello to his own brothers and sisters.

"With introductions out of the way, I would like to turn the attention back to you: those that have been selected to participate in this year's Magicians Trial," Aephes began, signaling for the Masters to return to the line. "You are here because your teachers have deemed you ready to take a great step forward in your training. You are here to prove not only to us, but to yourselves that you are worthy of the title 'Magician'. The road to get here has been long and paved by your hard work. However, this is not your final destination. No, each of you should aspire for mastery of the gift you have. To completely control every aspect of your being with grace and strength. In that spirit, we have elected to do something a little new this year: we will be having a friendly duel, right now, between two of our Mages to show you all what true mastery looks like."

The crowd rallied in crazed applause and cheers. Isaac clapped as loudly as he could along with them. There was no way he was missing out on a chance to see two Mages fight.

"Mages! Any volunteers?" Aephes turned and looked at the line of masters behind him.

"I volunteer." A large, broad-shouldered man who made Aephes look tiny stepped forward. The movement of his lips was barely noticeable from behind his scraggly beard. The Kitsune tattoo appeared massive on his dense forearm. His bulky physique and scruffy appearance made him stand apart from the other Mages.

"Ah, Darnel," Aephes said with a pained expression. "I'm not entirely surprised."

Isaac nudged Olfen to ask him a question but stopped when he saw the worried look on his face.

"What's wrong?" Isaac whispered to the brothers.

Olyen answered first. "Darnel, he... He loves to fight."

"What's wrong with that?" Isaac asked.

"He's been quite vocal about his opinion of the other Mages, saying they are beneath him. Recently, he's made quite the commotion demanding to be given the Archmage title, but the Elders won't allow it. Hell, they've even thought about kicking him out but haven't, just so they can keep an eye on him."

"He's that bad?" Isaac asked.

Olfen nodded. "So for him to step forward now, he wants to fight someone, and there's only one person here I could think of..."

"And who would—"

"Jack. Fight me," Darnel demanded, marching over to Jack.

Jack smiled and put his hands up in front of him. "Surely, there must be someone else you might have in mind. I'm only here to observe, nothing more."

"Cut the shit," Darnel snarled, now standing face-to-face with Jack. Despite Darnel's impressive size, and standing a whole head taller than Jack, somehow, Darnel seemed smaller than he did before.

"You are the last obstacle I need to overcome. I have almost defeated every Mage here yet, despite my power, the Elders refuse me. If I were to defeat *you* before everyone here, then what more could the Elders say to deny me the title I deserve?"

"Well, surely it wouldn't be your magnetic personality," Jack said with a sly smile.

Darnel's face contorted in anger. "Don't you think it'd be a worthwhile lesson to the Magicians-to-be, to see the next Archmage and the man who *could've* been Archmage, fight?"

Isaac looked back and forth between Jack and Darnel. He had to hand it to Jack; despite Darnel's attempts to provoke him, Jack remained completely passive. Isaac would be lying to himself though if he said he wasn't excited to see Jack fight Darnel. Isaac had never seen Jack fight anyone before, save for sparring matches at the Manor, but those hardly amounted to him being serious.

"You make an excellent point," Jack replied calmly. "I accept your challenge, Darnel."

Aephes cleared his throat. "I ask that all the Mages clear the stage, and also for the audience to move back, as we prepare for this *friendly* match." As Aephes shouted, a strong force of wind began pushing the crowd begrudgingly backwards several hundred feet. The Mages lined up in front of them, facing the arena. A glistening crystal wall projected out from them, forming a barrier between the stage and the onlookers.

"Mages!" Aephes shouted at Jack and Darnel, who now stood opposite each other on the stage. "The winner will be decided when either one forfeits or one of you is unable to continue. There shall be no killing *or* maiming." Aephes glared at Darnel, who waved his hand dismissively.

"Are you two ready?"

"I've been ready for a long time," Darnel said, cockily rolling his shoulders. "Fight me seriously, Jack, or you will regret that you didn't."

"Of course." Jack smiled at Darnel.

"Begin!" Aephes shouted.

Whips of blue flame erupted in Darnel's hands, the heat was so intense they could feel it even through the warding. Lightning crackled around the fire in Darnel's hands, and water pooled above him, forming a sphere of churning water. Jack made no movement to use his magic, standing and watching, still smiling.

What is Jack doing? Isaac thought frantically. *Isn't he going to attack?*

"I'm going to burn that stupid smile off your face," Darnel growled and went to lunge at Jack.

But he didn't move.

Darnel stopped dead in the middle of the stage, his body motionless.

Isaac watched as Darnel tugged at his limbs, trying to get them to move. The air behind Darnel flickered as another Jack appeared behind Darnel, the tip of an ice spear pressed lightly against the back of Darnel's head. Isaac could just make out a long, solid black line connecting Darnel and the Jack that stood in front of him together.

Isaac heard the crowd murmur in the same confusion that Isaac felt.

"What the hell happened?" Isaac asked Olfen, who didn't respond, his eyes glued to the stage.

Darnel roared in anger as he attempted to move his body, his magic thrashing around him trying to reach the Jack that stood behind him. Darnel's magic bounced off a shimmering crystal warding that Jack had surrounded himself with.

"You were quite right that this would be a great opportunity for the students to learn, Darnel." As the second Jack spoke, the appearance of what Isaac thought was the original Jack dissolved into a mist, leaving behind a stone golem.

"Shadow linking is a useful, if not overlooked, technique of Umbrakinesis. Shadow Arcanists, do well to not forget the basics!" Jack continued, looking at the crowd. "Warding magic can be dangerous if you're unprepared for the consequences; however, I was confident that I would be able to hold out against at least some of Darnel's attacks. For Abjuration Arcanists, do not overexert yourself when using your warding, or you'll leave yourself too exhausted to fight. And finally, for my Illusion Arcanist brothers and sisters, at first you may only be able to recreate one of the five senses. But advance far enough, and you can trick all five and make some truly devious illusions."

Jack turned his attention back to Darnel, who was still struggling like a caged animal. "I would like to call this match finished, if that's alright with you."

Darnel shook with rage. "*No,*" he bellowed. "No. I will not lose like this."

Jack looked at Darnel with a pained expression. It looked like he felt sorry for him. "I'm sorry to say, but you have already lost, Darnel."

The spear in Jack's hand melted, and the golem dissolved into the earth, the shadow link fading away.

Darnel fell to his knees, his magic disappearing around him.

"Now, *that* was a display of mastery!" Aephes announced. "Omnis Arcanists in particular, take note! *This* is what awaits you at the top of the mountain! Thank you, Jack and Darnel, for your demonstration! Please, join us here for some final words to the Trial-goers."

Jack extended a hand to Darnel. "Come, brother, put your ego aside and let your fellow Arcanists help you grow into the man we know you can be. Perhaps then we can have a proper match. Deal?"

Darnel pushed himself to his feet, his face a mix of anger and shame, and spat on the floor in front of Jack.

"You can keep your pity and shove it up your ass. We'll have our rematch alright, and next time *I'll* be the one extending my hand out to you." A portal opened before Darnel, and in the next moment, he was gone.

"Well... again, nicely done, Jack," Aephes said, breaking the awkward silence that followed. "If you would, please." Aephes motioned to the line of Mages next to him. Jack nodded, teleporting down to the line with Aephes.

"Now, then, Trial-goers..." Aephes began, smiling, but his face stoic and serious. "What you have gathered here for is the opportunity to achieve the rank of Magician. It is the first of four ranks that denote to your fellow Arcanists, and to yourself, your experience and your strength. It is the doorway to learning and achieving greater things. You all should be proud of just having made it to this point. Many of your friends may not be here with you today, and even fewer will be there as you progress to mastery.

"Tomorrow, you all will undergo a test of skill, strength, and endurance. Your task will be to survive in a forest of our design for the allotted time. That's it. If your skills are not honed; if your magic is not strong enough; or you do not have the stamina to endure, then you will not survive the Trial and you will not receive the rank of Magician. Healing Mages will be on standby for those who need it after the trial has concluded. The test will last for two consecutive days. After such time, the Arcanists remaining will be given their new rank. I implore you all to treat this Trial as if it were a matter of life or death. We are lucky here to be able to train and practice rather carefree, but when we go out into the world, we can only bring what we have trained ourselves to use. So please, give it your all. I sincerely wish to see all two hundred of you standing on stage with me at the end of the Trial."

Quiet murmurs started sprouting throughout the crowd. A few Arcanists scoffed behind Isaac, unimpressed by the Trial.

"Last year, they all had to fight their way out of a collapsing cave with these invisible snakes chasing after them. *That* is a real test," one voice said.

Isaac was inclined to agree at least slightly; simply surviving in a forest for two days couldn't be that hard.

Could it?

There was the matter that they had no idea what would be lurking in the forest with them. Though given the presence of the Conjuration Mage, there would be summoned creatures from the Domustiar, the plane of existence where unspeakable atrocities live, stalking around the forest.

No matter what, he couldn't underestimate what the Order had in store for them—that was the surest way to fail before he'd begun. Isaac had every intention of treating this Trial as life-or-death: he had to prove to himself that he could survive on his own. He had to prove that he was capable, that he wasn't helpless.

Isaac took in a deep breath. A lot was riding on the Trial. He was both excited and incredibly nervous.

For now, all I can do is try.

"You have the rest of the evening to do anything you wish," Aephes continued. "For our visitors: enjoy your time here. You all must gather here at sunrise. Once everyone is in attendance, the Trial will commence. Enjoy your night."

A portal opened behind the line of Mages and, one by one, each walked through and disappeared to the other side. Jack was the last one to make his way to the portal. He stopped as he was about to step through, scanning the crowd. His eyes locked with Isaac's, and he gave him a reassuring smile. Isaac could just make out Jack mouthing "Good luck" to him before he passed through his portal.

As soon as all the portals closed, the crowd erupted into chaos. People were trying to talk over one another, shouting to each other, and generally freaking out about tomorrow's events.

Like Isaac, Olfen seemed a little apprehensive about the Trial, but Olyen could not be more excited.

"C'mon, brother, lighten up a little. Have some fun!" Olyen teased.

"I'll 'lighten up' once this Trial is over. This is serious," Olfen said, running his hand nervously through his hair. Olyen laughed at his brother's anxious twitching.

"What'd you think, Isaac?" Olfen asked, his eyes pleading with Isaac to side with him.

"Well... to be honest, I agree with you; we need to take this seriously. Creator knows what they have in store for us."

Olyen shrugged. "Just destroy whatever is in your way."

Oh, to have your confidence. Isaac smiled.

"So, what'd you want to do for the rest of our time then?" Olfen asked. "Hadn't realized it 'til now, but I am fucking starving. Just about time for supper." Olfen patted his stomach.

Isaac looked at the amber sky, the sun slowly falling into the horizon. Olfen was right: time had gone by quickly.

"I've always wanted to see the Order's dining hall."

Olfen grinned and slapped him on the shoulder. "It is grand, trust me! Come! Let's see what the Order has arranged as our last meal."

Isaac followed Olfen and Olyen as they led him through the Order's keep. They walked through long hallways adorned with exotic paintings of places Isaac had never heard of before, and what Isaac assumed were past Mages. Eventually, they came upon a set of giant double wooden doors with polished golden handles. Olfen pushed the doors open, and immediately Isaac was hit by the smell of cooking meats and vegetables and the sound of jovial laughter and mugs clanging against wooden tables. The dining hall was gorgeous: the floor was composed of dark walnut wood, and the walls made of a slate gray rock that had colorful bolts of light streaking across it. Long benches littered the floor, with large Magelight floating just above them. A grand fireplace took up most of the back wall. The roaring fire gave the dining hall a comfortable, welcoming warmth. The hall was already packed with people; it seems everyone else had the same idea.

"So, where do we grab food from?" Isaac asked, glancing around at the tables. There was no buffet of food at any of them. Nor was there any sign of someone bringing food out to you.

"We'll show you." Olyen led them to an empty bench and plopped himself down.

Olyen held out his hands before him and, almost instantly, a ceramic bowl filled to the brim with the most delicious-smelling stew Isaac had ever encountered appeared in his hands. Setting the bowl down, Olyen held out one of his hands in a half circle, and a pint filled to the brim with ale appeared, the handle slapping against his palm. Olyen nodded his thanks to the air and grinned.

"How did you do that?!" Isaac asked eagerly, sitting down opposite Olyen.

Olfen laughed at Isaac's mystified expression. "The cook has a familiar, a little bird, that flies around the rafters of the hall and communicates with him. The cook can see through his familiar's eyes, and he teleports food to us accordingly."

"That's incredible," Isaac said in awe.

"Go ahead, try it," Olfen said, holding out his hands, a bowl appearing a second later.

Isaac did as he was told and held out his hands in front of him. He felt the air around his hands tingle for a moment before a bowl of stew appeared in them.

"Awesome." Isaac grinned. "Why does he teleport it to people? Why not set it out himself?"

"Good question. We wondered the same thing when we got here," Olfen said between bites. "Rumor has it that the cook is disfigured and doesn't allow anyone to see him, or her. Hell, no one even knows their name, so they're just 'the cook.'"

"That's sad." Isaac frowned. "I can understand their desire not to be seen. It's just surprising that no one has managed to catch a glimpse of them yet."

"He keeps himself hidden enough," Olyen spoke in his usual whispering.

"So, what'd you think of the food? As good as I said?" Olfen asked, clearly eager for Isaac's response.

Isaac smiled as he gulped down more stew. "Better. Thank you."

Olfen clapped Isaac on his shoulder again, a habit Isaac was sure was going to either give him constant whiplash, or incredibly strong shoulders.

"G'evening, twins," a soft, boyish voice said from behind Isaac.

Isaac turned his head to find a short, extremely pale fellow standing uncomfortably close to him. His pitch-black hair fell in shaggy tufts over his eyes. His clothes matched his hair in color, and his robe was no different.

"Hey, Fraunt, how are you? Enjoy the little display earlier?" Olfen asked.

"I liked it. I liked that Jack showed my magic during his fight. It made me happy." Fraunt's lips moved into some horrifying version of what Isaac assumed was his smile.

Olyen nodded, twitching in his seat. "It was exciting to see Jack... please, join us." Olyen gestured to an empty spot next to him.

"Okay," Fraunt responded flatly, seating himself beside Olyen.

Isaac cast a sideways glance at Olfen, who just shrugged.

"Where's your sister?" Olyen nudged Fraunt, who sat staring unblinkingly at Isaac.

Isaac made brief eye contact with Fraunt and shuddered. Something about him was incredibly creepy.

Fraunt shrugged, prompting Olyen to frown.

"Fraunt's a man of few words," Olfen explained.

"I know many words," Fraunt protested.

"That's not what—" Isaac began to argue but stopped when Olfen held up his hand.

"Yes, you do, Fraunt. You probably know a lot of words," Olfen said.

Fraunt nodded. "Yes. Many words."

What the hell is with this guy?

"There you are, Fraunt! I've been looking for you! Why'd you leave me behind like that?" A chipper, singsong voice rang to the left of them.

A petite girl in an ocean blue robe, with snow-white skin and curly pitch-black hair, ran up to the table.

"Ah, there you are, Meri." Olfen smiled. "Fraunt here was just talking our ear off, telling stories."

"You still have your ears," Fraunt stated.

Isaac's eye twitched in annoyance.

"Oh, I bet he was." Meri laughed. "Fraunt, you were supposed to wait for me. We were going to get food together!"

"I got hungry before you. So, I came here."

Meri frowned. "How could you possibly know that you got hungry before me?"

Fraunt shrugged. "Because I did."

"Please, join us." Olfen smiled, patting the bench beside him.

Isaac caught Olyen looking back and forth between Meri and the table, before eventually settling on staring at his feet.

What was that about?

"So, who's your friend?" Meri asked as she sat herself down, extending her hands out to receive her dinner.

"I'm Isaac Grey. It's a pleasure to meet you." Isaac nodded to Meri and smiled.

Fraunt visibly tensed. "Grey?" Fraunt leaned across the table to Isaac, his body practically in Isaac's bowl. "You're a Grey?"

"Yes..." Isaac picked up his bowl and scooted back slightly.

Meri examined Isaac and hit herself softly on the forehead. "Of course. Should've noticed by your cloak." She giggled. "That's amazing! You must have so many stories having lived with Jack. Have you always been with him?"

Isaac nodded, doing his best to ignore Fraunt's intense gaze. "I was adopted into the Greys when I was a child. I don't really know how I got there, but I've been with Jack since then, and he's taught me everything I know."

"I'm sorry to hear that you were orphaned. That must gnaw at you a little bit. But at least Jack was able to give you a good home!" Meri said.

"Thanks, but I don't honestly remember anything about my life before Jack, and I haven't thought about it in some time."

Meri cast a sad smile at Isaac before reaching across the table and smacking Fraunt on the forehead with her palm.

Fraunt leaned back on the bench, holding his head. "Ow," he said flatly.

"Mind your manners and other people's space, Fraunt. How many times have I told you?" Meri chided.

"I wanted to look at the Grey man."

"Look at him from where you are now. Besides, aren't you hungry?"

"No. I am no longer hungry."

Meri frowned. "Then just sit there."

Isaac mouthed a quiet thank you to Meri as Fraunt retreated back to his side of the table.

"So... is everyone ready for tomorrow?" Olfen asked, glancing around the table.

"Nervous, but ready," Meri said, her hands shaking a little as she lifted her spoon to her mouth. "Though, I'm not sure how I'll fare by myself."

"That's how I feel," Olfen said. "But, I'm sure they wouldn't throw anything in there that we couldn't handle, right?"

Olyen piped up. "I'm sure we can handle it." He cast a nervous glance over at Meri before returning his gaze to the table.

"What if we all worked together?" Isaac offered.

Everyone seemed to mull the idea over for a moment.

"Isn't that cheating?" Meri asked.

"Cheating isn't good," Fraunt whispered.

Isaac shrugged. "They never said anything about people working together. If we're all nervous, maybe working together can help alleviate some of that? Take some of the pressure off? You can't tell me other people aren't thinking the same thing. It's going to be a challenge no matter what, so I doubt it'll be an issue."

Olfen nodded. "He has a good point. I'm sure our classmates are going to try to band together, and so should we. We should stick together as much as possible."

"So... we're teaming up?" Olyen asked, his eyes lighting up as he glanced across the table again.

"Yes, a team effort," Olfen agreed. "Is that okay with you, Fraunt?"

Fraunt was quiet for a moment, his eyes glazed over in a trance-like state.

"Yes," Fraunt said finally. "I will protect Meri."

"That settles it then," Isaac said, slapping the table. "We'll huddle together at the grounds before the Trial starts. If any of us get separated, we'll try to find the others as soon as possible. Above all else, we should aim to pass this Trial. Deal?"

Everyone nodded.

Olfen clapped Isaac on the shoulders and stood. "Alright, I'm going to retire for the evening. I suggest everyone else does the same. Good luck everyone. See you tomorrow!"

CHAPTER TEN

THE AIR CRACKLED AND SNAPPED as a swirling purple and black portal appeared. Adara stepped through it, finding herself inside the now all-too-familiar castle of the individual she, unfortunately, had aligned herself with.

How she *loathed* his arrogant, pompous attitude.

If it wasn't for her master's pleading, she might have abandoned this partnership some time ago out of sheer frustration.

Just stay focused. She thought. *It's only temporary.*

Her footfalls were silent as she glided across the cold stone that made up the entire castle. The stone had a shining, snake-like quality, like scales glittering in the light, giving the castle a mesmerizing, if not disorienting, appearance.

Dragon-rock. Appropriately named. She traced a finger along the wall and felt the rough, yet slick, edges of the rock.

Adara stopped in her tracks as a chilling scream rang out through the hallway that made the hair on her neck stand on end. Another cry echoed closely following the first.

What the hell is he doing? She sprinted toward where she thought the sound had come from: the conference hall, where she was supposed to meet with him to discuss their next steps. Adara burst into the room, the wooden door flying open and crashing into the wall behind it. The room was rather bare, save for some tables, squat chairs, and torches lining the walls. His subordinates lined the walls of the room, huddled against each other, and as far away as they could get from him. Adara chuckled to herself. Some of these people were cold-blooded killers, yet now they looked like children watching a monster tear apart their friends.

And that is exactly what was happening.

Her ugly, disgusting-looking partner stood in the middle of the room. He was completely bald, with dark, sickly gray skin and beady white eyes. His looks reminded Adara of a gargoyle. On the ground at his feet were the charred remains of two people: a small, petite woman with her left hand missing and the hulking form of a man. Adara couldn't help but wince as she looked at them. She could assume who they were: Azrael and Djaro, the two who were sent to collect the artifact. Had Adara not known, though, there were no distinguishable features left on their bodies to tell who they used to be.

"Adara," he said without turning. His voice was eerily calm; his accent was thick but hard to place. "The rest of you, get out of my sight. Let this serve as motivation for you all."

The huddled mass of bodies slowly filtered their way out through the door that Adara had come in, the last one to leave quietly shutting the door behind them.

"What are you doing, Zet?" Adara asked once she no longer heard footsteps outside the door. If she questioned him openly in front of his subordinates, it'd just give him more of a reason to be an insufferable ass.

"Punishing," Zet said flatly as he ground his foot into Azrael's ashes. "Perhaps more punishment on myself than on them."

Adara scoffed. "If you had listened to me in the first place, then this wouldn't have happened and we would have the artifact right now. I told you to send *at least* three Arcanists. And you send two. I thought you were supposed to be smart."

"Mind your tongue, woman!" Zet's lips curled in a snarl. Even though he yelled, he was not enraged. Adara could feel the authority he felt over her roll off his words.

"I admit that I had too much confidence in my recruits, something that will not happen again. Fortunately, this has given me ample information about the abilities of the involved parties, and the appropriate people will be sent next time."

"And why kill them?" Adara asked, the smell of burning flesh beginning to numb her throat.

"Despite my miscalculations, they should've been able to defeat an old man. If they cannot do that, then what hope do they have against the rest of that accursed family?"

Adara had seen enough cold, arrogant leaders in her time to be unsurprised by the callousness with which they treated their subordinates. But, even so, the way Zet looked at their charred corpses and spoke about them, she could *feel* that he genuinely thought of them as nothing more than tools.

Adara sighed. "You're going to have to listen to me more if you want any hope of killing Jack. What do you suppose we do now, then, that Jack has the artifact safely tucked away in his collection? Perhaps we wait until he turns it into a museum, then we'll be able to steal it from there!"

"For someone so insignificant, you make a lot of noise." Zet turned to her, his colorless eyes glaring at her with a building annoyance. "This is a setback, nothing more. We still have the first piece: the knife. Perhaps this misfortune can be turned into something positive."

Adara chuckled. "Care to explain?"

Zet strode over to her and scowled, his tall frame casting a shadow over her. "Jack studies artifacts all the time, correct?"

"Yes, relentlessly," Adara said.

"At any time, you have access to his collection, yes?"

Adara nodded.

"So, then, given time, Jack could do the work *for* me, figure out how to work the artifact, and we will steal it and move against him. It is a change from me working with the artifact myself; however, adjustments must be made... When the time is right, I will take the artifact and eliminate Jack Grey and his family. Do you understand this?"

Adara gritted her teeth and nodded again.

"Ahh, good. So you do understand something."

Adara clenched her fists and stared at him with fire in her eyes. If she didn't need this asshole to achieve her goals, she would've had him killed a while ago.

But for now...

"So, the plan remains the same? And after this, we go our separate ways?" Adara asked, straining to keep her temper under control.

"Yes. We will continue to recruit and make preparations. We have waited this long, so we can wait longer for Jack to do the hard work for us. Once Jack and his family are dead, then you can claim the Dragon Heart artifact from his collection. Unlike my father, I have no desire to share my power. Let me be clear with you, woman. Beyond our current mission, I have never intended, nor would I care, to sustain a contract with you. Frankly, even this engagement I find incredibly infuriating given your lack of utility. Jack, I'm sure, has asked you questions, so make yourself useful: drop hints, but not too many. And bait him long enough until he figures out the artifact."

Adara smiled as she tried to picture herself somewhere that wasn't here. Somewhere that made her calm.

At his side. She thought, feeling a wave of serenity wash over her. *This is all for him. Endure this insufferable monstrosity and work for him... It will all be worth it.*

"I will delay him as long as I can while keeping up appearances. It is a fine balance I must maintain. The only difficulty would be the old man, Sigmund, that your men failed to kill. He will need to be dealt with."

"Then deal with him. Figure it out."

Adara snarled; she could feel her anger rising up her spine. "I will let you know if there are any developments," Adara said, turning to leave.

"As will I," Zet responded, returning his attention back to the burned bodies of Azrael and Djaro.

Damn this asshole. Adara thought as she slammed the door behind her. Despite his cockiness, he was right about some things, one of which being that Jack was the forerunner in understanding Primis artifacts. If anyone could figure out how to work it, and quickly, it would be Jack.

Perhaps he has a point then. She thought as she walked through the castle. If they had retrieved the orb, it would've taken much longer to dissect it. But with it being in Jack's possession, it only accelerated their timeline.

And they were ready for it.

Zet had been working tirelessly, with Adara's aid, to find every weakness and crack in the Grey family and find people who could exploit those weaknesses. Alone, these bandit Arcanists wouldn't do much against the Greys. But together...

Together, they all stood a chance.

So, she would let him revel in his self-assurance and endure his bravado. Once Jack was out of the way, he was going to die anyway: her master had told her as much. He had no need for someone like Zet in the world.

Soon everything would fall into place. Adara smiled. She could already hear her master's voice praising her for the good work she'd done.

Soon.

CHAPTER ELEVEN

THE MORNING SUN STUNG ISAAC'S EYES as it reflected blindingly off the white stone of the keep. Everyone in the training grounds stood huddled close to each other, ready for the Trial to start.

It was clear to Isaac by scanning the crowd that everyone was a mixture of excited and anxious, some handling it much better than others. Isaac himself was beginning to break out in a cold nervous sweat.

He looked down at his shaking hands. He had never really been this nervous about anything before. But a lot was riding on this event.

He needed this.

He looked between his new friends: Meri's normally smiling face was downcast and solemn. Olfen, often the talkative one of the group, was quiet. Fraunt and Olyen, on the other hand, didn't seem to be phased at all. In fact, Olyen's eyes had a cheery and excited glow to them, and Fraunt had a creepy grin on his face.

Several portals popped into existence on the stage in the middle of the training grounds, and through them the Mages from yesterday—excluding Darnel—stepped forward with Aephes leading them.

"Good morning, students!" Aephes called.

"Good morning, Master Aephes!" The crowd called back; everyone's attention was now glued to the stage.

"It is now time for you to begin the Magician's Trial. As I said last night, this test will last forty-eight hours. There will be no breaks. You will need to be constantly aware if you want any hope of passing. You will most likely encounter things foreign to all of you. Push past that discomfort and unease. Hold fast, stay strong, and you will make it to the other side. Is everyone ready?"

Isaac scanned the row of Mages behind Aephes, searching for Jack. He found him and locked eyes briefly, Jack's face uncharacteristically serious. Jack nodded his head to him.

Isaac nodded his acknowledgment back.

Jack wouldn't have brought me here if he didn't believe in me. I can do this!

"Good luck, students!" Aephes clapped, and a giant portal appeared beneath them, causing everyone to fall into the magical abyss.

Isaac's vision blurred as he fell through the rift, his body tingling from the energy that surrounded him. He was spat out unceremoniously onto a forest floor unlike any he had ever seen. Almost all the vegetation, from the grass to the shrubbery, was charcoal black. The trees were covered in blood-red thorns and grew long needles from their branches. The clouds were a dark red, distorting what little sunlight made it through them and casting a red misty haze over the ground.

What the hell is this place...? Isaac looked around, trying to get his bearings, but everywhere he looked, everything looked the same.

Isaac felt his heart sink as he finally noticed something he should've been immediately aware of.

I'm alone.

Isaac cursed under his breath. He probably should've known better than to think the Masters wouldn't separate the students from each other. He would try to find them when he could.

For now, he had to get moving. He wasn't going to pass the Trial just standing still.

It did not take long for Isaac to come face-to-face with the creatures that the Conjurer had summoned into the forest. A hulking, muscular corpse shambled its way in front of him. Old, rusted metal armor hung loosely off its body, its skin blackened from decay. It stared at Isaac, its empty eye sockets were small orbs of darkness inside its skull. Despite its grotesque appearance, the creature easily carried a large battle axe in both hands, seemingly undisturbed by the weight of the weapon.

"Draugr," Isaac breathed. He had read about them as a child: they were undead creatures normally summoned to guard treasure or a king's tomb. This time, the only thing it was guarding was Isaac becoming a Magician.

The Draugr groaned and swung its axe at Isaac's head. Isaac's eyes widened as he flung himself to the ground, narrowly dodging the Draugr's attack.

It's so fast. For something undead, it moved surprisingly quickly.

The creature swung the axe around its head, carrying the momentum from its previous strike, and brought it down toward Isaac. He reached out to the mana in the ground and commanded the earth to rise. The rock shot up around him in a dome-like shape, catching the axe on its descent and trapping it between its rocky grasp.

The Draugr groaned in what Isaac could assume was annoyance and yanked on its weapon, trying to free it. As it struggled, the creature began to double in size, its tugs on the axe becoming stronger, and its axe growing with it.

Uh-oh.

Isaac pushed his hands through the air, directing them toward the Draugr's legs. Two stone spikes shot out from the ground into the Draugr's legs, penetrating them at the shin. Isaac willed the spikes to grow thicker and longer until they severed the Draugr's legs completely. The Draugr fell to the ground with a loud thud, desperately clawing at the dome that surrounded Isaac.

Isaac opened a small hole in the dome and slowly crawled out. He watched the mindless creature, now much larger than it was before, attempt to crawl its way over the dome toward Isaac. He held a hand out toward the Draugr and ignited the air in front of him, showering the Draugr in a torrent of flame. The decaying body of the Draugr caught fire quickly. The smell of burning flesh soured the air and immediately made Isaac nauseous.

Isaac quickly back-pedaled as the Draugr swiped at his legs with its large hands, still desperate to kill him. The Draugr let out a guttural roar as the flames continued to burn, before collapsing motionless. Isaac poured on the fire for a little longer after the Draugr had stopped moving, just to be sure. The last thing he wanted to do was turn his back on this thing, only for it to take him out a second later.

Isaac wiped his forehead with the back of his hand, already sweating. It took a lot more to kill them than he thought. He knew he got lucky with this one, though; it seemed like it was a simple creature. He had read about other Draugr who could think and control lesser Draugr. This one was just a Pawn separated from its commander, wandering directionless.

At least he knew now what he was dealing with.

Isaac walked aimlessly but cautiously through the forest, unsure of where to go. The only thing he knew for sure was that the longer he stood still, the longer his friends remained alone. He killed any of the Draugr he encountered with minor difficulty. After his first encounter, he was getting better at figuring out how to deal with them more efficiently.

Isaac stopped and dropped to the ground as a shrill, ear-piercing shriek echoed from somewhere to his right.

Another Arcanist?

He quickly finished off a Draugr that stepped out in front of him and made his way to the source of the sound. As he drew closer, the sound of moans and groans of the Draugr grew louder. Isaac stopped a few feet away from the huddled mass of corpses and watched as a short, stocky man in electric-blue robes, who looked to be a few years older than Isaac, attempted to break free of the circling horde. Isaac watched as arcs of blue electricity danced through the air and shocked the Draugr nearest him. The Draugr he attacked shuddered for a moment and fell to the ground, but as soon as one Draugr fell, another one took its place. The man desperately let loose a torrent of electricity around him, electrocuting the Draugr that got too close to him.

But they just kept coming.

A low, deep growl came from the middle of the horde. A Draugr with glowing white balls of light for eyes marched to meet the Arcanist.

A Draugr Knight... Isaac cursed. Knights were the leaders of the Pawns. They were intelligent, calculating, and much stronger than the fodder they commanded.

Another Knight appeared behind the man.

And another one.

And another one.

Until the Knights surrounded the student on four sides.

"Get away from him!" a female voice cried, her Southeastern accent making her voice sound rough and throaty. Isaac looked up to see a large, muscular woman with jewels embedded in her long, braided black hair, and a red cloak flapping in the breeze, soar through the air before crashing into the Draugr horde in an explosion of fire.

"Drew, I'm coming!" The woman yelled.

"No, Sasha, stay away!" Drew protested as he attempted to shock the Draugr Knights around him, but his magic seemed to bounce off their skin.

Time to move. Isaac charged into the fray, wind whipping around him as he used it like a blade to tear through the Draugr's bodies. Isaac battled through the Draugr using every weapon he had in his magic arsenal as he raced toward Drew in the center of the horde.

Drew let out a frustrated cry as the Knights continued to slash and cut at him, narrowly missing mortal blows but still getting grazed. He released another torrent of electricity, the lightning singeing the air around him. This time, one of the Knights stopped in his tracks as the magic flowed through him.

But the other three continued advancing.

There was still a thick wall of Draugr between him and Drew, and now even Sasha looked like she was being slowed down by their sheer numbers.

Crap, we're not gonna make it.

Isaac willed the earth around him to rise like a wave before crashing down on the Draugr around him, briefly opening a small path forward.

Just in time for him to see the axe of one of the Knights swinging toward Drew's neck.

"No!" Isaac yelled, sending a blast of air toward Drew to try to deflect the blow.

As the blade of the axe was about to touch Drew's neck, a purple swirling portal appeared under him, and he fell straight through the ground, disappearing completely.

What the hell...?

Even the Draugr Knights seemed confused as to where their prey had disappeared to.

With Drew gone, two of the Knights turned their attention toward Isaac, and the other two honed in on Sasha, who was frozen in shock.

All at once, the Draugr horde around them split to follow their respective masters as they charged at Isaac and Sasha. Isaac dodged and ducked through the swings of the Draugr, killing them as they came. Isaac turned to face the next Draugr and ducked as the sword of one of the Knights whistled over his head. The next Knight came at him from his side, jabbing at him with a spear. Isaac felt slashes erupt across his body as he attempted to dodge both the Knights and the other Draugr that surrounded him.

Sasha's fiery attacks had become worryingly infrequent and less intense.

If we don't figure something out, we're both done for. Isaac thought, desperately back-pedaling.

The Knights were coordinated, moving as if they were one being; one would swing its sword or stab with its spear, and the other would move to intercept Isaac wherever he moved. And if they couldn't trap him, they pushed him toward the horde where the Pawns eventually succeeded in landing small cuts across his body. So far, none of the attacks Isaac had tried against the Knights seemed to work. Besides slowing them down or pushing them backwards, he couldn't seem to damage them.

Isaac took in a deep breath to steady himself. He could feel the unease in his mind growing louder the longer this battle dragged on.

If this were real, I'd be dead already. And I wouldn't have helped anyone. His mind whispered.

He shook his head, trying to free himself from those thoughts. If he didn't focus, he was going to find himself quickly eliminated. He could see why Drew was struggling: the Knights were tough. He couldn't afford to hold back here.

"Treat this like life or death," Aephes' words rang in his mind.

Then that's exactly what I'll do. Isaac thought.

He couldn't afford to give this any less than his maximum effort.

Taking a page from Sasha's book, Isaac let the air around him ignite, covering himself in a burning aura. He pushed the fire outward, forming a large ring that surrounded him. The fire's intensity was enough to set the Pawns ablaze instantly, slowing their movements. One by one, the Pawns around Isaac dropped dead. The Knights staggered backwards, pushed by the strength of the flames, but otherwise remained unscathed.

Isaac pushed the ring out further, and made the wall of fire thicker, so that any of the Draugr that stepped forward would be dead by the time it walked through. Isaac gave himself enough space for him and the two Knights to fight undisturbed, the wall of fire he created incinerating the Pawns that shambled into it.

This should make them easier to deal with.

Isaac charged at the Knights, electricity crackling down his arms. The sword-wielding Knight swung his blade in a large arc at Isaac's torso. The spear Knight followed its brother and came at Isaac with a series of quick jabs. A wall of earth shot up at Isaac's side, deflecting the sword Knight's strike and separating the two Knights from each other. Isaac compressed the air around the spear, forcing it into the dirt. The ground reached up around the spear, swallowing and trapping it in the earth. The spear Knight growled in what Isaac assumed was frustration as it let go of its weapon, and swung a massive fist at Isaac as its body doubled in size.

Isaac ducked, the creature's knuckles grazing the top of his skull. Isaac placed his hands on the spear Knight's body and let the electricity he had been storing on his arms flow through it. The Draugr shuddered as Isaac willed the electric current to intensify. The spear Draugr fell to its knees, its eyes beginning to fade. The stone wall beside Isaac exploded as the sword Knight crashed through it. Isaac felt his body fold unnaturally backwards as the sword Knight landed a hard punch on his back, sending him skidding across the dirt, stopping just before he met his wall of flame.

Isaac got shakily to his feet. His back was red-hot with pain, and his breath caught hard in his chest every time he breathed.

The spear Knight pushed itself up from the dirt, yanking its spear free from the ground. Both Knights had doubled in size, their hulking bodies towering over Isaac. What's worse, their weapons grew with them.

Great... Isaac spat blood into the dirt.

"I got one!" Isaac heard Sasha cry out, followed closely by a loud crash.

Good for her. Isaac thought sarcastically.

The two Knights charged at him, swinging their weapons wildly. Their destructive power had grown alongside their size and strength.

However, as Isaac noticed, they were also much slower.

The spear Knight stabbed at Isaac again, who rolled under the blow, and was met by the downward stroke of the sword Knight. Isaac flung himself to one side, positioning himself so that he was between the legs of the spear Knight.

The spear Knight attempted to stomp on him but, once its foot met the earth where Isaac had been standing, it sank into the ground. The spear Knight dropped its weapon to steady itself, but the earth around it was growing softer by the second, slowly swallowing more of its body. The sword Knight swung at Isaac as he darted out from under the spear Knight's legs. Isaac dodged to one side, the sword accidentally taking a chunk out of the spear Knight's calf. Its last foothold gone, the spear Knight fell forward, its torso now completely swallowed by the ground. The spear Knight thrashed against the soft earth, unable to pull itself back up.

The sword Knight roared and slashed madly at Isaac, who dove under the sword Knight's legs. He ignited the air around him, sending scorching flames upwards, engulfing the sword Knight. The Knight cried out as its body burned like dry timber. The light in the sword Knight's eyes finally went out, and the creature fell to its knees.

Isaac commanded the air to push the falling Knight onto the spear Knight, crushing it beneath the weight of its partner. The ground shook as their giant bodies slammed into each other, killing the spear Knight as well.

Isaac allowed himself a tired smile.

I did it. He was proud of himself. He wanted to jump and cry for joy, but he couldn't celebrate just yet: he had the rest of the Trials to finish.

And he had to help Sasha.

He let the ring of fire around him die as he charged forward to where Sasha had been. Her fire had returned to its previous intensity, stinging Isaac's eyes and making it harder to breathe as he got closer. Isaac burst through the crowd of Draugr just in time to watch her flames lick harmlessly off the last Knight's shield. She dodged backwards as the Knight slashed at her with its sword. Sasha looked over at Isaac and nodded before charging at the Knight again. Isaac was surprised that she was still able to move as well as she was: her body was covered in long, deep gashes.

Sasha let loose a torrent of fire at the Knight, its shield raised, once again blocking her flames. Isaac darted around to the Knight's side and willed the earth to rise beneath the Knight's shield. A stone wall shot up from under the Knight, crashing into the shield and knocking it upward. Sasha charged at the creature, her body covered in an aura of fire. She pummeled the Draugr with her fists, each strike leaving a smoldering hole in its body.

The Draugr swung its sword down, but was caught by Isaac's air magic, stopping it mid-swing. Sasha's fists blazed hotter as she grabbed onto the Knight's skull and let loose a stream of fire at close range, her fire enveloping it completely. The Draugr let out a rattling cry as its skull was reduced to ash, its body falling to the ground, charred and lifeless.

Sasha staggered backwards as the Knight fell and flashed a confident but tired smile at Isaac. "Let's finish this."

Isaac nodded and went to work, doing his best not to get in Sasha's way. She was hyper-focused, and her control over her magic was extraordinary. Each flash of her flames was controlled and powerful. If she hadn't had to deal with these Knights, she probably could have wiped out this entire horde by herself. Isaac scorched the last Draugr, its smoldering body thrashed against the dirt before falling still.

"You're pretty impressive," Isaac panted, collapsing on the ground beside Sasha.

Sasha grinned, brushing blood-matted strands of her brunette hair out of her face. "You're not bad yourself... As I would expect from one of Jack's." She pointed at his cloak and chuckled. "What's your name?"

"Isaac."

"I'm Sasha. It's nice to meet you." She stood and wiped dust and ash off herself. "Well, I suppose I'll be on my way. I thank you for your assistance there."

Isaac stood with her, confused. "Wait, would you want to stick together? I have some friends that we could meet up with—"

Isaac stopped as Sasha held up her hand. "Thank you, but no. I only stopped to help Drew because he was my close friend, but I have no intention of completing this Trial with others. To prove myself as a warrior, I must finish this alone."

Isaac nodded. "I can respect that. I hope our paths cross again sometime."

"Likewise," Sasha said, smiling. They shook hands briefly before Sasha darted off into the woods.

Isaac looked over himself and was horrified at the number of slashes he had on him. His clothes were in tatters, including, much to his dismay, his cloak. The true strength of these Draugr, he was realizing, was their sheer number. While the Pawns, and perhaps to some degree the Knights, could be dealt with easily enough on their own, if you got enough of them crowding around you, it was only a matter of time before you took a hit.

Isaac looked carefully around, wary of any remaining Draugr.

I should probably take this opportunity to heal myself a bit while I can.

Unable to find any stragglers, he found a tall tree nearby and climbed a few branches up off the ground, just high enough so that, unless you were looking for him, you would miss him as you passed beneath.

Isaac sat back against the tree and started the slow process of healing himself. He wouldn't be able to patch himself up completely. That would likely be too time-consuming, and it would also drain his stamina too much. He would just have to slow the bleeding for now.

It was clear now that the Mages would allow the Draugr to go *almost* to the point of actually killing you. They'd let you feel the pressure and then teleport you out at the last second. It was safe to assume then that if you got whisked away like Drew did, then you failed the exam.

I wonder how everyone else is doing now.

All he could hope for was that they were still in the Trial.

He'd started making his way around the forest again once he was patched up a bit. It wouldn't be wise to run out unprepared and exhausted. Isaac continued to mend his wounds, watching the ground below.

CHAPTER TWELVE

The sound of something heavy shambling below him caused Isaac to stir. Isaac shook himself awake, forcing his heavy eyes open. He hadn't even realized that he had fallen asleep. He squinted at the sun's piercing light that now hung over him. The last he knew, it had been early morning, so he had only been out for a few hours. His eyes darted around, looking for the source of the sound. He eventually spotted a Draugr who had, somehow, lost its legs and was dragging itself through the dirt.

He raised a calm hand at it and set it ablaze, incinerating it within moments. Isaac shimmied down the tree once he was confident the Draugr was dead.

It was time for him to get moving.

He took off at a light jog, feeling refreshed after his brief rest, being careful to keep his footsteps light. He didn't want to attract any more Draugr to his location yet.

Isaac ran and walked until the sun began casting a comforting evening glow, turning the red haze into a warm pink. As he was wandering, he ran into increasingly fewer Draugr. Before his encounter with the Knights, he'd encountered one every few hundred feet. But now, he was lucky to see one every couple of hours.

Perhaps we took out the biggest horde in the area? Isaac wondered. The four Knights commanded a large number of Draugr, so it's not entirely impossible that this section had been cleared out of the undead.

He'd just have to keep his guard up and hope for the best. For now, he'd enjoy the reprieve and recover his stamina.

"Isaac!" a woman's voice called out from behind him.

Isaac froze, his eyes darting around, trying to find out who had called him.

"Isaac?" this time, a man's voice.

Isaac turned around, spotting two familiar faces peeking out from behind a tree.

"Meri? Olfen?" Isaac squinted.

Meri and Olfen smiled and ran out to meet Isaac. The three of them embraced, thankful to see that they were all still in the Trial.

"How have you two been holding up?" Isaac asked, pulling away. "You both seem to be doing fine for yourselves. Not a scratch on you!"

"Well, thankfully, we landed rather close to each other," Olfen responded.

"We were holding onto each other before the Trial portal opened, and that allowed us to drop in around the same spot."

"I'm glad you two were able to stick together." Isaac smiled. "Any trouble dealing with the Draugr?"

Olfen and Meri both shook their heads.

"We've been doing our best not to help each other too much," Meri began.

Olfen nodded. "We want the Mages to know we can handle things on our own and that we're both worthy of the Magician title. Thankfully, we haven't encountered anything either of us can't bring down by ourselves."

"I'm glad you've both been doing well."

"What about *you*?" Meri eyed Isaac up and down. "Your clothes are ruined."

"Looks like you were met with some resistance," Olfen noted.

Isaac rubbed the back of his neck. "I got a little tied up."

Olfen clapped Isaac on the back. "I'd expect nothing less from a Grey."

"It's good to see you guys again. Even though it's only been a few hours, it's certainly felt much longer," Isaac said.

"Time sure does move funny in this place, doesn't it?" Olfen agreed.

"Now that we're together, we should look for Fraunt and Olyen. I'm sure they're just as lost and confused as we were."

Olfen scoffed. "I'm sure Olyen is having the time of his life right now. He *loves* to brawl, the scrappy bastard."

"Fraunt too... he gets kind of scary when he's fighting. I'm sure they're both doing fine!" Meri said, "But, you're right, we should probably get moving."

"Let's go." Isaac took off again, with Meri and Olfen tailing closely behind him.

They wandered for the rest of the day, encountering a few Draugr here and there that they dispatched together. Isaac was impressed with Olfen and Meri's use of their magic. Like Sasha, their techniques were full of a finesse that Isaac felt like he didn't possess. Meri used her water magic like a whip that constantly hovered around her and snapped at anything that came close. Her movements were quick and fluid like a dancer's. Olfen moved similarly, but his lightning magic moved around him as if he were wielding a staff, spinning in large arcs, and crashing with thunderous force.

So, these are what Arcanists trained by the Order look like?

They stumbled upon a shallow cave as Ieia was appearing in the sky with Aiei faintly visible behind its sister.

"We should rest here for the evening and continue looking tomorrow," Isaac offered.

Meri looked at the ground, a frown forming on her lips.

"What's wrong?" Olfen asked.

"Nothing, I just... I was trying hard to be positive earlier that they were both doing fine but... We couldn't find them, and we were searching all day... Do you think they are still in the Trials?"

"There is no need to worry. Like you said, Fraunt is strong. Same with Olyen. I bet they're both trying to find a place to sleep right now too," Olfen reassured her, placing a comforting hand on her shoulder. "We'll find them. Don't worry."

Meri nodded and entered the cave with Olfen. It was barely big enough for the three of them. Isaac sealed the entrance behind them with a wall of stone, leaving just a crack to see the night sky.

Meri and Olfen sat against a far corner of the cave. Meri rested her head against Olfen's shoulder, and Olfen laid his head atop hers.

Isaac couldn't help but smile. They made a cute pair.

Watching them made him miss Alison. They had always done everything together. It felt very foreign, almost wrong, not to have her with him right now.

He couldn't wait to see her again and to tell her everything about the Trials and the Order's Keep and how spectacular everything had been. Hopefully, they'd both be able to come here next year for her trial.

Isaac smiled, leaning against the cave wall.

CHAPTER THIRTEEN

Isaac, Meri, and Olfen were up and ready at the crack of dawn, too nervous and too high-strung to get any meaningful sleep. Even though Isaac had protected them by sealing off the entrance to the cave, it was difficult to settle one's nerves when there were creatures wandering around looking to attack you.

And with less than twenty-four hours left of the exam, they were all eager to pass and get the hell out of this forest.

They set out quickly, scouring every inch of forest as they went. There were more Draugr present than last night, with quite a few small battalions of Draugr and their commanding Knights marching around the forest. Thankfully, the Pawns posed no real threat now, at least when handled carefully enough, and the Knights were falling faster with their coordinated attacks.

The three of them made quite a good team.

As the day progressed, the number of Draugr began increasing exponentially, until there was nothing but a wall of them that stretched on for miles in any direction.

They ducked behind the remnants of a bush and eyed the horde. All the Draugr were looking in the same direction, their backs to Isaac, Meri, and Olfen, unmoving.

"Whoa..." Meri whispered.

"What'd you think is in the middle of all this?" Olfen asked.

"Nothing good," Isaac concluded. "The biggest group I've seen had four Knights leading it. But this... This doesn't even compare."

Olfen nodded. "It'd be wise to make our way around them."

Isaac led the two of them carefully around the edge of the horde.

Surprisingly, the Draugr did not seem the least bit interested in what was happening behind them. Meri had cracked a branch beneath her foot loud enough to startle Isaac, but none of the Draugr reacted. They just kept staring off into the distance.

Something isn't right. The Draugr, Isaac thought, were supposed to go after any sign of movement. It's how they were created. What good is a guard, after all, if it doesn't go after intruders? But the way these Draugr were behaving, it was as if someone was commanding them to stay in one place.

Whatever it was, Isaac was not eager to find out.

"Where is she?!" a boy's voice cried as they neared the edge of the horde. The three of them stopped and dropped low to the ground.

"What was that?" Olfen asked.

"It sounded like Fraunt." Meri's ears perked up, her eyes hopeful.

"Olyen, *move!* That is *my* Draugr!" the voice called again.

"They're both in there!" Olfen said, carefully observing the crowd. "We should go get them. I wouldn't be able to live with myself knowing I heard them but did nothing."

So much for avoiding the horde.

Meri turned to Isaac, her eyes full of determination. "Are you coming?"

Isaac looked at the Draugr and nodded nervously. He couldn't let them charge in there on their own. "We'll have to go in fast, get them, and get out. It wouldn't be good to get stuck in that mess."

The three of them quickly dove out from the tree line and began cutting their way through the throngs of Draugr and Draugr Knights. They stuck close together, taking special care to guard each other with enemies coming from every direction. Much to Isaac's shock, the Draugr remained motionless until they were right next to them, giving them more than enough time to kill the Draugr.

However, the path they had cut was quickly being closed by Draugr shuffling in to fill their fallen comrade's place.

That's going to make getting out of here trickier...

As the sound of Olyen and Fraunt's struggle grew louder, the three of them began pushing harder through the crowd in a flurry of water, lightning, and fire, taking on two or three at a time when they could to speed up their pace.

Eventually, they burst through the horde, and into the small clearing that was littered with bodies. Fraunt stood with his back to Olyen, one arm lamely dangling at one side, while Olyen frantically tried to fend off the encroaching Draugr.

"Olyen! Fraunt!" Meri and Olfen shouted in unison as they rushed to their brother's aid. Olfen began helping his brother beat the horde back while Meri tried to comfort and assess the damage done to Fraunt.

"Isaac! I need you!" Meri called.

Isaac rushed over and looked at Fraunt's arm. It was badly mangled and twisted, so healing it would take some time.

Time they didn't have.

Isaac shook his head. "It's fixable, but not here. Not right now. We have to protect him. Can you still fight?"

Fraunt blinked slowly. "I am awake. So I can still fight. Why wouldn't I be able to fight?"

Meri sighed. "He's fine. Just... be careful, Fraunt."

Fraunt tilted his head quizzically at his sister. "Why would I not be careful?"

Meri began to stand up and face off against the Draugr once more when Fraunt grabbed her hand, stopping her.

"I am glad you are okay," Fraunt said. Meri's head jerked backwards in surprise at Fraunt's uncharacteristically direct sentence.

"Let's go," Meri smiled. "We have to make it out of here."

"Nowhere else to go," Fraunt declared, returning to his normal demeanor.

"No kidding," Isaac said.

Olfen and Olyen had done a fantastic job of fending off the Draugr while they saw to Fraunt. Olyen's pestilence magic was superb at keeping the low-level Draugr at bay. With the Draugr being so close together,

Olyen's flesh-eating decay spread through the Draugr ranks like wildfire as infected Draugr touched their healthy friends, allowing the pestilence to spread quickly to another host.

"Anyone remember which way we came in?" Isaac asked as he crushed a Draugr beneath the earth.

"That way!" Olfen pointed behind Meri. "Follow me."

They began pushing their way slowly back out through the horde, their progress much faster now with five of them, even with Fraunt being injured. Fraunt's shadow magic, while not incredibly deadly yet on its own, could freeze some Draugr in place by shadow linking them together, allowing everyone else to dispatch them even easier.

We just might be able to pull this off. Isaac thought hopefully.

Suddenly, the Draugr stopped, some of them even mid-strike, and stood still before backing away from them, creating a wide empty space.

That can't be good. Isaac looked around and saw everyone's equally confused faces.

"What's going on…?" Meri asked warily.

Isaac could feel the soft rumble of heavy footsteps through the ground as something approached. As it drew closer, the wall of Draugr split open to reveal a taller, wider, more intimidating opponent. This Draugr wore a cracked gold crown on its head and had a scraggly white beard that was teeming with beetles. It held two rusted swords limply in its hands as it stared at them with a mixture of malice and indifference.

A low growl came from behind the newcomer as a massive lion with shimmering gold fur strode up next to the Draugr.

"Is that what I think it is…?" Olyen asked in his hushed tone.

"A Draugr Lord…" Isaac said breathlessly. Draugr Lords are above and beyond the strongest type of Draugr. From what Isaac had read, there were only a few left around. And for one of them to be here in the Trials, with a pet Nemean Lion at its side no less…

Well, it certainly wasn't good.

The Draugr Lord looked at them one by one, pausing for a moment to peer at Isaac with his cold, eyeless glare.

"Mortals…" The Draugr Lord spoke in a raspy, whispery voice, as if it had not spoken in some time. "Surrender now, and I will allow you to join my army. Deny me, and I will stick you on a spike outside my castle."

Silence.

Like Isaac, they were probably too stunned to speak. Everything about the Draugr Lord was different from the Pawns and the Knights. There was something about the Lord that made Isaac's mind scream at him to run. But he couldn't; he felt completely frozen, unable to move.

"Very well. I elect to take him first," the Draugr Lord said as it closed the distance between it and Fraunt in an instant.

Isaac watched as the Draugr Lord masterfully swung its swords at a bewildered Fraunt, the rusty, chipped blades screaming faintly as they cut jaggedly through the air.

The shadows beneath the Lord shot up in thin tendrils, coiling around its legs and snaking up its body, wrapping around the Lord's arms in a desperate attempt to stop the Lord's strike. The Draugr Lord remained undeterred; the shadowy threads snapped as soon as they were formed under the sheer strength of the Lord.

Just as the blades were about to make contact, the same portal that had appeared under Drew appeared under Fraunt, swallowing him.

The Draugr Lord groaned, visibly annoyed. "Taken from me? Very well, I will kill them faster than they can be whisked away."

The Draugr Lord advanced on Meri next, who stood frozen in shock. In a flash of blue light, Olfen appeared before the Lord, blocking his path toward Meri, lightning magic racing around his arms in wild arcs as he brought a series of punches down on the Lord's body. The Lord didn't move as Olfen's magic danced harmlessly off its body.

Shit, I have to help. Isaac thought, finally snapping out of his stupor. He reached out to the mana in the earth beside the Lord and commanded it to form a stone spike and thrust it toward the Lord. Olyen moved as well, his pestilence magic shooting out from his hands in a greenish-black blob.

The Draugr Lord let loose a chilling, airy whisper that Isaac assumed was laughter. A faint, shimmering field of energy appeared around the Lord the moment before Isaac and Olyen's magic was about to hit him, their magic vanishing instantly as it touched the barrier. Olfen looked up in shock as his lightning magic was extinguished as his fist drew closer to the Lord. The Lord grabbed Olfen's head and kneed Olfen in his side before throwing him like a discarded toy against the wall of Draugr.

"Abjuration magic," Isaac cursed.

"Observant," the Lord rattled.

Great. Not only was this creature physically superior, but its magic could cancel out other magic. Their only hope now was to try to overwhelm the Lord's barrier and cause it to shatter. That plan seemed impossible enough as it is, but it would be made increasingly more difficult if his pet intervened.

Isaac's eyes slid over to the Nemean Lion, who was pacing impatiently back and forth, chunks of meat from its last meal still hanging between its bared teeth.

Should be no problem at all. He thought sarcastically.

The Draugr Lord rushed again, this time at Isaac, catching him off guard. Isaac desperately back-pedaled, using air magic to push himself further away from the Lord. Isaac tumbled along the ground for a moment before rolling to his feet. The Lord was on him immediately, with Meri and Olyen attempting to intervene. The Lord spun around, slashing at them both. Olyen dove to one side, barely dodging the blow, while Meri's water shield shattered under the weight of the Lord's strike.

Olyen threw more of his pestilence magic at the Lord, his magic evaporating instantly as it hit the barrier around its body. The Lord ignored him as it swung both swords at Meri. Isaac buffeted Meri with a burst of wind, throwing her out of the way of the Lord's blow. Meri tumbled to a stop close to Olfen, who was struggling to stand.

The Lord turned its attention back on Isaac, assaulting him with a flurry of blows. Olyen frantically tried to help, pummeling it with his pestilence magic to no avail. Isaac did his best to dodge the Lord's strikes, but quickly found himself covered in shallow cuts as the Lord's attacks grew more frenzied. The Lord kicked Isaac in the stomach, sending him careening backwards. As Isaac tumbled, he could just make out the Lord bearing down on Olyen, with a desperate Olfen and Meri attempting to save him.

The Lord slashed at the three of them, knocking Olfen to the ground and opening a gash in Meri's leg. Isaac watched as Olyen caught a quick slash across his chest and fell backwards, a portal opening up beneath him.

The Lord turned back to Olfen and Meri. Lightning crackled around Olfen as he infused his body with lightning magic, briefly enhancing his own speed as he grabbed Meri and dashed out of the way of the Lord's blows.

Isaac regained his balance and got to his feet, quickly joining Olfen and Meri as the three of them surrounded the Lord, unsure of how to proceed. The Lord looked at them indifferently before craning his head back to the Lion.

"Pet..." The Lord pointed a blade at Olfen and Meri, "Hunt."

Fuck.

The Lion let loose a predatory roar and bounded toward Olfen. Isaac stepped in to intervene, but the Draugr Lord cut him off.

Even without eyes, Isaac could feel the piercing, malicious glare of the Draugr Lord.

"You are mine... I've never had one of you before."

The Lord's statement made Isaac pause.

What is this thing talking about? Does he mean a Grey?

Not giving Isaac any time to think, the Draugr Lord leapt at Isaac, its powerful legs kicking up dirt as it pushed forcefully off the ground. Instinctively, Isaac summoned a thick wall of earth between him and the Lord, hoping to stop its advance altogether. The Lord burst through Isaac's wall, its blades slicing through it as if it were made of paper. Isaac dodged backward, summoning fire this time in thick torrents from his hands. The Lord was completely unfazed as the barrier magic around the Lord extinguished Isaac's flames instantly.

Abandoning the fire tactic, Isaac quickly closed the gap between him and the Draugr Lord.

Time to take a lesson from Sigmund. Isaac thought as his fists became coated in a thick sheet of ice. He sidestepped one of the Lord's slashes and brought his fist to its skull. Isaac's blow bounced harmlessly off the barrier, the ice evaporating from his hand instantly.

The Lord quickly swung its blades in a vicious upward slash, catching Isaac across the body before he could even attempt to move.

Isaac felt his skin being separated—no, ripped apart—by the jagged edge of the Draugr Lord's blade. His skin stretched and screamed in violent protest as the sword cut through it, letting forth a steady drip of crimson from his body.

Isaac stumbled backwards, then summoned a blast of air to throw himself away from the Draugr Lord, desperate to heal his wound and put distance between them. He now knelt several feet away from the Lord, his clothes slick with blood.

Just slow the bleeding. I won't have much time. He eyed the Draugr Lord, who stood watching and waiting patiently, like a hunter eyes its prey before striking. The Lord began a slow, methodical, confident walk toward him.

Isaac worked quickly to stitch himself back together the best he could. He couldn't afford to waste too much energy healing himself; he'd have to do the bare minimum and hope that would be enough. Isaac winced as he felt the flow of blood slow. Every beat of his heart throbbed painfully in his wound.

Isaac felt a fresh wave of anxiety roll through his mind.

Can I really handle this thing? His magic wasn't effective against it, and it had already eliminated Olyen and Fraunt. It was just a matter of time before he was too.

Isaac shook his head.

No. I have to do this. He pushed hard against the swirling doubts in his mind and tried to refocus.

He was just going to have to be smarter if he wanted to take down the Draugr Lord. He'd have to come up with some way to push the Lord's Abjuration magic to its shatter point.

And there was also the problem of the Lord likely not using all of its strength just yet...

Isaac glanced over at Meri and Olfen, who were also in the fight of their lives with the Nemean Lion. Meri had five long, thankfully shallow, gashes across her back, and Olfen had a similar, but deep, scratch on his left thigh. Olfen landed a series of blows against the Lion's hide, but to no avail; the Lion turned and swatted at Olfen like a fly. Meri's attacks had a similar effect: her water magic was like a refreshing splash to the Nemean Lion.

And how the hell are we going to kill that thing? Isaac thought to himself as he got to his feet.

One thing at a time. He reminded himself as he turned his attention back to the Draugr Lord.

It was gone.

Panic filled Isaac. He foolishly took his eyes off his opponent to check on his friends.

Fuck.

Behind him, he heard the Lord's blade screaming through the air. Isaac flung himself forward, raising the earth up under his feet at the same time to catapult himself further away from the Lord. As he jumped, he willed the earth under him to rise quickly, catching him, and forming a sort of pillar that, for now, kept him out of the Lord's reach.

The Lord did not hesitate as it swung its swords, slicing through the earthen pillar Isaac had constructed. Isaac leapt off the pillar at the last moment, commanding the air around him to soften his fall.

The Lord was on him immediately, not giving Isaac any time to breathe. Isaac scrambled backwards, narrowly ducking beneath a horizontal slash. Isaac threw himself to the side, propelling himself with air magic once again, as he opened the ground wide beneath the Lord. The Lord fell into the crater Isaac created, and Isaac quickly sealed the fissure, burying the Lord beneath hundreds of pounds of dirt.

Meri's scream pulled Isaac's attention over to his friends once more.

Meri had another gash, this time on her side, and was bleeding heavily. She sank uneasily to her knees, tears mixed with blood as they streaked down her cheeks. It was clear that she was slowly losing consciousness, with her head bobbing forward and her eyes struggling to stay open. Another portal appeared beneath her, whisking her away just before the Nemean Lion's maw closed down around her skull.

Only Olfen was left now.

Olfen stood up wearily, his body covered in lacerations and teeth marks. He was bloody, bruised, and visibly tired.

Yet his determination and fury shone through his eyes like a raging fire. Olfen's body became coated in electricity as his lightning magic shrouded him in a thundering aura. He glared at the Nemean Lion with unwavering resolve, the lightning around him intensifying in response.

For someone who doesn't like to fight, he has a hell of a fighting spirit.

But Isaac could see beneath the cold, piercing stare of his. Olfen's body was shaking, and it was apparent that each step was becoming more difficult.

He wasn't sure how much longer Olfen could hold out for.

I should help him.

The ground shaking beneath Isaac made him pause as the Draugr Lord burst through the earth, now double its previous size. Isaac didn't have time to react before the Lord's enormous fist crashed into his chest, sending him flying into the wall of Draugr behind him. Isaac's body slammed through the Pawns, his body obliterating a few of them like a cannonball before he tumbled to a stop.

Isaac lay in the dirt. His body felt like it was being crushed by some unseen weight. Isaac let out a wet cough, blood spurting from his lips. His breathing had turned raspy and labored, his ribs creaking with every breath. He tried to push himself up, but his chest screamed in protest.

Isaac watched as the Draugr Lord returned to its normal size and began its slow, predatory walk over to Isaac, assured of its victory. Out of the corner of his eye, he saw Olfen get tossed through the air like a plaything, disappearing into the crowd of Draugr.

At least the Trials are over for him. Isaac thought as the Nemean Lion stalked back over to its master.

The Draugr Lord pointed at Isaac with one long, decaying finger. "Hunt."

The Lion roared as it bounded over to its prey. Isaac closed his eyes and waited for the feeling of the portal to take him away from the Trials.

Instead, Isaac heard the Lion frantically gnashing and growling at something. He opened his eyes to see a bloodied and battered Olfen holding the Lion in a sort of chokehold. The Lion looked as surprised as Isaac felt as it clawed and thrashed against Olfen's grip.

"Giving up so easily?" Olfen flashed a tired smile. "That's not Grey-like behavior."

Olfen roared and threw the Nemean Lion to the side as a lightning spear crackled into existence in his hand.

"I don't have much left in me, Isaac, but I'm taking this beast out with me if it's the last thing I do. Do whatever you need to do while I fight this, but don't you dare stay down there."

Olfen briefly glanced over his shoulder before charging after the Lion, the Lion roaring and leaping to meet Olfen in combat. As the Lion lunged at Olfen, maw agape, Olfen slammed his spear down the creature's throat. The Lion tried backpedaling, but Olfen shoved the spear deeper down the Lion's gullet, lightning magic erupting down the spear and into the Lion's body in wild arcs. Olfen let out a determined cry as his lightning magic intensified, thunder booming from each crack of electricity. The Lion's body convulsed violently, the smell of scorched flesh burning Isaac's nose.

The Lion shook once more as both it and Olfen collapsed to the ground. The Draugr Lord walked over to Olfen, the tip of its blade dangling over his neck. The Lord plunged the blade downward as quickly as it could, yet the portal was faster, taking Olfen away before the Lord could add him to his army. The Draugr Lord grunted in annoyance, turning its attention back toward Isaac.

Isaac balled his hands into tight fists, clutching at the grass beneath him, and tore them from their roots as he struggled to force himself up.

Olfen was right. For some reason, they hadn't removed him from the Trials yet, so that means he still had a chance to finish the fight. He glanced over at the Lion's corpse, its body still twitching from all the electricity that Olfen had pumped through it. If Olfen could kill that thing, then there was a *chance* that he could take down the Lord.

He had to try.

Isaac began slowly mending his chest as he tried desperately to push himself to his feet. The Draugr Lord was watching him carefully as it continued its self-assured walk over to him.

I will not—I cannot—fail here...

Isaac's body jolted as he felt a rush of energy course through him, as if he had just been struck by lightning. He could feel something like drops of water leaking through a cracked dam, each drop bringing a surge of strength through him.

His healing sped up exponentially, his magic working faster and more efficiently than ever before. His ribs cracked and popped as they slid back into place, the weight on his chest suddenly lifted.

What is this...? Isaac looked down at his hands as if they were not his own. The energy welling inside him felt strangely familiar, despite the sensation being unlike anything Isaac had ever felt before.

The Lord must have had some understanding of what was going on, charging at Isaac before he could get off the ground.

Isaac flicked his hands at the Lord, sending an intense burst of flame—so strong that it shocked Isaac—that scorched everything around the Lord. The Draugr Lord seemed to be surprised too as it, for the first time, hesitated after it began using its Abjuration magic. Fire surged from Isaac's hands again as he bathed the Lord in flame as it advanced. The Lord leapt through the fire, unscathed, its abjuration magic glinting against the flames and its swords poised to strike.

Isaac summoned the earth up around him in a sort of cocoon before driving himself deep into the ground, trying to put distance between him and the Lord. Isaac pushed and pulled the earth around him, dodging the Lord's strikes, as the Lord cut into the ground with strength that could only come from the Lord taking on its larger form.

Isaac shot out of the ground, using both air and earth magic to propel himself high into the air above the Draugr Lord, and continued to use air magic to keep him suspended above the Lord for as long as possible. The Lord stood in the middle of a carved-out crater that it had created chasing Isaac. Isaac raised the cut-up earth around the Lord, commanding it to wrap tightly around its legs. But the Lord's barrier kept the magic-controlled earth from touching it. Just as the Draugr Lord turned to face Isaac, he sent another powerful stream of fire at it, using air magic to fan the flames and increase its intensity.

The Draugr Lord's barrier, for a moment, flickered.

Isaac did not have time to celebrate as the Draugr Lord's sword met him in the air. He summoned a gale of wind to shove himself backwards, narrowly missing being cut in half, as the Lord's blades cut across his abdomen. Isaac tumbled through the air, using what magic he could to try to cushion his fall.

The Draugr Lord was on him immediately, giving Isaac no time to recover. Isaac clutched at his stomach, blood pooling between his fingers and rolling over them. Every movement brought fresh, hot pain into his stomach, as if his insides were on fire. It took everything he had to duck out of the way of the Lord's frenzy of slashes.

But there was hope: he had seen the limit of the Lord's Abjuration magic.

He just had to keep pushing that limit until it broke.

Isaac threw himself toward the Lord, rolling between its massive legs and summoning a barrage of stone spikes as he went. The barrier, once again, stopped them all.

Isaac dove out of the way of another sword slice, feeling the wind whip at his neck as it barely missed decapitating him. He turned to face the Lord, reaching out to the mana around him, and holding the image of lightning in his mind as he commanded the mana to obey. In his hands, two spears made of pure electricity crackled into existence.

Slowly, another appeared floating above his head.

The Lord launched another barrage of attacks at Isaac, swinging his swords in a never-ending series of slashes and stabs.

A cut landed across Isaac's arm.

Another spear appeared above him.

Isaac attempted to dive out of one of the Lord's swings, earning a deep gash on his back.

Another spear appeared until half a dozen lightning spears surrounded Isaac.

This is for you, Olfen.

Isaac flung his spears at the Lord as it turned to slash again at him, grabbing another spear from the air as one left his hand. Thunder roared across the battlefield as the spears slammed into the Lord's barrier. Isaac staggered away from the Lord, its blade lacerating his leg as his last spear collided with its shield, shattering it.

The Draugr Lord stumbled backward, its skeletal face contorting in what Isaac thought must be disbelief. Seizing this opportunity, Isaac summoned the earthen spikes once more to pierce the Lord's body and, at the same moment, he let loose a stream of fire and a vortex of wind at the Lord, entrapping it in a maelstrom of elemental magic.

Isaac continued the assault until he began to shake from the effort. He released his hold over the mana and slumped to the ground, feeling more tired than he had ever felt before in his life. Isaac clutched at his stomach again as he lay in the dirt, half of his shirt slick with blood. He felt the world begin to spin around him as his blood loss finally caught up with him. He sucked in air sharply as he slowly mended his wound, the feeling of his flesh stitching itself back together bringing jolts of pain through his abdomen.

Isaac looked over at the Lord as it lay, unmoving, blackened and riddled with holes in the middle of the scorched crater. Around him, the

Pawns and Knights stood still, as if frozen in place, their eyes downcast, staring blankly at the ground, almost as if in mourning.

He eyed them carefully, weighing his options. He wasn't sure how long they would stand comatose like that, and he'd rather not stick around and find out. Plus, the surge of energy that he felt earlier was fading, as if the dam in his mind was being patched. Soon, he'd be defenseless against the horde that surrounded him.

Isaac stumbled as he stood, his vision briefly flooding with millions of black stars. The gash on his stomach still burned like a roaring fire, but he had stopped the bleeding almost completely. It was all he could do for now. He had to get moving.

Isaac froze as the ground began to shake beneath his feet.

No... Impossible. Isaac turned, staring in disbelief as the Lord's charred body rose slowly.

Isaac balled his hands into tight fists, his shock quickly transforming into anger. He took an uneasy step forward toward the Lord.

I will not lose here.

I can't.

Not when I'm so close...

Isaac could tell that the Lord was just as tired as he was. It was no longer walking with a calm self-assuredness. Instead, it was stiff, and weary. Shattering Abjuration magic took an immense toll on the Arcanist, so even the Lord would be feeling strained now.

Isaac roared determinedly, half-running, half-limping toward the Lord, fire blazing to life in his hands. The Lord's Abjuration magic flickered around it as it watched Isaac approach. Isaac pointed his hand at the Lord, a stream of fire erupting in front of him. The Lord made no motion as Isaac's fire licked against his barrier, coating him completely in a cocoon of flame.

The Lord's barrier flickered.

Just a little more...

Isaac pressed forward, stoking his flames with air magic. The fire streaming from his hands roared in response, engulfing the Lord so completely now that he could barely see its cold eyes above the fire.

The Lord's barrier disappeared.

Yes!

Isaac stumbled backwards as something sliced the top of his left shoulder, followed by a loud crash as something heavy struck the Draugr behind him. He dropped to his knees as fresh pain exploded through his shoulder. He clutched at his wound, feeling warm blood quickly seeping out between his fingers.

Isaac looked up just in time to see the Lord's massive fist slam into him, sending him tumbling across the ground, stopping only after he slammed through several lines of Draugr.

Isaac shuddered as he lay in the dirt. His body suddenly felt too heavy and cold to move. He was just barely able to crane his neck toward the Lord as it approached him, wielding only one sword.

And that's when he saw it.

Out of the corner of his eye, Isaac saw the Lord's other sword lodged into several Draugr like meat on a spit. The Lord's barrier hadn't shattered again like he had thought. It had used Isaac's flames to conceal its movements and, in his desperation, Isaac hadn't considered why the Lord wasn't moving. He had been too focused on shattering its barrier again to notice that he was being lured into a trap.

Isaac wheezed as he struggled to breathe, the air stinging his dry, blood-caked throat. The grass felt like small daggers against his skin, and the light from the moons brought a deep pain into his eyes.

He couldn't move. His entire body ached with a sharp, indescribable pain that throbbed with each softening heartbeat. All he could do was watch as the Lord returned to its normal size and hobble over to Isaac. It stood smugly over Isaac's shattered body. Its remaining sword dangling over his throat.

Tears welled up in Isaac's eyes. Despite everything he tried, he couldn't defeat it. No matter what he did, the Lord just kept coming, relentlessly. In the end, he wasn't strong enough.

He lost.

Isaac closed his eyes as he waited to feel the cold pull of the portal. He wasn't ready to face everyone, knowing he had failed. But he desperately wanted to go back home.

Go back to Alison.

Isaac felt the world get sucked away from him, his body tingling and cold, as the portal transported him away from the Trials. He landed in a soft, welcoming bed, his head settling gently onto a pillow. The silky sheets and comfortable bed brought waves of comfort crashing over Isaac, his body sinking into the mattress. Someone was there with him, a Healing Mage most likely, huddled over his broken form, seeing to his wounds. It was too dark to make out exactly who it was, and he didn't particularly care. He was just happy to feel the deep pull of Healing magic slithering throughout his body.

Isaac winced as he tried to breathe, his ribs slowly clicking back into place. Somehow, despite the pain, he was drifting off to sleep.

Or maybe it was unconsciousness. He wasn't sure which one was coming first, but he welcomed it anyway.

As he drifted between wakefulness and sleep, his mind became flooded with torrents of traitorously destructive thoughts.

Am I ever going to be strong enough?

If this were real, everyone would be dead. And I couldn't help them.

I'll never be able to live up to Jack...

Becoming a Mage is a foolish dream...

Give up now before I actually *get other people killed...*

Stop...

Isaac forced his eyes tightly closed as fresh tears ran down his cheeks, the doubtful voices growing fainter as he slipped into unconsciousness.

CHAPTER FOURTEEN

Alison let loose another torrent of buffeting winds, slicing away at the vegetation that stood in their way. Even though they had been to the Temple just a few days before, it did not seem to make the trip any easier. They had passed through the mountains again easily enough, but the forest surrounding the damn Temple seems to have grown exponentially. If Alison had thought the underbrush was dense before, she was sorely mistaken. Even Sigmund had to help occasionally now, snap-freezing the plants so that it was easier to cut away.

At the rate they were going, they wouldn't be back in time for Isaac's return from the Trial.

"There is no way it was like this before," Alison protested.

"No. It wasn't," Sigmund grumbled, clearly as frustrated as she was.

"What do you think happened? The forest seemed to fight against us before, but this...?"

Sigmund simply shrugged. "Don't know. Perhaps the forest surrounding the Temple reacts to intruders, making it more difficult to enter the next time."

"That's certainly possible," Alison mused. The Temple acted like a stronghold for the artifact, so it wasn't impossible to consider that the Ancient Ones would have also made the Temple's environment part of the artifact's defenses.

"How do you think Isaac is doing in the Trials?" Alison asked, trying to keep any form of conversation going. The long, endless silence from Sigmund was driving her insane. She hadn't realized just how much she would miss the constant chatter with Isaac. Plus, it felt... different being out here without him, like there was some big part of her that was missing.

Sigmund shrugged again. "He's doing fine," he grumbled, as if saying that was painful.

"I just hope he doesn't put too much pressure on himself. He's always pushing and pushing, never taking the time to reflect on how far he's come."

"He's fine."

Alison felt her eye twitch. Leave it to Sigmund to brush off any sort of sentimental conversation. But, to his credit, Sigmund saying that Isaac is doing *fine* is quite the compliment. Normally, Isaac was an idiot, a buffoon, a knucklehead, or any other colorful term Sigmund had handy that day. So, by comparison, *fine* is Sigmund's equivalent of 'great'.

Alison's air magic sliced another bit of underbrush away, revealing the clearing they had come to before.

There it is... A shiver went down her spine as she stepped out of the forest and peered up at the Temple. They had returned much sooner than Alison would've liked. Her personal preference would've been never, but here they were. The flashbacks of the fight between Sigmund and the other two made her heart race.

Alison shuddered.

Let's make this quick.

"Start looking," Sigmund ordered as politely as he could.

Alison set about scouring the field, looking for any sort of clue their attackers might have left behind. She groaned in frustration at her fruitless endeavor. The only things she had found were shreds of fabric and tiny bits of steel from metal clashing.

"What are we even supposed to be looking for, anyway?" Alison called over to Sigmund, who was holding something grotesquely purple and decaying. A piece of cloth from a sleeve still covered the back of the severed hand slightly; dried blood had crusted the fabric in place.

"That's... disgusting." Alison grimaced. She could handle a lot of things: blood, guts, dismemberment, all fine. But something decaying and rotting like that made it feel like her stomach was learning acrobatics.

The fabric and skin crackled and popped as Sigmund removed the dried, bloodied cloth. On the back of the hand was a seared brand of a giant letter 'A' with a slender dragon wrapped all around it. The 'A' was surrounded by some form of uneven, octagonal shape with what looked like vines growing toward the middle.

"Whose symbol is that?"

Sigmund shrugged. "I have an idea. But Jack will have to confirm it."

Sigmund sat in the grass and retrieved a piece of parchment, his quill and ink, and quickly redrew the symbol.

At his behest, Alison used her magic to quickly and gently dry the ink until it was safe to roll up and transport.

"Come." Sigmund stood, making his way toward the path they had created. "It's time we get out of here."

She couldn't agree more.

Alison gazed out at the deep red horizon, and the twin moons that were beginning to appear in the east. Darkness would certainly make traversing the enchanted forest much more difficult, and it was clear that Sigmund was eager to leave. She didn't blame him. She'd rather be locked in a room with Isaac's clothes after a day of intense training than sleep in this forest.

Alison paused for a moment before following Sigmund to take in the Temple one last time. She again recounted everything that had happened, a deep pit forming in her stomach. She did her best to keep moving forward no matter what but, if she was being honest with herself, she was afraid. Afraid of what was lurking in the shadows, waiting for them. And coming back here brought all the raw emotions that sat in the back of her mind front-and-center. The fear that she felt from watching Sigmund struggle and Isaac desperately try to help...

It was as fresh and real as it was then, wrapping around her neck like a snake and choking the life out of her.

Alison took in a shaky breath, doing her best to calm her pounding heart.

"It's okay to be afraid, but it's not okay to let that fear control you," Jack had once told her.

Alison glared at the Temple with a renewed sense of determination. Jack was right: she couldn't let fear control her.

"Alison," Sigmund called, snapping her out of her trance.

"Coming!" she replied. She twisted her face in disgust at how much the sunset-soaked stones of the Temple resembled fresh blood. She rushed after Sigmund, turning her back on the Temple for what she hoped was the last time.

CHAPTER FIFTEEN

*D*AD! ISAAC SCREAMED. *HELP ME!*

Isaac felt a cool tingling sensation fall over him as he felt his body get pulled through something. He opened his eyes and saw a shimmering outline of a man with short black hair and kind silver-gray eyes.

"Dad?" Isaac reached out to him, but his grasp passed right through his father's body. Isaac looked up at him, confused; his father's eyes were dark with melancholy.

His father cast a soft, sad smile at him. "I'm sorry... It has to be this way."

Suddenly, the purple-black world was whisked away from him, and Isaac found himself outside of a home he didn't recognize. A tall, lean man with earthy-brown hair and a warm smile greeted him, standing there as if he had been expecting him.

Isaac felt his throat tighten as tears welled in his eyes.

Mom...?

Devlin...?

"It's okay, Isaac," the man said as he knelt in front of him and laid a gentle hand on his shoulder. "You're safe now. I'll take care of you. I promise."

The man looked up at the sky and repeated, "I promise."

Isaac felt a pinch deep in his skull, his vision suddenly narrowing and turning dark as the world began to spin. He felt himself falling forward into darkness, his limp body slamming against the ground.

* * * * *

Isaac shot straight up out of his bed, gasping for air. He was drenched in sweat, and his heart felt like it was trying to punch its way out of his chest. He lurched forward, feeling disoriented. A gentle hand caught his shoulder, stopping his fall.

"Isaac, are you all right?"

Isaac turned toward the familiar voice. Worry painted Jack's usually smiling face. He sat on a wooden stool, one that was much too small for a man his size, close to Isaac's bed.

"Jack!" Isaac blinked in surprise. His heart had settled somewhat, but his breathing was still shaky, making it difficult to speak without some strain. "I'm sorry. It was just a bad dream."

Jack leaned back in his chair. "Do you remember this one? Do you think it's the same nightmare that you had before the Temple?"

Isaac's head cocked to the side. He hadn't told Jack about his nightmare. "How'd you know about that?"

Jack smiled. "Alison told me. She worries about you, you know."

Isaac felt his cheeks grow warm. "I appreciate her concern, but no, I don't remember this one either. I don't think they are the same, though. This one felt... different. It's hard to explain. I'm sorry."

Jack shook his head. "No need to apologize! I just wish there were some way to help you remember them. If you have another nightmare, or certainly if you remember it, let me know. Alright?"

Isaac nodded.

"Now!" Jack clapped his hands together, his usual brighten-up-the-room smile returning to his face. "Get dressed. I prepared fresh clothes for you." Jack lightly tapped the table next to Isaac, where his new clothes lay neatly folded. "I'll tell Aephes that you're awake so we can proceed." Jack stood, making his way to the door.

"Wait! Jack, what's going on?"

Jack's smile grew wider. "It's the Ranking Ceremony, of course! It's time for those who passed the Trial to receive their ranks. Aephes allowed extra time for everyone's recovery from the Trial. You just took a bit longer than most. About a day, in fact. Healing you had been quick, but your body clearly needed more time to recuperate. But now that you're awake, we can proceed with the ceremony! So, up and at 'em!"

Isaac's gaze turned toward the bed. *Shit... I had almost forgotten...*

"Everything alright?" Jack asked, one eyebrow raised questioningly.

Isaac met his gaze and smiled lightly. "Yeah, I'm fine. Still just tired, I think."

Jack nodded slowly, his eyes narrowing at him. "That's understandable. You went through a lot. When you are ready, meet us at the training grounds. We won't start without you." With that, Jack slowly closed the door and disappeared.

Isaac got shakily out of bed, his legs wobbly and weak. He wasn't looking forward to this. He didn't want to be formally confronted by his failure.

After a few minutes of struggling to get dressed, Isaac began the difficult process of navigating from the Order's infirmary down to the training grounds. After a seemingly endless series of never-ending hallways and dead-ends, Isaac finally found his way outside to the training grounds. He had come out in a different place than before. He was overlooking the grounds this time from an elevated perch, with stairs on either side that led down to the grounds themselves. Everyone had already gathered and were huddling together at the foot of the stage. All the Mages from before—except for Darnel—waited patiently on the stage.

"Finally, he has decided to grace us with his presence!" Aephes's booming voice shifted everyone's attention straight to Isaac. He felt heat rise in his cheeks as he smiled nervously.

Aephes laughed heartily at the sight of Isaac's embarrassment. "I jest!" Aephes beckoned with his hand. "Please, come join us!"

"Oi, Isaac!" A hand shot up through the throng of people. "Over here!" Olfen called to him through the middle of the crowd. People pushed themselves, and each other, out of the way to reveal Olfen, Meri, Fraunt, and Olyen all huddled together, smiling at him—besides Fraunt, who simply looked curious—, beckoning Isaac to join them.

As Isaac made his way through the crowd, a large paw of a hand clapped down onto his shoulder. Isaac stopped and had to crane his neck to look up at the tall woman who had stopped him.

Sasha smiled down at him kindly. "I'm glad to see you have recovered. I hear that you fought hard until the end. I'd expect nothing less from someone like you."

Isaac cocked his head. "A Grey, you mean?"

She shook her head. "A warrior. Like me and my people. I commend you."

Isaac felt his face grow warm again. "I uh... Thank you. That means a lot to me coming from someone as skilled as you are. Your control over fire magic is incredible!"

Sasha flashed him a wide grin. "I can control the fire because I *am* the flame. I can feel it deep within me that my soul is a blazing inferno. Remember that as you grow, my friend. You do not control magic; the magic is a part of you."

Isaac smiled thoughtfully back at her as they shook hands. "I'll try to keep that in mind." They waved their goodbyes, and Isaac continued his journey through the crowd, finally reuniting with his friends.

"It's about time you woke up!" Olfen clapped Isaac hard on the back, eliciting a grunt from him.

"We were worried about you," Meri added in her usual sweet tone.

"Grey man in bad shape," Fraunt chimed.

"Thank you all for your concern, but I'm okay." Isaac smiled and patted himself lightly. "Good as new."

Aephes cleared his throat, his way of politely asking everyone to be silent. The crowd shuffled closer together as everyone anxiously waited for Aephes to begin the Ranking Ceremony.

Everyone except for Isaac.

"Welcome, *everyone,*" Aephes winked at Isaac, "to the end of the Magician's Trials. This was a long and brutal forty-eight hour test. A test that was designed to push your abilities to their limits, and I am proud of the effort that every single one of you put forward. Before I announce the newest Magicians, allow me to explain how we judged your strength, and ultimately determined if you are to be named Magician. First: the monsters you encountered, the Draugr, were created to directly measure your abilities. The Pawns that you fought were slightly *below* the level of a Magician.

"The Draugr Knights, on the other hand, were on par with the level of a Magician, and only a Magician-level Arcanist would've been able to defeat them. To successfully complete the Trial, an Arcanist must meet two criteria: successfully remain in the Trial for all forty-eight hours, and defeat the Draugr Knights. If an Arcanist could not do *both* of these things, then they have failed the exam. With that being said, of the two hundred of you that took the Trial, only forty have passed."

Aephes paused for a moment to let his words hang over the crowd, as silence filled the grounds. Isaac was surrounded by a sea of shocked faces and defeated downward gazes. Isaac felt a heavy pit form in his stomach as he was faced with the harsh truth that he had been bracing himself for.

Even though he had been able to defeat the Knights, it didn't matter. He hadn't been able to defeat the Lord, and he didn't survive the length of the exam.

He failed.

Isaac looked over at his friends, their heads hung low in a mixture of sorrow and disappointment. Olfen, however, had a twinge of anger on his face, his fists clenching and unclenching. Isaac certainly couldn't blame him for being angry. Had that Draugr Lord and his damn Nemean Lion not shown up, they *all* might've passed.

"However..." Aephes began, immediately catching the attention of Olfen and Isaac. "Some of you had enough good fortune to encounter the *one* Draugr Lord and his pet, the mighty Nemean Lion, during the Trial. The Lion is considered to be between a Magician and Sorcerer's skill level. The Lord was the strongest creature in the Trial, being almost at Sorcerer-level strength. With this in mind, those of you who encountered Draugr Knights and defeated them soundly but were defeated *only* by the Draugr Lord and his pet will still be awarded rank today. Very few Arcanists could have hoped to perform as well against these mighty beasts as you did. Be proud of what you have done, Meri, Olfen, Olyen, Fraunt, and Isaac."

Isaac locked eyes with them in stunned disbelief.

What...?

Aephes continued, "Further, the Order would like to acknowledge two Arcanists in particular for their stunning performance. First, to Olfen, the Lightning Arcanist, who dealt the killing blow to the Nemean Lion! A feat of strength not to be understated. And to Isaac, the Omnis Arcanist who fought against the Draugr Lord, who shattered its Abjuration Magic, and demonstrated his proficiency and tenacity in his hard-fought battle with the Lord. With that being said, while awarding a higher rank from a lower Trial is not allowed, as Warden it is my honor to formally recommend that *both* of you take the Sorcerer's Trial is just two years' time, a full decade ahead of your peers. Truly, a job well done to both of you!"

The crowd around them erupted in raucous applause and cheers. They quickly became assaulted with playful shoves and pats on the back. Isaac locked eyes with Jack, too stunned to move. He had a proud, ear-to-ear grin on his face.

Congratulations. He mouthed, clapping.

Aephes held his hand up after a few moments, and the lively crowd slowly returned to the quiet huddle they were moments ago.

"For those of you who passed, when I call your name, please make your way up to the stage with the Masters." As if on cue, a short staircase suddenly extended from the stage. Aephes rattled off the short list of forty names and, one by one, each of them made their way up and stood, facing the crowd.

"Would the Arcanists on stage with me awaiting rank, please display their left forearms."

Isaac slowly rolled up his sleeve. Aephes stood before them and held one hand up. A blue, shimmering outline of a phoenix flared to life in front of his palm.

"It is with great pleasure and honor, to grant you the rank of Magician! The symbol of the Phoenix symbolizes your rebirth: rising from the ashes of who you were before the Trials, and the journey that lies ahead of you as you work to realize your full potential. Congratulations, all of you!"

Aephes waved his hand across everyone on stage. At the same time, Isaac felt a sharp stinging sensation on his forearm. There, emblazoned in bold, black strokes, was the tattoo of a phoenix, its wings spread wide and its mouth open in a triumphant screech as it looked upward toward the heavens.

The crowd broke out into more deafening cheers and applause; this time even Aephes was helpless in quelling the noise.

"The rest of the day is yours, students of the Order! Remember that regular training will resume tomorrow!" Aephes called out feebly before finally giving up.

Isaac and everyone else on stage were swarmed by people wanting to shake their hands and congratulate them. It was a surreal experience that Isaac hoped to burn into his memory forever.

Isaac glanced over at his friends and was surprised to see Jack greeting them all and congratulating them. Olyen looked so excited that Isaac thought he was going to pass out from hyperventilating, and Fraunt, well, his stare was as intense as ever.

Isaac looked down at his tattoo, running his fingers gently over it.

I passed...?

"Young Mr. Isaac Grey," Aephes' voice boomed behind him, making him jump.

Aephes laughed. "Sorry. I didn't mean to scare you."

Isaac turned, not realizing how large Aephes was up close. Like Sasha, he had to look up to look him in the eyes.

What the hell are they feeding people here...?

"I wanted to congratulate you personally. Jack has done a fine job in training you, not that I would expect anything less. It feels like not so long ago that I was watching in awe as Jack practiced outside in this very courtyard."

Isaac's jaw went slack. "You were here when Jack attended?"

Aephes nodded. "Of course. I was a Warlock at the time, but Jack was far above me in strength even then. I remember the discussion the Mages had over the outcome of Jack's Magician Trial and whether it was possible that he had cheated." Aephes let out a hearty, belly-filled laugh. "It only took one look at Jack to know that he did *not* cheat and he was every bit as powerful as everyone said he was. He learned so quickly that the Masters then didn't know what to do with him. And Jack back then was quite the handful, always getting into trouble."

Isaac scoffed in disbelief. "Jack? A troublemaker?"

"Oh, yes." Aephes chuckled. "He got himself into all sorts of trouble. Constantly disobeying the Masters and going against Order mandates. He was a handful indeed..." Aephes' voice trailed off, as if lost in a fond memory.

"At any rate," Aephes continued, "Jack was a sight to behold. The pride on his face when he used his magic made *me* feel proud to be an Arcanist. And the determination in his eyes when he set his mind on something was inspiring, even if he was determined to do the *wrong* thing. I saw that same determination and pride in your eyes during the Trials when you fought the Draugr Lord. Be proud of what you have done. I do not know of many Arcanists who could've taken on the Lord as you did. I look forward to seeing you grow and hearing of all the great things you accomplish, Isaac." Aephes smiled and patted Isaac on the shoulder before walking off to the next new Magician.

Isaac was at a loss for words. Everyone's excitement and now Aephes's remarks made him feel like he could do anything, and being compared to Jack—even just a little—meant the world to him.

I can't wait to tell Alison all about this. Isaac beamed, beyond eager to share his accomplishments and celebrate with her and everyone else back home.

"Isaac!" Olfen bear-hugged Isaac from the side. "We are gathering for drinks at the Twisted Wyvern Tavern if you would like to join us!"

"Please, join us!" Meri called from Isaac's other side.

"Actually..." Jack called from behind them. "If you all wouldn't mind, I have quite the party planned at the Grey Manor for *everyone* who participated in the Trials. Aephes loves the idea, and everything has already been prepared. Would you care to join my family in celebrating your accomplishments?"

"*YES!*" Olyen shrieked excitedly, before awkwardly clearing his throat.

Olfen released his hold on Isaac. "A trip to the Grey Manor? Absolutely! Can't wait to rub it in everyone's faces later!"

Jack beamed. "Splendid! Let the celebration begin!"

Jack clapped his hands together and, a moment later, they were all outside of the Grey Manor.

Isaac was surrounded by giant tents made of beautiful white cloth, adorned with roses and lilacs near the poles. On each tent was a famous scene from the battles written about in *The Age of Formation*.

A tent to his right showed the final battle between the Elves and the Orx as the Elves defended their great capital, Nivandeer.

Another tent depicted the Fasismach, the Orxish duel to the death, between Ithu'k the Decapitator, a great Orx War Chief, and the Vaccar Rubort, the Phantom of the West, who had come to stop Ithu'k from claiming land from the Kingdoms of Man.

Beneath the tents were tables upon tables of food: meats, breads, pastries, fruits, practically anything you could think of was there. Mugs of ale sat on tables near the food, each one filling automatically whenever someone grasped the handle.

A great, shimmering banner floated around the manor with '*CON-GRATULATIONS ALL*' twinkling in the middle.

And amidst it all was the Grey family, waiting eagerly under and between the tents, smiling earnestly. Then, all at once, everyone began to cheer and shout their congratulations.

Isaac felt his cheeks grow hot. He definitely wasn't used to getting this much attention.

He scanned the crowd, looking for his family. After a moment, he could see Margaret off in the distance in her usual spot standing next to Jane, with a cocky, but proud, grin on her face. He spotted Sigmund standing closer to the front of the crowd, with his arms crossed and his face like stone. But when he locked eyes with Isaac, he gave him a light nod and brief applause.

Isaac almost gasped.

Sigmund? Showing an explicit and *direct* display of approval?

He's growing soft in his old age. He chuckled to himself.

He kept searching the crowd until he was finally able to locate Alison. She was pushing her way through the crowd to get to the front, cheering and screaming as loud as she could. She sprinted at him and locked him in a tight embrace that pinned Isaac's arms to his side.

"Ain't that cute," Olfen teased.

"Shut up," Isaac coughed out.

"Everyone, please, enjoy yourselves! My home is your home. Congratulations to everyone who passed the Magician's Trial. For those who were not able to this year: keep training. Nothing is out of your reach. I believe in you." Jack's voice boomed even over the cheering crowd, his trademark bright smile etched onto his face.

Olfen patted Isaac on his shoulder. "We'll catch up later, yeah?"

Isaac nodded, and Olfen pulled Meri, Fraunt, and Olyen to the tables of food and then quickly into the Grey Manor. Alison released her death-grip on Isaac a moment later, her face beaming. "Congratulations! I knew you'd be able to do it!"

Isaac rubbed the back of his neck absent-mindedly, suddenly at a loss for words. "Thanks. It definitely wasn't easy."

"Well? Let's see it!" Alison demanded, grabbing for his left arm.

Isaac backed away from her. "Gimme a second! Sheesh, here." Isaac pushed his cloak to one side and flipped his forearm over, exposing the Phoenix tattoo.

"Whoa..." Alison breathed, tracing the lines of the feathers with her fingers, her touch sending shivers down his spine.

"I wonder what new magic you'll learn as an Omnis now that you're a Magician. Oh, I can't wait to see what new techniques I am introduced to once I pass my Trial..." Alison stared dreamily at the tattoo. "I am *definitely* going next year."

"You think you'll be ready in a year?" Isaac teased, a cheeky grin settling on his face.

Isaac let out a hard wheeze as Alison punched him in the chest. "Don't think that just because you got a title before me that you're better than me. I'll still beat your ass."

Isaac smiled. *Always the competitive one.*

"I have no doubt about that. I'm confident that Jack will have you test next year."

"That's what I thought." Alison clapped her hands together, her mood turning much more chipper in an instant. "Anyway, I want to hear all about the Trial! And I'm sure Margaret, Jane, and Sigmund do too. Oh! And who are your new friends?"

She pulled Isaac by the hand through the growing crowd of people, asking him what seemed like an endless number of questions. And he enjoyed every one of them.

Seeing Olfen and Meri together at the Trial had made him miss Alison more than he had realized. Being back with her now, it felt like he was complete again. Everything somehow seemed brighter and more exciting when he was with her. Even though their separation had only been for a couple days, it had seemed like an eternity since he had last seen her.

It's good to be home. He thought with a smile.

Isaac took in a deep breath and let himself take it all in. He took a sizable chunk out of a leg of meat he grabbed off the table, savoring the smoky flavor. Isaac scanned the crowd between bites of food and answering Alison's questions and spotted Olfen and Olyen having what appeared to be a mutton-eating contest, and it looked like Olyen was actually *winning*.

Isaac shook his head in disbelief, spotting Meri desperately trying to pull Fraunt away from a startled group of Greys. He was staring so intensely at them that Isaac was sure that Fraunt was going to drill a hole through them through sheer concentration. Off in a corner, Jack, Adara, Aephes, and even Darnel were gathered in a circle, chatting and laughing at something, though, Darnel seemed to more painfully chuckle than laugh.

Jack looked up, caught Isaac's gaze, and smiled at him warmly. Jack's eyes flicked back and forth between him and Alison and, for a brief moment, Isaac had seen something in Jack's eyes that he had never seen before.

Regret.

Pain.

It lasted only for a moment before being replaced by his usual jovial gaze, now also accompanied by pride. Jack offered a brief head nod to Isaac.

Isaac's eyebrows furrowed together in confusion. *I wonder what that was about...*

Time seemed to move at a distorted pace; the once midday sun was now waning to the west, ready for the sister moons to relieve it of its duty. Margaret and Jane had just joined them at the pastry table, Alison going for her fourth helping of cake and Isaac his third. Margaret stared in disbelief at how much food they were both able to eat.

"You two eat as if you've been starved all your lives," Margaret said, bewildered.

"I'm a growing boy." Isaac grinned cheekily with his mouth still full of chewed food.

Alison smacked the back of his head. "At least swallow your food before speaking."

Isaac bit off another chunk of a delicious crème-cinnamon dessert and stuck his tongue out with the bit of food balancing in the middle.

Alison smacked him again, followed by Margaret.

"Hey!" Isaac shouted, the dessert falling from his mouth. "Only one of you can hit me at a time; you have to at least take turns!"

"Whose rule is that?" Margaret raised her hand to smack him again, but was stopped by Jane's cane, smacking Margaret's hand away.

"Ow," Margaret hissed, rubbing her hand.

"I thought you had something you wanted to say to the boy, Margaret?" Jane raised a stern, questioning eyebrow at her.

Margaret grumbled like a pouting child. "Fine. Yes. Isaac, you did better than I gave you credit for. Congratulations on not being a disappointment."

Jane smacked the back of Margaret's head with her cane.

"Ow! Damn it!" Margaret hissed, rubbing her skull. "Alright, alright. Isaac, you did good. We heard it was a hard test, and you fought tooth and nail to the very end. Congratulations."

"Yes, congratulations, dear, on a hard-earned rank!" Jane added cheerfully.

Isaac laughed as Margaret flashed Jane a scathing glare, which Jane seemed to ignore completely with a quiet smile.

The Draugr Lord's scorched face looking down at him flashed in his mind as the Trial played over in his head at a frantic pace.

And with it, the overwhelming feeling of vulnerability that he had felt then flooded him now, sucking away the jovial buzz he had felt all evening. He had been so caught up in the excitement that he hadn't had time to stop and think.

He looked around the party once again, seeing the 'Congratulations' sign fluttering in the breeze, and everyone celebrating in the new Magicians' honor.

In *his* honor.

He looked down at the phoenix tattooed on his arm.

Did he really deserve this?

Despite all the praise, he hadn't *really* been able to win.

How could he say he was worthy of being a Magician if, had this been real, he would've been helpless to stop that monster from killing him and his friends?

It was no different from what had happened at the Temple.

For the second time in his life, he had been powerless against an overwhelming force. He had been shown again just how ill-prepared he was for the life that Jack had spent training him for. If he couldn't at least live up to that simple expectation, what hope did he have of reaching Jack's level?

"Isaac? Hello?" Alison waved her hand in front of Isaac's face, ripping him free of his thoughts.

"Huh?" Isaac looked between them, all three staring at him questioningly.

"Everything okay?" Alison asked worriedly.

"Yeah, why the long face? Didn't like my compliment?" Margaret crossed her arms indignantly. "I even had to compliment you twice."

"I appreciate your kind words, both of you," Isaac insisted, forcing a smile. "I'm fine. Must've had too much to eat. Feeling a little nauseous is all." He patted his stomach.

"Right..." Margaret looked at him skeptically. "Whatever. Congrats again and all that." She waved goodbye, quickly grabbed a pastry, and pushed her way through the crowd with Jane following and scolding her as they went.

"Are you okay?" Alison questioned, locking eyes with him.

"Yeah... I'm okay. I just... I don't know. I got hit with this wave of emotion... I was just thinking, do I *really* deserve this?"

Alison jolted back. "What the hell are you talking about?"

"Keep your voice down, please," Isaac pleaded, taking a deep breath before he spoke again. "It's just... I still feel a little shaky after the Temple is all. I was *really* hoping for a big win with the Trials. I wanted to prove to myself that I wasn't helpless. That I could help and save other people. But then the fight with that damn Draugr Lord... Well, it just made me feel like it was the Temple all over again. I feel vulnerable, useless, and... And I don't know what to do."

Isaac let out a long sigh and slumped forward, feeling the crushing weight in his mind ease a bit.

Alison looked him over carefully and gave him a soft smile before placing her head on his shoulder.

"It's okay, Isaac. It was a terrifying experience, and I'm still scared too. I know how you feel. It was scary, for the first time, to see our mentor, the man who had protected us all our lives, struggle. It's... unnerving to see just how vulnerable we can be. But we can't let that feeling control us. Don't you remember what Jack said?"

Jack's voice rang in Isaac's head. *"It's okay to be afraid, but it's not okay to let that fear control you."*

Isaac shook his head. "I know what he said... but it's not that easy.

He's the strongest Arcanist to *ever* live, so of *course* he wouldn't have to be afraid of anything. What would *he* know about feeling helpless as your friends are getting hurt, and you can't do anything about it?"

Isaac trailed off, realizing that he was starting to talk louder. Alison looked at him worriedly. He had never openly challenged Jack's advice before. He had always hung on Jack's every word.

This time, though, it was just harder for him to accept.

How could the most powerful man alive know what it's like to feel helpless?

"I'm sorry," he said, frowning a little. "I'm just—"

"I know," Alison said, placing a gentle hand on his cheek. "It's okay. Why don't you talk to Jack about it? You say he doesn't understand, but I'm sure he will if you explain to him what's going on."

Isaac unconsciously leaned his head into her hand. "That's probably a good idea."

"I have a lot of those," she teased. "Just remember that you are not alone in this or anything else you go through. We're all here for you. Your family, your friends, everyone. We'll work through this together, okay?"

Isaac nodded half-heartedly. Sharing all of that with Alison had helped. He felt a little lighter, and the chaotic tidal wave in his mind had calmed somewhat, but he could feel something churning under the currents, slowly building...

"What's all this talk I hear of doubting yourself, eh?" Olfen clapped Isaac on the back, completely taking him by surprise.

"By your logic, we would all be dead right now." Meri came around the left side of him.

"We did not die. We are alive, sister. Stop with your foolishness," Fraunt agreed in his own way.

Olyen appeared close to Meri and quietly nodded. "We're all still here," he whispered.

Isaac looked at them each in shock.

"Well, if you don't want people standing close to you to hear your business, *maybe* speak a little quieter?" Olfen winked at him. "Listen,

Isaac, *you* are the one that went up against that Draugr Lord. Alone. And you almost won!" Olfen said plainly.

"Yes, but if you hadn't been there, the Nemean Lion most likely would have gotten me anyway," Isaac protested back.

Olfen smacked Isaac on the back of the head. "But I *was* there. And you still distracted the Lord long enough for me to figure out how to kill it. I'd listen to her if I were you, and have a little faith in yourself."

Isaac looked between them, each of them smiled reassuringly back at him. Isaac dared not look over at Alison. He could just *feel* her "I told you so" face.

Isaac let out a long sigh. "I will—am—working on it. I promise."

"I'll hold you to that." Olfen stepped between him and Alison, wrapping his thick arms around their necks. "Now, enough of this kind of talk. We have a party to get back to, eh? Would you two care to join us for a round of drinks?"

"It would be our pleasure," Alison choked out from Olfen's tight grip.

"Olfen! Be careful, you're going to strangle the poor girl." Meri appeared at Alison's side, grabbing her by the arm, and walking with her as Isaac was practically dragged by his neck.

Time seemed to melt away as Isaac and his friends drank and shared stories and laughed as if they had been friends all their lives. Any stories involving "Grumpy Sig"—a nickname affectionately given to Sigmund by Meri—seemed to be the favorites. Isaac had been particularly interested in Meri's upbringing. Since Meri's parents were both Sorcerers in the Order, she was the only one that Isaac knew of that had a generational link to the Order.

"It definitely made for a more involved childhood," Meri said, taking a sip of her wine. They had all gathered on long benches around a small fire. "I grew up learning how to use magic, outside of the Keep, of course. It was just a part of our daily lives. I never experienced any discrimination for being an Arcanist, so when I heard it was common, it was hard for me to believe at first. But then we found Fraunt."

Meri glanced over at Fraunt, who was staring unblinkingly at the fire.

"My family and I were traveling to Emberion so my parents could visit some friends, and we stumbled upon a young boy who couldn't have been much older than ten, wandering the woods alone. We still don't know how long he was out there. But judging by the loose tatters of clothes that didn't fit him anymore, and how skinny and dirty he was, he must've been alone for a long time. Maybe years. My parents think that his parents abandoned him after he began displaying his magic. Can you imagine? Years out in the wild all alone? All because your Vaccar parents didn't want an Arcanist?"

"Never alone. Darkness was my friend," Fraunt said, his eyes still fixed on the fire.

"And now we're your friends," Meri said, smiling.

Fraunt nodded. "Yes. Friends."

Isaac couldn't help but feel a sort of companionship in Fraunt now. For one reason or another, they both had been left behind by their parents, and an Arcanist family willing to raise them had graciously taken them in. Isaac couldn't remember his family, but they at least had brought him to Jack's doorstep. But they also very easily couldn't have. Isaac could've been in the exact same situation as Fraunt. Alone, confused, definitely afraid. It was no wonder he had the quirks he did.

"Gray man, stop this staring immediately."

Isaac blinked and realized that Fraunt was looking at him intently. "It is not polite."

"Sorry, Fraunt," Isaac said, wondering how long he must've been staring at him. "I got lost in thought for a moment."

Fraunt scoffed. "Lost? Gray man never moved. Ridiculous..." Fraunt turned his attention back to the flames.

Aaand there's that quirkiness...

* * * * *

As the night went on, guests slowly began saying their goodbyes, and fewer people hung around the Manor grounds.

"Isaac." Olfen pulled him in for a tight hug. "It has been a pleasure. If you need anything at all, you know where to find us."

"And be sure to write and visit!" Meri added, hugging Alison.

"Goodbye for now," Olyen spoke just barely above a whisper and gave Isaac and Alison a soft, tepid hug.

"Byes are not good. Frankly, they are terrible," Fraunt chimed.

Isaac sighed. "Yup, I'll miss you too, Fraunt."

Fraunt's eyes narrowed. "How will you miss me? Did you throw something at me?"

Isaac chuckled and shook his head. Fraunt really was something else.

The four of them waved and made their way toward the glowing, purple-black portal that shimmered in the air like a hole cut in the fabric of reality at the far end of the Manor grounds.

"Oh, and Isaac." Olfen turned to face him. "Make sure you take to heart what we said earlier, yeah? Trust yourself, have faith, everything else will work out fine." He flashed a toothy grin and waved again, ushering everyone down the hill. Olfen and Meri walked close together, their hands interlocked.

Isaac watched them go, Olyen keeping some distance away from Meri and Olfen. He could see Olyen take careful, quick glances up at Meri and watch her for a few seconds before looking away. Even at a distance, Isaac could make out the sad, downcast look on his face. Yet despite that, he could just barely make out a small smile on his quiet face. As if he were happy just to see her happy.

"Must be hard for him, seeing the girl he likes with his brother," Alison said, standing next to Isaac.

Isaac nodded. "I don't even want to imagine anything like that."

"Yes, lucky for you, I just plain don't like you." She winked and waved once more as their friends disappeared through the portal.

"See you guys again soon," Isaac whispered.

"I like them!" Alison announced in a chipper tone. "We should *definitely* visit them before my test next year."

"Definitely."

Alison yawned and stretched, cat-like. "It's been a hell of an evening. I think I'm going to retire. Are you coming too?" She grabbed his hand and pointed to the Manor.

Isaac hesitated. "Actually... I'm going to go talk to Jack for a bit." Isaac nodded over to where Jack was waving his goodbyes to Aephes.

Alison beamed at him. "Good idea! I'm proud of you. Well, let me know how it went in the morning, alright?" She wrapped her arms around his neck and pulled him into a tight hug. He wrapped his arms around her in return, pulling her closer to him. Isaac felt a wave of calm wash over him as the heat from her body bathed him in a comforting radiance. All the tension he had been feeling seemed to vanish, and the dark fog that he could feel building in his mind parted for a moment, letting in a serene silence he had not felt since before the Temple.

"Good night." She looked up at him. "And congratulations again. I'll see you in the morning."

Isaac smiled and watched her walk to the Manor doors. Isaac took in a deep breath, readying himself.

He made his way over to Jack, who piled quite a number of desserts onto a plate.

"Hey uh... Jack, can I talk to you for a second?" Isaac asked behind him.

Jack turned, a half-eaten cheese-filled baked roll in his hand, and the other half tucked in his cheeks as he continued chewing.

He smiled at him and laughed after he swallowed. "Well, you caught me at a bad time. Ha!" He set down the plate on the table, careful not to accidentally dismantle the tower of sweets. "I'll be back for those later... But of course, we are welcome to talk. Come! Walk with me. No reason for anyone to hear any private business."

Jack set off at an easy-mannered pace down the path away from the Manor. The two of them walked in silence for a few moments, as Isaac admired how the moonlight cast everything in a silvery, otherworldly glow. Even in the dark, the Manor seemed to teem with light.

"So, what's on your mind?" Jack broke the silence.

"Well... a lot of things," Isaac admitted.

"Start wherever you want."

Isaac was silent again, mulling over exactly how he should go about expressing what he was feeling. He didn't know why he was so nervous—so hesitant—to talk to Jack. He had never had a problem asking him about anything before. So, why now?

Was he afraid of admitting that he felt weak to him, who he felt expected so much of him?

Or was it more that he was afraid that Jack, the all-powerful Arcanist, the man who could've been Archmage, wouldn't understand where he was coming from after all?

Perhaps a mixture of both?

"Take your time, son. There is no rush. Just know that, no matter what it is, I cannot—or will I ever—judge you. It is impossible for me to be disappointed in any respect. Whenever you are ready, you can begin. Otherwise, I am quite content with spending a quiet evening beneath the stars." He flashed his warm, understanding smile.

It's like he can read minds too... Isaac thought, and then sighed.

"Alright, here it is. At the Temple, I was shown just how powerless I really am. I had to watch as Sigmund struggled against two powerful Arcanists, and I could do nothing about it. And when the attention was drawn to me and Alison, we were completely helpless. Sure, we managed to take one of them by surprise, but had Sigmund not been there again to save us, we would've died for sure.

"And then you invited me to the Magician's Trial, and I was so desperately hoping that it would help me shake this feeling of vulnerability that I've been having... But then that Draugr Lord dashed those hopes away, and I was shown *again* just how unprepared I am for what the world has in store... I don't know if I can be the Grey you want me to be, Jack, and I'm scared of feeling powerless again and I'm scared I won't be able to be there when people need me."

Jack was quiet for a long time, long enough for them to loop the perimeter of the Manor grounds twice before he spoke again.

"I know exactly how you feel, Isaac," he said, looking at him with a soft smile, then laughed at Isaac's bewildered expression. "Yes, hard to believe, I'm sure. Perhaps to best tackle this, I'll address this first: the only thing I have ever expected from you, or anyone else in this family, is for them to try their best. I ask nothing more than for everyone to put their best foot forward and be the strong, capable Arcanists I *know* they can be. Don't *ever* worry about not living up to my expectations. As I said earlier, it is impossible for you to disappoint me. You live up to all that I could hope for and more. Do you understand?"

Isaac nodded slowly.

"Good... Now, as for the other thing..." He took in a deep breath and sighed. "I'm sure after your visit to the Order you had heard some things about me that left you with some questions. I'm sure Olfen told you about my declination of the Archmage title, and surely he mentioned whispers of the Primis Beast, did he not?"

Isaac smirked despite himself. "He mentioned all those things, actually, yeah."

Jack chuckled. "I thought as much... When I was younger... I felt like I had the world in the palm of my hand. I was an arrogant, brash fool who let my power go to my head much too often."

"Aephes did tell me that you had been a troublemaker."

Jack laughed again. "I'm sure he did. And he wasn't wrong. Oh, I can remember the Mages' faces when they would see me breaking the Order's rules... But... despite all my bravado and my strength, I couldn't avoid the consequences of my own actions... And how low they would bring me."

Isaac looked at Jack questioningly. He just smiled in a sad, understanding sort of way, a portal appearing before them.

"I imagine you're wondering how I could be made to feel powerless... helpless... Well, come with me, Isaac, and let me show you the height of my arrogance."

CHAPTER SIXTEEN

"W HAT IS THIS PLACE?" ISAAC WHISPERED, gazing at the forest around him.

The woods were dense and slightly crowded, the trees twisted as if someone had used both hands to stretch and pull them. Their leaves were jagged like shark's teeth but were a dazzling shade of ocean blue that glowed like gems in the moonlight. The slightest breeze caused the leaves to dance enchantingly, bringing the sound of waves gently lapping against the shore echoing around them. A twinkling yellow sap slowly oozed out from where there were holes in the trees. Even the grass was a strange color: mostly green, but with a faint orange tip. The air was salty and sharp, burning Isaac's nose with each breath.

Isaac's eyes drifted to a tombstone placed near one of the tallest trees. The tombstone was made of polished white marble with round-ed corners. In thick black lettering, the name 'Rose Greimendoor' was scrawled across the headstone. On either side of the marker were two small bushes: one rose and one lilac.

"Jack... what is this place?" Isaac repeated, his eyes pinned to the headstone.

Jack cast a melancholic smirk. "We are in the Forest of Waves, in Drahkul, not too far from the Order. This was her favorite place to visit..."

Isaac watched as Jack knelt before the headstone and placed both hands on top of it, holding it as if it would break if he wasn't careful. At that moment, Jack seemed to deflate; he became smaller, somehow. The larger-than-life figure Isaac always knew him to be seemed to shrink to the size of a normal person.

He looked... vulnerable.

When Jack looked back at Isaac, Isaac was surprised to find lines of fresh tears beginning to slowly roll down his face, catching in the dimples of his half-smile before falling silently to the ground.

"I suppose I have much to share with you," Jack began, his voice cracking a little at the end.

Isaac stood there absolutely dumbfounded. He had always seen Jack as this legendary figure that was above the problems of regular people.

Jack cleared his throat before speaking. "Perhaps I should start from the beginning. As you have heard, I had a different temperament back then. When I was brought to the Order, I was full of youthful arrogance, honed through years of using my abilities to crush any opposition before me."

Jack chuckled to himself. "Yes, I definitely did not have an issue with self-confidence. I was overflowing with it. How could I not have been? A young child born with so much latent power that the world itself seemed to bow to him. Eventually, my escapades around Eutrox caught the Order's attention, and an Omnis Warlock, Raetelle, was sent to fetch me. I refused him at first, repeatedly. But he and the Order *insisted* that I join them so that I might hone my abilities. But what would I, someone so strong, and so far unchallenged, need with people like them? So, when Raetelle refused to take no for an answer, I challenged him to a duel. If he won, I would go to the Order. If I won, he, and the Order, were to leave me alone."

Isaac's eyebrows furrowed. "And he beat you? How?"

Jack smiled. "For all my power, my technique was... unrefined. I had no sense of strategy. Raetelle had both of these, and it was with his cunning and skills that he was able to beat me. I would find out much later that, unsurprisingly, Raetelle was Aephes's predecessor. He was being groomed to be the next Warden. At any rate, I despised the fact that he had beaten me, but I kept my word, now actually eager to join the Order if for nothing else than to learn how to beat Raetelle the first chance I got. I am thankful that this stubborn man was able to best me, for it was through him I not only learned discipline and skill, but I also met her."

Jack turned back to the tombstone, gently running his thumb against the smooth stone.

"Raetelle allowed me to stay with him and his family while I adjusted to life at the Order. And it was the first night at his home, where I had a real supper for the first time in my life, that I met his daughter, Rose."

Jack paused and smiled, gazing dreamily off into the trees as the leaves danced in the breeze. The sound of ocean waves gently churning echoed around them.

"I knew from the moment I saw her that I was under her spell. I had never met anyone who made me feel nervous. Rose was everything that I wasn't: kind, compassionate, optimistic, and she had this child-like wonder about her that made everything seem so much more exciting. And her smile—ah, her smile—she had this large, beaming grin that could have beckoned the very mountains to move if she so chose...

"It was by some miracle that she seemed to feel the same way, about me of all people. We became practically inseparable, constantly doing everything together. Rose is actually where my interest in Primis—the Ancient Ones—came from and their relationship with the Luminare. She was fascinated by their history, and she wanted to know everything she could about them. Partially out of an interest in their magic, but also to learn from what they had done and work to repair the damage they had caused between Vaccars and Arcanists. That was her dream: to make the world whole again. While mine was simply to beat her father."

Jack closed his eyes and listened as the breeze picked up once more, the oceanic sound roaring around them like a stormy sea. Isaac watched as tree branches whipped violently, the blue leaves shimmering and fluttering madly in the wind, the salty scent becoming stronger. Something wet gently hit Isaac in the face, making him reach up and touch his cheek.

Jack smiled at him. "This forest experiences a phenomenon where, as the wind grows in strength, some of the excess moisture from the plants gets pulled out from the leaves and sprays you. Almost like the real ocean."

The wind grew stronger for another moment before dying down, spraying Isaac with more droplets.

Jack turned his attention back to Rose's grave. "Rose's fascination would eventually lead her—and subsequently me—to Primis's prized possessions: their artifacts. She had read about them in plenty of Primis stories, and we were eager to go out and find one for ourselves. The very thought of going after one was exhilarating. However, the Order had strict rules against this, of course. No one was allowed to disturb the Ancient One's artifacts. In the Order's opinion, they were too dangerous and best left alone. We had made such a fuss about going after the artifact that the Archmage, who was Virua at the time, had to come speak to us directly to warn us.

"Of course, we did not listen. Despite my time at the Order, my overconfidence had actually *increased*. The other Arcanists were taking notice of my strength and circulating new rumors, all accumulating into a heightened renown that fed my ego terribly. Even Virua seemed hesitant around me. And it was with that ego that I pressured Rose into hunting down an artifact with me. Rose was rightly hesitant, but I reassured her that *I* could protect us no matter what. Unfortunately, she believed me."

"No one tried to stop you before you left the Order?" Isaac asked.

Jack shook his head. "No, we were both Magicians at the time, and ranked Arcanists can come and go as they please. Besides, no one would have stopped to question me. They wouldn't have dared. I was a dueling fanatic back then and was undefeated except for Raetelle..."

Jack lightly pinched a rose petal between his fingers, rubbing his thumb over the petal. "So, we began our journey toward the Mausoleum of the First, a burial site for all of Primis' first members, and the location of an artifact that was said to act as a key to another dimension. We found the artifact—a hand-sized, pyramid-shaped object—hidden deep within the Tomb without much issue. But everything changed once we touched the artifact. The artifact did not behave in the way the books at the Order hypothesized... No, the supposed 'key' should have never been activated without us explicitly wanting it to. However..."

Jack stopped, his voice quivering. His smile had receded into a flat, grim mask. His eyes lacked the light Isaac was so used to seeing behind them. Now, it was as if a murky fog clouded Jack's eyes, blocking the light.

Jack coughed and cleared his throat again. "... Rose was the first to touch the artifact. That 'key' immediately lit up like the sun, quickly enveloping Rose in a thick violet haze. The sheer force of whatever magic was stored in there was enough to throw me backwards through several walls of the Tomb. When the haze cleared and my senses recovered, Rose had been... transformed... twisted into a Klythini..."

"Klythini..." Isaac whispered to himself, recalling his conversation with Olfen. "Is that the Primis Beast?"

Jack nodded. "Yes. The 'Primis Beast' as the Order refers to it. The Klythini was a creature created by Primis by combining different parts of different animals and using the Luminare as glue to hold the creature together. Once Rose had touched the artifact, it triggered the trap laid by Primis, and she became the catalyst for the newest Klythini. The creature had dragon-like scales, an eagle's wings, tiger's paws, and three scorpion tails. Poor Rose's beautiful face was contorted into an almost bear-like appearance with razor-sharp fangs..."

Jack winced and peered up at the night sky, releasing the rose from his grasp.

"Before I could fully recover, the creature fled, leaving me alone in the Tomb. I rushed back to the Order, screaming for Virua and Raetelle. Once I found them, I told them everything that had happened. I can still see the look on Raetelle's face. He looked at me as if I were the most insignificant little pest he had ever had the misfortune of putting up with. I had never felt so small.

"It wasn't long until reports started flooding in from Order Arcanists from northern villages stating a Klythini had appeared. Virua quickly summoned other Mages and Warlocks—including Raetelle—to go after Rose. I begged them to let me help. *Pleading* with them to let me go, so that I might fix my mistake. The Archmage forbade it and trapped me in an enchanted barrier much like the one we have around the Manor. However, being the stubborn child that I was, I eventually overpowered Virua's prison, and I fled from the Keep to the village. But by the time I had arrived..." Jack's voice trailed off again. He let out a heavy sigh and ran his hands over his face.

"What happened?" Isaac asked, now kneeling beside Jack.

"By the time I arrived, it was a bloodbath. All the Arcanists who had been sent to subdue or kill the beast were dead. Bodies were thrown everywhere like discarded dolls. I got there just as the Klythini killed Virua; her eviscerated body lay spasming at its feet. And Raetelle... Well, Raetelle had been cut in two. I had only ever found his torso, his face partially caved in. With Virua, and everyone else, dead, it was up to me to deal with the Klythini. At first, I tried to see if I could reach Rose somewhere within the monster, but the beast slashed and flared its magic at me. If Rose were in there, she was buried deep beneath the consciousness of the Klythini.

"I fought the Klythini for hours until it eventually landed a near-fatal slash across my back. As I fell to the ground, blood pouring out of my wound, I looked up at the Klythini, its gaping maw inches from my face. Then something changed in the Klythini. Its face contorted and shifted back into Rose's. For a split second, she was there, crying and pleading with me to stop her. At that moment, I summoned all of my strength and used every school of magic that I knew at once to rip through the beast's side and pierce its heart."

Jack clenched his fists tight, his knuckles turning a bright white. While Jack was telling the story as level-headedly as he could, Isaac could hear the gnawing regret he felt for what happened that day. Isaac couldn't blame him. If he had been responsible for something happening to Alison, like he almost had been in the Temple...

Isaac shuddered.

"The Klythini became enveloped in that haze again and, in its wake, it left Rose's near lifeless, bleeding body. I crawled over to her, desperate to save her. When I pulled her limp body closer to me, I could feel the life slowly draining from her. But she refused my help. In her last moments, she asked only that I lay there with her, and so I did. I held her as she slowly faded away, reassuring me she didn't regret a thing. I watched as the familiar light in her eyes I had become so enchanted with slowly dimmed as she took her last raspy breath.

"I woke up in the infirmary a week later, shaken to the very core of my being. I was forbidden from attending regular lessons, and the infirmary became a sort of prison as the Elder Mages and the rest of the Order decided what to do with me. The time I spent there, waiting for my punishment, gave me a lot of time to reflect on myself. I questioned every decision I had made up to that point, wondering if I had done something differently, even slightly, would the outcome have changed. I drove myself to the brink of insanity with those questions, all the while trying to push down this terrible feeling growing inside me. For the first time, I had been utterly powerless to stop something from happening. With all my natural-born power, I couldn't save her. I couldn't contain the Primis Beast, and I couldn't save my fellow Arcanists."

Jack took in another shaky breath. His eyes had welled with tears again, creating long wet streaks on his cheeks. "For the first time, I felt I did not have control, and that frightened me—angered me—and I wanted to get that control back."

"So what'd you do?" Isaac asked, inching closer to Jack.

"Well, it took me a long time to realize that, in order to get my control back, I had to change my way of thinking. I couldn't focus on what I couldn't do then, or entertain the 'what-if' scenarios that ravaged my mind relentlessly. I had to focus on what I could do now. It was with that revelation that I took control back. I decided then that I would become the man that I think Rose had always seen in me, and I wanted to make her dream become a reality. In doing those two things, I felt like I might make my way toward some form of repentance.

"I requested an audience with the Order and announced my plans to further Rose's vision of healing the relationship between Vaccars and Arcanists, and that I would hunt down the Ancient One's artifacts and house them and study them so that none might experience what Rose had to endure. To my surprise, they granted my request, and I was allowed to continue my studies, though everyone was more hesitant around me after the Primis Beast incident. Once I finished my studies at the Order, I founded the Grey family to facilitate both Rose's dream and my mission. Somewhere along the way, the Greys became a sort of family for those without a home, and I think Rose would've liked that."

Jack was silent again, with a sad half-smile on his face. Isaac sat there in silence, completely dumbstruck at what he just heard, and feeling a little ashamed of what he said earlier.

He glanced over at Jack, who looked like a shadow of his former self from just an hour ago. Jack wore his pain like a thick, melancholy cloak that shrouded his entire being in a muted air. Isaac could clearly see the pain in his eyes, the indescribable pain that tears at the edges of your soul after you lose someone precious to you. It was a nauseating, dizzying feeling that seemed to strike Jack to his core.

Isaac didn't want to even begin to imagine the levels of torment that Jack had to go through to get to where he was now. But, just knowing that even Jack had gone through something like that, *and* had managed to work through it then, perhaps, Isaac could too?

But how was it that Jack was able to push down the thoughts that sought to paralyze him as they do Isaac? How was it that he was able to twist his mind into obeying him, and not cave under the weight of his own anxiousness? The Temple had brought to the surface a raging undercurrent of fear that had been exacerbated by the Trials that Isaac didn't quite know how to contain.

Jack said it had taken some time, but how much time? Would it take days? Months?

Years?

Isaac shook his head. From what he could tell, it seemed like something he would have to figure out, in part, on his own.

Right now, however, he had an idol to console.

Isaac placed a reassuring hand on Jack's shoulder.

"For what it's worth, I think Rose would be proud of everything you've done, Jack. You've done everything you've set out to do and more. I'm sure she's happy."

Jack offered a half-smile and patted his hand. "Thank you, I appreciate that. I have certainly tried, for what that's worth. I hope that this was helpful. If you take nothing else away, remember not to let your emotions control you. You have to shift your mind away from fears and irrational scenarios and focus on what you can do in the moment. It may take some time, and I know how insidious those thoughts can be, but you will get there. Does that all make sense?"

Isaac nodded and smiled. "Yeah, I got it. And this has helped. Thank you."

"Are you ready to head back?" Isaac stood and offered a hand to Jack.

Jack waved his hand away politely. "I think I might stay a little longer. It's been a while since I last visited. I can send you back though, don't worry. It has been a long day for you."

"Good night, Isaac." Jack offered a soft smirk and waved his hand through the air, Isaac disappearing from the forest as his hand passed over him.

* * * *

Jack turned back to the gravestone and took in a deep breath, allowing the scent of the roses and lilacs to fill his nose.

Her favorite. Jack thought as he carefully examined the flowers. He frowned, noticing some dying branches on the rosebush. A pair of pruning shears appeared in his hand, and he carefully began clipping away the dead parts of the rosebush before doing the same to the lilac. He worked hard to keep the bushes looking as neat and lively as possible.

He owed Rose that much.

Jack smiled as he thought back to what Isaac had said. He sincerely hoped that he was right. Jack had devoted his life to trying to set things right, and he could only hope that he was building the world that Rose had always envisioned.

A few drops of water splashed against Jack as the wind rustled the leaves around him. He could still recall vividly the first time he and Rose had come here, and how she was instantly enchanted with this place. Her face had lit up in awe, with her usual ear-to-ear grin and her eyes as wide as saucers.

Someday, Rose, we'll see each other again... when my work has finished.

Jack looked between the bushes and, satisfied with his work, the shears disappeared from his hands. He let out a relaxed sigh as he leaned against the tombstone and closed his eyes, feeling the cool night air run over his body in calm pulses. He sat there in silence for a long time, trying his best to ignore the nagging thoughts in the back of his mind.

Someone had attacked his family and attempted to take an artifact. Something had to be done about that.

And something will be done. Jack told himself. *After I allow myself these few more minutes of peace.*

After some time, Jack stood, gazing down at the marker.

"I'll come back to see you again soon, I promise. But there is some important business I must take care of first. Good night, Rose."

Jack turned away from the grave, disappearing in an instant, leaving the fading moonlight to cast a soothing glow upon her resting place.

CHAPTER SEVENTEEN

"Thank you both for your help." Jack smiled gratefully at Adara and Sigmund. Jack leaned forward in his chair, elbows on his desk, and fingers laced tightly together. Adara lounged in a chair across from him, her legs kicked up over one arm. Sigmund opted to stand, leaning against the wall closest to the door.

Adara returned a tight-lipped, serious smile. "Of course. What's family for?"

Sigmund grunted and nodded.

"Sigmund, we'll start with you. Were you able to find anything at the Temple?"

Sigmund reached under his armor, retrieving a neatly folded piece of parchment paper and placed it on the desk. "Have a look."

Jack's eyes widened as he unfolded the parchment. His finger traced over the slim, sleek dragon that wrapped around the emboldened 'A', and then the twisting vines that grew toward the middle of the symbol.

"What is it?" Adara sat upright, craning her neck to see.

Jack flipped the parchment around and held it up for Adara.

"Are you sure this is what you saw?"

Sigmund nodded.

"Isn't that the Anguis family crest?" Adara asked. "Didn't you and Queen Hestia destroy them years ago?"

Jack nodded. "Yes. The Anguis family used their twisted power to oppress and abuse the people of Drahkul. Kenna and her rebellion had reached out to me asking for help. I was more than willing to assist. We had taken great care to ensure that none of that family survived..."

"Someone did." Sigmund jabbed his finger into the symbol. "Someone is working under this banner. Including the traitor in our family. Coincidences do not happen."

Jack gave Sigmund a slow nod. His old friend was right, of course. If Jack had learned nothing else in his long life, it was that Sigmund was seldom wrong. He didn't want to think about one of his own willingly betraying them, but his instincts told him that, whoever this person was, was acting of their own free will and not being coerced. And as for the person using the Anguis Crest... Jack had been so careful in the Anguis eradication, surely no one could've survived.

Could they?

"Adara." Jack turned his gaze to her. "I apologize for the short timetable. But were you able to find anything?"

Adara stretched in her chair and shook her head. "On the traitor front? No, unfortunately. The people I have looked into, which included Sigmund, Alison, and Isaac—sorry—" She shot Sigmund an apologetic look. "Have not given me any indication of betrayal."

Jack smiled. "I agree with your assessment of those three. I doubt they would be capable of such a thing."

"However, I *did* hear some rumors that have been circulating. I reached out to my contacts across several kingdoms, and they all confirmed what you heard initially: someone was recruiting Arcanists for a job. I was able to cobble together a rough description of whoever this is: they're said to have grayish skin and an almost snake-like appearance. At first, I thought perhaps it was a sort of were-creature, but now..."

Jack leaned back in his chair. "Gray skin, eh...?" he mused. Every member of the Anguis family had discolored skin. It was a byproduct of their fusion with dragon blood and a reflection of the race of dragon they had fused with. However, despite the Anguis members he had fought, he had *never* encountered a gray-skinned one.

Blood magic is tricky, especially when fusing powers from two completely separate beings together. And the greater the disparity between the two beings in the fusion, the more dangerous the process is for both of them.

It would stand to reason, then, that perhaps why he didn't see anyone with gray skin was because the process to make them was too difficult or had failed in the past. So what then could this survivor have been mixed with?

Jack drummed his fingers on his desk, and then sat upright as a thought occurred to him. *There is only one race of dragons that might turn someone's skin gray...*

Scattenwerz.

If someone were fused together with a Scattenwerz, the race known for their pitch-black scales, the result would most likely produce an individual with gray skin.

"What is it?" Sigmund asked.

"I think I'm beginning to put the pieces together..." Jack began.

"Care to share?" Adara leaned forward in her chair.

Jack smiled. "Whoever is recruiting Arcanists I believe, in all likelihood, is this Anguis 'survivor', as we're calling him. And I believe he was fused with Scattenwerz blood."

Adara shuddered. "Scattenwerz? How'd they manage to get a hold of one of them?"

"Most likely from the Dragon Heart artifact that I took from them," Jack explained.

"But fusing with something *that* powerful, something that has Archmage kind of strength, wouldn't that be... hazardous?" Adara questioned.

"Terribly. The success rate would be unpredictable. But if it were to work, it would make quite a powerful individual. When Kenna and I took Dragon's Respite, we found a dead Scattenwerz mother in its underkeep. They must've been trying for quite some time."

"Why do they need the orb then?" Sigmund interjected. "If they are so strong already, why bother with it?"

"That's a good question," Jack said. "I think their plot, potentially, is to challenge me. Why else would someone go after that particular artifact, given the mythology surrounding it? I think that whoever this is, is gathering power to take me—and my family—on."

"What's their goal, then? To kill you? To retake their home? Both?" Sigmund pressed.

Jack shrugged again. "I'm not sure yet. It would make sense for the survivor to want to reclaim their home."

"And it would make sense that he would see you as the biggest threat to that goal, or even to himself," Adara chimed in.

Sigmund nodded. "So, right now we are the targets. Can we handle it?"

Jack looked down at his hands, balling them into tight fists.

Could they handle it?

Even just a few years ago when Jack and Kenna had marched on Emberion—then Dragon's Respite—, he had asked himself that same question. A lot of their plan that day had relied on him. Many of the Anguis members were too powerful for Kenna's soldiers to handle, and even Kenna herself—despite her being a Fire Mage—was outclassed by some of the Anguis members. Luckily, they had carried out the mission with minimal losses. But he could *feel* the pull inside of him, the sinking pit into the abyss where his vitality was being drained.

Every day he felt the weight of that pit increase.

Every day, he felt a bit of himself slip away.

A few years ago, he would have just been hesitant, but he knew what the passage of time meant for him.

And now, thinking about how his family would handle this survivor with strength equivalent to, or beyond that of an Archmage, well...

He would have to be very careful indeed.

But if Raetelle could stand up to Jack despite their differences, then Jack believed *anyone* could hold their own against any power with the right mindset.

If nothing else, that's exactly what he'd bring to the table.

He looked up from his hands and noticed Sigmund and Adara eyeing him suspiciously.

"Everything alright?" Adara asked, tilting her head.

Jack smiled warmly at them. He had too many people relying on him. He couldn't afford to doubt himself now. They needed him to be the strong anchor in the storm that was coming.

They needed their leader.

Whatever may come, he would deal with it, one way or another.

"Yes, sorry. Got swept away for a second. Yes, I believe we can handle it just fine. We have plenty of talented Warlocks here, and a plethora of Sorcerers and Magicians."

"What of the Order? Should we involve them?" Sigmund inquired.

Jack winced. "No... I'd like to keep them out of it as much as possible. This is my fight, and now, unfortunately, it is all the Grey's as well. We can handle it. Trust me."

Sigmund and Adara both looked at him with disbelieving, suspicious glances.

He could tell that they thought he was holding something back.

He could count on one hand all the people who knew of his predicament, and he intended to keep that number small. If word got out...

There would certainly be a shift in the hierarchy of power.

With everything going on, did he owe it to them so that they might not put so much faith in him? Or, by spreading this information, did he risk the traitor finding out and relaying it back to the survivor?

For now... I'll keep it to myself.

"Are you sure not involving the Order is wise?" Sigmund questioned.

"Given Jack's history with them, I think it's understandable why he wouldn't want to drag them into something like this," Adara said.

"I understand that, but we have more at stake here than pride and reopening old wounds." Sigmund retorted.

"It's not a matter of pride. It's—"

Jack raised his hand, cutting Adara off. "I value both of your opinions deeply. However, Sigmund, I won't be calling on the Order. It was just a few decades ago that they finally rebuilt themselves with all the Mages that they lost from the Klythini incident. I won't burden them again with another of my blunders. Do you understand?"

Sigmund opened his mouth to question further but stopped and snorted his displeasure.

It was quiet in the study for some time. The only noise was the soft crackle of the slowly dying fire.

Jack cleared his throat. "With the Trials done, I can assist with our search for the traitor. I want all of us working together to figure out who this turncoat is and find out more about this Anguis survivor. We'll share information as we progress. Is everyone okay with this?"

Adara nodded, and Sigmund agreed reluctantly.

"Good. If there is nothing else, I would like to meet with Isaac briefly if you would send for him."

"Sure, we'll get him." Adara stood from her chair and patted Sigmund on the arm.

"I hope you know you can trust us with anything, Jack. Especially now, there is no need to keep things from us."

Adara shot him a skeptical glance, Sigmund mirroring her gaze.

Jack smiled. "I know, don't worry. I appreciate your concern."

Adara and Sigmund exchanged unconvinced looks and shuffled out the door.

Jack ran his hands over his face and let out a heavy sigh.

Adara was right, of course. He should be able to trust them with this knowledge but, with the traitor still in their midst, he wanted to be as cautious as possible. Once he had more information and a clearer understanding of the threat, he'd reassess his decision.

Not that he suspected that either of them were the traitors, but someone hearing a whisper through the door at the right time could spell disaster.

Jack shuddered as his mind flashed back to his fight with the Klythini. He had told Isaac much of the story, but not all of it.

He had left out the haze that settled over his body after he killed the Klythini.

And the deep, burning sensation that he felt at the core of his being as it sank into him, as if his soul were set ablaze.

Since that moment, it has been a race against time. Fighting the curse that was so intertwined with his existence that even the Elder Mages could not remove it, for it would kill him instantly. If it weren't for Aura magic and being able to manipulate his life force, he never would've been able to stay the curse's toll for so long. An ordinary man, or even an untrained Arcanist, would've been dead within a year. Jack had survived hundreds of years, despite this parasitic curse.

But it was catching up with him now.

He could feel it.

The strain of sustaining his life was becoming greater with each passing day.

Each hour, he felt more of his vitality and strength slip away, like sand between his fingers. If he were lucky, he was perhaps half as strong as he used to be. And that was a generous estimation.

He took a steadying breath. His match with the Anguis survivor was inevitable. But for now, he had to focus on more immediate, pressing issues. For starters, he had to figure out more about the survivor, how they had survived, and confirm or dispel his suspicions of his merging with a Scattenwerz. Then there was the issue of this traitor. What was their goal, and how was that linked to this survivor?

A quick succession of short, rapid knocks echoed from his door.

"Come in!" Jack called in a chipper tone, leaning forward in his chair and flashing a warm grin at the door.

Isaac all but threw the door open and stepped inside. "Just can't get enough of talking to me, eh?" He smiled cheekily.

Jack chuckled. "Never. Now, I called you in for a couple of reasons. First, in light of our conversation last night, I think it's important that you go out there and get some of your control back, without having someone watching over you. Doing minor tasks, like perhaps some bounties from Beignknost, can help build that sense of control back into you. With that being said, please feel free to take someone with you, though I can guess who you'll choose."

Isaac said nothing, his face turning red.

Jack laughed heartily. "I knew it. Alright then, you and Alison can leave as soon as you'd like. And if anything happens, remember that you are not alone. You have her and other people to rely on and help you through it. Understood?"

Jack smiled as Isaac nodded eagerly, his eyes lighting up in anticipation.

"Oh! And before I forget again..." Jack held out his hand and a large, black, scaly egg appeared in his palm. The weight of the egg caused Jack's arm to buckle slightly.

Isaac's eyes grew wide. "Is that—"

"A dragon egg?" Jack grinned. "Yes. Do you recognize it?"

Isaac ran his fingers along the edges of the scales. The egg seemed to hum and grow warmer in response to his touch. "This... I remember seeing it in your artifact room."

Jack nodded. "Correct. When you were younger, you would follow me around endlessly. One day, when you had followed me into the artifact room, your attention was immediately drawn to the egg." Jack chuckled, "It was actually quite difficult prying you away from it. I reclaimed this egg from the Anguis family, its mother dead in the underkeep, and the last of its kind that I could find there. This egg had been tucked under her wing in her attempt to hide it from her captors. I attempted to hatch the dragon myself by pouring magic into the egg as the mother might've done, but, try as I might, the egg would not hatch. There are Draconic tales of eggs that will only hatch under certain circumstances. So, given your magnetic attraction to it when you were younger, perhaps it is your fate to discover what those circumstances are."

Jack placed the dragon egg in Isaac's hands. "I had considered waiting to give you this when you achieved Mage, but, to be honest with you, I was too excited and I couldn't wait until then. Just don't expect a dragon egg for every rank." Jack winked at him.

Isaac stood silently for a moment, running his hands over the scales, and watching it intently. "Thank you, Jack, I... I don't even know what to say."

Jack smiled and waved his hand dismissively. "Best way to show your appreciation is to figure out how to hatch it, and then teach me. I have moved a special container for the egg into your room so that you can house it in your trunk for safekeeping. Now, I believe Beignknost is waiting for you..."

Isaac grinned from ear-to-ear, nodding emphatically. He turned to leave, but stopped, his eyes locking onto the parchment on Jack's desk.

Isaac's eyes narrowed. "What is that?"

He snatched the paper off the desk and held it up in the candlelight. "Is that the weird symbol Alison was talking about that she and Sigmund had found?"

"Indeed. It's the Anguis family crest. A family that I had thought to be long dead."

"So... one of them is alive, then."

"It would seem that way, yes. But don't worry. I am working on it with Adara and Sigmund."

"What are they after?" Isaac asked, returning the parchment to Jack's desk.

"We have a few working theories."

"What can I do to help? Does anyone else in the family know? What about Margaret and Jane?" Isaac's eyes were wild and alert as he leaned over the desk.

Jack offered a soft smile. He could appreciate Isaac's enthusiasm for helping. Isaac had always been one of the proudest members of the family since the day he arrived.

But this problem was no longer his to deal with.

"No, only we—and now you—know about this. I don't plan on sharing anything until we know more. The best way you can help Isaac is by working to become the best version of yourself. I appreciate your concern, but let us handle this. You'll hear as soon as we know something."

Isaac's eyes narrowed on Jack. He opened his mouth to say something, but stopped. Finally, Isaac sighed and made his way to the door. "Fine, but I want to know as soon as you hear anything. We were there when this all started, so you owe us at least that much."

Jack raised his hands. "You have a point. Like I said, I promise I will let you know as soon as I learn anything."

Isaac nodded, still not entirely content with that answer. "I'm off then. Thanks again, Jack, for everything."

Jack smiled. "You're welcome. I look forward to hearing about your travels to Beignknost."

* * * * *

Isaac smiled in return and waved his goodbye. Throwing the door open and slamming it shut behind him as he sprinted down the hallway toward Alison's room. Isaac was equal parts excited and nervous at the prospect of going out on a mission with just Alison.

What would happen if they encountered something like the Sigmund clone at the Temple again? Could they handle that all on their own? Their recent history didn't give Isaac much hope. Just imagining what could happen made him anxious.

Isaac shook his head. Jack was right: he couldn't let the what-if scenarios run rampant in his mind. He had to just focus on what he could do.

Easier said than done. Isaac thought.

It would be hard for him to control his fear, and Jack had told him as much, but it would be especially difficult now with the events of the Temple, and now whoever this Anguis person was, looming in his mind. Jack had told him not to worry about it, but how could he not? They were attacked trying to retrieve the artifact, and it was safe to assume that whoever was after it wouldn't give up trying to take it for themselves.

But the likelihood of anyone getting anywhere near the artifact now was laughable. No one would be able to brute-force their way through the barrier Jack had created around the Manor grounds. That at least offered him some comfort.

Focus, Isaac, one thing at a time.

Isaac stopped abruptly in front of Alison's door, almost running face-first into it. He had been so lost in thought that he hadn't noticed how close he had gotten to her room. Isaac rapped his knuckles against her door softly.

"Alison? You there?"

He heard a quiet shuffling, followed by a loud thud and a series of exclamations and profanities, before the door opened a second later to a smiling but frustrated-looking Alison. The early morning sun was beaming in from her window, giving her a radiant glow that made Isaac's heart skip a beat.

"Good morning! What's—" Her eyes slid to the dragon egg under his arm. "What is that thing?"

"Are you going to say something or wait for a fly to land in your mouth?" Her voice dripped with sarcasm, her eyes sliding to the dragon egg under his arm. "What is that thing?"

Isaac grinned. "*This* is my dragon egg!"

Alison's eyebrows furrowed. "How the hell did you get one of those?!"

"Jack gave it to me as a gift for achieving the Magician rank," Isaac said proudly.

"If he gave that to you, then *I* should get an entire family of dragons when *I* make Magician," she teased. "But that is really something. Are you going to try to hatch it?"

Isaac shrugged. "Eventually, maybe, but it doesn't seem like it's ready yet... I can just kind of tell that it's not the time."

Alison raised an eyebrow. "Anyway, did you come to brag about your gift or were you just dying to see me?"

"Can't it be both?" Isaac smirked cheekily. "In all seriousness, I came here for a reason: after speaking to Jack, he is encouraging me to take on bounties in Beignknost to help me work through my confidence issues. He said I could take anyone I wanted with me, so, obviously, I picked you! If you want to go, that is."

Alison clapped her hands together excitedly. "Of course I'll go with you! I'm going to need all the experience I can get if I want to take on the Trials next year. Besides, who is going to watch out for you if I'm not there? Just don't get me stabbed this time, okay?" She winked.

Isaac winced, the scenes from the Temple briefly flashing through his mind.

"I will do my best." Isaac rubbed his neck awkwardly. "But maybe it's best if I don't make any promises."

Alison chuckled. "Good enough for me. When do we leave?"

"I was thinking as early today as possible. I'll go back and pack my things now. Meet in the foyer in a couple hours?"

"I will meet you there. Oh, how wonderful! I love Beignknost…" Her voice trailed off as she turned briskly and slammed the door in Isaac's face.

Isaac frowned. *She can be so rude for someone so nice.*

Isaac turned and rushed down the hall to his room to gather his things.

CHAPTER EIGHTEEN

Sigmund and Adara walked together in silence around the halls of the Grey Manor for some time, stopping only briefly to inform Isaac that Jack wanted to see him.

Sigmund didn't talk much as it was, but now that his mind was busy playing different scenarios over in his head—all of which ended terribly—his silence was even more prolonged.

Their conversation with Jack troubled him. Jack had said all the right things, sure, but it was his body language and the look in his eyes when he saw the Anguis crest that bothered him. It was there only for a moment before his usual demeanor returned, but, for that second, Sigmund could clearly see the fear that Jack was desperately trying to hide.

"I'm worried about Jack," Adara's voice was barely above a whisper as they stepped out onto the Manor grounds.

"He seemed quite startled by that symbol, don't you agree?" Adara continued, as if she had been reading Sigmund's mind. "I've known him all my life, and not *once* have I seen him bat an eye at, well, anything, but now, well, something is different."

"Indeed," Sigmund responded quietly, clasping his hands behind his back as they walked the perimeter of the grounds. Adara smiled and waved as they passed other Greys walking around the gardens. The grounds seemed busier than usual; the warm sun and gentle breeze had pulled people outside to enjoy the nice weather. Some played games while others sprawled out on the grass, taking in the sun.

Sigmund grunted. *Let them enjoy this time while they have it.*

"What do you think it is then?" Adara asked, pulling Sigmund away from his thoughts, "What reason would he have to be afraid?"

Sigmund shrugged, ducking beneath a branch.

Adara chuckled. "Not very helpful, are you?"

"There are many possibilities to consider, both with Jack and this traitor. I believe our time is better spent investigating and finding concrete information than discussing our worries."

"Ah, so it does speak!" Adara's words were playful, but lightly dipped in condescension. "You're right, of course. Our efforts should be focused on gathering information. So then, what is our next course of action, Siggy?"

Sigmund cast her an annoyed side-glance. "I will take over the investigation into the traitor, picking up where you left off. Since your contacts seem somewhat privy to the survivor, perhaps it's best if you looked into that further."

Adara cheerfully clapped her hands together. "Splendid idea! My resources have been quite helpful, haven't they? And with your tightly wound, paranoid nature, we'll find the traitor in no time!" Adara's eyes darkened and her hands balled into tight fists. "Just promise me that when you do, I'll get first crack at them."

"After they give information about the survivor, they are all yours."

Adara raised her index finger, a small flame lighting at the tip. She traced her finger lazily through the air until the drawing of the Anguis family crest hung in fire before her. She stared at the symbol with unwavering hatred and annoyance before eventually speaking. "He must have quite the devout following for his underlings to brand themselves willingly with this... ugly symbol."

Time seemed to stop for a few seconds as Adara's words hung in Sigmund's mind. He had to resist the urge to stop dead in his tracks.

What did she say...?

Had he mentioned that the symbol he drew had come from a brand?

No, he was sure he hadn't mentioned that detail to her or Jack. Why would he mention something so insignificant?

How does she know?

Is it her?

The question caught in Sigmund's mind like a fish in a net.

Could it really be Adara, of all people?

Sigmund fought to maintain his usual stoic, non-reactive manner as he felt time catch up around him. If Adara was truly the traitor, it was imperative that he not give away her slip. Once they parted ways, he'd look into her first.

Sigmund simply grunted his displeasure.

"An ugly symbol indeed," Adara repeated, waving her hand through the flames, dispelling it. "Not as pretty as the Grey family symbol, and even that could've been made better if Jack had allowed me to adjust the design a bit." She paused, sighing. "At any rate, I'll dig into a few more leads of mine to find out more about this gray-skinned fellow. An associate of ours in Tefik, Kenta, reported she had news for me that could not be put in writing. I swear, if it's more gossip about Elvish politics, I'm going to smack her... Once I'm done with her, I'll look into my other sources. Where will you begin, Sigmund?"

"I'll start with anyone who might've been involved with Jack and Queen Hestia's attack on the Anguis throne several years ago. They might have gotten connected with the survivor that way."

"Ooh, how clever!" Adara cooed mockingly. "Best of luck to you, Siggy. If you need any help, just let me know." She strode past him, playfully smacking him on the cheek as she went. A portal opened briefly before her and disappeared just as quickly as she stepped through it.

Sigmund didn't relax until after the portal had closed.

Could Adara really be the traitor?

He could not overlook or dismiss any possibility, no matter how much he might not want it to be true. However, while Greys typically are away quite often, none are gone more than Adara, who can disappear for months on end on some assignment.

And none held a position higher in the family than her.

She was the only other Mage the Grey's had and functioned as Jack's second in command.

Sigmund cursed under his breath. If this betrayal were true, it would absolutely devastate Jack. Jack had taken a special interest in Adara, perhaps because he saw a lot of his younger self in her. The two were quite close.

But why would she turn her back on her family, on Jack, who had helped her realize her strength, given her purpose, and a home?

Sigmund shook his head. Her reasoning wasn't important right now. His suspicions would only get him so far, especially where Jack was concerned.

He needed proof.

In order to do that, he'd start by retracing her steps and verifying her accounts of where she had been the past few months, starting with her most recent assignment to aid Queen Hestia.

Ideally, he'd like to investigate everything in person to avoid any communication being intercepted. However, it would take a month at least to ride across the Seven Kingdoms, and that's if he never stopped for anything. Sigmund made his way back toward the Manor, specifically to the Raven's Nest.

Perhaps Margaret would be willing to aid me.

But what if there is another traitor?

The thought gave Sigmund pause. It would be foolish to think that there would be only one turncoat in their mix. Until he could prove otherwise, it was safer for him to assume that the entire family was compromised.

He'd have to accept the risk of sending out letters requesting information and riding where he could. He'd just have to be incredibly careful about his wording to avoid giving anything away.

Sigmund eventually came to a black door with a feather delicately carved in the center and pushed it open. The Raven's Nest was the hub for most of the Grey's communication with the outside world. Here, letters would drop in either through teleportation or by carrier bird.

The Raven's Nest was massive, housing around forty or more birds at a time. There were two desks with parchment, quills, and ink on either side of the room. Wooden beams ran high and low across the room, offering places for the messengers to rest after a long flight.

A particularly large, black raven sat perched on one of the highest beams. Jack's raven, Umbra, eyed Sigmund curiously before letting out a welcoming *caw*.

Sigmund nodded to it before crossing the room to where his hawk, Yaln, perched. Yaln clicked his beak together as Sigmund approached, his feet shifting eagerly on the wooden beam. Sigmund lightly ran a finger over Yaln's head, the bird's beak clicking together again.

Sigmund grabbed some parchment and quickly dipped the quill in ink and began furiously writing a letter to Queen Hestia. He did not sign it, but still requested to speak with her and sealed the letter with hot wax and stamped the Grey family symbol into it. Sigmund slipped the message into the smaller leather backpack strapped across Yaln.

"To Queen Hestia's kingdom in the North, Yaln. Go! With haste."

Yaln cocked his head in understanding and let out a fierce screech as it took off into the air, his powerful wings beating hard against the wind.

In the Raven's Nest, another hawk let out a shriek in response to Yaln. Sigmund turned to see Isaac's hawk, Qurem, hopping excitedly on its perch on one of the lower beams. Alison's dove, Pairul, chirped blissfully beside Qurem.

Sigmund's mind wandered briefly to Isaac and Alison as they began their first mission without him. The three of them had been together as a team for almost thirteen years. He would be lying to himself if he said he wasn't worried about them, especially now, but he knew they couldn't be coddled forever. And despite how aggravating they—mainly Isaac—could be, he came to enjoy their companionship.

Be careful, you two. We do not yet know what lurks in the shadows, waiting for us.

CHAPTER NINETEEN

Adara peered down over the city of Emberion or, how Zet knew it before, Dragon's Respite. They stood at the edge of a cliff—his decision—that gave them a spectacular view of the mountainside-turned fortress that Zet used to call home. Emberion was built out of the same dragon rock Zet lined his hideout with, and here it shone white against the snowy caps of the mountains that it was built into. The climb to Emberion was steep and often treacherous, depending on the time of the year. Now, during the spring thaw and the runoff of water down the mountain from the icy caps, the hike was slippery and difficult.

"Reminiscing, are we?" Adara goaded.

"You find yourself quite funny," Zet responded flatly. "Though perhaps you are right. I am sort of 'reminiscing.'"

Adara followed the cobblestone path with her eyes as it wound through the flat plains past several watchtowers and up to Emberion. Dragon's Keep—the giant castle sat in the middle of the city—was aglow in the evening light. It was the only thing in the city that was constructed from the actual scales of a Blaphir dragon, giving the castle its rich glistening blue color. Small specks of light popped into existence as torches were lit around the perimeter of Emberion.

Zet let out a long exhale, one that almost sounded like he was relaxing.

"So then, Adara, to what do I owe the unfortunate pleasure of you interrupting my evening?"

Adara had to almost literally bite her tongue. No matter how many times she spoke with him, his pompous attitude never failed to piss her off.

Prick.

"My sincerest apologies for interrupting you, my lord," Adara mocked, earning her a disdainful glance and scowl from Zet. "I come bearing updates from my meeting with Jack and Sigmund."

Zet let out an exasperated sigh. "Out with it then."

"Well, to begin with, Jack has figured out that an Anguis member was behind the attack on his family. But we anticipated he would start putting pieces together, didn't we?"

"Yes, Jack Grey is quite smart and resourceful. Would you like me to stroke your ego next after I'm done with his?" Zet snarled, his growing agitation making Adara smile.

"No, I would prefer if you did nothing relating to stroking involving me, thank you," Adara responded. "To continue, I've been charged with finding out more information about, well, you. So, as previously discussed, I'll continue leading them along until we are ready."

"Is the entire point of you coming here to recite what we have already discussed? If so, perhaps I need to instruct you on what an 'update' actually means."

Adara's lips curled into a knowing grin. "I do indeed have an update. Right now it's more of a suspicion, really, but one I will be digging into. At the mention of the Anguis survivor, Jack began acting... strange."

Adara's smile grew wider as Zet's head perked up. His eyes left Emberion for the first time since Adara arrived.

"Strange? How?"

"He seemed... worried. It was just for a brief moment. A lapse in his persona, perhaps, but the look on his face showed doubt, not confidence."

Zet looked at her expectantly. "And what does this mean, then?"

"I think he's hiding something and, whatever it is, it must be quite a big deal for him to try so hard to mask it. Hopefully, it's important enough to turn the tide more in our favor. Between the anti-magic knife, the orb, and your power, I figured we should be set, but this... Well, I think it'll lend itself to be incredibly useful."

"Perhaps even *you* can be useful every now and then," Zet said coldly before turning his attention back to the city. "This is indeed fascinating. Look more into this and report to me as soon as you hear anything. We may have more of a chance after all."

"I'm sure I'll have little problem pulling the information from him. I am his favorite, after all."

Zet closed his eyes in annoyance and took a deep, steadying breath. Adara smiled. Irritating him had become quite a fun game.

"Anything else?"

Adara shook her head, her mind instantly going to Sigmund. She was hoping he hadn't noticed her slip earlier, but it was unlikely that someone like Sigmund wouldn't have noticed. You couldn't get anything by that old oaf.

She'd have to keep a close watch on him to see what he uncovers. She can't afford to have him discover anything too important before she and Zet were ready. And getting rid of him would be no simple task either.

She'd let her contacts know to be wary, and to inform her if Sigmund started asking around. She put too much coin in their pockets for them to be anything but loyal to her.

"Nothing I cannot handle," Adara said confidently.

"We shall see about that," Zet said, his stone-gray skin taking on an ethereal shine in the sunset. "As for where we go from here. I have been collecting information about the Grey family for some time now. With your information, I have been able to task my followers with carefully stalking them while they are out on their assignments, and I believe I am getting a greater grasp of their abilities. My men are ready at a moment's notice to pounce on any of the family I have them tailing. With the information you brought, this plan can now serve two purposes: first, when we are ready, I will have them strike and thin the herd. Second, this plan could send Jack into a panic and get him to divulge whatever secret he is hiding, if you cannot coax it out of him in a timely manner."

"Do not forget the other part of our deal, Zet—" Adara began, but Zet swiftly cut her off.

"Yes, girl, I'm aware. 'Not the boy.' I do not understand your annoying infatuation with him, but I can promise you that, in light of recent events, the correct man has been selected for the job. His guardian will not be able to protect him this time."

Adara looked at Zet unconvinced, but slowly nodded. While she hated him, she knew Zet wouldn't be so arrogant as not to learn from his mistakes. So, for him to send only one Arcanist this time, this one *must* be different.

As long as her master got what he needed, she didn't care.

"If there is nothing further, then the plan will proceed as follows: I will, unfortunately, have to wait for you to report back to me before I tell my men to act. Find out what Jack is hiding. That information will set the rest of our plans into motion, one way or another."

For once, Adara actually agreed with Zet. His plan was well thought-out and showed a measure of restraint that Adara hadn't known Zet was capable of.

"I will let you know as soon as I learn anything."

Zet simply nodded, his eyes locked onto his former home.

A portal opened behind Adara, and she slipped quietly through, finding herself in a cold, dark slum in Triol. Where she stepped, rats scurried and ran for the nearest cover. The ground was covered in mud, and judging by the smell, *something's* feces.

A small ball of light flashed into existence at her right shoulder, revealing emaciated, huddled bodies outside of the decrepit buildings that lined the street. The people shuddered and grew tighter together, as if they found the light repulsive.

None of these sad creatures were who she was here to see. Her contact, Kenta, had been lifted out of this poverty thanks to Adara's generous payments for her information. It was her duty to have eyes and ears everywhere. Her master wanted to track gossip as closely as possible, and squash it where he could.

But such acts were quite expensive. Especially the counter-gossip. No good informant would purposefully spread false information cheaply. If someone caught them in a lie, it would cost them their livelihood.

Fortunately for Adara, Kenta was willing to take the risk.

As she made her way down the winding street toward the only building with windows that weren't boarded shut, she felt almost giddy with excitement. Things were beginning to fall into place, and the world she envisioned didn't seem too far out of reach. If Jack had listened to her, none of this would've happened. If he had listened, perhaps her master would've even let Jack into the fold too.

But no.

Jack's ideals were too steadfast to be changed.

No matter. Soon, her partnership with Zet would come to a close, and she'd be one step closer to realizing her goal.

To realizing *his* goal.

Adara flashed the guards a smile and stepped into the building.

All a matter of time.

CHAPTER TWENTY

"Ahh, at last! Beignknost!" Isaac peered down at the large, bustling village from the top of the rolling hill. The hills surrounded the town like a giant hand that cupped the village in its palm.

They had made great time, taking only a couple of hours to reach Beignknost, much of that was because of Alison rushing them. She had been adamant about arriving as early as possible to look around at the vendors before heading to the bounty board, a prospect that Isaac couldn't argue with. He was just as interested in seeing the different exotic goods as she was.

"It feels like it's been a lifetime since we were last here," Alison said, her eyes scanning the roughly built stone houses and their thatched roofs. Isaac smiled as he watched her face shine with excitement. Alison absolutely adored quaint village architecture, and she had a great deal of respect for the Vaccars, who had to do everything without the aid of magic. Living the life that they did made it easy to forget that other people will never experience magic, and it made them both appreciate their lives and respect the Vaccars more.

"No kidding. So much has happened since then..." Isaac stared off into the distance for a moment, years' worth of events dancing across his eyes in an instant. "Let's see what Beignknost has in store for us this time!"

Alison smiled. "Let's go! I'd hate to miss anything."

They began the final short stretch down to Beignknost, pushing and shoving each other out of the way as they both desperately wanted to beat the other to the town.

With one last shove, Alison tossed Isaac out of the way as she crossed the threshold into Beignknost. Isaac tumbled through the grass, his bulging backpack slowing his momentum.

Alison laughed boisterously as Isaac pulled blades of grass out of his hair and, much to his disgust, wiped something slimy off his pant leg.

"Thanks for that," Isaac said between gags as he tried not to smell the slime that now coated his hand.

"Don't mention it." Alison beamed and turned toward Beignknost.

For a small town, it was surprisingly busy. Beignknost is one of the closest villages to Alric and acts as a sort of testing ground for merchants to peddle their wares before bringing them to the capital to sell to the wealthier residents. The market was built right in the middle of Beignknost, with rows upon rows of vendors, each insisting that you needed their wares.

People rushed back and forth carrying water, food, or some trinket they had just bought from the market. Children ran through the wide streets, screaming and playing as they went. An odd, aromatic mixture of freshly baked goods, foreign perfumes, and kicked-up dirt blanketed the entire town.

Isaac appeared next to Alison and smiled with her as he watched people hurry past them. A few of the townspeople waved as they went and shouted their greetings.

Isaac unconsciously touched his Grey cloak, his hand hovering over the insignia. Many towns they visited took an aggressive stance towards Arcanists, where the slightest hint of magic was met by an armed mob.

But not Beignknost.

Beignknost was one of the few towns that were, for the most part, always welcoming to Arcanists. Given their proximity to the Grey Manor, a lot of Greys traveled to Beignknost for day trips to help the people there. It took some time, but eventually a majority of the town became quite welcoming not only to the Greys, but to any Arcanist that passed through.

"Come on." Isaac smiled, taking Alison by her hand and leading them through the crowd.

One particular vendor caught their attention. Unlike the other merchants who were shouting and begging for their attention, this peddler was quiet and stood humbly behind his wares. The Dwarf merchant was, like all Dwarves, short and stocky with thick arms and legs. He had a happy, approachable smile and red-brown curly hair that was held back with a thick piece of black cloth.

His stand was laden with just about anything someone would want, from hatchets and pickaxes to carefully crafted wooden bowls. But it was the weapons in particular that had really caught Isaac's eye.

On another table next to the tools was a spread of weapons, each made from Dwarven steel that could only be found deep in the mountains behind the Dwarven capital, Behaldur. Isaac picked up one of the swords, surprised at how light it was; for being the most durable metal, he had assumed it would be much heavier. He rotated the sword in his hand; the orange-blue hue of the Dwarven metal flashed in the sunlight like a fledgling flame. Isaac ran his finger over the edge of the sword and saw blood pool up almost immediately.

Beautiful, sturdy, and *sharp.* Isaac smiled. He shouldn't be surprised; Dwarven craftsmanship was legendary. Their skills in the forge were second to none, and that made *any* of their products extremely valuable and highly sought after.

With that being said, they had nowhere near enough coin to buy anything he was selling.

Someday...

Isaac healed his small cut and wiped off the sword before begrudgingly placing it back on the Dwarf's table. The Dwarf nodded his thanks, and Isaac and Alison continued down the busy street.

They paused as the sharp sound of clay pots shattering erupted to the left of them.

Isaac looked and noticed a large crowd already beginning to gather around two of the stalls.

Alison gripped his hand tight. "Let's go see what all the excitement is about." She flashed him a grin and practically dragged him along the congested path. Alison ignored people's exclamations of displeasure as she not-so-politely charged her way through them. As the two broke through to the front of the crowd, they immediately understood why the crowd had gathered so quickly: two Orx merchants were getting ready to fight.

The Orx were quite a formidable sight. They were both built like mountains: impossibly tall and wide. They had a deep, rich red-brown skin tone and thick ivory tusks that protruded from their lower lips and curled upward. The points of their tusks had been cut off and filed down, and Isaac could barely make out engravings in their tusks that had been partially sanded away.

"What's wrong with their tusks?" From what he knew of Orx culture, their tusks were a significant symbol of pride and showed which tribe they belonged to. No Orx would willingly allow someone to abuse their tusks in that way.

"They are Disavowed," Alison said. "They were kicked out of their tribes and exiled. It takes a lot, and I mean *a lot*, for a Tribe Chief to think one of his Orx brought shame to their clan. They must've done something particularly terrible."

Isaac cast Alison a questioning glance. "Well, well, someone has been reading up on their Orx culture."

Alison chuckled and shrugged. "Their culture is interesting! They value strength, strategy, and power above all else. They're *constantly* fighting for the stronghold Urithal, which they see as the ultimate seat of power and status. Tribes constantly battling with each other, never-ending wars! It's interesting to read when you're not a part of it," she added sheepishly.

"Oh! Look, they're preparing for Aghkni!" Alison pointed at the Orx as they began pouring red sand in a circle around them from a dusty leather pouch while muttering something in Orenic.

"They're doing what?" Isaac asked.

"Aghkni. All Orx disputes are settled by combat. Whether or not it's to the death depends on how much they feel their honor has been attacked."

Alison tugged at his hand. "We should go. These matches, from what I've read, can get quite rowdy. Plus, I don't want to see them beat each other senseless."

Isaac nodded, then paused as Alison began to lead them back through the crowd.

"What is it?" Alison asked, looking back and forth between the two Orx, who were now standing toe-to-toe with each other.

"Just noticed that one of them has a statue of Archangel Utriel." Isaac pointed to the small, gold statue of a man clad in armor, his helmet bore a resemblance to a gorilla's face, with large, feathery wings protruding from his back. The statue held a giant claymore in its hands, the tip of the blade facing the earth.

"And the other has a flag with Xyteres' crown on it." He moved his finger to point at a small, tattered black flag gently flapping in the breeze that depicted a blood-red crown made of weapons and shields, and two curved, devilish horns sprouting up from either side of it.

"I wonder if that's what they're fighting over... the Archangel of Strength versus the King of Hell," Alison said thoughtfully.

"*Former* King of Hell, since Ranatrael took that title from him. I wonder who would win..."

The two Orx lunged at each other suddenly, earning a gasp from the crowd as the Orx's hulking forms desperately tried to wrestle the other to the ground.

"We may never know," Alison retorted. "Time to go."

Isaac nodded and followed Alison as she led them back through the crowd. As they walked, they passed by more stalls that had similar golden statues like the one the Orx had. Two were feminine figures, one with a helmet designed like an owl's head, who wielded a small dagger, and the other had a helmet modeled after a jaguar's head, her bow drawn.

"Archangel Emiliel and Archangel Felicitiel," Isaac whispered as they passed by. The vendors had their backs turned to them, with their heads bowed, in the middle of prayer.

Isaac paused at the last statue they saw. This Archangel was of a man with a helmet modeled after a hawk's head, with a double-ended spear balancing nonchalantly across his shoulders. Its painted silver-gray eyes had a weird sort of glow that pulled Isaac in like a vortex.

"... And Aethaniel, the last living Archangel," Alison added, stopping to look at the statue with Isaac. "The Archangels of Peace, Order, and Truth. An appropriate trio to pray to."

Alison's words seemed distant as Isaac's gaze remained locked on the statue of Aethaniel. Those ethereal silver-gray eyes looked as if there was some form of intelligence behind them. The glow of the statue's eyes became brighter suddenly, becoming like small suns.

Alison waved her hands in front of Isaac's face, startling him. "I don't think staring at it is going to do you any good," she teased.

Isaac chuckled and looked back at the statue. The glow he had seen a moment ago was gone, its eyes staring blankly back at him.

What the hell was that?

"Everything okay?" Alison asked, this time stepping in front of him.

"Yeah, sorry," Isaac began, then sighed. "Just thinking."

"Anything you want to talk about?" She asked, stepping closer and placing a hand on his chest.

"No, it's nothing," Isaac said, glancing back at Aethaniel again. "Truly, it's nothing."

She shook her head and began leading them through the crowd again. He took one more glance over his shoulder, hoping to feel the weird sort of presence he had felt before, but, again, nothing was there. As they walked away, he could faintly hear one of the women who was praying at Aethaniel's feet singing part of the Song of the Betrayer.

...

Heaven's warriors came down to speak,
To negotiate their terms of peace
Ranatrael, the new King of Hell,
Bitter about how he fell
Refused them at the gate,
And drew his sword to seal their fate

*The mighty Archangels knew
Just then what they must do
With their lives, they'd end the war,
And seal the betrayer forevermore.*

...

Aethaniel, the last Archangel... Isaac thought. The statue's glowing eyes were seared into his mind. *Could you be watching over these people after all?*

A horrific screech sounded through the town, followed closely by shouts and the clang of metal. People began surging past them, knocking into Isaac and Alison and jostling them around. They turned to see a large, elephant-like creature with rough, purple skin and bone-like spikes that protruded all over its body, and three massive horns that stuck out from the top of its head. One long, thick nail stuck out from its front two feet, making clicking sounds as it shuffled angrily.

"What the hell is that thing?" Alison asked, her eyes narrowing.

"I... I think that's a Reltuant," Isaac said. "But only a Conjurer or an Omnis can access the Domustiar and make contracts with the creatures that live in that dimension. So, for that kind of creature to be here..."

"Then there must be an Arcanist over there somewhere," Alison said. "Come on, we need to get closer."

They pushed through the stream of people that seemed to try their best to prevent them from going toward the Reltuant. They burst through the last throng of people to see a short, stocky man with night-black hair and a Conjurer Arcanist's distinctive burnt-orange robes surrounded protectively by the Reltuant's trunk. A small, tan-colored creature perched itself on the man's shoulder, its wide leathery wings flared out. It spat out a small burst of fire defensively at the mob of people that stood opposite them.

"A drake too?" Isaac asked in awe. His eyes slid to the mob, and he recoiled when he saw they were all staring at him and Alison now. There were perhaps twelve men, each carrying either a bucket full of rocks or a farm tool that was clearly recently sharpened.

And they looked *pissed.*

"Easy, Grover, Trui." The man looked at the drake and then up at the Reltuant. He had a gentle Eastern accent that rolled each vowel. He reached up to pet the drake called Grover on the head, revealing the griffin tattoo on his forearm.

"And a Warlock at that," Alison said, almost sounding impressed.

"What's going on here?" Isaac asked, stepping closer to the man.

Isaac ducked, narrowly missing getting smacked in the head by a fist-sized rock.

"Another fucking Arcanist, eh?" the man in front said, and spat on the ground. "As I was just telling this one, you and your kind need to leave. You're not welcome here."

"I think we've been quite welcome here before," Isaac retorted, feeling his irritation slowly creep up his spine. "Who are you to tell him, or anyone else, what to do?"

The man stepped forward, quickly brandishing a knife from within his coat.

"Last warning: leave, or we will force you out."

Isaac felt his eye twitch. It's not like they were strangers to this kind of treatment. Hell, in most towns they visited, they had to tuck their cloaks away in their packs to avoid being chased out, but Beignknost had always been kind to them.

"I appreciate your help, but please, this isn't worth the fight," the Conjurer spoke behind him. "I will leave if that means it won't come to blows." To Isaac's surprise, the man appeared to be more hurt than angry.

Isaac glanced over his shoulder at him. "No, they are the ones that will be leaving."

"I don't know who you think you are, but—" Isaac took a step forward, but was caught by Alison.

She pulled him back toward her. "Listen, we can help him, but we have to do it *calmly*. Okay? Look around you."

Isaac looked around him slowly, and there were still other townspeople watching the events from their homes or shops nearby. They were all waiting to see how everything would play out.

"We need to show them they have nothing to fear. We can't turn into what they think we are."

Isaac nodded and took a deep, steadying breath before stepping forward again. She was right; they had to handle this tactfully. If he acted too rashly and antagonized this mob, then he could end up being the reason why Arcanists are no longer welcome in Beignknost.

"Look, I don't know what started this, but this doesn't need to end in violence. Let's just all go home, alright?"

A flurry of rocks sailed over the leader and smacked hard into Isaac and Alison.

"Nah, I don't think we will," the man said as he charged at them.

A wall of air erupted behind the leader, stopping the assault of rocks mid-air before returning them back to the throwers, knocking most of them off their feet or sending them scrambling for cover. Isaac and Alison danced backwards as the man sliced at them with reckless abandon. Isaac feinted to one side, then side-stepped around him, grabbing the arm holding the dagger. Alison spun around Isaac and brought her foot hard into the man's stomach, causing him to drop his weapon as he doubled over. Isaac let go of the man's arm and brought his leg behind the man and swept him clear off his feet, slamming him into the ground with one swift motion.

Alison plucked the dagger off the ground with a simple flick of her wrist and held it dexterously in her hand.

"Leave," Isaac commanded, then looked at Alison. "So much for the diplomatic route, eh?"

Alison shrugged. "He attacked first. We just defended ourselves."

The man scrambled away from them, clutching his stomach, only standing when he was a good distance away. "You Arcanists aren't fooling anyone," he hissed. "You can't hide what you truly are. These people will see again soon, don't worry…"

He grabbed one of the other men and hefted him off the ground. "We're done here." The mob retreated down the street like a pack of beaten animals.

Slowly, the townspeople crept back onto the main road, all of them eyeing Isaac and Alison.

"Sorry about that, everyone," Alison said, smiling as sweetly as she could. "Please go about your business."

There was a brief spurt of murmurs going around the crowd before people began milling about again as if nothing had ever happened.

"Thanks for steppin' in." An elderly gentleman placed his hand on Alison's shoulders. "Frank n' his boys... well, they're rowdy and we offen don't know what to do wit 'em, so thank you for puttin' 'em in their place today." He clapped Alison on the shoulder and shuffled off.

They both let out a relieved sigh before turning to the Conjurer.

The Reltuant's trunk had relaxed a little, and the Conjurer smiled at them. "I appreciate your help. That was nothing short of amazing." He bowed his head, and the Reltuant and the drake imitated his movement.

"It's not a problem," Isaac said. "We couldn't just sit by and let them get away with that. What got them so riled up anyway?"

"Nothing more than a group of unreasonable individuals. They must've gotten mad at the show I was putting on. I was demonstrating to a group of children all the wonderful things Grover and my small midnight truko, Ber, could do. I suppose someone had told them what I was doing, and they didn't like it very much. Poor Trui appeared on his own, which is quite unlike him, but he meant well."

"People can be ignorant," Alison stated flatly.

"Indeed." He nodded.

"So what is a Warlock like you doing in Beignknost?"

The drake on the man's shoulder leapt and glided gracefully onto Isaac's arm, where he began to slowly climb up to his neck.

"He's a good judge of character, that one," the man said with a chuckle. "I'm just a man of travel. Can't see the world behind the walls of the Order. I love to explore and spread the knowledge of magic any way I can, especially to the Vaccars. I think if we can understand each other, there isn't as much to fear. Jack inspired that in me, I think. Despite the recent outburst, I think a lot of good has been done."

Isaac felt himself admiring the Conjurer. He had the same calming presence as Jack, and he sympathized with his desire to explore and see the world. Honestly, the idea of traveling and showing the Vaccars magic was both fantastic and stupid. After being surrounded by Arcanists for so long, it was easy to forget that a majority of the population cannot use magic, so maybe by exposing them to it can help mend the relationship between Arcanists and Vaccars that much faster.

Or he could be chased out of a town, detained by an unfriendly King, executed...

There were plenty of things that could go wrong.

The Warlock turned and waved his hand at Trui, the Reltuant disappearing into a glistening blue cloud. "Well, I believe it's my time to head to the next town. Anyone with a good sense can tell when it's time to move on."

Grover jumped off Isaac's head, where he had briefly found it amusing to perch, and glided back over to the man's shoulder, where it nuzzled against him.

"Sorry again about what happened. Hopefully next time your visit will be a little better." Alison offered an apologetic smile.

"Oh, that's quite all right. Things will change, with time, as the old ways die and the unreasonable ones disappear until it's all a primitive, hazy memory remembered only by a few."

He reached inside his cloak and pulled out a small white stone pendant that glowed softly. Isaac recognized it immediately as an Aura stone, an item commonly given out by the Order to its students to help extend their lifespan through Aura manipulation. Omnis Arcanists could learn to do this on their own, but other Arcanists needed an enchanted item.

"And thanks to the Order, I will be around to see many wonderful changes come to this world. Ah, I'm excited to experience it all." He smiled thoughtfully and scratched under Grover's chin.

"At any rate," he continued, "I'll be off. It was a pleasure meeting you two! Uh... I don't believe I caught your names."

Isaac blinked, realizing they had neglected to introduce themselves. "Ah, sorry, I'm Isaac."

"Alison."

He nodded and grinned. "I'm Alystaer. I hope our paths might cross again someday. 'Til then, take care." Alystaer waved a cheerful goodbye while Grover spit a small flash of farewell flames, and the two disappeared into the busy street.

"I don't remember Beignknost being so... rowdy," Isaac said.

"It certainly made for an interesting visit. Now, should we get to what we actually came here for?"

Isaac shrugged. "I suppose so. Time to go to work."

They walked around town for another few minutes before finally coming up to the Beignknost bounty board at the easternmost entrance. The board was cluttered with bits of parchment, some yellowed and deteriorating from age. All were desperate calls for help that went unanswered for Creator knows how long. It made Isaac uncomfortable staring at the board with all the uncollected bounties up there. He reached out to catch an old contract just as it dropped from the board. It was a job to kill a cyclops in Efona.

"There's so many," Alison said, frowning. "No one's done these in a while."

It was painfully clear that the Beignknost bounty board had not been getting much, if any, attention from bounty hunters in at least the past few years, leaving the peoples' call for aid unanswered.

Isaac nodded solemnly. "It feels abandoned. I wonder why."

"Regrettably, most of us have been pulled to a much larger hunt, leaving most other duties temporarily left undone." A man in dark robes and even darker leather armor stepped up to the side of the board. His voice was as gruff and as unrevealing as his stoic features, with an accent similar to Alystaer's. He had sand-blonde hair pulled back into a tight ponytail and deep, ocean blue eyes that made his face appear to be the sea and the sand all rolled up into one person's features. A jagged, long scar that could only come from a forceful, dull blade went straight across his forehead over his left eye.

The stranger shrugged off his pack and placed his long sword down on the ground with it before leaning against the board.

Isaac's eyebrow shot up in confusion. "And you are...?"

"Aye, right, should probably introduce myself." The man took a step back and cleared his throat into his fist. "I am Mikael Gilano, of the Venatores. At your service." His arm swept across his body, bowing low. He acted and spoke as if he were in front of some grand court.

Isaac cast a questioning glance at Mikael, who was still bowing. Who acts like this in public?

Crazy people. Isaac thought.

Alison, however, clapped her hands together excitedly. "No way," she all but squealed.

"You know this guy?" Isaac pointed with his chin toward Mikael.

She nodded enthusiastically. "How can you not? He's a *Gilano*, for one. You know, like *King* Gilano, ruler of Ahntwen?"

Isaac smacked his forehead with his hand. "Ah... yes, *that* Gilano."

"*That* Gilano," she continued, turning toward Mikael. "His entire family are members of the Venatores. The largest group of bounty hunters across both Eutrox and Aesus that take on all sorts of jobs. But what's *really* cool is that they have members from all the Mortal races, they employ Arcanists, *and* they have were-creatures too! There is no other organization in the world where all of these individuals willingly work together. Am I right?"

Mikael chuckled lightly, finally coming up from his bow. "Aye, couldn't have said it better myself. Mortals from all walks of life come together to take on one common enemy."

Isaac smiled and rolled his eyes at the excitement gleaming in Alison's eyes. It was cute to see her so giddy.

"And who might you two be?"

"I—"

"Alison Grey," she blurted out, interrupting Isaac. "And this is Isaac."

Isaac waved a nonchalant hello.

"Ah, Greys! Aye, should've recognized your cloaks." Mikael clapped his hands together. "Yes, we've helped Mr. Jack Grey a couple of times in the past. Well, 'help' is perhaps not the right word. *Partnered* would be more appropriate. Jack handles more... human affairs, whereas we handle the things that go bump in the night for the Vaccars. But there have been times when our paths have crossed."

Jack knows these people too, eh? Isaac made a mental note to ask Jack more about them later. The more he got out into the world on his own, the more he saw just how much of it Jack had touched. It seemed like there wasn't a corner of the world that Jack hadn't found his way into.

"Looks like you Venatores haven't been here in a while," Isaac said, pointing at the board. "What brings you back now?"

"Aye, it seems only a few hunters have been through Beignknost for quite some time. Something I am hoping to rectify by journeying out here. In truth, I am here to recruit new members for the Venatores. As I mentioned, most of us are currently entangled with an incredibly pressing issue that has taken up all of our time. So, I've been sent to recruit new members to try to fill in some gaps. Would you two be interested in joining? I know the rest of the Venatores would be honored to have some Greys finally join the ranks."

Isaac hesitated. The idea of joining the Venatores certainly sounded exciting enough. But was he really ready to commit himself to an organization that would depend on him to hunt nightmarish creatures? He still hadn't gotten over his loss at the Magician's Trial. This bounty exercise was supposed to help give him some confidence back and help him focus on things he can control over the things he can't.

He wasn't ready to take on anything else. Not yet. He needed more experience, and he needed to get his mind sorted first.

Isaac looked at Alison, who was staring at him with a determined fire in her eyes, her lips curved into a permanent, excited smile. He didn't want to speak for both of them and deny her this opportunity that she was clearly thrilled about. But at the same time, he couldn't ignore his own feelings on the matter.

"You obviously do not have to tell me right away," Mikael held up his hands. "You can certainly inform me another time. I would, however, like to accompany you both on whatever bounty you decide, if you would have me."

Alison squeezed Isaac's hand. "What'd you think? This might be good for you."

Isaac looked between Mikael and Alison a few times before sighing. "He can come with us, but I'm *not* committing to anything, got it?"

Mikael smiled dryly. "Of course, no need for anything binding right away. Now, have you decided on a contract?"

Isaac shook his head. "There's too many to choose from; it's hard to know where to begin." Isaac tore off another old bounty—the parchment yellowed and the ink incredibly faded. This one was for a Gorgon supposedly living in a cave between Beignknost and Alric.

"What about this one?" Alison tore off one bounty that looked much newer than the others and held it out so all three of them could see it.

Hurried, almost unintelligible writing covered the note in long, shaky scrawls.

MISSING : PLEASE HELP!

Isaac squinted, trying to make out the script. "Can't read this writing that well to understand much more besides someone is missing."

Alison brought the paper closer to her face, straining to read the bounty. "I think someone's wife has disappeared. A man named Thomas, who lives on the outskirts of town... will have a yellow cloth hung over his door for us to find him. I can't make out more than that. We'll have to ask him in person once we get there."

"If it's not already too late," Isaac added.

"We won't know until we try. This one seems new, so hopefully we can help in time." Alison contended.

"So, it's decided then?" Mikael slung his pack and sword over his shoulder.

They both nodded.

"Good. Disappearances are time-sensitive matters. As you have pointed out, we do not have much time. So we need to get moving before we aren't able to find her."

Isaac and Alison exchanged worried looks before the three of them took off toward the outskirts of Beignknost, following to the best of their ability the directions Thomas had provided: from the center of town, head North of East for five-hundred paces, then head North of West for the rest.

Alison and Mikael chatted as they hurried through the streets of Beignknost, Mikael answering all of her questions with the same patience a teacher would an eager student.

"How long has your family been in the Venatores?" Alison asked excitedly.

"Since the beginning, or at least close to it. The Gilanos have always served a prominent role in the Venatores' functioning. In fact, my family conquered the East solely to be closer to Aesus, where the Venatores reside."

"Do you normally hunt by yourself?" She continued.

Mikael shook his head. "Not always, no. Bigger hunts require more people."

"Like the large hunt you mentioned earlier," Isaac chimed in, pushing past a group of children huddled together playing a game of sticks.

"Aye, like the one I mentioned earlier. That particular hunt is a Venatores-wide effort."

"Can you at least *hint* at what it is you're hunting?" Alison asked almost pleadingly.

Mikael's stoic face turned grim as he spoke, "Something very old and very hungry. It is a great threat to mortals everywhere, but right now, its main target is Mankin."

Isaac's eyebrows furrowed as he cast a questioning look at Mikael. *What kind of creature is he hunting...?*

Before Isaac could press further, they came to the small collection of houses Thomas had described in his note.

The houses on the fringe of Beignknost looked like they were from a different world entirely. The wood was clearly weathered and rotting from its center, and holes littered the poorly thatched roofs. Dirt, mud, and animal excrement littered the ground, making it difficult to walk without getting something stuck to the bottom of your feet. A thick cloud hung over the village, reeking of refuse and rotting meat.

Unlike Beignknost's lively atmosphere filled with hundreds of sounds, this place was as quiet as death. The only sounds were the flies buzzing and the soft crackle of someone's fire as he passed by a house.

"Be on the lookout for a yellow cloth." Alison reminded them, trying her best to stifle a gag as they split off and began searching.

This is no way to live. Isaac winced as he went from door to door. The longer they stayed in the town, the dirtier it seemed to get.

Perhaps many of those bounties are from these people... and no one took them because they thought they couldn't pay for the service.

This seemed to be the only logical answer in Isaac's mind. Beignknost being the hub that it was, even a casual bounty hunter would be foolish not to at least browse over the bounty board. But if they think the requester can't pay up then, unless you have a bounty hunter with a heart of gold, they'll just move on.

"I believe I have found it," Mikael's voice called from somewhere to his right. Isaac caught up with Mikael at the same time as Alison. Mikael pointed to the dirty yellow cloth crudely nailed to the door, just as Thomas had said.

Mikael rapped his knuckles hard against the door.

"Hello? Thomas?" Mikael called.

No answer.

Mikael knocked again, harder and louder this time.

"Thomas? Are you there?"

Again, no answer.

"Should we take a look inside?" Alison offered.

Mikael shrugged and pushed the door open slightly. They were immediately hit with the smell of an old fire and overcooked meat, which thankfully was drowning out the smell of the rest of the town. The inside was small, but surprisingly well kept, with a modest bed to one side and a small table across from the fire. Embers still glowed in the fireplace below a wide cauldron.

"It appears he might've just left," Mikael concluded. "We stay in town and wait for his return and see what information we can get from him when he does. In the meantime, we'll talk to his neighbors and see if they know anything. Don't stray too far, though. We don't want to miss him again. Meet back here by sundown if one of us hasn't noticed his return by then, got it?"

They both nodded. Isaac looked up at the sky, shielding his eyes with his hand. They only had a couple of hours of daylight left, so they had to hurry to get as much information as they could from the neighbors.

"Right, we'll get going then."

CHAPTER TWENTY-ONE

Isaac stood outside of Thomas's home, rubbing his sore knuckles. Having gone to so many doors, he felt like he had met most of the town. Some people were nice and somewhat helpful, but others…

Isaac brushed at the dirt imprint of a broom on his buttocks.

Others were not so helpful.

The rest of the day had slipped away, and only slivers of light remained as the moons now dominated the sky.

And still no sign of Thomas.

If he didn't show up soon, they'd have to try again tomorrow. But at that point, too much time would've passed, making his wife's chances of survival much slimmer. He could only hope that Alison and Mikael were able to find out something that was useful so they didn't have to delay any longer.

Speaking of…

Alison and Mikael rounded the corner and were soon in front of Thomas's home.

"So, what'd you find out?" Mikael began, fixing his ponytail that had somehow come undone.

"His wife's name is Cela, and she went missing yesterday evening. Heard people say she went outside but never came back," Alison said, now leaning against Isaac.

"I heard that she's not actually missing, but that she left Thomas to be with someone else, but then I *also* heard that those two were deeply in love." Isaac shrugged. "But everyone I spoke to said they heard a scream come from around Thomas's house and then everything was quiet."

"I heard that as well," Alison agreed. "Some people are beginning to speculate that Thomas had something to do with this."

Mikael nodded as he listened. "Sounds like we all heard similar things. Though, I have my own theories about what actually happened that Thomas may be able to confirm."

"Care to share?" Isaac asked.

"Certainly, I—"

"Wait, who's that?" Alison interrupted, pointing down the wide, winding roadway.

A disheveled-looking man was shuffling down the street, holding something tightly to his chest, weeping softly as he went.

"Must be Tom," Mikael concluded.

Isaac looked at Mikael with wide-eyed sarcasm. "You don't say."

Thomas looked up as he approached and started sprinting after he saw the three of them standing there.

"Happy run?" Alison whispered to Isaac.

"I certainly hope so."

Thomas stopped just shy of crashing into them, desperately trying to catch his breath between fits of shaky sobs. He was a tall, somewhat burly man with messy short black hair and a scruffy beard. His deep blue eyes were like glass, and wet from a continuous stream of fresh tears.

"Are you here for my Cela?" Thomas asked with such desperation that Isaac felt his chest tighten.

"We are." Alison stepped forward, smiling softly. "We're here to help."

Thomas fell to his knees and began to cry even harder, muttering "thank you" repeatedly.

"Thomas," Mikael said, kneeling beside him. "We need your help to find her. Is there any information you could give us?"

Thomas looked down at his hands and stared at the ornate jade necklace he had been holding on to so frantically just a moment before.

"This was hers... it was in her family for many years..." Thomas mumbled.

"Thomas, focus." Mikael placed his hand on Thomas's shoulder. "What happened to Cela?"

"It should've been me..." Thomas said, just barely above a whisper. "I wasn't home then... I came back too late..."

Isaac watched as Mikael and Alison both tried to get Thomas's attention. His mind was awash with emotions as he couldn't help but think about Jack and Rose.

And him and Alison.

And the pain of having a loved one stripped away from you so suddenly. Thomas had the same tortured look in his eyes that Jack had when he told him about Rose.

Isaac glanced over at Alison. The thought of her being ripped away from him made his throat grow tight.

It was paralyzing.

He wouldn't know what to do with himself if she were gone, and he was sure that Thomas felt the same way about Cela.

Isaac clenched his fists.

We'll find her.

Isaac knelt down with Mikael. "Tom. I—we—want to help you. But we need to know something, *anything,* about what Cela might've been doing when she went missing. So please let us help. Where would she have been heading? We need to find her."

Thomas looked up at Isaac with, for the first time, clear, focused eyes. "It was evening, so..." he sniffled. "She makes a late-night run down to the river just behind our house. Not two hundred paces."

"Do you know why anyone might want to hurt her?" Mikael asked.

Thomas looked down at the necklace again. "We've lived in many places before this... Many people did not like my wife because she is not like us." He pointed at his ears.

"She's an elf?" Alison asked, surprised.

"I see." Mikael stood, beginning to walk toward the back of the home. "Thomas, if you could please wait at home until our return, we'd be most grateful. If it's necessary to leave, only do so during the day. Understood?"

Thomas nodded solemnly. Isaac grabbed Thomas gently under the arm and helped him to his feet.

"Don't worry, we'll bring her back to you. I promise." Isaac squeezed Thomas's arm comfortingly.

Thomas nodded his head and patted Isaac's hand.

"Can you give us a description of her, Thomas?" Alison asked quietly.

He nodded curtly. "Long, dark hair, and amber eyes..." His grip tightened on the jade necklace. "Short, petite-looking woman and, you know, an elf."

"Thank you, Thomas. We'll do what we can." Alison patted his shoulder reassuringly. Thomas nodded once more before shuffling inside his home.

"Alright, let's not waste any more time," Isaac said as he and Alison jogged to catch up to Mikael, who was waiting for them by the tree line. "What were you saying about your theories?"

"Ah, yes," Mikael began as they started making their way through the forest. "Well, we can assume that Thomas is not the guilty party here. We do not know, however, whether this was a targeted attack or if she was a victim of circumstance. Though I am fairly certain that she was not the target, at least this time, of a racially motivated attack."

Alison shot a questioning look at Mikael. "How do you know?"

"Well, at least in my experience, in racially motivated crimes, the aggressors also target the spouse to make an example out of them to serve as a warning to anyone else. Since Thomas is unharmed, it must be something else."

"So, it's some creature then?" Isaac asked.

"That is my guess. Though what creature, I do not know. Many creatures like to take their prey back to a dwelling before eating them, some storing months' worth of food at a time. Some love attacking people for the joy of hunting. But we will know more once we get to where she was taken and start tracking her."

"Let's hurry then."

Mikael grabbed Isaac's arm as he began to jog.

"I admire your urgency, but on a hunt one must move quickly but *quietly,*" Mikael stressed. "We may very well startle the creature and not be able to track it properly. So please stick with me and follow my pace."

Isaac nodded begrudgingly and fell into line behind Mikael.

Alison walked up beside Isaac with a soft smile. "It's cute seeing you care so much about this. I guess you do have a heart under all that sarcasm."

Isaac's cheeks flushed, eliciting a laugh from Alison.

A few minutes later, they arrived at the river Tom had described. The water ran quietly down a small hill, lapping against the rocks underneath. The water was so clear and pristine that the shallow bottom could easily be seen. The fading sunlight glinted against the stream, sending dazzling yellow and orange gleams of light across the forest around it.

It was calm, almost eerily so, that it looked like someone had brought a painting to life.

"It's easy to see why she got water from here." Mikael knelt beside the river and, cupping his hands, drew a small amount of water to his lips.

Mikael stood, scanning the woods. "Look for anything of interest: crushed foliage, scratches anywhere, drag marks, and, the obvious one, blood."

* * * * *

They had been searching for hours without much sign of anything being out of place. The only clue they had been able to find so far was a scuff mark in the dirt on the other side of the river. And now that it was nighttime, their search would be made that much harder, even with the glow of the magelights that Isaac had created for them.

How does a person go missing but not leave anything *behind?*

Isaac paused as his eyes caught a splash of red against the green underbrush. He directed his magelight closer to him and could barely make out a faint trail of crimson splattered on the ground and the surrounding foliage. The vegetation had been slightly bent out of place, so slight that if someone wasn't looking at it directly for long enough, they'd surely miss it.

"Mikael! Alison!" Isaac called, beckoning them over with his hand. "I think I found something."

Mikael rushed over and knelt down beside him, examining the blood-soaked grass.

"Aye, good job, lad." Mikael nodded his approval. "We'll follow it. Let's go."

Mikael led a slow, careful march through the forest, stopping every so often to reorient himself to the trail.

"Wait." Mikael held up his hand and crouched low. "Dim the lights."

Isaac did as he was asked, and the magelight grew dimmer.

"What is it?"

"*Sh*," Mikael responded sternly, holding a finger up to his lips.

It was quiet all around them, except for the sound of crickets and mice darting through the grass. Mikael's head was tilted to one side, clearly straining to hear something. They sat crouched for several more long, excruciating seconds as Isaac waited for something to lunge at them from the trees.

But nothing did.

"Let's keep moving," Mikael said, slowly making his way through the thick underbrush.

Isaac brightened the magelight once more. They stopped and started again over and over until they finally hit the end of the trees, and a small mountain lay a few hundred feet from them. Directly in front of them was the mouth of a cave. It was black, uninviting, and seemingly endless.

"Stay close to me," Mikael said, slowly moving forward. "There's no telling what could be lurking in this cave."

The three of them crept up to the cave, the magelights creating just enough light to allow them to see right in front of them. They hugged the walls, being careful not to accidentally trip any traps or make too much noise. The cave was long and winding and appeared mostly naturally made, but, as Mikael pointed out, the stones were too jagged and uneven in some places, as if someone had chipped away at them.

They came to a three-pronged fork in the cavern, all leading to the same blackness they had been met with outside.

"Any ideas?" Isaac asked in a hushed tone.

Mikael looked carefully at the ground in front of them, kneeling for a moment. "This way." He pointed to the leftmost trail. "This path is more recently worn, look."

Isaac squinted hard, and he could just barely make out the slight displacement in the sand of the passage Mikael chose. He found it incredible that Mikael could notice such a small detail so quickly.

Hunter indeed. Isaac admired.

"Are you a Vaccar?" Isaac asked.

Mikael nodded. "For those of us born without magic, honing our physical abilities is the best thing we can do. So, we made do with what we have."

"You do very well for yourself," Isaac said.

"Almost like I do this for a living." Mikael smirked. "All members of the Venatores are taught the same skills, all without relying on magic. We learn to hunt, fight, and survive without magic. Those that are Arcanists just have an easier time once training is done, but the lessons are invaluable all the same."

The passageway soon gave way to a massive open space with crudely put together wooden structures and rusting metal cages scattered around. They stood at the top of what appeared to be a man-made crater, overlooking everything around them. Bodies writhed in the blackness, the quiet moans of pain filling the room.

"What the hell...?" Isaac asked shakily. "Who did this to these people?"

"We're going to find that out right now. Split up and look for Cela. I'll try to see if anyone is coherent enough to give us any useful information."

They split off, each taking a section of the cavern.

He knew he had to look at them to see if any matched Cela's description, but Isaac couldn't bear to bring himself to meet any of their eyes. They were husks.

Dying flesh on brittle bones.

Flies buzzed around their poor, broken bodies. Most were so emaciated that he could make out almost every bone in their bodies. It was clear that some had been down here for quite some time, while others still had a supple liveliness to their skin.

The one thing that all of those still alive had in common was the same glassy-eyed stupor, staring out into nothing.

These poor people...

"Isaac. Alison. Come over here immediately." Mikael's serious and hurried tone startled him. Even though he had only met him a few hours ago, Isaac could already tell that it took a lot for something to shake Mikael's stone-like façade.

They rushed over to where Mikael was kneeling over a dying man. His breathing was raspy and shuddering, the effort of just staying alive shaking his entire body.

"Look at this." Mikael held up the man's arm and pointed to two puncture marks on his forearm.

"Is that—"

"Vampires," Mikael confirmed, cutting Alison off. "Vampires that have been here for a while." Mikael shifted so he could look all around them. "I think we stumbled upon a nest. Nests are temporary hiding places for vampires that typically serve a larger Coven, mainly used to supply the vampires until whatever their objective is has been accomplished. If I had to guess, I'd say this nest has been here for..."

Mikael looked down at the man again, inspecting his frail body. "Perhaps a couple of weeks. It doesn't take long for them to completely drain a human. In terms of their mission, given all of these cages, I'd say they were capturing humans to be used as cattle for their Coven. If they've taken to killing off the ones not chosen to feed the rest of the family, I'd say they are preparing to leave. And soon."

"So, what do we do?" Isaac asked.

"We have to leave quickly, and go send for help," Mikael said matter-of-factly, dropping the man's arm.

"Are you serious?" Isaac questioned incredulously. "We can't just leave them here. We have to help them. And we have yet to find Cela!"

"Isaac," Mikael said in an almost cautious tone. "Look at all the bodies here. There were enough human cattle here to feed twenty or more vampires. And the healthy ones that remain are most likely the last shipment back to the Coven. It will be very difficult for us to take on twenty vampires at once, especially since you two have no experience killing them, correct?"

Isaac slowly shook his head.

"I thought as much. This operation here seems massive, and I'm wondering if this might have something to do with the larger hunt that I was telling you about before. We are in over our heads here. We *must* get assistance before we can help them."

Isaac looked around at all the comatose bodies and felt sick to his stomach at the thought of abandoning them. Was he really just supposed to leave them behind?

Isaac glanced at Mikael. The whole point of the bounty was to help Isaac regain some sense of control, but, so far, it has proven the opposite. It was just showing him that more things were out of his control than he thought, and how over his head he was when it came to real-world problems.

He didn't like the idea of leaving these people behind, but Mikael was right. There was no way the three of them could handle that many vampires alone. They had to call in more hunters.

"You're right," Isaac said finally. "We need help. So, let's get out of here and go get it."

Mikael nodded his thanks, and they began their quiet, slow trek back through the passage they had come in from. As they walked, a strange green mist began to slowly fill the tunnel.

Isaac heard a thud in front of them as Mikael's body hit the floor, his body writhing as he struggled to speak.

"What's happening?" Alison gasped as she fell to her knees in front of Isaac.

"What the hell is going on?" Isaac rushed to her and, as he did, his body began to feel heavier and completely unbalanced, driving him to the floor along with them.

"Alchemy," Mikael finally choked out. "They've returned."

Isaac watched as Mikael and Alison struggled to stay awake as he crawled desperately toward them. Mikael's body suddenly went limp, his head rolling to one side. Alison held out her hand weakly toward Isaac, before feebly falling to the dirt in a puff of dust.

A pale, slim figure walked into the light of Isaac's dimming mage-light, his hood and dark clothes obscuring his features.

"You've held out for much longer than most people. You should be proud," the man said, kneeling beside Isaac. "Now, sleep..." Isaac felt his awareness slipping away from him like sand between his fingers. Soon, everything was consumed by a murky, uneasy darkness.

CHAPTER TWENTY-TWO

I SAAC STRUGGLED TO OPEN HIS EYES as he felt consciousness slowly return to him.

Everything felt heavy and immobile. Even breathing seemed to require extra effort on his part. He managed to open his eyes a little to squint at his surroundings, but everything was foggy and out of focus, as if he were looking through poorly refined glass. His nose still stung from whatever the gas was made of.

Shadowy figures passed by him, moving so quickly it was disorienting to watch. One paused to kneel down in front of Isaac and smile.

"Awake already?" It was the same man as before in the tunnels. "You're certainly more persistent than your friends," the man said, grabbing Isaac's face and turning his head so he could see Mikael and Alison beside him. Their packs were gone, and their hands were bound by a thick rope around their wrists. They sat there unmoving in a deep, undisturbed slumber.

"No matter," he said, holding up a small beaker of iridescent green fluid. "Go back to sleep." He blew on the top of the glass, a fine mist coating Isaac's mouth and nostrils. Isaac could immediately feel the clouds in his mind becoming denser and his senses deadening as he was dragged back to unconsciousness again.

The cycle of awakening and being put back to sleep happened several times, and each time Isaac would wake up much quicker, and less dazed, than before. And each time the same man, with growing impatience, came and put him back to sleep.

He was just beginning to stir again now. He had caught enough of his surroundings from waking up previously to know that they were not in the cavern anymore. Rather, they appeared to be in some stone structure—a small castle or tower, perhaps. But with no windows or openings in sight, he couldn't determine where they were or how long they'd been held.

"I cannot dose him much more."

Isaac's ears perked up at the sound of the Alchemist's voice.

"If I keep putting him under, he will reach his overflow point, and Vladimyr made it clear that we were to bring any hunters back directly to him. Alive."

Overflow? He had never heard that term before but, then again, he had also never practiced Alchemy before. Whatever it was, based on the conversation, it seemed like a death-sentence if someone reached it.

Luckily for him, it sounded like their boss wanted them alive, at least for now, so the Alchemist wouldn't be pressing his luck any time soon. He glanced over at Mikael and Alison; both of them were still deep under the effects of whatever potion the Alchemist had used.

How the hell are we going to get out of this? His heart started to pound in his chest. Here he was again, at the mercy of an overwhelming force that was leagues above his current abilities. It was like the Draugr Lord and the Temple all over again except, this time, no one else was here to miraculously save him.

There was no Sigmund, and there was no possibility of teleporting away.

They could die.

Isaac pressed himself against the wall as his breathing became short and rapid, his mind flooding with poisonously anxious thoughts.

What if they separate us?

What if I reach my 'overflow' point?

What if...

What if...

Isaac hadn't even noticed the Alchemist approaching him again, and didn't see his hand flash before his eyes until he felt a sharp sting across his face. His head spun as his skull slammed into the wall behind him.

The Alchemist leaned in, holding up the vial of green liquid again. "Why don't you stay asleep?!" he snarled and blew into the top again.

Isaac felt the pull into slumber once again, his head rolling forward as the vampire walked away. But this time, he awoke practically instantly. All the panic and worry he felt before came rushing back into him, almost blocking out the pain he felt from the slap.

Just focus on what you can do right now. Jack's voice cut through his mind.

Easier said than done. Isaac scoffed as he tried to take some deep, steadying breaths. Trying to wrangle in his thoughts was like trying to tame a dragon with nothing but a ball of yarn.

Okay, okay, so... What can *I do...?*

Isaac looked down at his bound hands and carefully examined the ropes. He was pretty confident that they were not enchanted with anti-magic. Jack had shown him an anti-magic object when he was younger, and the feeling he got just by being near it was not something he could easily forget. It had felt as if his body was struggling not to rip itself apart.

Anti-magic items are incredibly rare and volatile, eating away at the mana in the world around them. It can even strip an Arcanist of their ability to use magic if exposed for too long. Because of their incredibly toxic potency and ability to kill even Vaccars, most Mortals stayed as far away from anti-magic as possible.

Of course, that did not stop some people from using it still, especially if they were hunting Arcanists. It is the best way to render them powerless, after all.

Thankfully, it didn't appear that these vampires had any anti-magic items in their possession.

He turned to the sound of a light groan. Mikael and Alison shifted a little, and looked like they were slowly waking up.

About freaking time.

An approaching shadow caught his attention. Isaac quickly slammed his eyes shut and let his head fall to the side. He was sure it was the Alchemist again, making sure that they—particularly he—were still asleep. He could feel the Alchemist leaning over him, carefully inspecting him.

"Ko, we're about ready to transport the last batch. Would you mind?" another voice called.

Isaac felt Ko—the Alchemist—retreat from him.

"Fine. We'll be departing within the hour then," Ko said.

Isaac waited for several minutes after Ko and the other vampire left before he opened his eyes again. Time was quickly running out. They had to move. Now.

He pushed himself unsteadily to his feet, his legs shaky and struggling under his own weight. Isaac shuffled his way over to Mikael and Alison, where Mikael was just beginning to wake up, his eyes barely cracking open. Alison seemed to be waking up as well, though slower than Mikael.

Isaac fell to his knees in front of them and attempted to conjure a small flame to burn away his binding. A tiny fire flared to life, igniting the rope and quickly burning through it without hurting his own skin.

"Hold still, I'll get you out of this," Isaac said as he steadied his hands over Mikael's, quickly burning through his ropes before doing the same to Alison's.

Mikael and Alison both sat up uneasily and still quite groggy. Isaac was definitely starting to feel the pressure of time slipping away. In their current state, it could take hours for them to recover completely. By that time, they would have been captured again, and Cela would be carted off to Creator knows where. Their window for escaping was quickly closing and, with their resident Venatores looking worse for wear, their chances didn't look too promising.

Their only chance was if they could get out of their stupor faster somehow.

Could they be forced awake somehow? Isaac contemplated. If a strong, external force jolted them, would it be enough to bring them out of their drug-induced disorientation faster?

Only one way to find out.

"You can be mad at me later," Isaac said, grabbing both of their arms. "Sorry."

Isaac willed the mana around him to become charged as electricity raced down his hands into Mikael and Alison's bodies. They both sat upright immediately as the electrical currents briefly assaulted them, their eyes wide with shock. Isaac sat back, releasing them from his grip. Their bodies still twitched from the shock, but they were both more awake it seemed.

And a hell of a lot angrier too.

"Fucking asshole..." Alison squeaked out. Mikael nodded in agreement.

"Yeah, you're welcome. Listen, we need to get moving. Can you guys stand?"

Mikael and Alison looked at each other with uncertainty before they both slowly started pushing themselves to their feet. Isaac grabbed both of their hands and helped steady them as they stood shakily. Even though they were awake, they were still feeling the aftereffects of the potion.

"Thank you for waking us." Mikael nodded his gratitude, leaning against the wall. "Now, first and foremost, we must get our packs back if we want to have any hope of making it out of here. I will need my sword if I'm to be of any use to you."

Isaac nodded. "Alright, in the meantime, if we encounter any vampires, how do we kill them?"

Mikael cocked his head to one side thoughtfully. "These vampires should only need to be burned alive or have their heads cut off with some kind of metal."

"*These* vampires," Alison scoffed. "There are some that are different?"

Mikael nodded. "Yes, the Pure Bloods, but none of them are here. Trust me, we'd know if they were. At any rate, be careful. I've known many hunters who underestimated the first vampire they went after, and it was the last mistake they ever made."

Isaac gulped. *What a pleasant thought.*

"Time to get moving then. Are you two ready?"

They both nodded and put on a brave front, but Isaac could clearly see the strain on their faces from just standing up. Their knees were still shaking, Alison's especially were on the verge of buckling, and they were both sweating heavily. Unfortunately, they didn't have much choice. They'd have to wait out the aftereffects while moving.

And while fighting.

Pushing an onslaught of unpleasant thoughts aside, Isaac led Alison and Mikael out of the cramped room they woke up in. There were four ways out, but Isaac opted to take the exit that Ko took every time he visited. It may not lead directly to an exit, but it may give them a path to Cela.

They hugged the wall as they progressed, crouching low and moving as quietly as possible. The deteriorating stone floors made walking silently a difficult task. Everywhere they stepped seemed to cause the stones to smack together noisily or send pebbles skittering across the floor. The walls weren't much better; brushing against them the wrong way sent chunks of rock tumbling down. The stench of decay and dried blood wafted from the next room as they drew closer, making Isaac gag, and eventually forcing all of them to cover their noses with their arms.

"What is that Creator-forsaken smell?" Isaac asked, his eyes watering as he tried hard not to vomit.

The room they found themselves in seemed like it used to be a dining hall of some sort, with plaques mounted on the walls and a grand fireplace, lit and crackling softly, in the center wall. Remnants of long wooden tables and several chairs were scattered around the hall, smashed to pieces. Old barrels were tipped onto their sides with gaping holes in them, and old potato sacks, dyed crimson and stiff as a board, littered the room like leaves on the forest floor.

In the far corner was a pile of bones and liquifying bodies, whose skin hung loosely off their decaying forms. They looked as if someone had thrown a loose coat of flesh over a skeleton to imitate what a person looked like. Others toward the top of the pile seemed much newer, their bodies shriveled and dried up like raisins, each with several puncture marks all over their bodies.

Isaac struggled to keep himself from throwing up the contents of his stomach.

"That's disgusting," Alison said, her voice muffled by her arm.

"Aye, these vampires are quite brutal," Mikael said, walking over to the pile of corpses, the only one with his mouth and nose not covered. He grabbed a deteriorating arm and yanked it free from the pile with a sickening squish, and began rubbing the detached limb over his clothing.

Isaac covered his mouth with his hand, forcing down fresh bile.

"What in the hell are you doing?!" Isaac asked, his voice muffled by his hand.

"Disguising my scent," Mikael said matter-of-factly. "Vampires have a fantastic sense of smell. It's better that we try to smell dead than alive and fresh."

Alison's hand on his shoulder stopped him from protesting. She certainly didn't look happy about the prospect of rubbing decaying flesh over her body, but she walked over and yanked a limb free and did as Mikael suggested.

How do I get myself into these situations...

Reluctantly, Isaac followed Mikael and Alison's lead and covered himself in the terrible-smelling juices of a dead person.

"Better." Mikael nodded his approval.

"Glad you think so," Isaac responded sarcastically.

"We should get moving... I'd prefer not to join them." Alison pointed at the pile of bodies.

"Agreed. Let's keep going," Mikael said.

They continued on to the next hallway and slowly made their way from room to room. All the rooms were much like the first one: piles of decaying bodies and remnants of a once-homey castle strewn all over. It was clear that, wherever they were, the vampires had been using this as a sort of nexus point for quite a long time.

The stench of death hung in the air like a thick, suffocating fog. Despite his reservations about smelling like a dead man's foot, he was glad for Mikael's suggestion. If they had continued on without trying to cover their scent, they would've stuck out amidst the sea of rot.

Isaac glanced back to check on Mikael and Alison. They were recovering quickly, thankfully. They didn't even need the wall anymore to hold themselves upright. There was still a bit of uneasiness to their steps though, like newborn calves walking for the first time.

At least they're showing progress.

"Wait," Mikael whispered, grabbing Isaac's shoulder. "Do you hear that?"

"Hear wha—"

Mikael covered Isaac's mouth with his hand as he cocked his head to one side. Isaac strained hard to hear whatever Mikael *thought* he was hearing. Maybe the potion had affected his mind—

Wait.

He *could* hear something.

Isaac closed his eyes and listened as intently as he could.

It was soft, but growing louder now. It sounded aggressive.

Angry.

It was... shouting.

They must've finally noticed we were gone. Isaac felt all the blood drain from his face.

Mikael held a finger to his lips and pushed Isaac forward. Isaac thought about saying something in protest, but decided against it. If the vampires' sense of smell was superhuman, it was safe to assume their other senses were as well. So any sound now, no matter how minute, would help them find their location that much faster.

Isaac felt Mikael's hand clasp onto his shoulder, his grip like iron, as he pulled him backwards into a nearby room. He moved him and Alison into a corner behind a stack of bodies and squatted low, careful to avoid any stray torchlight. Before Isaac could question what Mikael was doing, he saw a small, pale head peek through the corridor. His breath caught in his chest as he froze. The vampire slowly scanned the room, methodically checking every corner. His heart was pounding so loudly in his ears, he thought for sure that the vampire would be able to hear it as well. Isaac looked around his surroundings. Were they tucked away enough? Could they fight him right now if they needed to? Should—

His mind went blank as he felt the vampire's icy gaze pass over him. *We're dead.*

He watched the vampire look over him once more and sweep the room again in the opposite direction, before slowly ducking out and disappearing down the corridor. Isaac let out a long, quiet sigh, his blood still rushing in his ears.

Isaac raised a questioning eyebrow at Mikael, who tapped on his ears. Somehow, Mikael had heard them coming. Mikael made his way carefully back into the hallway, with Isaac and Alison following close behind.

Mikael stopped abruptly, almost causing Isaac and Alison to bump into him. They had been walking for quite some time, wandering through the castle's seemingly endless hallways in search of their gear. Mikael had paused outside of an octagon-shaped room that was littered with large wooden trunks, packs, and other random items thrown haphazardly all over the place. This seemed to be the vampire's dumping ground for their prisoners' belongings. Now, if they could just find theirs...

Isaac squinted. There in the far corner, Isaac thought he could just make out the tuft of fur from his bedroll poking up from behind a chest. Mikael pointed in the same spot that Isaac was looking, confirming his suspicions. Mikael motioned forward, and they slowly crept into the room with Mikael in the lead. He stopped occasionally, sweeping the floor gently with his hand or foot before continuing on. Their pace was slow and nerve-wracking, with each of their steps sounding like thunder as their feet slid on the dirt-ridden floor.

After several long minutes, Mikael reached the chest and tossed Isaac's pack to him, which he almost fumbled and dropped to the ground. Mikael shot him an annoyed look before tossing Alison hers, which she caught effortlessly with a satisfied wink at Isaac. Isaac stuck out his tongue at her. Mikael shook his head as he slung his gear across his back and secured his sword down at his waist.

Mikael started forward down a hallway next to the room they were in, with Isaac and Alison close behind. There was a lot of noise ahead:

Isaac could hear people yelling, and others screaming, followed faintly by what he assumed was the sound of metal scraping against metal or a rough surface. Isaac felt an odd mixture of fear and eagerness swirling inside of him. While he was afraid of coming face to face with the vampires, he desperately wanted to save Cela, and anyone else that might be trapped here. It was an odd feeling to be terrified, yet full of energy.

Isaac took a cautious step forward, but was stopped by Mikael, who shoved him and Alison into another room, and back into a corner behind a tall stack of chests. Mikael pressed them against the wall, tapped his ear again, and waited.

Isaac strained to hear whatever it was Mikael could be picking up on. There was so much noise coming from the other room, what could he possibly be hearing?

He closed his eyes and tried to focus harder on the sounds around him. There was one there that he thought he might've heard earlier when the other vampires had left the room they were hiding in. It was so faint and high-pitched you might miss it. But it sounded like...

... like a banshee screaming.

Isaac opened his eyes and saw Mikael staring at him intently. He nodded his head and looked toward the door. There was a vampire approaching the room from the hallway they had come from, and approaching fast.

They crouched low, peering out from between the crates. A flash of black whipped into the room, the vampire's complete form only taking shape once he was standing still. He glanced around the room before slowly stalking around, sniffing at the air like a bloodhound, and throwing chests and crates out of his way.

Isaac and Alison exchanged worried looks. They wouldn't be able to hide from this one. If they just sat here, they would be found for sure. But had they all recovered enough to fight yet? And if they fought, how much noise and attention would that bring to them?

Mikael tapped on their shoulders and held a finger up to his lips and pointed to the vampire. The vampire had begun looking through the chests opposite them, tearing each of them apart. Mikael held up his hand, stopping Isaac and Alison from following him as he began to carefully maneuver his way toward the vampire.

Isaac watched as Mikael carefully crept behind the creature, every moment slow and calculated. As Mikael drew closer, he quietly unsheathed his sword, the blade sliding out of the scabbard noiselessly. Isaac's jaw went slack at the sight of Mikael's weapon. The once unassuming sword was composed of dwarven metal and folded steel, giving it a beautiful orange, blue, and silver color that swirled in lazy circles from guard-to-tip. A line of runes appeared on the gold crossguard. One rune that looked like a fang with a line cut through it glowed a faint blue.

The sword ignited into a glorious flame in Mikael's hand as he cleaved through the vampire's neck, separating its head from its body in one swift motion. The vampire's body caught fire immediately, its flesh crackling sickeningly as it was consumed by red-hot flame. Mikael caught the vampire's severed head like a falling ball and braced the sizzling body with his own to prevent it from falling over.

Mikael smiled at Isaac and Alison, who were completely out from behind their cover now, and shared the same confused expression. Mikael opened one of the chests, carefully laying the vampire's still-burning body inside, before turning back to them and tapping on his guard where the rune was still glowing.

The enchantment only works against vampires. Isaac smirked, and Mikael smiled back.

So, this is a Venatores Hunter...

"*NO!*" a woman screamed, echoing from deep within the old castle.

Mikael took off at a brisk pace down the hallway with Isaac and Alison close behind. They weren't moving as quietly as before, but, judging by that scream, the time for stealth may be over.

Mikael stopped and tapped his ears.

More are coming? Isaac closed his eyes and focused, trying to find that banshee-like sound again.

His eyes snapped open. He could hear it! But was it louder this time? No, that wasn't it...

Isaac locked eyes with Mikael, who nodded at him understandingly.

He was right; it wasn't that it was louder.

There were more of them coming.

And they were all heading directly toward them.

"No point in being quiet now, I suppose," Mikael said begrudgingly. "There are perhaps three or four of them heading this way. Stick close to me and remember: either burn them or cut off their heads. And be quick about it. You don't want to engage in a war of attrition with a vampire."

Isaac nodded, but stopped himself as he was reaching for his swords. Could he really stand toe-to-toe with a vampire? Mikael was able to confidently hold his own against them after probably years of training and experience. It'd be foolish of him to think that he could handle a vampire in close combat right now. No, it'd be better if he tried to keep his distance and burn them. Though even that would be a difficult task. The hallway was only wide enough to fit the three of them shoulder-to-shoulder. Certainly not wide enough for a handful of people to be fighting all at once.

They'd just have to make do.

"Remember, you have us here to help too," Alison said, smiling. "We've got your back."

Isaac smiled lightly back. He was glad to have her here. Despite everything going on, she made him feel safer.

"Thanks."

"Here they come," Mikael said, his grip on the sword tightening.

Isaac readied himself, fire igniting in his hands, his eyes locked on the hallway in front of them. Any second now, they would—

A flash of black whipped in front of Isaac's eyes, and suddenly he felt himself go airborne. He slammed into the wall sideways, gasping as the air was forced out of his lungs before tumbling and skidding across the stone floor.

What the hell was that? All he could remember was seeing black flash across his eyes. Isaac winced and held his side as his ribs groaned in protest with each breath. He turned his face up from the dirt to see the vampire looming over him, its hands balled into tight fists. Alison groaned beside him as she struggled to her feet, her lip already busted open.

Mikael was engaged with two other vampires a few feet away from them, one wielding a spiked mace and the other a pair of daggers. Mikael dodged and parried their blows, his flaming sword keeping them from getting too close. Isaac cursed as he fought to his feet. Mikael wouldn't be able to assist them, not when he had two of his own to deal with.

They'd have to handle this one by themselves.

Another brief flash clouded Isaac's vision before his head cracked against the wall behind him, followed by what he assumed was the sound of Alison's body being thrown hard against the wall again. His vision went dark for a moment as his mind spun. Isaac sat against the stone wall, his body shuddering under the barrage of blows from the vampire. All he could make out was the same flash of black followed by excruciating pain. His body slowly began to collapse under the fury of the vampire's strikes. And no matter how hard he tried, his body refused to move. It was as if he were shutting down.

He was done for.

He—once again—had failed. This time, though, with much harsher consequences.

He and Alison were dead.

So much for control...

"Djaro's arrows fired faster." He heard Alison scoff at the vampire, the assault on Isaac's body pausing. He thought he heard the vampire move again but, this time, when he heard something get thrown, it was Alison who was *cheering*.

"Ha! I knew it," she declared victoriously.

Isaac looked over at where the vampire had been tossed. Even with his one eye almost completely swollen shut, he could tell that the vampire was stunned.

"If you see the black flash, you're already too late," Alison said as she grabbed Isaac by the arm and helped him to his feet. Isaac felt his knees buckle and almost collapse under him. His entire body felt like it had been crushed by a boulder.

"Just after they move, there is a slight blur where they were standing and where they are currently. It's faint, but noticeable if you concentrate. You have to anticipate a little where they're going," Alison said confidently as the vampire disappeared from his vision again, only to reappear a second later, thrown back against the same wall as before by a strong burst of wind. Alison looked at Isaac and smiled self-assuredly.

"Just trust your instincts and let's kill this thing. I can't do this without you."

Isaac turned shakily toward the vampire, who was pacing in front of them like a predator about to pounce. It was clear that the vampire hadn't been expecting the non-Venatores to be able to put distance between them.

A blur as they move? Isaac thought back to when Djaro had fired his arrows at them and how they had seemed so imperceptible at the time. Even now, he wasn't sure he would be able to confidently dodge any of his shots. But, Isaac *had* been able to see them once before, when he dove to protect Alison.

Isaac moved his stiff, almost broken body. He could hear his bones creak and his muscles groan with every twitch. He rolled his shoulders. While his body screamed in pain, it didn't hurt more than when he had fought the Draugr Lord. It had been much worse then.

If he's dealt with worse before, could he handle this now?

Only one way to find out...

The vampire disappeared again before being forced backwards by Alison. The vampire hissed like a feral sabertooth, his hands clenching and unclenching in frustration.

"Did you see it that time?" Alison asked.

Isaac nodded slowly. He'd seen a slight distortion in the air a few seconds after he couldn't see the vampire anymore.

"I think I got this," Isaac said, glancing over at Mikael, who had dispatched one of the vampires, its body burning against one wall while its head rolled down the hallway.

"We'll finish this and help Mikael," Isaac said, and Alison nodded.

Fire ignited in Isaac's palms, the flames licking eagerly at the air around it. Just as he was about to unleash a torrent of flames, the vampire disappeared from his sight again. Isaac searched frantically for the blur, hoping to find any indication of where the vampire was going.

Out of the corner of his eye, he caught a slight distortion in the air.

There he is. Isaac could barely see him through his swollen eye, strafing to the left trying to get behind them. Isaac moved his hands in a semicircle around him, fire leaping from his palms and fanning out in an arc. Alison was quick to follow up as the vampire jumped back. A blade of air, white and thin, shot from her hands and arced out toward the vampire. The vampire's eyes widened as he twisted through the air, narrowly avoiding being bisected.

Isaac smirked. *She can do more than just push you back.*

Alison's hands whipped through the air as she pressed her attack on the vampire, each air blade that missed creating long gashes in the hallway walls. Isaac let fire stream forth from his hands, bathing the air between him and the vampire in unrelenting waves of flame. The vampire did his best to dodge out of the way, with each of his attempts to get closer blocked either by fire or a barrage of air magic. Frustrated, he surged forward, leaping over the flames and narrowly missing being slashed by Alison's magic. The vampire rolled as he hit the ground and sprung at Alison like a wolf bounding after its prey.

Alison smiled as the vampire bore down on top of her, unleashing another barrage of air blades, cutting its legs off at the knees.

The vampire howled in pain and shock as he landed on his severed legs and tumbled along the floor. Isaac dashed after him as he recovered, pushing his hands together and creating a growing ball of flame. As Isaac drew closer, he raised the now small boulder-sized ball of fire above his head and slammed it down on top of the vampire. His undead flesh caught fire immediately like dry kindling. He screamed as he crawled towards them on his hands and stumped-legs. Isaac shivered at the grotesque, spider-like sight. The vampire collapsed a few feet in front of Alison; most of his body had already turned to ash.

The last vampire fell to his knees in front of Mikael, his severed head bouncing against the wall and his body going limp as fire consumed it. Mikael wiped his forehead with his sleeve and nodded at them approvingly.

"Nicely done for your first time," Mikael said, wiping the blood off his sword in the crook of his elbow. He glanced over at Isaac and winced. "I wish I could tell you it will only get easier from here. But, the truth is, these were fourth or fifth generation vampires, and they don't move as quickly or hit as hard as their lower generation siblings."

Isaac's eyebrow shot up questioningly. "They don't all possess the same amount of power?"

"Not at all," Mikael began, walking down the hallway. "The further away from the Pure Blood source you are, the weaker the vampire. Conversely, as you move closer to the Pure Blooded vampire, the stronger the vampires become. So, stay on your guard."

Isaac and Alison exchanged uneasy looks. They had barely kept up with the vampire they had just killed.

Hopefully, all the stronger ones stayed home. Isaac thought wishfully.

Isaac turned to look back down the hallway as the sound of approaching vampires filled his ears.

"Get ready. We're not going to let them slow us down this time," Mikael said, his grip tightening once more on his sword.

Vampires came rushing in at a steady pace in groups of two or three at a time, and each time Mikael would take one or two of them and cut them down with a few skillful sword strokes. Mikael's techniques were beautiful and precise, almost like a dance. His years of experience were on full display, and the confidence he emitted was almost tangible. When Isaac caught sight of Mikael between his own blasts of fire, he could see the same confident gleam in Mikael's eyes that Sigmund would have whenever they encountered trouble.

Somehow, they continued to push forward. Despite his injuries,

Isaac was able to dispatch the vampires that came after them with Alison's help. As they battled their way down the corridor, the stream of vampires slowed until Mikael slew what seemed to be the last one, its corpse joining the hallway that was already littered with the flaming bodies of decapitated vampires that lit up the corridor like grotesque bonfires.

The sound of a heavy wooden door creaking shut echoed from further down. Isaac and Alison followed as Mikael sprinted off toward the sound, just in time for them to see a large door being pulled shut. Something heavy fell against the door, and it stiffened slightly as it became braced from behind.

Mikael scratched at his chin as he drew closer to the door. Isaac could barely make out the muffled sound of orders being shouted and chains rattling from the other side.

The prisoners were on the other side, no question about it.

"Any chance you two could blast through this?" Mikael asked, stepping back to give them room as if he already knew the answer.

Alison cracked her knuckles excitedly. "Of course. Ready?" She looked at Isaac, who nodded.

"You might want to cover your ears," Isaac said to Mikael. To create enough force to blow in the door in this tiny space would be deafening. The last thing they needed was to incapacitate their lifeline.

Mikael placed his hands over his ears and took a couple more steps back.

Isaac stood shoulder-to-shoulder with Alison, their hands leveled at the door. The wind began to whip and howl around them, as Isaac reached out to the mana in the air, working it into a gale-force frenzy. Isaac smirked despite himself, enjoying the harsh wind snapping against him, as the door began to rattle violently. With a flick of their wrists, the wind slammed into the door, causing it to buckle and begin to splinter from the center. Isaac could feel the brace start to fall away just before the door exploded inward in a shower of wooden shards and chunks.

Mikael charged ahead of them as soon as the door had caved, leaving Alison and Isaac to trail behind him. Isaac was shocked to see only three vampires waiting for them on the other side. The room appeared to be an old carriage station. It was partially open to the outside, which allowed castle visitors to pull their wagons up to the castle without being exposed to the elements. There were two old, rickety horse-drawn carts with large metal cages, filled with the emaciated bodies of barely alive prisoners, chained to the cages. The moonlight streaming in from the large windows overhead gave them all a ghostly, haunting appearance. Huge, muscular horses sat at the front of the carts, their heads shaking impatiently.

Mikael wasted no time in killing two vampires as he rushed into the room, fire streaking behind him, creating a vortex of flame as he spun and decapitated them.

Only one vampire remained in the room: Ko. Who, despite now being the last vampire standing, glowered arrogantly as Mikael approached. He snatched three vials of glowing, colorful liquid from a pouch at his side and quickly downed them.

Isaac's eyes narrowed on Ko as his lips curled into a devious smile. He thought he saw something flash in Ko's eyes, a color change of the iris, perhaps. But there was something different now...

Something's wrong. Isaac stopped his sprint, causing Alison to almost slam into him. Instead of Ko cowering away from the Hunter that killed his entire battalion, *he's waiting for him.*

Eagerly.

"Mikael, wai—" Isaac felt something large shoot past him, and suddenly Mikael was no longer standing in front of him.

Isaac turned around to groans coming from behind him. A human-sized hole now decorated the wall, with Mikael's arms and legs hanging limply out of it, his sword still clattering noisily against the stone floor.

When did—

Isaac felt his body collapse around a fist buried in his stomach as he was thrown backwards into the wall opposite Mikael. He slammed into the brick, causing dust and debris to shower him as he fell hard to the dirt. Isaac heard Alison's startled yelp followed by a heavy thud as her body slid to the ground.

What the hell had happened? Isaac rubbed dust out of his one good eye and squinted at Ko, who was pacing back and forth like a cornered predator. His fangs had elongated, and his body was suddenly very muscular. His eyes looked crazed and bloodshot.

"I should've killed you outright. To Hell with Vladimyr, no cattle are worth this amount of trouble..." Ko hissed, saliva dribbling down the sides of his mouth.

Isaac winced as he struggled to his feet. Ko looked more like a feral dog now than a vampire, which must've been thanks to whatever potions he had taken.

What else did those potions do to him...?

Mikael was just beginning to stir, albeit slowly, pulling himself out from the wall.

Isaac felt his throat tighten as Ko glanced back and forth between him and Mikael. He didn't see Ko move last time. He was way faster than the others they had killed getting here. Hell, he was even so fast that *Mikael* didn't see him. If Ko decided to come after him, he was done.

What can I do? Isaac thought frantically.

He almost had to laugh at himself. First mission on his own, and he dies.

Here lies Isaac Grey. Died on his first real mission.

Ko's gaze landed on Isaac, and he snarled, revealing a strange set of serrated teeth.

Isaac closed his eyes tightly and looked away.

I'll see you in Heaven, Alison.

Isaac felt the wind whip around him, kicking up small rocks that assaulted his body and roaring in his ears like a tornado.

Isaac opened his eyes just in time to see Ko get lifted off his feet and tossed backwards away from him and Mikael. Ko attempted to rush back toward them, but the vortex that Alison had created around them was slowing him down and pushing him back.

Alison limped over to the center of the room, and the air around her seemed to hum as she exerted her control over it.

"He's like a rabid animal," Alison coughed. "He's stronger now, sure, but he has a narrow focus. Look! You can tell by how he couldn't decide which of you to go after next instead of just killing you outright... We can do this."

Isaac slowly rose to his feet, his eyes locked on Ko, who was snarling and struggling against the wind that Alison was commanding. Ko's eyes went back and forth between the three of them, his teeth gnashing together in frustration.

He really has lost his reason.

Across from him, Mikael was finally rising to his feet, one arm held tightly to his side, and his sword held tightly in the other hand.

With Alison's help, we might be able to do this...

"I can slow him down, but I can't hold him like this forever," Alison said, raising her hands as the wind howled louder, even grains of sand picked up by the current felt like daggers digging into Isaac's exposed skin. "You two better figure out how to kill him now. Good luck!"

Ko began to push back against the wind restraining him and dashed toward Mikael, who dodged backwards away from Ko's wild slashes with his claw-like fingers, and attempted to counter with his own strikes, though his sword remained unlit.

Isaac started to make his way to help Mikael, but hesitated.

Mikael must've realized, as Isaac did, that they wouldn't be able to rely on fire to kill Ko. If a fire were to be lit inside this cyclone, it would either be quickly snuffed out or—and this was Isaac's favorite alternative to think about—they'd all be burned alive in a fiery tornado.

So their only option was decapitation. And given how easily Ko, even now, has been able to deflect Mikael's blows, it would not be an easy task.

Isaac reached down to his sides and drew his swords with shaky hands and ran over to Mikael's aid. The last thing he wanted to do was fight toe-to-toe with the vampire but, at the very least, Alison's work had reduced his speed down to the vampires they were fighting earlier. However, the problem remained of how to kill him. Without being able to use magic, Isaac felt that he wouldn't be of much use. What could he do besides serve as a distraction?

What about slowing him down more?

The thought struck in Isaac's head like a gong as his first slash clanged feebly off Ko's metal vambraces. He backpedaled, narrowly ducking out of the way of a vicious slice from Ko that would've slit his throat clean open.

He could still use magic here. Alison proved that. Even if her magic couldn't outright kill Ko, she was doing everything she could to make his life inconvenient. So why couldn't he do the same?

Isaac sheathed one of his swords as Ko lunged at Mikael, who parried and narrowly missed slicing off Ko's arm. Ko fell to his knees as the ground under him turned into a thick sheet of ice. He flung himself to one side, avoiding Mikael's attempt to cut off his head. Ko rolled across the ground and sprang forward off his hands and feet like an animal toward Isaac.

Isaac threw himself backwards, the ground shooting up between them, catching the vampire in the stomach and sending him tumbling back toward Mikael. Isaac rolled and rushed back toward Ko, lowering the wall he just created before quickly raising it again underneath himself, springboarding off it high above Ko and Mikael as they clashed.

Isaac briefly locked eyes with Ko before the vampire maneuvered toward his almost blind left side. Isaac hit the ground and rolled again just before feeling his body fold over a hard kick to his side. He skipped across the dirt like a stone across water.

Isaac quickly recovered, rolling to his knees and now holding his left side. The ground beneath Ko froze once more, his slip this time allowing for Mikael to land a cut across his face.

We're getting closer.

Isaac fell back to his knees as he tried to stand, his breath catching in his chest, a sharp pain erupting across his abdomen.

My fucking ribs. He hissed as another breath made him hug his side even tighter.

Isaac looked up to check on Mikael, who was covered in small scratches and was bleeding in several places. He was doing very well on his own against the powered-up vampire, but it was clear he was beginning to tire.

His hair was matted down to his skull from sweat, and his face looked haggard and exhausted. His movements were starting to slow, and Ko was beginning to take notice, catching Mikael where he left himself exposed.

We're going to have to finish this soon... Isaac forced himself to his feet, sheathing his remaining sword to use his only free hand to use magic.

Mikael would have to be the one to kill Ko, but how could Isaac give him that opening? If Ko truly was a mindless, bloodthirsty animal right now, then perhaps they could use that.

Isaac hobbled toward Mikael, walls of stone erupting around Ko that trapped him on three sides, with the only open side facing toward Isaac.

And, just as Isaac thought, Ko turned his feral attention right onto him. *Good boy.*

"Mikael! Be ready!" Isaac shouted as Ko charged at him, slashing and catching him where he was too slow to react. Isaac continued to raise walls around him and Ko, encasing them in a sort of never-ending hallway, blocking Ko's peripheral vision. At the same time, Isaac kept freezing the ground beneath Ko to keep him from getting too close to him.

Ko snarled as his feet slid across the ice. Ko leapt into the air and kicked off the wall Isaac had just created, avoiding the icy path trap Isaac had set. Isaac threw himself to one side as Ko landed on top of him, claws at the ready.

"Mikael!" Isaac shouted, one of the walls opening to allow Mikael to charge in. Isaac watched as Ko looked up just in time to see Mikael's sword sever his head from his shoulders, showering Isaac in warm blood. He shielded his face with his hand; the blood was so hot it felt as if it were burning him. He heard Ko's head and body hit the floor seconds later.

Isaac wiped his hands off on his pants and frowned at his now grayish-red cloak. He gagged as the smell of warm, decaying flesh assaulted his nose.

Disgusting... Isaac's nose twitched at the awful smell of vampire blood.

"Crazy bastard." Mikael reached down to help Isaac to his feet, which he happily accepted. The wind around them had returned to normal, and Alison quickly appeared at Isaac's side, hugging him tightly.

Isaac felt his ribs groan in protest, and he started to wheeze.

"I can't breathe," he said, patting her back.

"Sorry," she said sheepishly, loosening her grip and stepping back to look at him. "I'm proud of you. Of us." She looked at Mikael. "We did it."

Isaac nodded and smiled. Somehow they had managed to pull it off.

But we won't always be this lucky, will we?

Isaac shook his head, trying to push down the thoughts flooding to the surface of his mind. He had to focus on other things right now.

Like finding Cela and freeing everyone.

Isaac glanced over at the huddled mass of bodies clinging, petrified, to the cells, none of them looking particularly eager to move. Many of them were having trouble standing, and most had several gashes or cuts somewhere on their bodies with blood still seeping out. If their wounds weren't already infected from their poor conditions, they would be soon.

"We should patch them up before we go anywhere," Isaac suggested. "Get them out of their shackles and give them the ability to move around, if they can."

Alison nodded. "I have some bandages in my pack. We can use whatever we have. Isaac, can you help heal these people at all?"

Isaac lightly pushed on his side and took in a sharp breath as stabbing pain shot through him. "I should be able to at least take their pain away after I mend my ribs a bit."

"We should wait until sunrise before we move these people," Mikael added, finally finished wiping off his sword and sheathing it. "There is a possibility that there are other, smaller nests located close by. The sunlight saps them of their abilities, making them no more than human if they're exposed to it for long enough. It'll be safer to move then."

"That'll give us plenty of time to see to everyone," Alison said as she walked over toward the carts.

"It's alright, everyone," Mikael said, doing his best to smile reassuringly. "All the vampires are dead, and we'll be getting you out of here shortly. We're going to tend to your injuries and get you out of your shackles. By morning, we'll be heading back to Beignknost."

The prisoners looked at each other skeptically. Isaac couldn't blame them for being doubtful. They had endured for Creator knows how long with the vampires, and suddenly three people show up and play hero?

I'd probably think it's a trap. Isaac admitted.

Alison stood next to one of the carts and held her hand up for someone to grab so she could help them down.

"We want to get you all home," Alison added. "But we want to make sure everyone is safe and can move around freely, so please, let us help you."

"Will we have to go back in these cages again?" A voice called out from the mass of bodies, echoed by murmurs of similar questions.

Alison frowned. "Only temporarily once we head out so we can bring everyone back."

The crowd shifted uneasily inside the cage. They clearly didn't want to be stuffed inside these cages again. Who could blame them? But, the fact remained that the only way to get everyone out of here was by having everyone sit in the cages.

How can we make them feel more comfortable?

Isaac eyed the cages and noticed long, thick chains hanging limply around the door with a giant metal lock dangling on one end.

Isaac walked over to the cage Alison was standing next to and yanked the chains off the door; the chain clanking against the metal sounded like an angry snake hissing. Isaac held the lock and several links of the chains and willed fire to ignite in his hands. He could feel everyone's eyes on him as the metal burned white-hot. It felt like he was holding two suns in his hands with how hot he was pushing his own flames. Alison had even had to take a few steps away from him because of the heat radiating off him. The lock was the first to soften and become jelly-like, before completely turning to a tainted liquid silver. The chain followed shortly after, leaving nothing but molten metal burning on the floor.

"We don't want to keep anyone a prisoner," Isaac said, looking at the people inside the cages. "You are free to go whenever you want. But if you let us, we'll get you at least back to Beignknost. Where you go from there is up to you. Though, no offense, some of you have seen better days. So maybe it'd be better if you trusted us for now?"

More murmurs erupted throughout the cages, with each of the prisoners looking at each other uneasily. Isaac glanced back and forth between the cages as the prisoners eyed them curiously.

Was I too forward?

One of them took a step forward—a small, frail woman—and reached out for Alison's hand, who grabbed it lightly and slowly helped them to the floor.

"... I have a gash in my thigh that I would like to have looked at, when you have the time," she said, limping over to Isaac.

Isaac smiled. "Of course. We'll see to it right away."

"Nicely done," Mikael said, placing a hand on his shoulder. Alison gave him an approving smile as she continued to help people off the carts.

"You remind me of my younger brother, in a way," Mikael said, smiling lightly. "It would be interesting for you two to meet someday." He patted Isaac on the back. "Come, we've much to do."

* * * * *

Time melted away as they aided the people out of the carts, removed their shackles, and tended to anyone's injuries. Many were just tired, understandably drained from their long journey and poor conditions. Others were bleeding from the rough iron shackles that dug into their skin. Some had been bleeding so frequently that their wrists and hands were stained a deep crimson.

They had gone through almost every other prisoner before finding Cela. Alison found her in the back of one of the carts, curled into a tight protective ball, shivering as if she were left out in the cold midwinter. Alison almost didn't recognize her. If it wasn't for her elf ears just barely poking through the wild mess of matted hair, she probably would've been overlooked as just another human.

"I found her!" Alison yelled, prompting Isaac and Mikael to rush over to the cage.

Alison was holding her now, almost like a mother would a child. Cela stirred groggily, shielding her eyes as she looked up at them as if the dimly lit room was far too bright to stand.

"Cela?" Alison asked softly.

Cela looked at her cautiously and nodded. Her mouth moved, but no words came out. Just raspy wheezing that turned into a short fit of coughs.

Alison smiled at her, laying her gently against the cage as she went about bandaging her leg. A long slash twisted from her calf down to her ankle. She wouldn't be able to walk for some time.

"Your husband, Thomas, sent us. He's the whole reason we came here," Alison said, trying to sound as sweet and reassuring as possible. "We're going to get you back to him, okay?"

Cela rested her head against the cage, and her cracked lips spread into a faint smile.

* * * * *

"Finally, that's everyone..." Isaac let out a satisfied sigh and plopped down on the ground next to Mikael. They had just finished seeing to everyone's injuries. Dawn was beginning to break, showering the earth in its welcoming golden rays.

He had never been so happy to see the sunlight.

The long night and its battles were weighing heavily on him. It was all he could do to keep his eyes open.

"This certainly was... eventful," Mikael said, running his hands over one of his bandages. Alison had patched him up last at his behest. "However, I think a good day's rest is in order."

"Or weeks." Isaac smirked, watching Alison as she made her way over to them.

He shook his head, his smirk turning into a smile. Even after all they'd done, she still looks just as bit as energized as she did when they first set out.

She was certainly incredible.

"Are you two done relaxing? We can probably start moving out now," she teased, crossing her arms over her chest impatiently.

"Aye, aye, you raise a good point." Mikael stood slowly, using the wall for balance. Isaac rose with him.

"So, we're ready to be off then?" Isaac asked, glancing over at the nervous faces staring back at him.

"Yup. Just have to load everyone back in and then we'll be good to go," Alison said confidently.

"Let's get to it then. Mikael was just complaining about how tired he was," Isaac said, grinning.

"Is that so?" Mikael raised an eyebrow.

"Too bad we don't have time to argue." Isaac walked over toward the crowd, Alison and Mikael trailing behind. "Everyone! It's time to get ready to head out and get you back home. Next stop, Beignknost!"

END OF PART 2

PART 3

THE MAN WHO WOULD BE ARCHMAGE

CHAPTER TWENTY-THREE

Sigmund couldn't remember the last time he had felt this anxious, his mind so wild and untamed with worry.

His fists clenched so tightly in anger.

He had to find Jack as soon as possible.

He rounded the corner into the hallway that led to Jack's study. Despite it being such a short corridor, the study had never felt so far away.

It had been almost three full days since he had last spoken with Adara, and in that time, he had launched as comprehensive an investigation as he could. Queen Hestia, by her good graces, agreed to speak to Sigmund by letter correspondence, though Sigmund never mentioned who it was exactly that she was speaking with.

Given his reputation for being both thorough and paranoid, he could safely assume that she knew.

She had confirmed that Adara had never been to Emberion, and there was no such report of highwaymen or bandits ravaging her people in outlying villages. If there were, she surely would've known about it.

Similar reports came back when Sigmund probed other contacts, whom Sigmund trusted, that Adara supposedly had dealings with recently. All of them said the same thing: they hadn't heard from Adara in several months.

His findings thus far, including her slip in their discussion, were enough to convince him that Adara, at the very least, was being less than honest about her extracurriculars. Indeed, it seemed she was the bug they had been looking to squash all along.

Sigmund flung open the door of the study, the knob slamming into the wall behind it with a hard thud.

The room was dark. The candle wicks were stiff, and not even embers remained in the fireplace.

Where could he have gone? Jack always left the candles in his study burning, only extinguishing them when he planned to step out for a long time. The last he knew was that Jack was looking for information about the Anguis survivor, but that left him with no clues as to where that could possibly take him.

Sigmund grumbled under his breath, all but slamming the door behind him as he stormed down the hallway. If anyone would know where Jack went, it was Margaret. With her teleportation magic, Jack always liked to inform her of where he was going in case of an emergency.

While Sigmund was fairly certain that Margaret and Adara weren't working together given their... complicated history, he could never be too safe.

He would just have to be careful not to tip his hand.

Sigmund came to her door with the crudely carved 'M' and rapped his knuckles hard against it.

No answer.

His eyebrows furrowed together. He knocked again, harder this time, the entire door shaking against the frame.

The door flung open a second later, revealing a very disgruntled Margaret, her eyes full of rage.

"Sigmund!" she roared. "Can I *fucking* help you? Didn't you hear me say I was coming?!"

"No," Sigmund said. "Where's Jack?"

Her eyes narrowed on him. She had always been quite hot-tempered, and it seems getting older hadn't quelled the fire inside her.

"You were about to break my door down, and interrupt *my* reading, just to ask where Jack is? You can't be serious."

Sigmund glanced over her shoulder. There was a book open on her bed, face down where she had paused reading, and a hot mug of tea—most likely lemon—perched precariously on the mattress.

"I apologize. It is urgent."

"So urgent that all your manners dribbled out of that old, thick skull?" A small portal opened up in front of her at the same time as one opened up next to her cup. She reached her hand through and yanked her cup off the bed through the portal and took a large swig.

She sighed before stepping back into her room. "He's not here, moron. He's in Aesus with Adara."

Sigmund felt the color drain from his face. Was he already too late?

"Do you know where?" Sigmund asked, careful to keep his tone steady.

"Somewhere on the Giltrean coast. Some small local town there. I've never been there before."

"Do you have a map?" Sigmund took a step into her room.

"Yes, but, Sigmund, what is this about? And no bullshit. Fucking tell me," Margaret said, glaring at him.

"I cannot. Trust me. All I can say is that time is of the essence."

She looked him up and down. He could tell that she was debating pressing for more details. Sigmund was always forthcoming with information when asked, so for him not to say anything...

Well, it said quite a bit.

She gave him one more angry side-eye before retrieving a large, rolled-up parchment from her bookshelf. She unrolled the map on her bed, slowly revealing the two giant, adjoining land masses of Eutrox and Aesus. Her finger trailed straight through the Seven Kingdoms of Man and into the Elves' home, Valestris, toward the Giltrean Sea.

"He's somewhere up there. I can get you close, but you'll have to find him on your own." Margaret took another sip of her tea.

Sigmund nodded. "Thanks."

"Yeah, whatever, just don't interrupt me again. It was just getting good." She flicked her wrist at him, and Sigmund felt the cool tingle of teleportation magic swallow him. A swirl of purple and white sparkling lights filled his vision for a moment before he was spit out, thankfully on his feet, into the golden forest the Elves called home: Valestris.

The trees that surrounded him were massive, stretching as high as they could toward the sun. So high, in fact, that Sigmund couldn't see the tops of them. Each was as thick as a Hydra's neck and cast a dazzling display of gold light all around him as the sun's rays kissed their bark.

Even the grass and flowers were tall, coming up to Sigmund's thighs. White, blue, and yellow lilies were in full bloom all around him, filling the air with the sweet aroma of a fresh spring. Perhaps Sigmund's favorite aspect of Valestris was how quiet it was. Everything was still and calm, with the gentle sound of waves breaking against rocks echoing from somewhere off in the distance. Sigmund had to squint and shield his eyes as he looked around, with the sunlight making everything sparkle like fine jewelry.

Unfortunately, he didn't have time to take it all in.

He had to find Jack.

With no clear direction, Sigmund opted to make his way toward the sound of the water and follow the coast until he found a town and ask around from there. Normally, the Elves did not take kindly to strangers—especially Mankin. But outside of the posh, tightly wound aristocrats of Nivandeer, most other Elves were pleasant enough to speak with.

Unfortunately, Elves living outside of their grand city were few and far between.

Sigmund trudged through the vibrant undergrowth, each blade of grass and branch clinging to his clothes in a soft passing embrace. A peculiar creature took interest in him, squirrel-like but with large bat-like ears; long, sharp claws; and a flat, leathery, pointed tail that twitched anxiously. It darted between Sigmund's legs and raced ahead of him, waiting for him until he drew closer, and then sprinting ahead again.

The creature continued this game until Sigmund came to a break in the tree line, where he came to the edge of a cliff. He peered over the edge, his eyes tracing down the sheer cliff face and to the rocky crags and cold water that waited below. The soft sea foam deceptively looked like a welcoming mattress to cushion the deadly fall. To his right, nestled between two sides of the cliff, was a small port town, built right on the beach. Simple straw houses and moored sloops littered the sandy alcove.

He looked down at the little animal, its nose twitching expectantly.

It was as if the creature knew that Sigmund had been looking for other people. Sigmund reached down and gently petted the top of its head.

"Thank you."

The animal chirped and then darted off back into the woods.

Sigmund turned his attention back toward the town.

Guess I'll begin there. He thought.

Sigmund stopped in his tracks as movement in the corner of his eye caught his attention. He turned to it and felt his breath catch in his chest. At the edge of a precipice not a few hundred feet away from him, in the opposite direction of the town, was Jack.

And beside him, Adara.

Sigmund took off toward them, carefully minding his footing. The last thing he needed was to make a stupid mistake and tumble down the bluff. He slowed to a walk as he grew closer; he didn't want to appear as if something was wrong.

Everything had to appear normal.

"What are you looking at?" he grumbled as he walked up behind them.

Jack, with Adara, turned to greet him. Jack's brief look of confusion broke into a wide, welcoming grin when he saw him. Adara offered her attempt at a sincere, tight-lipped smile.

"Sigmund!" Jack exclaimed with surprise. "What brings you out here?"

Sigmund looked carefully between Jack and Adara. He had to choose his words carefully. He couldn't risk tipping Adara off, assuming his showing up here hadn't done that already.

"I have been hitting dead ends," Sigmund said, making sure to keep his tone neutral. "I did not want to wait for you to return to discuss whether you had found anything. Margaret mentioned you were in Aesus and helped me get here."

"Getting a little too impatient in your old age, don't you think, Siggy?" Adara chuckled.

Jack smiled, but this one was not warm and reassuring.

It was tight-lipped and serious.

"Well, I do have some updates, so your trip out here won't be wasted. I was going to tell you when I got back, but since you're here..."

Jack stepped forward, closer to the edge of the cliff, and gazed out at the Giltrean Sea, his back to them. The afternoon sun made the water sparkle like millions of stars twinkling beneath the waves.

"As I was telling Adara, I started looking into the Anguis family by first going through old records of their history that I had taken from what's now Emberion. These books contained their long-held traditions, rituals, and beliefs that I found revoltingly fascinating. I figured that if something, *anything*, would help me understand how one survived, it'd be in their books. Indeed, in my research, I stumbled upon a rite of passage that all Anguis members that successfully merge with the dragon's blood must undertake before they are allowed back into the Anguis family.

"All 'reborn' must hunt and kill a dragon of similar, or greater, strength to the dragon they had just been merged with. The gray-skinned survivor was a clear indicator to me of someone successfully merging with a Scattenwerz. The Scattenwerz are the strongest of all the dragon species, with their power being said to rival that of an Archmage. They are also the rarest, making finding a living one, let alone an egg, no easy task."

Jack paused as the waves crashed noisily against the rocks below, coating them in a fine spray of sea mist.

"With that knowledge, I began searching through recorded Scattenwerz sightings from the Order's library, from around the time Kenna and I invaded the then Dragon's Respite. Sure enough, there were reports of a Scattenwerz flying across Ahntwen. I began my digging there, moving from town to town asking anyone old enough who might remember seeing a large dragon fly overhead. Eventually, I was able to trace the creature to this spot, roughly, next to this humble port town." Jack pointed down to his right to the small village nestled cozily in the sand, the same one Sigmund had seen when he arrived.

"The people here told me a wonderful tale of a great battle several years ago between a tall, gray-skinned man with a Scattenwerz so large and black, they were convinced it was a monster that had sprung from the depths of Hell itself. They told me that their fight lasted several days before the gray-skinned man finally slew the dragon. Unfortunately, their story was more than just a tall-tale…"

He pointed now to his left side, on the other side of the cliff, shielded from the view of the townspeople. On the rocks and sand were the decaying remains of a dragon, its carcass too heavy for even the strongest current to pull into its maw. The bones were mostly sun-bleached, with bits of color remaining where sinew and muscle held limply to the bone. The Scattenwerz once proud, midnight black scales, were dim and flaking away in the breeze.

"It was reality. This event—this rite of passage—is why this Anguis member was not home when Kenna and I were eradicating the Anguis family. When they did return, however, there would've been a lot of change they weren't prepared for."

"If he was so powerful, then why wait? Why didn't he attack immediately and be done with it?" Adara asked, stepping up closer to Jack.

"If your family of powerful dragon-blooded Arcanists was wiped out while you were away, I doubt you would attack and take revenge immediately. You don't know what you're up against. It would not take much asking around to figure out that I was involved, and my reputation would be enough to give him pause. Since then, it seems he's been preparing and searching for ways to kill me. The artifact, if the rumors are true, would certainly do that."

"So, what do we do now?" Sigmund finally asked, breaking the long silence that followed.

"It should be no problem for us—and especially you, Jack—to squash this man like a bug. Especially since we have the artifact this Survivor was after," Adara reasoned.

Jack smiled solemnly again, a smile that was beginning to set Sigmund on edge. There was an air of reticence about him, as if he were holding something back, debating whether or not it should be said aloud.

"Perhaps at one point in time, yes."

Sigmund froze.

What did he say?

"... What do you mean?" Adara questioned. Sigmund could hear the slight twinge of excitement in her voice.

Jack turned so that he could see both of them. He offered them a soft, melancholy smile.

"I have tried my best to keep this secret for a long time, out of fear—rightfully so, in my opinion—that if others knew of my dilemma that I'd bring more disaster to my home. To my family. Only a few members of the Order know of this, but that was because they were there when it happened..."

Jack looked back out over the water again for a moment. He stared out at the sea, admiring it, as if he were seeing it for the first time.

"After I killed the Klythini, something happened... It didn't just disappear. Something came from that Beast's body and burrowed into not just my body, but my *soul*. The Elder Mages helped me when I finally woke up, and they were the ones who were able to deduce what had happened to me. I had been cursed. A curse so intricate that it became part of my very being. Any attempt to cleanse myself of it would either kill me outright, or leave me comatose for the rest of my days."

"What is this curse?" Adara asked, leaning forward in anticipation.

Sigmund forced down his growing irritation. Surely Jack could see the way she was acting too, right?

"This... curse, over time, drains me of my strength until there is nothing left. With the Elder Mages' guidance and Aura manipulation, I have been able to keep the curse's effect at bay. But it has always been a race against time, and each day it takes more and more of me. It's like a dam that's beginning to crack under the pressure of the water it's trying to hold back..." Jack turned to them again, looking at each of them, a melancholy smile creasing his lips. "I'm dying."

In that moment, while Jack was speaking, everything seemed to fade away and slow down to a crawl. It suddenly felt like someone had dropped a mountain on top of him.

The sun seemed to cast a tired glow on Jack's face. Had he always looked so old? So fragile?

"What does this mean for us? What happens with the Survivor?" Adara asked carefully. She had put on her best look of shock but, beneath it, Sigmund could see what she truly felt.

Joy.

Excitement.

A sense of victory.

And it made his blood boil.

"I am uncertain about my ability to defeat this Survivor. Even back then, when Kenna and I stormed their home, I had my doubts that I would be strong enough to do my job properly. Thankfully, Kenna was there to help offset my weakness, but now, well... I'm not sure." Jack's voice trailed off as he turned his attention back to the sea.

"Could we ask for Queen Hestia's help again?" Adara asked.

"And what of the Order?" Sigmund asked, hoping to reason with Jack one more time. "Would they not help us?"

Jack shook his head. "No, as I said before, I won't drag others into this. The Order is inherently passive, mostly unwilling to be involved directly in worldly affairs. Besides, I have taken too much from them already from my past actions. As for Kenna, her kingdom is too new. Too fragile. I cannot ask her to involve herself in something like this."

"So instead you decide to damn your own family out of what? Pride? Fear?" Sigmund pressed through gritted teeth. "If we called on them for help, surely—"

Jack turned and held up his hand, cutting Sigmund off.

"No, Sig, I cannot—*will not*—involve anyone else in this. Our family—at its core—was founded on helping others. To defend others in exactly this type of scenario. And while I have grown weaker, I still believe we'll have a chance."

"How do you figure?" Adara asked, crossing her arms over her chest. "I hate to admit it, but I agree with Siggy—we're going to need help if this guy is as strong as you claim he is."

Sigmund restrained himself from shooting Adara an angry look.

Jack smiled. "For two reasons: first, I figured out how to use the Orvtu."

Adara's eyes narrowed. "The what?"

"The Orvtu," Jack repeated. "I found some ancient Elvish lore on the orb we had found, and they called it that. Regardless, I have figured out how to work it. So, if he was planning on using it against us..."

"Then we can use it against him," Adara concluded, smiling.

Sigmund watched Adara carefully. Why did her eyes light up so much when Jack mentioned the Orvtu? If he was able to work it, surely that would mean trouble for her and her benefactor. It was as if she had been waiting for this very moment.

"Precisely," Jack nodded. "What's more, I hold another advantage over him, I think."

Sigmund met Jack's eyes. "What is that?"

"I won't be facing him alone." Jack's eyes slid back to Adara. "I need your help. Even with the Orvtu, there is a chance that he could overpower me and take it for himself. With your help, we should be able to eliminate his family line once and for all. What do you say, Adara? I can think of no one I'd trust more at my side for the battle to come."

"I—" Adara stuttered, looking genuinely shocked. "It'd be an honor, Jack. We'll put an end to this monster once and for all."

Sigmund found himself utterly dumbfounded.

Jack...

It's her! He wanted to yell. Sigmund couldn't shake the growing feeling that, with this conversation, the fate of the Grey family had been sealed.

He couldn't prove it exactly. But he could *feel* it. Every instinct in his body was screaming the truth.

And he had never been wrong.

But Sigmund knew how close Jack was to Adara, so would he heed him?

"What now then?" Sigmund questioned, trying to maintain his composure.

Jack smiled at Sigmund. "Always getting to the point. Right, well, Adara was able to narrow down the Survivor's location to somewhere out in Sakreed."

Adara nodded proudly. "It wasn't easy, but he has been leaving quite a trail behind for people to follow. Within the next couple of days, I should have a better understanding of precisely where he is."

"This is good news," Sigmund grumbled.

"While Adara is finishing her investigation, I will help you flush out the traitor. All of this planning will be for nothing if the Survivor knows we're coming."

"Agreed," Adara chimed.

Sigmund grumbled and nodded, trying hard not to scowl at Adara's painted innocent face.

"Adara, if you don't mind, please report back by nightfall every day. I do not doubt you can handle yourself, but I fear if we get too close too soon, he may attack if he feels cornered."

"Of course! I'll hopefully have good news when I get back. I'll head out now then if you don't mind." She flashed Sigmund a knowing smile.

"Good luck, Siggy," she said, then disappeared in a flash of purple and black.

Sigmund felt the blood drain from his face.

She's won, and she knows it.

"Are you okay, Sig?" Jack asked, placing a concerned hand on his shoulder. "You look paler than usual."

"Jack. Listen to me, and listen carefully," Sigmund's usual grumble turned into a low roar.

Jack's eyebrows furrowed together. "What is it?"

"Adara *is* the traitor. She slipped the last time she and I spoke, revealing information that she would have no way of knowing. I've investigated all of her recent reports of where she's been and what she's been doing. Jack, it's all a lie."

Jack was silent for a long time, his finger lightly tapping his upper lip as he thought.

"Are you sure about this?" Jack asked reluctantly.

"I have never been wrong, Jack," Sigmund said sternly.

Jack hesitantly nodded his agreement. "Even so... part of me doesn't want to believe this, Sig. It's *Adara*. She loves this family, and I can't believe that she would betray us like this. I'll have to look over the evidence you acquired and verify this. I must see it for myself."

"You know as well as I do that we might not have that kind of time," Sigmund pressed, taking a step closer to Jack. "Especially now that Adara knows that you know how to work the Orvtu *and* you're not as strong as you once were. We are in a race against time here, and we do not have the luxury of hesitating. We need to go back and prepare everyone for an attack, and quickly."

"I am not hesitating, Sig, I just... I have to be *sure*," Jack countered. Sigmund could see the struggle in his eyes as Jack wrestled with what to believe.

Sigmund scoffed and tossed his hands into the air. "You're risking losing your family over taking the time to verify my reports. You should be thinking about how we're going to protect everyone at the Manor. What about the family that are out on missions? Will they be targeted? How do we protect them?"

Sigmund paused as he felt a deep sense of dread well up inside him. *Isaac and Alison haven't reported back yet.*

They're still in Beignknost somewhere.

"Get me to Beignknost," Sigmund commanded suddenly, startling Jack.

"What for?" Jack asked.

"I have a family to protect, and I refuse to sit idly while you contemplate what to do. Get me there *now!*" Sigmund snarled.

Jack nodded, a portal flashing open behind Sigmund.

Sigmund paused before he stepped through. "You'd better make up your mind quickly, Jack, before it's too late. But I fear it may already be," he grumbled and disappeared through the gateway.

* * * * *

Jack was speechless as Sigmund vanished through the portal. He had seen Sigmund angry before, but nothing like this, and never directed toward him.

Is it hesitating if I verify his findings? We need to be sure before we accuse someone.

But... if this were someone else, would I have taken Sigmund's word without question?

Jack stepped out to the edge of the cliff, watching as the waves crashed against the rocks and slowly retreated back into the sea.

It was no secret that Adara was one of his favorites. They had a lot in common, after all.

They were both the only survivors of a ransacked village, with so much power at their fingertips that the Vaccars of their towns had feared them. Perhaps rightly so.

When she was younger, she even had the same bad attitude.

Jack had raised her like a daughter. He hoped that he could help prevent her from making the same mistakes that he had. He thought, at the very least, he had tried his best.

Why, then, would she betray not only him, but her entire family? It didn't make sense.

Yet, there was something in Jack that knew the truth. Adara had been gone a lot more recently, without giving him much information on where she was going. Her reports were vague and uninteresting. Nothing like her former writings. But Jack had trusted her.

And then Sigmund investigated her. Sigmund was as thorough and paranoid—or prepared, depending on who you ask—as they come. For Sigmund to present Jack with this information meant that he conducted as thorough an investigation as possible.

Sigmund had said it himself: he was never wrong.

Jack watched as an Elvish skipper—sleek and golden—glided effortlessly across the water.

But something still didn't sit right with him. He couldn't shake the feeling that something grander was at work. Adara's motivations surely couldn't be exactly aligned with this Anguis Survivor. The Survivor's motives seemed straightforward: revenge. He may even want his home back.

If Adara *is* the traitor, what are her motivations? What is it exactly that she wants?

Jack ran his hands through his hair and interlocked his fingers behind his head. If only he had more time, he might be able to dig up more information.

Sigmund was right again; however, they most likely didn't have time to spare. But with Adara gone for now, Jack had no choice but to wait for her to return to confront her. In the meantime, he would have to let everyone at the Manor know what was going on, and to have them prepare for a fight. He would have to send letters to those still out on missions giving them the same warning, but that would take some time.

A portal opened beside Jack, his study appearing on the other side. There was still more work to be done with the Orvtu as well. There was something off with it, and he needed to figure out quickly how to resolve it. And there were Sigmund's reports that he needed to go over...

Jack hesitated before stepping through the gateway, taking in the sun-speckled water and the skippers gliding across it one last time.

He passed through the portal into his study. There was much to do.

CHAPTER TWENTY-FOUR

Adara stepped into Zet's fortress for what she hoped was the last time. She was quite eager to deliver the good news to her "partner." Finally, their arrangement would come to an end, and her master would be one step closer to his return.

Adara smiled as she strode down the long dragon-rock-paved hallway, her heels clicking against the stone. Blue-flame torches blazed on the wall, making the sparkling dragon-rock twinkle like the night sky.

The poor, arrogant fool didn't know that he was simply a means to a greater end. She almost felt sorry for him.

Almost.

He should be honored, in a way, that he helped progress the world toward a better future. Even if inadvertently.

She came to his door—large, dark, and imposing—and threw it open.

He sat in a high-backed, throne-like chair with red cushions and golden arms, pushed in tightly to a dark wooden desk with scrolls sprawled out all over it. A luxurious-looking bed was pushed into one corner, and balls of magelight floated lazily around the room.

"What do you want, woman?" Zet asked flatly, not looking up from the scroll in front of him.

Adara ignored him. Not even he could trample her good mood. "Jack Grey is dying."

Zet paused and looked up, locking eyes with her. For the first time since Adara had known him, and perhaps even for only the second time in his life, Zet appeared shocked.

"What?"

Adara took a step closer to his desk and grinned. "Jack's strength is failing him. What's more, he's figured out how to use the artifact—the Orvtu, he called it. He expects to use it, and me, to beat you. However, with the Orvtu in your possession and with him at half his strength, without my help..."

"We can kill him..." He sat back in his chair. "Perhaps you're more useful than I originally thought."

Adara thought she could see a faint, tight-lipped smirk forming on his unsightly face.

"I suggest we make our move soon," Adara said, placing her hands on Zet's desk.

"For once, we agree," Zet responded. "We need to move quickly before Jack can make any solid preparations against us. Our plan remains the same, but we will attack today. As discussed, I require that you allow me and my people inside that damn bubble of his, *and* secure the orb. Are you capable of that?"

"Certainly, Zettie," Adara teased, earning her a hideous scowl from him. "And you still have him going after the kid and the girl, correct?"

"Do not address me so casually, woman," Zet snarled. "Yes, the Butcher is in position and awaiting my orders. I fail to see their importance. But then again, I do not care. I keep my bargains."

Several small portals opened up around Zet along with small balls of fire waiting beside each one. The portals slammed shut as the fireballs shot through them.

"The signal has been given," Zet said, standing from his chair and walking to the front of his desk.

"Make any last preparations you need quickly. We will be leaving shortly," he hissed, appearing suddenly more reptilian-like. "Rejoice! After today, the Grey family will cease to exist."

CHAPTER TWENTY-FIVE

Sigmund took off in a frantic, mad dash around Beign-knost, waving or nodding to people as they called out to him as he passed. He had no clue where Isaac and Alison could be, but he was bound to run into them eventually if he kept looking.

The conversation he had with Jack weighed heavily on his mind. Sigmund could understand Jack's hesitancy; part of Sigmund didn't want to believe it either. But the facts do not lie, and it is useless to resist the truth, no matter how painful it might be.

He could only hope now that Jack would make preparations to confront Adara before it was too late, if it wasn't already. However, Jack's hesitancy wouldn't stop him from saving what he could of his family. All he could do now was do the best he could.

That's all he's ever done.

Sigmund passed through the town square for perhaps a third time and, with still no sign of Isaac or Alison, decided to expand his search to the outskirts of Beignknost before circling back into town. He was relieved that, so far, he hadn't seen anything out of the ordinary. But what was worrying him was that he had not seen Isaac or Alison anywhere. They had been out on assignment in Beignknost for the past three days and had heard nothing from them since. He had even stopped to ask around, but no one had seen anyone matching their description recently.

It was quite possible that whatever their contract was was taking much longer than they expected, but Sigmund couldn't shake the dread he felt welling up inside him.

Something was wrong. He could *feel* it.

Sigmund ran through the west entrance of Beignknost and into the forest, searching along the trail in case they decided to rest off the path.

A flash of black caught the corner of his eye. Sigmund turned around just in time to catch the gleam of a short sword bearing down on his skull. Sigmund reflexively grabbed his claymore and swung it around his body, the force of his deflection knocking his attacker back.

The man was cloaked in black from head to toe, with only his eerie yellow, cat-like eyes visible through the folds of darkness that enveloped him.

A soft chuckle muffled out from behind the black cloth. "They were right: you *did* show up. No matter." His grip tightened on his short sword. "I was assigned for that very purpose."

They?

Sigmund's eyes narrowed on his attacker. Sigmund's hunch had been right: members of the family abroad were not safe. It is very likely that other Greys are facing off against an assassin of their own, sent by Adara and her compatriot. It was probably also safe to assume that, like the Temple, whoever they were fighting was most likely able to counter their magic. The last time, however, it took two of Adara's men to give Sigmund a hard time, and now they only send one.

They wouldn't make the same mistake twice.

Sigmund tightened his grip on his claymore.

What is his counter to me?

He could see a slight crease of a smile form from behind his mask as the man started to walk nonchalantly around Sigmund. Sigmund moved without hesitation, swinging his sword in a large arc, attempting to cleave him in half. Sigmund's eyes widened as the man jumped high over his slash, his sword passing harmlessly under him.

The man continued walking toward Beignknost, his stride unbroken. "I do not waste my time on already dead opponents."

What? Sigmund looked quickly around himself, and over his body, but found nothing. He had no markings, no cuts, or abrasions. Not even a hair was out of place.

A hoop of water formed around Sigmund. It churned as if it were a wave contained in a glass tube. With a flick of his hand, the water snapped out like a whip toward the figure. Again, the man leapt nonchalantly out of the way of Sigmund's attack with Elf-like agility, landing on a low branch before jumping to the next tree. Sigmund raced after him, one hand balancing the claymore on his shoulder while the other launched ice spikes at his opponent.

Yet the man kept evading his attacks, even with his back turned. He seemed to be dodging faster each time.

Or was it that he was getting slower? There was a weight to his movements, a sluggishness coming over him that was foreign to his senses.

Poison.

If he were a Pestilence Arcanist, when could he have poisoned him? He hadn't touched him, had he? At least he hadn't *felt* his touch. Nor had he touched anything that Sigmund was touching. So, if it was poison, when did it happen?

Sigmund felt panic shoot through him as the west entrance came into view beyond the tree line. He couldn't let him find Isaac and Alison.

The man nimbly landed on a tree stump and spun around to look at Sigmund.

"I commend your persistence," he said, his eyes flitting between annoyance and pity. "You have lasted longer than I thought you would. However, I can't have you following me into town..."

So he did poison me. Sigmund eyed him warily. The man jumped onto a nearby tree, disappearing from Sigmund's sight once more. Sigmund spun around, watching for any sign of movement, but he couldn't see or hear anything. Not even the leaves rustled.

Where is he...

"I was told that you were quite sharp, so I will confirm your suspicions: yes, you are getting slower, old man."

Sigmund spun around, coming nose-to-nose with his opponent.

Another smile creased the cloth covering his face. "Yes, you may as well be moving through waist-deep mud."

The man caught Sigmund's upward slash with his bare hand, as if Sigmund's strike was nothing more than a leaf blowing in the wind.

"Weaker, too," he chided, turning Sigmund's blade toward him despite Sigmund's efforts to wrench it free of his grasp.

"Look." The man pointed at a small swirling black and green dot on his claymore where their blades had clashed previously. He tapped on the sword, and cracks spread like wildfire across the claymore, before shattering into thousands of shards, leaving only a jagged, tooth-like blade near the guard.

Sigmund staggered backwards, dropping what remained of his sword as his vision began to narrow and spin. He felt a hot liquid begin to pool in his mouth. He dabbed the corner of his lip with his finger, and saw that it was smeared with blood.

Sigmund fell to his knees, all the strength in his body evaporating in an instant. Sigmund balled his hands into tight fists as he tried desperately to stand up, rejecting his body's cries to stay on the ground.

The man knelt and patted Sigmund on the back. "What you failed to realize is that, during our brief exchange, I was able to make contact with you. The moment our swords clashed, my free hand had touched yours ever so lightly. And that was all I needed. All that running you did allowed my toxin to burrow into your body faster."

Sigmund's body burned hot as hellfire. Whether that was from his rage or the poison, he wasn't sure. The man stepped over Sigmund and continued in a slow, measured manner toward Beignknost.

"You were dead as soon as you crossed swords with me."

Sigmund fell face-first into the dirt as he reached feebly after him. His vision had become a pinprick, and he could feel the pestilence magic swirling around inside of him, infecting every cell it touched. His body began to spasm uncontrollably, his limbs and head knocking against the hard earth.

He squinted hard, trying to maintain sight of the assassin.

Sigmund shuddered, and spat out a glob of blood onto the ground, coating the vibrant green grass a healthy shade of red.

He took a deep, steadying breath.

Get up.

He scoured the ground and reached shakily out to his broken claymore. He dug his sword, once proud and heavy in his grasp, hard into the dirt as he attempted to push himself to his knees. His arms and legs gave out almost immediately, sending him sprawling to the ground once more.

Get up. He spat out more blood, his vision returning slightly, but the shakiness remained. Once more, he ground his sword into the earth to try to leverage himself up, even for just a moment.

And once more, he fell.

Sigmund growled like a feral animal, every stubborn fiber of his being screaming in unison for him to stand.

To struggle.

To find his way back to his feet.

Get. Up.

Sigmund stabbed at the dirt once more and pulled himself forward with all his might. He did this several more times as he slowly crawled to the nearest tree. Each time his body moved, it felt like he was being stabbed with thousands of hot knives. His joints began to lock up, and his muscles felt as if they were going to rip clean off the bone.

But Sigmund didn't care. He had a job to do. A family to protect.

An assassin to kill.

He dug his jagged blade into the body of the tree, drawing sticky sap from the wooden wound, and grasped with desperate fingers with his free hand.

Now fucking stand up.

Sigmund groaned and heaved himself up the side of the tree, his knees buckling like a newborn calf.

Get up and get to Isaac and Alison.

He slid down the side of the tree, his sword stopping him halfway down.

Stand.

He moved his foot under him, finally finding solid ground.

Move.

Another foot found a solid hold on the spinning earth beneath him.

Sigmund stood straight up, the world like a whirling haze around him. He took a shaky step forward and almost fell to his knees again, but caught himself on the tree beside him.

Now, go kill him.

Sigmund yanked his broken weapon free from the tree's clutches and made his way to Beignknost. With each step, he felt as if his bones were going to be reduced to dust. The pain was almost unbearable.

But he could bear it. Despite the haze and the agony, Sigmund's mind had never been clearer about what he had to do.

Kill him.

Protect them.

He was going to bring them both home safely. No matter what.

Kill him.

Protect them.

I am coming, Isaac...

Kill him.

Protect them.

I am coming, Alison...

Kill.

Protect.

Just hold on.

* * * * *

"Easy does it." Isaac gently lowered another enfeebled man off the cart. They had gotten back to Beignknost surprisingly quickly, stopping only three times as they chased the stars back to the town. It was times like these that Isaac was thankful for Sigmund's insistence on learning how to navigate by the cosmos, and not always relying on a map.

He'd never say that to him though, didn't want to give him any more reasons to say he was right all the time.

Isaac joined Mikael and Alison as Alison helped Cela down out of the cart. Mikael sat, leaning against one of the wheels, his eyes heavy, with deep purple bags under them.

"Last but not least." Alison smiled as she grabbed both of Cela's hands, steadying her as she took a tentative step to the ground.

"Are you ready?" Alison asked, slinging Cela's arm around her shoulder as they began walking toward her home.

Cela nodded enthusiastically. Her health had drastically improved since they had left the old castle. The color was starting to return to her Elvish-olive skin, and she was much more alert and attentive.

Isaac offered his hand to Mikael. "C'mon, deadweight, we have a contract to complete."

Mikael smiled tiredly and grabbed Isaac's hand, standing with his aid.

Mikael looked like hell. Then again, they probably all did. They had been awake for at least two days, too fearful that if they stopped to take a break, someone would sneak up on them and capture them all again. It had been a very careful and paranoid trip back.

Alison knocked on Tom's door. Not a second later, the door swung open wildly, revealing Tom with bloodshot-eyes and wild hair. He looked like he had been awake for as long as they had. Tom's jaw went slack when he saw Cela cradled next to Alison. Tom caught Cela as she stumbled forward, wrapping her up in his massive arms in a grip so tight, it was as if he were afraid she'd blow away if he didn't hold her down. Their bodies shook with sobs and disbelieving laughter.

Isaac smiled and lightly squeezed Alison's hand. She looked at him and smiled back. He could only imagine what Tom and Cela had been going through, being separated from each other for so long, neither of them sure if they were going to see each other again. Isaac being separated from Alison during the Trials he thought was bad enough. But being taken and almost used as cattle for vampires?

He shuddered at the thought of that happening to him or Alison. But they were together again, and that's all Isaac had hoped for throughout this contract.

Job well done.

But what if... The thought chilled him, freezing him in place momentarily.

Isaac shook his head and shoved the growing chorus far into the back of his mind.

Just enjoy this moment.

Cela and Tom pulled back from their embrace.

"We cannot thank you enough," Tom said, his voice cracking.

Isaac held up a hand as Tom reached shakily into his pockets.

"No, keep it. This was payment enough," Isaac reassured.

Tom passed them all a questioning glance. "... Are you sure?"

"Absolutely," Alison agreed. "We didn't really do this for any money."

"Aye," Mikael added. "Spend it on yourselves."

"Thank you," Cela said, her voice, for the first time, clear. Her Elvish accent was light and airy, as if the wind itself were speaking.

They bade farewell to Tom and Cela and looped back toward the eastern side of town where Mikael had stabled his horse. Mikael and Alison talked at length, reflecting on the contract. Isaac tried to join in, but his mind constantly wandered elsewhere.

Back to the cold thoughts waiting for him.

"So... when would you two be willing to take on another bounty?" Mikael asked as they approached the stable, waving at the stablehand to prepare his horse. "The Venatores would be more than welcoming to the Greys."

Isaac hesitated, the chorus of thoughts growing louder, warning him away and gnawing at any shreds of confidence he might've gained from the contract.

He glanced over at Alison, who was staring back at him with determined eyes and a wicked smile, as if she were daring another challenge to come her way. When all he wanted to do was hide, she was still pushing, eager to take on the next mission.

Why was this happening? Shouldn't he be excited to take on another contract? To help more people? But instead, all he could focus on was the difference in capabilities between him and the vampires. Hell, there were even stronger ones that Isaac hadn't encountered. Would he be able to deal with those if he had to?

He doubted it. They barely survived the encounter with *this* generation of vampires, and the alchemist—if not for Alison—would've killed them all. The entire time they were there, he was struggling to find any facet of reality that he could say was under his control. Where was he supposed to apply what Jack said? If not for Alison and Mikael, he would be dead. Where's his 'sense of control' in that?

What if next time Alison and Mikael aren't there to help him? What if there are more of them? What if...

Isaac clutched at his head as thoughts ran through him like a stampede of wild horses. His chest grew tight, and his throat felt like it was beginning to close. He reached for his neck, as if to brush away a hand that was choking him.

"Isaac?" Alison's concerned face filled his vision.

Isaac blinked, looking back and forth between Mikael and Alison, both of whom exchanged worried looks with him.

"Is everything all right?" she asked, inching closer to him.

Isaac nodded hesitantly. He should tell her what he's thinking, but would she understand? She was so strong, so brave, so... like Jack. And here he was, quivering like a field mouse.

"Yeah," Isaac managed. "I'm fine. Just tired, sorry."

Mikael nodded his thanks to the stablehand as he handed off the reins to him. A large, black mare with a chest as wide as a tree and an ornate white and blue saddle trotted up beside Mikael.

"Rest up then, you two," Mikael said as he hefted himself up into the saddle, his horse neighing and shaking its head.

"Congratulations on a job well done to the both of you. We did something truly great, and I hope it inspires you to keep going," Mikael said, locking eyes with Isaac. "Many things could have gone wrong. I have seen many Venatores that have perished on their first mission, yet you both handled it masterfully. We adapted and overcame what was in front of us. As my father once told me, 'When faced with difficulty, it is your reaction that determines your outcome.' And it was your combined strengths that allowed us to succeed and free these people."

"If ever you two are looking to work together again, do not hesitate to contact me in Haentu. I will always welcome your company, and the Venatores will have seats with your names on them, I assure you. Safe travels back to your Manor, my friends."

Isaac nodded and smiled half-heartedly. "Thank you."

"Yes, thank you, Mikael. We'll be in touch, I'm sure." Alison added.

They waved as Mikael took off, kicking up dirt as he sped off toward Ahntwen, the afternoon sun at his back.

"Are you okay?" Alison stepped in front of him again, softly taking his hands.

Isaac felt his heart skip a beat. He hated making her worry.

He didn't answer.

"C'mon, Isaac, you've always been able to tell me anything. Is this about what we talked about at the party?"

Isaac nodded slowly.

"Did you talk to Jack about it? Did he help?"

"Yes, I did. I think it helped... well... maybe. I'm not sure." Isaac ran a hand anxiously through his hair.

"What do you mean?"

"I..." Isaac trailed off. "It's not that I don't think Jack's advice worked. It's just that I'm not sure how to apply it. He said to just focus on what I can control, and ignore everything else. But how am I supposed to do that when literally *nothing* has been in my control since the Temple? How am I supposed to shake this feeling if I'm always outclassed by my enemy? I don't know, maybe it's all nonsense..."

"Isaac." Alison gently cupped his face. "Just by fighting back puts you in control. You are taking an active role in what's going on around you. Sure, there were some things out of our control, but that's life. We can't be in control all the time. Just focus on the things you *can* do. And be patient with yourself. It was only the first time. I'm sure this will take time before it gets any better. Just allow yourself that time and work at it little by little each day. Eventually, you'll get there."

Isaac leaned into her hand. She sounded so much like Jack. Everything they had said made sense, but how long would he have to continue with this pit that was building in his stomach? How much longer could he endure second-guessing every move he made? Weeks? Years?

"Isaac, I'm afraid too. What happened at the Temple it... it scared me. When Sigmund and I went back there, it was like I was returning to Hell. But I made a choice. I decided that I wasn't going to let that fear stop me from doing what *I* wanted to do, and you have to do the same. It's all about your perspective. But give yourself time. As much time as you need. I'll be here to help you through it, always."

She gave him a quick kiss and hugged him tight. Isaac rested his head on top of hers and hugged her back. It was obvious now that, whatever he was dealing with, it would take some time to get over. Even Jack said that it took him a while to fully come to terms with it. So if it even took Jack some time, then he shouldn't expect himself to get over it any faster.

Part of him knew he shouldn't give any heed to the thoughts popping up in his head, but they were insidious and tantalizing. They offered him a weird sort of comfort where he thought he had none...

He turned his wrist so he could see his Magician's tattoo while still holding Alison. What was supposed to be a proud symbol of his accomplishments seemed to remind him only of how much he had failed.

How powerless he truly was.

Isaac took a deep breath. If that's how he felt now, then he would have to work toward earning it. He didn't want to feel this way, and he would continue trying, if for nothing else, for Alison. She deserved someone she could rely on. He would do his best for her.

Hopefully nothing tops the Temple. Isaac dreaded the thought. If something worse were to happen, would he be able to continue trudging forward?

He wasn't so sure.

Deal with that if it comes. Isaac reminded himself of Jack's advice. *Little by little, right?*

* * * * *

"C'mon." Alison led him by his hand. "Let's get moving. It's a couple hours' walk back home. I don't know about you, but I could use a bath."

Isaac scrunched his nose. "Is that what that smell was?"

She punched him on the arm, ignoring his cries of pain, and began leading him back through town.

Beignknost was busier than usual, with bards singing and people dancing up and down the street in eccentric costumes. Every alley they walked down displayed a banner of the six Archangels, with their likenesses emblazoned in gold. Children chased after jesters, crowding the already bustling streets.

Alison beamed as she glanced around at the decorated shops and colorful costumes. She had been so caught up in the bounty that she had forgotten what today was.

"Imputio," Isaac said, his eyes glued on a beast master with a hawk perched on his right arm.

The Day of Reckoning. The day that five Archangels gave their lives to seal away Ranatrael for all eternity, saving all mortalkind and the Divines from his tyrannical ambitions. Alison didn't care much for the history of the day—unlike Isaac, who found the Divine Civil War incredibly fascinating. No, she preferred the colors, the parties and, of course, the food. The smell of freshly baked bread and cooling pies wafted tantalizingly into her nose. They definitely had to get home soon if she wanted to have any of Jane's famous chocolate cakes. She did not want to get there after Margaret devoured them all.

Again.

An ear-piercing shriek rang out from the crowd, followed closely by the thundering sound of footsteps as people pushed past each other. The joyful, uplifting tunes quickly turned into a cacophony of shouting and the sound of people stampeding around them. A bard closest to them stopped mid-falsetto and darted off with the crowd. Alison felt like a stone amidst a river as a mass of bodies rushed past them.

Alison squinted, trying hard to see what everyone was running from. Far down the cobblestone path, she could see a man, cloaked in black, walking at an easy-going pace toward them.

Behind him were the bodies of townspeople, convulsing against the ground, clawing desperately at their throats before falling still.

The hair on the back of Alison's neck stood on end. The man looked familiar, vaguely, but from where...

The contract board!

There had been a wanted poster there, with the sketch of a man looking just like him. A Pestilence Arcanist wanted for multiple murders.

"The Butcher," Alison said breathlessly, before taking off in a sprint toward him, Isaac following closely behind and shouting after her. She winced as a hot, stabbing pain shot through her leg. Isaac had stopped the bleeding, but the muscles that had been cut were still healing and tender.

But that didn't matter. She had to stop him before he killed anyone else.

Alison locked eyes with him as they drew closer. The faint outline of a smile beneath his mask sent a chill down her spine.

He looked as if he were expecting them.

The Butcher rushed toward them, his movement a wild black blur, almost as fast as the vampires they had fought earlier. Gusts of wind rolled off Alison as she sent a blast of air at the Butcher. The ground beneath the Butcher's feet gave way and rose around him as Isaac tried to funnel him into a sort of hallway. The stone walls Isaac erected crumbled to dust as soon as the Butcher touched them, allowing him to dodge out of the way of Alison's attacks.

He bounded in between them, his hands glowing a sickly greenish-black as he swiped at the both of them.

Crap! They were too close to him to dodge in time. But if they didn't do something, they'd end up just like the other people he had killed.

What if...? Alison hit Isaac with a gale and directed another at the ground beneath her, launching her and Isaac away, narrowly missing the Butcher's grasp.

Alison's satisfaction was dashed away as she saw the Butcher looming over her as she rolled to her feet. She launched herself into the air again, streaking past the Butcher. A wall of flame erupted behind her as Isaac attempted to cut the Butcher off from them. Alison rolled as she hit the ground, slamming into the town well. She cried out as she felt something in her shoulder pop.

She'd have to learn how to land if she wanted to continue to move around like that.

"Are you okay?" Isaac asked, helping her to her feet.

Alison nodded and scanned the courtyard. The Butcher was nowhere in sight. Did he abandon them for his true target? Did they present too much of a hassle for him to kill?

Her gaze fell upon a hole in the ground opposite the fire as she felt the earth beneath her crumble to dust. She and Isaac stumbled and fell as the Butcher shot up from beneath them, his glowing hands poised to strike.

The sound of rushing water roared down an alleyway moments before a tidal wave crashed into the courtyard they were in. The water churned and raced toward the Butcher, slamming into him like a battering ram and carrying him away until he was out of sight down the street.

What was that?

She looked over at Isaac, whose eyes were fixed on something behind her. Alison raised herself onto her knees and turned around, her breath catching in her throat at the sight of him.

It was Sigmund.

No, it couldn't be him. This was just an old man with a white beard dyed red, his skin a sickly green and sagging as if it were slowly falling off the bones. His eyes were dark and sunken, and his sword was broken, hanging limply in one hand.

"S-Sigmund?" Isaac's voice cracked.

That can't be him. Alison tried to reason.

It can't be...

Sigmund leaned weakly against the side of a house, pushing himself into the middle of the street. He shambled toward them unnaturally, as if he were a puppet on strings.

"Out of my way," Sigmund grumbled.

"Sigmund, what's going on?" Alison questioned, standing and starting toward him.

Sigmund held up his hand, stopping her, and continued to walk by them, his body shuddering with every step. "Pestilence Arcanist," he said simply, and then added, "Elf."

"They had warned me that you would be difficult," the Butcher said, dropping down from a nearby rooftop. His clothes tattered and his mask stripped away, revealing a handsome face.

"Leave," Sigmund barked. "Go back to the Manor and warn Jack that it's started."

Alison's jaw dropped. He couldn't be serious. He had to know what kind of shape he was in. Did he really expect them to just leave him here?

"Sigmund, don't be an idiot!" Alison protested. "Let us help you."

"Leave!" Sigmund commanded, turning his head to look at them out of the corner of his eye. "Now! Tell him Adara has enacted her plan."

Adara? What on earth did she have to do with this?

Alison was about to protest further, but Isaac stopped her.

"Alison..." Isaac grabbed her shoulder, his eyes never leaving Sigmund. "If something is happening, we need to get back and tell Jack."

Alison couldn't believe what she was hearing. How could Isaac be okay with this? She wasn't going anywhere. They were going to stay here and kill this bastard, *and then* they were *all* going back to the manor. She wasn't about to abandon Sigmund and leave him to die alone.

She closed her mouth as she was about to speak, locking eyes with Sigmund. His usual discontentment had been completely replaced by the pleading eyes of a dying man. In them she could see that he was begging for them to save themselves and to let him finish this.

He wanted to protect the kids he helped raise one last time.

Sigmund turned back to face the Butcher, his sadistic smile reaching his eyes.

"Go," Sigmund grumbled once more. "Go and do not come back here. Do you understand?"

Alison didn't like it, but she didn't have much room to argue. If something else really was going on, someone had to tell Jack. Sigmund had given them one more mission, and she didn't want to let him down.

Goodbye, Sig. We love you.

* * * *

Sigmund glanced behind him, catching a glimpse of Isaac and Alison as they disappeared around the corner.

Run... Run back as fast as you can.

He turned back to face the Butcher. Sigmund's body trembled. The tremors were getting worse.

He didn't have much time left.

The Butcher moved to dart around Sigmund but, much to his surprise, Sigmund cut him off.

The Butcher leapt onto a low roof and ran toward Isaac and Alison. A pool of water exploded beneath Sigmund's feet, shooting him toward the Butcher. The Butcher threw himself to one side and rolled along the shingles and off the roof, back onto the street.

Sigmund growled. Water spun around him like a whirlpool as he ripped the moisture from the air and condensed it around himself. Waves of water rolled away from Sigmund, rushing after the Butcher like a stormy sea, with Sigmund at its epicenter. The water crashed through buildings, ripping doors from their hinges and tearing smaller stone buildings apart.

He would not let him get away.

"I see, old man," the Butcher yelled as he nimbly jumped from building to building. "You're using the water in your body to pull yourself along like a marionette, even as your body fails. Very clever."

A wall of ice rose to meet the Butcher just as he was about to jump to the next house, a barrage of ice shards shooting out from the wall like archers on a battlement. The Butcher backpedaled in surprise, diving behind a chimney to try to dodge the shards. The chimney was quickly ripped to shreds by the icy onslaught, and the ice shards found their mark. The Butcher cried out as several shards impaled him, his body becoming covered in a dense patch of ice, freezing him in place.

Sigmund joined the Butcher on the roof, puppeteering his body limply over to him.

The Butcher cackled as Sigmund approached, his head the only thing not completely frozen. "Stubborn indeed. Ha! At the very least, I—"

Sigmund drove the shattered remains of his claymore through the Butcher's skull, his head lolling forward lifelessly.

The water around Sigmund subsided, the moisture returning to the air as he slid shakily down the outside wall of a nearby building. He had caused quite a bit of destruction chasing after him. There was a mess of wooden beams and stones scattered everywhere, as if a tornado had ripped through Beignknost.

Sigmund grunted and spat up more blood. He'd raze entire kingdoms if it meant saving them.

I hope it's not too late.

He gazed off toward the afternoon sky. Everything seemed so vibrant now. Had the approaching evening sun always been this beautiful?

Sigmund shivered. His entire body felt like it was on fire yet, at the same time, he felt cold.

So incredibly cold.

Even that gorgeous sun beaming down failed to warm him now.

His vision turned a glassy red, and soon the entire world was ablaze with crimson before going dark completely.

Isaac...

Alison...

Margret...

Jane...

Jack...

Images of them popped into his head one by one.

Sigmund grunted as his body convulsed, his head rolling back to touch the cool stone wall behind him.

The rest is yours...
Be well.

CHAPTER TWENTY-SIX

Jack set down the orb in frustration. His desk was a mess of letters and unfurled parchment and, at the center, was the Orvtu, glowing a bright, indignant white.

Jack had spent the last several hours pouring over Sigmund's exchanges and working more with the Orvtu. During that time, he had discovered two things. First, Sigmund had been right to suspect Adara. After reading the communications he had between their contacts—especially Kenna—, confirming she had not been where she said she was, Jack couldn't really find any argument to be had against Sigmund's conclusion.

It certainly seemed like Adara was the traitor.

But he could do nothing about that until she returned home. She should be back in a few hours, but if she were the traitor, she certainly wouldn't come alone. Not after everything she had learned today.

But his family would be prepared. He owed Sigmund that much.

Jack ran his hands through his short hair, eyeing the Orvtu. If one problem weren't enough, the Orvtu wasn't responding as he anticipated. Normally, the Ancient One's items responded to some type of magic. In the Orvtu's case, it was Aura magic. Which, admittedly, was a strange magic to react to. Regardless, the Orvtu came to life, and Jack could immediately feel the pull of the dense magic inside the orb. It felt as if the Orvtu had latched onto him, slowly draining his strength. It was clear that, once activated by the user, the Orvtu operated like a parasite, feeding off its host while providing them with unfathomable amounts of power.

However, the problem was that it didn't seem to stop. As long as Jack wasn't touching it, he was reasonably sure he was safe since he didn't feel the pull on his strength anymore. But no matter what he did, the Orvtu would not stop glowing.

Moreover, it seemed to be glowing brighter.

Jack shook his head and left his study. Hopefully, a few moments of reprieve would provide him with some clarity.

He ambled down the hall, smiling as he passed each door. He never could have imagined that when he first started the Grey family, it would take shape in the way that it had. The Greys had become more than just a group that supported his mission. It had turned into a place where the wayward sons and daughters of the world could call home.

Rose would be proud. Jack's smile grew at the thought. It was always Rose's dream to see Vaccars and Arcanists standing arm-in-arm once more. Now, thanks to the Greys, that dream was becoming a reality. Sure, there were still people who held onto their rigid beliefs of Arcanists being evil, but it is impossible to eliminate such prejudice completely. Generally though, it seemed the world was finally healing after the damage done by the Ancient Ones all those thousands of years ago.

He was honored to have played a small part in it.

Jack's mind slipped to his conversation with Isaac as he passed his room, his door slightly ajar, revealing a mess of haphazardly thrown dirty clothes and an unmade bed. Jack chuckled and shut the door. No matter how many times Alison, Jane, or Sigmund prodded him to clean his room—even standing over him and watching him sometimes—it always ended up looking like a tornado had run through it.

I wonder how he and Alison are doing now?

After their conversation, Isaac seemed to understand at some level what Jack was saying. Jack knew it would take some time for the lesson to truly sink in, and he also knew that Isaac's impatience would probably make things much more difficult. But he hoped that by Isaac taking on bounties by himself that it would help bolster his confidence.

The Temple had understandably shaken him. Realizing how vulnerable you truly are can be a frightening thing. It can take some time to overcome that.

Isaac was a smart, capable young man who could face down any challenge he set his mind to. He just had to see that for himself.

"*JACK!*" A pain-filled voice cried out from the foyer.

Adara?

Jack raced to the entrance, the blood draining from his face as he caught sight of her, battered and bloodied, lying on the floor, her breathing fits of wheezing gasps.

The worries he had earlier melted away as he knelt beside her, trying to heal her wounds. It couldn't be Adara now. Why would the Survivor have attacked her like this if she were working with him?

Jack's eyebrows furrowed together. Her wounds weren't closing.

Adara clutched at Jack's cloak. "I—he found me, Jack. I don't know how, but... he cut me with something, and I can't heal the wounds..." She choked out through raspy breaths.

"It's all right, Adara." Jack picked her up, cradling her like a child, smiling warmly. "Let's get you to the medical ward, and I'll take care of you there. Don't worry, we'll figure this out."

* * * * *

She smiled weakly back at him.

Adara wasted no time in slowly removing the small knife she had hidden in her sleeve, the cloth she had wrapped around it falling away as she grabbed the handle. Even though it wasn't touching her directly, she certainly felt sicker with the anti-magic knife being so close to her.

The knife had been one of the very few suggestions Zet had ever offered that she agreed with. While the Orvtu might've helped secure their victory before, and even more so now with Jack's weakened state. The knife served as an insurance policy to ensure that Jack would be rendered too enfeebled to put up a fight.

Adara spun the knife, angling it behind his shoulder blade. As she brought the knife down into Jack's flesh, she knew she was doing more than just killing the man who had been like a father to her. She knew she was doing more than destroying the people she had once called a family.

She was severing her ties to them forever.

If only he had listened to me.

Adara thought she had seen all the cruelty the world was capable of when her town was burned to the ground by Orx invading from Aesus. But as she grew older and traveled, she learned that she had been wrong.

No, the world was much more unfair and unforgiving than she had previously imagined.

Since the day her first home was reduced to cinders, Adara had a single-minded focus on eliminating anyone like the Orx by any means necessary.

Forever.

No more pain.

No more suffering.

She wanted to create a paradise across Eutrox.

She thought that Jack had thought like her, sharing the same lofty ambition.

But no.

He was content to watch history repeat itself.

For the past two hundred years, it has always been the same.

Go here.

Help these people.

Leave.

Something bad happens.

Go back again.

Over and over again she'd see the same damn towns and villages, helping the same people with similar problems. Yet, despite all his power, Jack refused to make a permanent change. To step up and bring everyone in line.

"I understand where you're coming from," Jack had said, smiling at her. "But I'd argue that's not the most effective method for change. Giving people something to hope for, bringing them light into what they think is a dark world. I'd argue *that's* the proper way."

His blatant disregard for reality still burned deep in her mind. Jack's dismissal of her plea was more than just him shooting down her goals, but it was a direct slight against her. That was the moment when she knew that Jack did not care enough to truly help the world. No, he was content playing the hero. But she knew she couldn't achieve her goals alone.

That's when a voice had reached out to her.

Quiet at first, like a whisper, but the more she paid attention to it, the louder it became.

In her mind, she could see the world that he—*they*—so desperately sought and promised that, with her help, he could make it a reality.

He had been waiting for someone like her who would be strong enough to help him, and she eagerly agreed to execute his plans to shape the world in their image.

Finally, she felt like she was following her true purpose.

But something stood in their way. A mortal powerful enough that, if he were to catch wind of her master's plans, he would do everything in his power to stop them.

So, Jack had to die.

Her master and his compatriots couldn't move openly without drawing unwanted attention to themselves, so he arranged for Adara and Zet to meet. He had brilliantly used Zet's quest for revenge to take a powerful player off the board, allowing for Adara to retrieve the dragon heart artifact and his nephew unimpeded.

So it was with this simple act that she would set in motion the first part of his plan, laying the foundation for a better world that *she* would help shape.

Adara jammed the knife as deep as she could behind Jack's shoulder and, with a hard heave and a quick burst of blue flame, snapped the handle off, leaving the blade stuck inside him. Jack howled in pain and dropped her. She landed on her feet, the illusion she had put around herself to appear injured fading away.

He whirled around, eyes wide with shock, as he dug desperately for the blade with his fingers.

"Zet," Adara said calmly, smiling. "I invite you."

A purple and black light flashed briefly next to Adara, replaced by a tall, gray-skinned man with black eyes.

"Jack," Zet snarled as an ethereal wolf-like beast appeared before him. The beast charged at Jack, fire crackling under its fur. It slammed into him and crashed through the wall, Jack and the beast both disappearing outside.

"Find the artifact and deliver it to me quickly," Zet instructed as he followed after his pet. "I will keep him occupied until then."

Adara took off in a mad dash down the hallway toward the artifact room. She would stop there first on her way to his study. Jack had annoyingly warded off any teleportation into the artifact room, save for himself, so getting in and out quickly wasn't an option. However, Zet should be able to hold off Jack until she found what she needed. After all, he was weaker *and* had the knife in him. Surely, Zet could handle that.

Adara smiled as she heard the crackle of portals being opened all over the manor, with Zet's men streaming in by the hundreds. The air was filled with the electric tingle of magic as, much to Adara's surprise, Zet's men were quickly engaged by the Greys.

Sigmund must've warned him... And Jack actually listened. Perhaps he's not a complete fool.

No matter. She thought as Greys streamed by her. Despite Jack heeding Sigmund's warning, no one had even given her a second look. Jack must've warned them only to be ready, but not for whom. This meant she'd have all the time in the world to find the dragon heart artifact, retrieve the Orvtu, and disappear without a trace.

There! She threw the door of the artifact room open. It was the only room in the house without a marking on the door. The room was dimly lit and lined with glass shelves and cabinets, with a single bookcase crammed into the back of the room with rolled-up parchment neatly stacked on each shelf.

The dragon heart artifact was nowhere in sight.

She began frantically pulling out drawers and knocking over other artifacts in her whirlwind search. Some—delicate and ancient—cracked or shattered as they toppled to the ground.

Where is it? Her pulse pounded in her skull as desperation began to settle in. She'd spent too much time here. She hadn't been in this room in a while, but had assumed the dragon heart would be easy to locate. Adara had to find it quickly before—

"Adara?" a voice called behind her.

Adara froze, slowly turning to face Margaret, who stood in the doorway, looking as pissed off as ever.

"What are you doing here?" she asked, her arms folded across her chest.

"Jack sent me in to retrieve one of the artifacts." She smiled, trying to think quickly. "He said it'd help push the intruders out. Would you mind helping me find it? I'm in a bit of a hurry."

"Horseshit," Margaret spat as she strode into the room, coming nose-to-nose with Adara. "No way Jack would have you rummaging through here when *you* could be out there helping, while I'm supposed to move the artifact room to a secure location. So what are you *really* after?"

No sense in hiding it now. Adara smirked as her shadow extended toward Margaret's, a solid patch of darkness connecting them. Margaret attempted to move, but was stuck fast to the floor.

"Now, be good and keep that sharp tongue of yours locked tight while I look for something," Adara said, turning away from her.

Adara saw a flash of purple and black as she was teleported outside of the Grey Manor.

"What?!" she screamed in disbelief, her voice lost in the cacophony of the battle that had spilled outside. Screams of pain or elation echoed all around her, accompanied by the bitter, metallic scent of blood that stung the back of her throat. Her body seemed to vibrate in response to the intense, constant hum of magic in the air. Parts of the Manor were already on fire, smoke billowing up in thick, black clouds high into the sky, blocking out the setting sun as if it were night.

In the distance, she could hear what she assumed was Zet and Jack fighting, the ground trembling with every clash of their magic.

Even weakened, he fights like a dragon.

She hurried back into the artifact room, slipping in and out of her portal seamlessly. Margaret stood there waiting for her.

"I did not know you were strong enough to use magic while shadow stitched," Adara mocked. "And here I thought you were nothing more than a Sorcerer."

"Just shows how little you fucking know." Margaret spat a fat glob of saliva at Adara. "I never did like you. Always seemed to be slinking around like a lost puppy looking for its owner. Seems like you've found your master, like a good bitch."

Adara felt the heat rise in her cheeks.

How dare *she speak to me this way.*

Did she forget who I *am?*

That arrogant little sh—

Adara inhaled deeply.

Focus. She had to get rid of Margaret before she moved the artifact room, or else she risked the artifacts being out of reach without more serious intervention. She also had to get to Jack's study and get the Orvtu for Zet. If Jack were somehow able to turn the tides before she could get Zet the orb, the entire plan would fall apart.

Adara gritted her teeth. She refused to let that happen.

Electricity crackled around Adara, lightning arcing off her body as she closed the distance between her and Margaret.

The room suddenly filled with opening and closing portals as Margaret slipped between them. The electricity raced after Margaret, following her through a portal only to be redirected back at Adara. Adara cursed, diverting her own lightning away from her. Electricity continued to arc around the room, chasing after Margaret as Adara froze the moisture in the air, creating tiny dagger-like shards of ice. She whipped these ice shards around like a blizzard, hoping to catch Margaret as she appeared from a portal.

More gateways opened around Adara, the ice shards disappearing through them.

Adara fell through a portal that opened beneath her, spitting her out above where she had just been.

What the hell?

There was a flash of black and purple light out of the corner of Adara's eyes followed by the hard pressure of knuckles smashing into her cheek. Her head whipped backwards as a second punch landed, blood spurting from her now-broken nose.

Another flash, and she was hit in the head with something heavy.

Another flash, and she felt her ribs crack against the blow.

Adara tumbled to the ground, the remains of her ice shards falling around her, and the electricity dying as she was pummeled by an endless volley of blows.

Clever little girl. Adara mused. *Using portals in this manner to overwhelm an opponent. Well done.*

Another flash came from her left but, this time, Adara was ready for it. Adara opened a portal of her own as a table leg, decorated in her hair and blood, swung through her portal and back into the one it came from. Adara heard the heavy thwack as the leg hit Margaret, followed by the leg clattering against the floor.

Adara stood shakily and eyed Margaret limping to a corner of the room. Adara stepped through a portal and appeared behind Margaret. As Adara raised her hand, a wave of water came up from the floor and slammed Margaret into the ceiling. Another portal opened behind Margaret, and beside Adara, as Margaret hoped to redirect the water back at Adara. Adara turned calmly, the waves maneuvering around her as they still carried Margaret. Adara sent electricity skittering along the waves, like snakes slithering along a river.

Margaret spasmed as she tried desperately to form another portal, each one flickering out of existence before it could be fully formed. Adara's electrified current curled around Margaret in a cocoon, suffocating and electrocuting her. Adara watched with quiet glee as Margaret's body violently jerked inside her watery prison.

The mana around her felt alive as they exacted their will upon it. It was as if the air itself were on fire, and Adara *loved* the sensation of this heat. It made her feel powerful.

Unstoppable.

Adara felt something wrap tightly around her throat before she was yanked hard backwards out of the room. She crashed through the outer wall of the manor and was slammed into the dirt. Whatever was wrapped around her neck pierced her skin like a wolf's fangs. She grabbed at the rope-like material around her neck, slicing her fingers open on the razor-sharp metal teeth.

Jane stepped through the hole Adara had just been thrown through, her whip held firmly in her hand. Adara's eyes slid to Margaret, who was recovering slowly on the floor, coughing up water and shuddering uncontrollably.

"Jane," Adara hissed. "Always have been Margaret's keeper."

Jane looked at Adara sadly. "I am so disappointed in you," she said as she joined Adara outside.

"Breaks my heart to hear that," Adara retorted.

"Margaret, I do not mean to rush you, but you had better move that room soon," Jane said. "I will give you as much time as this old body can muster."

Margaret gasped and nodded at Jane. Purple and black light appeared waveringly around Margaret like an aura before slowly expanding out and starting to cover the room.

No! Adara attempted to teleport to Margaret, but was quickly yanked back by Jane's whip, its teeth slicing into her skin. A layer of ice formed between Adara's neck and the serrated whip, pushing the teeth out of Adara's skin as the ice expanded, allowing her to slip out of its grasp. She teleported back into the room and was met by a large, imposing snake-like creature with a thick, feathery body and a leathery yellow dewlap.

The Sylin lunged for Adara's throat, missing by mere inches as it passed through her portal to the other side of Eutrox. Another creature, panther-like with orange fire burning visibly in its belly, appeared beside her. The Puntar's mouth glowed white-hot as it spat a torrent of roasting fire at her. She dove to the side, only to be met by the snake again. Adara leapt backwards, narrowly dodging the Sylin, Puntar, and Jane's thrashing whip.

Everywhere she appeared, the Sylin and Puntar were there to meet her, followed closely behind by Jane's whip.

The artifact room was almost entirely coated in teleportation magic now.

Adara cursed. She was running out of time. The longer she spent here, the more she put the plan in jeopardy. She would *not* be the reason why this plan failed.

She would have to rethink her strategy. If she couldn't get the artifact now, perhaps she could ensure she could later. It would change the plan a bit, but he would understand, wouldn't he?

Adara teleported back to the room again, the ground behind her splitting and heaving upwards as a thick stone wall rose from the depths of the fissure, separating Adara from Jane and her pets.

Margaret and the artifact room were a shimmering mess of purple and black, with the protection runes that Jack had placed on it swirling ethereally in the air, like leaves gliding across a pond. Adara placed her hand flat against one wall of the now mostly transparent room. In her mind, she searched her Encitary, the internal book of enchantments that housed all of an Enchanter or Omnis Arcanist's knowledge over their lifetimes. She hurriedly flipped through the Encitary's yellowed pages, years of enchantments blurring by her mind's eye in moments as she scoured it for the proper enchantment.

There.

In her mind, she could see a set of glowing blue runes, twisting, jagged, and primitive. The Encitary fell away from her vision as the same runes appeared briefly beneath her palms before joining the swirling sea of Jack's runes.

Adara knew that she couldn't break the enchantments that Jack had placed on the room. And she was too late to stop Margaret from teleporting away. However, she *could* stop anything from leaving the room and prevent it from being moved again.

While it would still be difficult to locate given the concealment enchantments, she made her odds that much better. What's more, she effectively made Margaret a prisoner of the room she so desperately wanted to protect.

I'll be coming for you. Adara smiled as Margaret and the room disappeared in a blinding flash of purple and black light.

Adara ducked as a set of talons cut the air just above her head. Another of Jane's creatures, a Hutak—a hawk-like creature, with blue and purple feathers, electricity crackling through its wings.

The Sylin and Puntar burst through the stone wall Adara had created, and they quickly bounded after her. The Hutak screeched from above and dove again, talons grabbing and slashing like swords, lightning crashing with every flap of its wings. Water appeared around Adara, violently churning as the whirlpool rose high into the sky and expanded around her, catching the creatures as they closed in on her before throwing them some distance away.

Jane's whip tore through Adara's vortex, wrapping around her left arm and nearly cutting her to the bone. Adara felt a strong pull as she was brought to her knees, the whip gnawing deeper into her skin. The whirlpool around her faltered as Adara's concentration broke momentarily.

Adara clutched at the whip, ignoring the hot pain and warm blood dripping down her hands, and sent a powerful jolt of electricity up the length of it. She could feel it as it reached Jane, the whip thrashing briefly before it relaxed. She slipped out of the metal and teleported over to Jane. More of Jane's pets—a lion made of ice and a bear carved from stone—greeted Adara as she stepped through the portal.

Adara scowled. *How many of these fucking things does she have?*

As the Icleo and the Rizlear lunged, Adara reached out to the Domustiar, the dimension of monsters hidden to all but Conjurers and Omnis Arcanists, using the mana around her to create a gateway to it. In her mind, she could see a doorway forming, glowing a wispy, ethereal blue, with tendrils of light curling off it like smoke from a fire. The only thing separating the Domustiar from the rest of existence was a pane of equally blue glass that took up the entire doorway.

On the other side, Adara could just make out the gentle dance of tall grass kissed by a breeze she could neither feel nor hear. It was dark in the Domustiar, the sky-blue glass giving everything a haunting, otherworldly glow. She placed her hand against the glass and shuddered as the cold wall of magic that kept the Domustiar isolated shot through her, feeling as if ice had formed in her veins.

"I came to call upon a contract," Adara said. "Swiltoc, I summon you to me."

The Domustiar faded away from her vision as the Icleo and the Rizlear were caught by long, monstrous tentacles. The Icleo roared, ice forming down the length of the tentacle, but it quickly melted away. The Rizlear clawed and gnashed, its body covered in razor-sharp points like a porcupine, but the tentacle remained undeterred.

Adara smiled as her creature, a large, octopus-bodied beast with black and yellow stripes and two snarling heads—one a wolf and the other a shark—smashed Jane's pets into oblivion.

Jane was up now and desperately summoning more creatures to combat Adara's Swiltoc, while defending them with her whip. But the Swiltoc, with its twenty appendages, was more than capable of dealing with Jane and her summons. Each creature Jane summoned was smashed mercilessly into the ground. Stone spikes shot up from under Jane, almost piercing her legs. Jane deftly danced backwards as Adara continued her assault. Jane spun, her whip slicing into one of the Swiltoc's tentacles as it tried to destroy another of her beasts.

As Jane turned to maneuver around more of Adara's spikes, one of the Swiltoc's tentacles slammed into her, sending her careening through the wall of the manor. The Swiltoc smashed its arm against Jane repeatedly like it was beating against a drum, kicking up a cloud of dirt and debris.

Adara held up her hand, halting the Swiltoc, as she strode over to Jane, her whip lying some feet away from where she now lay. Her body was bloody and shrunken, her breathing coming in short, wheezy gasps for air.

"Adara..." Jane wheezed. "How co—"

Fire erupted from Adara's fingertips, engulfing Jane in an inferno.

The sound of the roaring flames almost drowned out Jane's final screams of pain as she thrashed helplessly about.

Jane fell still. Her body a charred, unrecognizable mess.

The Swiltoc slowly vanished back into the Domustiar, along with Jane's creatures as she died.

Adara staggered and leaned against the wall, her vision narrowing and nausea hitting her so strongly she could barely stop herself from vomiting. She took a steadying breath and began to slowly heal her wounds. There was not one inch of her body that did not ache, especially her arm, which Jane had almost successfully severed.

Fuck that old bitch. Adara spat on Jane's charcoal corpse.

This was not the outcome she, or her master, had hoped for. But she did what she could to salvage the mission. That was what's important, right? If the plan changes, adapt with it?

Did I fail him? Will he be upset with me?

She shook her head. He wasn't one to get angry, even over something of this magnitude. She made the best of the situation she was in, so she knew he'd understand that.

As for the others... The other two would not be so forgiving.

But fuck them. She didn't need their approval.

Only his.

Adara looked out of the hole in the wall and watched as Zet's men continued to clash with the Grey family. Desecrated bodies and pools of blood littered the grounds like macabre decorations.

Speaking of Zet... Adara had wasted enough time trying to get the damn dragon heart artifact. She had to at least make good on her arrangement with Zet so they could kill Jack. If he were left alive, the entire plan could fall apart. She hobbled through the Manor, through the rubble, and into Jack's study, snatching the Orvtu and Jack's notes off his desk.

Now to find that dragon freak and be done with him.

CHAPTER TWENTY-SEVEN

Jack was too stunned to move as the beast Zet had summoned carried him straight through the walls of the Manor and out into the forest, thrashing him about as they went. Even though it happened right in front of him, and the evidence Sigmund had gathered pointed to it, he *still* didn't want to believe it. Right until the end, he had hoped that Sigmund was wrong this one time. He'd have to apologize to him once he dealt with Zet.

Blue flames ignited around Jack and spread quickly over the creature's body. The monster roared and dropped Jack into the dirt as it flailed about, trying to snuff out the flame. The fire burned hotter, turning almost white, before the beast fell still and disappeared back into the Domustiar.

Intense pain shot through Jack's back, almost bringing him to his knees. He sucked in air sharply as he dug his fingers into the wound, desperately trying to rip the blade out. Jack leaned against a tree and panted, his arm swinging back down to his side, fingers glistening with blood.

No luck. He couldn't get a good grip on it.

What felt like cold jolts of electricity shot through him, radiating from the wound. His hands began to shake, and he felt simultaneously cold and warm as the anti-magic slowly cut off his connection to the mana around him.

He had to figure out a way to get this knife out of him. The longer one stays near anti-magic, the stronger the anti-magic's poisonous aura becomes. If too much time passed...

Jack shook his head. He couldn't worry about what-ifs. He knew what he had to do.

A giant ball made of jagged rocks suddenly parted the clouds above him, treelines flattening as it exerted a tremendous amount of air pressure as it approached. Jack reached a hand out to the ball. The wind whipped around him as he slashed at the stone with sharp gusts of wind, slicing the giant rock into millions of tiny pebbles.

"We finally meet."

Jack turned around to face the gray-skinned man he had seen moments ago, small stones still falling like rain.

"I hope it has become quite clear what I am here to accomplish, Jack," Zet said, clasping his hands behind his back.

Jack was taken aback by his formality. While his appearance was much more akin to that of an animal, he spoke with a royal-like pointedness.

"You killed my family many years ago," Zet continued, his voice growing in intensity as he spoke. "You took my home from me. These are transgressions I simply cannot allow to go unaddressed."

"Your family were monsters," Jack said. "The people of Drahkul were your slaves. You murdered dragons. You exercised your power in ways *I* couldn't allow."

Zet stomped his foot on the ground, and a large fissure opened beneath Jack. Jack teleported himself away, only to be met by Zet wielding a crackling bolt of lightning like a spear. Jack called lightning into his own hand and slammed it into Zet's spear, creating an explosion that sent them flying backwards away from each other, the trees around them bending as a thunderous boom shook the area.

Jack tumbled through the air and teleported himself back to the ground before slamming into a tree, stumbling only slightly as he caught his footing. He could see Zet recovering some distance away. Jack could already tell from just that brief exchange that whatever ritual the Anguis had performed on him had been well worth the risk. He absolutely reeked of power.

The air shimmered behind Zet as a large, gorilla-like creature with a pearly-white exoskeleton and yellow, pulsating light that raced all over its body appeared. The Apgor roared and pounded its fists together before taking off at a sprint toward him. Jack summoned his Weltur from the Domustiar, a wolf-like creature with three heads, a long barbed tail, and bat-like wings, and sent it bounding after the Apgor, the two beasts crashing into each other with animalistic fury.

Zet and Jack clashed relentlessly in a maelstrom of elemental magics, as Zet sent a sea of water crashing down around Jack, only to be evaporated away by a ring of blue flames so hot that the ground around them started to smoke and boil. A wave of shadows slithered underneath Jack before rising up around his ankles, clawing at him with the desperate hands of the abyss as they tried to drag him down into darkness. Jack placed his hands down against the shadows as they grabbed at his arms, pulling an enchantment from his Encitary. Two runes composed of several horizontal lines intersecting two circles lit up a bright blue on the black, shadowy canvas. Beams of white light shot out from the runes in an explosion of light, scattering the shadows away from him.

Jack dodged nimbly backwards before teleporting away as Zet struck at him, his hands dripping in the sickly glow of pestilence magic. Zet chased after him, and the two went back and forth, teleporting after the other, their magic clashing in bright flashes of power. Jack thought he could hear the mana around them scream as they exercised their wills on the world. Every time they collided, space seemed to quiver as the ground heaved and split, trees incinerated, and ash fell like snow from the sky.

And with each exchange, Jack could feel his strength beginning to buckle. His shakes were becoming more intense, and he could barely hold himself upright. Zet swatted at Jack with his pestilence-covered hands. Jack ducked and raised his abjuration magic between them reflexively to block the strike.

As Zet's attack met Jack's barrier, Jack was forced to his knees as a large crack went through his shield. Jack dropped his barrier as Zet blasted him with hurricane-force winds that sent him flying through the desecrated forest. Jack tumbled in the air for a few moments before summoning an air current to catch himself. When he landed, he fell to his knees, his vision beginning to narrow as the knife burned hotter in his back.

Jack panted; the smoke-filled air stung his throat and made his eyes water. The once ancient forest that surrounded his home had been reduced to ash and dirt, with what little trees that remained either charred and cracked or still burning. He could hear his family battling against the men Zet had brought in the distance. The Manor was in shambles. The smoke rising from the battlefield almost completely blocked what little evening sunlight there was left.

Jack gritted his teeth and forced himself shakily to his feet.

"You are frustratingly resilient." Zet stared out at the charred landscape, his lips curling into a snarl. "But, I should expect as much from the man who could've been Archmage. Can you feel it, Jack? The tightening around your throat as the hand of fate seizes hold of you, forcing you to face the consequences of your actions... Me."

The air shimmered like heat waves next to Zet as another Zet appeared next to him.

And then another appeared.

And another until there were a handful of Zets standing before Jack. Jack eyed each of them carefully as illusions of himself appeared next to him to match Zet's. Jack rushed at the Zets, his illusions following suit as he searched for the true Zet.

Jack threw himself backwards as a lightning bolt screamed past him. Another Zet appeared to his right, blue fire erupting from his mouth. The earth shot up in front of Jack in a protective half-circle around him, the Zet bathing his wall in intense flames. Jack teleported behind the Zet, fire igniting in his own hands as he slammed his fist into the back of that Zet's skull. The illusion flickered before disappearing in wisps of sensationless mist.

Jack stumbled forward as he felt something needle-like pierce his back. He teleported away and looked back to see another Zet with a long bone extending from his finger, the tip covered in blood.

Another Zet appeared on his left, unleashing a torrent of hurricane-force wind at Jack. As Jack raised another stone wall to protect himself, another Zet appeared at his side. Jack saw the blue flash of a rune activating before he was hit by a violent explosion that sent him careening through the wall he had just created. Jack landed in the dirt some feet away, the earth under him suddenly withering away, oozing and becoming almost liquid.

Pestilence! Jack cursed, teleporting himself away, only to be met by the Apgor that Zet had summoned earlier. The creature raised its giant arm and smacked Jack hard into the dirt before kicking him across the forest like a ball.

The world spun as Jack pinwheeled across the forest, coming to a stop against the remains of a tree. He pushed himself up and coughed into his hand. He winced as he felt the wet squelch of blood hit his palm. The Apgor paced back and forth in front of him. His Weltur lay off in the distance, whimpering and struggling to stand.

The Weltur disappeared in a haze back to the Domustiar.

Go home girl, you've done your best.

Jack convulsed as the pestilence Zet had placed took hold. His exposed flesh became inflamed and fell away as if his skin were being melted. Jack tried to heal while he could, but combating Zet's magic would take more time than he had.

A line of Zets appeared beside the Apgor. All of Jack's illusions had been beaten by Zet's, leaving Jack exposed and still unsure which of the Zets in front of him, if any, was the real one.

I'll just have to keep taking them out until the real one appears.

Jack's breath caught in his throat as Adara appeared behind the line of Zets in a flash of purple-black light.

Holding the Orvtu and his notebook.

And she was injured. He could just barely make out a circle around her bicep where something had cut into it deeply. The rest of her was caked with blood and dirt, her hair a matted mess. He and Adara locked eyes briefly, her appearance changing as they did back to her usual, un-injured self.

Adara, who did you fight to look like that?

Who did you kill?

Another Zet appeared next to Adara, taking the Orvtu from her.

"No!" Jack yelled, teleporting to them, attempting to snatch the Orvtu out of Zet's grasp. But Zet was faster, his illusions appearing around him, vines and shadows shooting up from the earth and wrapping around Jack's body like chains before throwing him backwards away from Zet.

Jack tumbled in the air before teleporting back to Zet. His illusions and Adara had disappeared, leaving only one eager-eyed Zet with the Orvtu glowing white-hot in his palm.

Tendrils of white light shot out of the orb, thrashing about like an enraged kraken. The tendrils wrapped around him, forcing him to the ground and pinning him in place. Whatever strength Jack had left was instantly sapped from him as soon as the tendrils touched his body. His body went limp and immobile, his breathing becoming ragged as if his lungs were becoming too weak to function.

Zet stood over Jack, his tight-lipped smile stretching unnaturally from ear-to-ear, giving him a snake-like appearance.

"What a magnificent artifact…" Zet stared into the Orvtu, the light making his eyes seem to glow. "The death of your family is on your hands." Zet lifted the Orvtu higher, and the tendrils lifted Jack's body before throwing him, discarding him like an old toy. Jack's body bounced off the trees and the ground like a ball before smashing into the Manor, where he finally fell still.

In the brief moments the Orvtu had touched him, he felt like he had aged hundreds of thousands of years. His senses had been all but stripped from him; his vision was a confusing mess of light and shadows, and what he could hear was nothing more than garbled muffles. Despite all this, Jack clutched at the earth and tried to force himself to stand.

He couldn't lose. His family needed him.

He managed to push himself onto his hands and knees before sliding back down again. His own bodyweight suddenly felt like it was crushing him, turning his already ragged breathing into fits of wheezing gasps.

Warm tears welled in his eyes as a heavy exhaustion came over him. The enticing allure of sleep beckoned him with its insidious siren call.

No... not yet... I can't.

Flashes of images flooded his mind of all the people who had joined his family. All of them would soon be slaughtered by Zet.

Zet had won.

And there was nothing he could do about it.

I'm so tired...

Jack felt himself drifting, as if he were falling asleep, as all feeling left him and he was pulled into darkness.

CHAPTER TWENTY-EIGHT

Isaac ducked under a branch, narrowly missing smacking himself in the face. He was running as fast as he could on a twisting, forested trail back to the manor. But no matter how fast he ran, he couldn't shake the feeling of moving in slow motion. He rubbed at where the strap of his backpack had been slapping against his shoulder. Their packs had been slowing them down too much, and they opted to throw them to the side of the road and return for them later. They couldn't afford to waste any time.

"I can hear Sigmund scolding us for not hiding our packs better," Alison said with a hint of a sad smile on her face as they raced along the narrow trail. Her voice held hints of reminiscing, as if Sigmund were already dead.

Which, unfortunately, was most likely true. The man that he saw back in Beignknost wasn't the Sigmund he knew. That man was just a collection of loose flesh and sinew holding bones together. Even if Sigmund managed to win against the Elf, Isaac doubted that he would be around much longer after.

Sigmund had put himself between them and danger *again*. He had always been there to save them when things got too intense. Always swooping in like some knight that kids hear about in stories.

And there he was again. When they were backed into a corner, he dragged himself half-dead into town just to save them. Despite his harsh exterior, Isaac never doubted Sigmund's adoration of them. It was clear from his actions that he loved his family deeply, even if his demeanor suggested otherwise.

He glanced over at Alison as she jumped over a thick tree root. Her face was hard and determined, but behind her eyes Isaac could see flickers of reservation and hesitancy.

Yet she pressed on.

They both pressed on, charged with a final mission from Sigmund: Get home and warn Jack about Adara.

Isaac couldn't even begin to imagine what Adara had done, if—

The sharp sting of smoke smacked him in the nose just before he saw black, billowing clouds rising above the hill. The setting sun made the black clouds burn a violent, foreboding red. Isaac felt his throat tighten as panic gripped him. He bounded up to the crest of the hill, leaving Alison behind with cries for him to wait for her.

He stopped at the top, his jaw slack, and he fell to his knees.

"What's going—" Alison stopped as she joined him.

The Grey family was locked in desperate combat with people Isaac didn't recognize. Bodies littered the once manicured lawn. Fire raged in the Manor, with entire sections of it already collapsed or reduced to rubble. The ground was blackened and cracked, and most of the trees had been incinerated or blown to pieces.

In the distance, Isaac saw flashes of bright, colorful light. He could feel the air tremble around him each time those lights clashed as shockwaves rolled across the area, almost forcing Isaac completely to the ground.

There was only one person Isaac knew of that could produce that level of power.

And he was fighting somebody.

"What the hell happened here?" Alison asked breathlessly. Isaac watched as her determined façade faded away, her eyes swelling with tears and her lower lip beginning to tremble.

"Could Adara really be responsible for all this?" Isaac asked, just barely above a whisper. He felt a deep, bone-chilling cold sweep through him as he watched everything he'd ever known be destroyed right before his eyes.

They had arrived too late—a few hours too late, by the looks of things.

Unbeknownst to Sigmund, they had been doomed to fail from the start. Even with that knowledge, Isaac couldn't shake the feeling that he had let Sigmund down. Maybe if they had run a little faster or stolen someone's horse, maybe they could've gotten back in time still. Maybe if—

Alison put her hand shakily on his shoulder. "We're here now, and that's all that matters," she said, as if reading his mind. "We have to do something."

Isaac nodded hesitantly, but her words rang hollow in his ears. How were they supposed to help? It was very likely that this was the same group that Djaro and Azrael were a part of. If that's the case, then an entire army of Sorcerer and above-level Arcanists were down there with the specific purpose of killing Greys.

They wouldn't stand a chance.

A loud boom drew Isaac's gaze back to the forest. The colorful lights had been replaced with brilliant rays of white that had consumed the forest around it, leaving an impenetrable veil of white like an isolated snowstorm. A gray speck emerged in the white light as it was ejected from it before striking the ground with a thunderous crash. The speck pinwheeled over the earth, stopping only after slamming into the Manor.

From where Isaac knelt, he could just make out the unmoving gray blot on the blackened earth. While he couldn't make out the face, he knew by the cloak who was lying there.

"That's Jack..." Isaac choked out. His body turned cold as if ice had been pushed into his veins.

Before Isaac could think, he was racing down the hill. He heard Alison call something to him, but her words were lost in the unusual stillness of his mind. He darted across the battlefield, magic crackling dangerously around him as the Greys fought their attackers.

He could hear the quiet chattering of fear whispering to him to hide or run away. But its cries were drowned out by something else. What it was, Isaac couldn't say for sure. All he knew was that it was driving him forward with a single focus: Jack.

Isaac leapt over magic-made fissures and clambered over rubble before he rounded the corner to the side of the Manor where Jack's body now lay. Isaac stopped, Alison almost crashing right into him. He hadn't even realized she'd been that close behind him.

Jack's skin was sunken and sickly, and his eyes were blank, empty glass plates that stared into nothing. One side of his cloak was stained red, and the rest of it was in tatters.

Isaac took shaky steps toward him, his knees buckling before finally giving out right next to him. He stared at Jack in disbelief, his stomach doing an uneasy somersault. Could this really be Jack? He looked so different now.

He looked... fragile.

Jack?

Isaac grabbed Jack's shoulders and shook him lightly. He didn't move.

Isaac's body became rattled with hard sobs that caught in his chest. His vision was blurred by the waterfall of warm tears that slowly fell from his cheeks and onto Jack's face, his unmoving eyes staring blankly back up at him.

Alison fell to her knees opposite him, her hands covering her mouth. She leaned forward, pressing her head against Jack's shoulder, her body shaking as she was taken by fits of sobs.

"Jack, wake up," Isaac pleaded, grabbing Jack's shoulders once more, his hand slipping against the pool of blood on his side.

Jack couldn't be dead... Could he? Was it even possible for him to lose?

No. Jack couldn't lose. If he were gone, then what hope did the rest of them have?

What hope did Isaac have?

"Ow!" Alison hissed, her hand recoiling from Jack's back. "What is that?"

She pushed Jack's cloak to the side, revealing a black mass protruding from behind his shoulder blade.

"It looks like a knife..." Isaac reached tentatively for it. His body spasmed as a sharp, cold jolt of pain shot through him as his fingers brushed the slick metal.

"Anti-magic," Isaac cursed, flailing his hand in the air, his fingers tingling.

Alison's face turned hopeful. "We have to get this out. Maybe if we remove it, he can—"

Isaac was already plunging his hand as deep into the wound as he could. He gritted his teeth and pinched the blade between his fingers as hard as he could and slowly began to pull. He had to pause several times to wipe the blood from his fingers and give himself a slight reprieve. Isaac grasped the knife again, and each time he did so it brought fresh pain coursing through him. His body ached with a deep cold he couldn't shake. He could feel his connection with the mana slipping away from him.

Had Jack fought like this the entire time...? Isaac wondered.

Isaac gave one last hard tug, wrenching the blade free with a disgusting squelch before throwing it as far away from them as possible. He clasped his hands together over Jack's wound and slowly began to mend it, ignoring the pain he felt blossoming inside him.

The blinding white light was flashing all around them now, followed by terrified screams or the soft thud of a body hitting the ground. Isaac could just barely make out the figure of a tall, gray-skinned man holding what looked like the orb they had recovered from the temple.

"Is that—"

"It has to be," Isaac said. The artifact they recovered was said to be able to take out entire armies. Evidently, the rumors had been true. But why didn't Jack have it? Was that Adara's doing?

Isaac shook his head, refocusing himself. He looked back down at Jack's empty, faraway gaze.

"C'mon Jack, get up..." He pounded Jack's chest with a fist.

Jack couldn't die like this. He had so much left to show him. He was supposed to have more time with his family. It wasn't fair for him to be taken from them now. The Greys still needed him.

Isaac still needed him.

Alison desperately clutched at Jack's cloak.

No, they couldn't lose him and Sigmund. Isaac refused to let that happen.

Please, Jack...

Get up...

CHAPTER TWENTY-NINE

J ACK COULDN'T QUITE DESCRIBE WHAT HE WAS FEELING.

He felt like he was floating down a slow-moving, ethereal river. The waves pushed him along like gentle guiding hands. The darkness around him suddenly vanished, replaced by a stark white expanse that stretched out infinitely in all directions. He was standing now. Wasn't he just lying down, floating a moment ago?

"What is this place?" he whispered.

"Somewhere you're not supposed to be... yet."

The light, high-pitched voice made Jack's heart stop in his chest. He slowly turned around, afraid that if he moved too quickly, he would somehow scare her off.

But she was there.

Her emerald green eyes shone like beautiful lanterns through the locks of her curly, vibrant reddish-pink hair. Freckles checkered her soft, pale face and framed her large, beaming smile that looked like an angel's welcoming grin.

"Rose?" Jack stammered.

"The one and only!" she responded. "It's so good to see you again, Jacky."

Jack wrapped his arms tightly around her, sweeping her up in his arms and spinning her around. He buried his face in her neck and let her warmth flood his senses, overcome with peace.

"I can't believe it's you," he breathed. "I've been waiting for this moment for..." He stopped and hugged her tighter.

Rose giggled. An all but forgotten sweet melody in Jack's ears.

"I'm happy to see you too." She returned his tight hug, her arms wrapped around his neck. "But, it's not your time to join me here. Not yet."

Jack released her from his embrace, but kept his hands on her waist. "What do you mean?"

She flashed him a patient smile. The same smile she would give him any time he was being an arrogant ass in the past but, this time, it held more sympathy.

"You still have something left to do down there."

Jack sucked in air sharply as he felt pain explode in his back. He reached behind him and examined his hand to find that it was now coated in blood.

Jack looked between his hand and Rose. "I don't understand."

She giggled. "You're in between right now. That Zet and Adara really had it out for you, didn't they? Between the Orvtu and the knife... Very unfair of them. That's why you have to go back and kick his ass!"

"Rose, I... I don't know if I can. The Orvtu—"

"I know." She smiled solemnly. "The knife doesn't help either. But! Not to worry. That should be taken care of soon."

Jack lurched forward as he felt the knife inside him shift.

"They're saving you," Rose said, placing a gentle hand on his chest.

Images of Isaac and Alison huddled over his body flashed in his head. Jack winced. Those poor kids. They didn't deserve to see him like that.

"So, do you know how you're going to beat him?" Rose asked playfully.

Jack thought for a moment before nodding. "It's the last card I have to play. I'm not sure if it'll allow me to kill him, but it should be enough to get the Orvtu away from him."

"I knew you'd have the answer." Rose beamed at him and buried her head in his chest.

Jack rested his cheek on top of her head and stared out into the white expanse. He had waited so long for this exact moment when he could be with her again. But now that he was here, he couldn't help but feel some pangs of guilt. There was so much work left to be done. So much more to show his family.

And then there was Isaac.

Jack had made a promise years ago to Isaac's father that he would watch over him. Help him live a normal life. How could he do that if he were dead?

"He'll be okay. They'll *all* be okay. You've taught them well enough," Rose reassured, as if reading his mind. "There is always more that could be done. But, tell me, did you spend your time wisely, Jacky?"

"Yes, I suppose I did," Jack said thoughtfully. "After I met you, anyway."

"Not surprising. I *am* the best thing to happen to you," Rose said cheekily. "Now, I think it's about time to go back."

Jack felt the knife get pulled free from his shoulder, followed quickly by the sensation of his flesh slowly stitching together.

"I'll see you again soon, Jacky." She stood on the tips of her toes and kissed his lips gently. In the next moment, the white space and Rose faded away from him as he felt a hard tug at the center of his being. He was pulled backwards through darkness before he felt himself slam into a familiar space.

* * * * *

Jack's vision slowly returned to him. Fuzzy at first, but he could gradually make out Isaac and Alison's faces, both wet with tears and covered in grime. Neither of them were looking at him as they knelt over him, their heads buried in their hands. He could still feel the slow lull of Isaac's magic flowing through him as his wounds continued to heal.

Jack smiled. "Thank you." His voice startled them, jolting them upright. They tumbled excitedly on top of him, almost crushing him to death with their combined weight.

A sad smile spread across his face as a memory flooded his mind. Alison and Isaac were children, clinging to his pant legs, refusing to let him go anywhere without them.

How they've grown...

White light flashed behind him.

Jack turned, feeling a deep burning rage well up inside him as he saw another Grey fall.

"Thank you again for your help. I can take it from here." They slowly pulled away from him as Jack stood shakily, his legs wobbling.

Isaac began to protest, but he quickly closed his mouth and looked at the ground. He could tell that Isaac wanted him to wait for more of his strength to return. If he looked as good as he felt, then he could understand Isaac's desire. Unfortunately, they didn't have that luxury.

This was just another part of the lesson that Jack hoped Isaac could learn sooner than he had. In life, there are very few things ever under your control. All you can do is accept that and make the best of the choices you have.

And this was the best option that Jack could think of.

"I am so proud of you. Both of you." Jack turned to them, flashing them one last beaming grin before teleporting them to the top of the hill overlooking the Manor before they could try to protest further.

Jack took in a deep breath and focused on the rune he had etched into his mind: a simple loop with no end, surrounded by three intertwining circles encased within a triangle. This rune had been keeping him alive all these years, manipulating his aura to prolong his lifespan. With what he planned on doing, he'd need to burn it all.

The rune flickered and grew dark as it crumbled away in his mind. Jack stumbled forward, the weight of all his years catching up to him in an instant. He focused on the mana coursing through his body, feeling the raging current flowing within him. He touched it and felt a surge of energy course through him. The air around him crackled as his body became engulfed in a bright green aura. His body tingled with warmth as if he were on fire. He hadn't felt this way in hundreds of years, not since before the Klythini.

He felt... powerful.

Jack had to hurry, though. This sensation wouldn't last long now that he was burning the candle at both ends.

Jack shot around the Manor grounds, teleporting so quickly he felt like he was in several places at once. Everywhere he went, he would teleport the Grey member to the hill with Isaac and Alison and kill whoever they had been fighting. Bodies hitting the dirt became a soft, melodic drumbeat as he raced across the grounds.

Jack bore down on Zet just as he was raising the Orvtu at another Grey. He teleported beside Zet, the wind whipping around him, slicing at the ground, and creating large claw-like gashes in the dirt before slamming into Zet, throwing him deep into the forest.

Zet reemerged moments later in a flash of purple-black light, his surprise somewhat masked by his scowl. Jack eyed Zet and his men carefully, as the remnants of his troupe slowly closed in on him from all sides.

Jack readied himself as Zet extended his hand out toward him. Stone spikes shot out from under Zet's men, splitting some of them in half, while the others slid down the spikes like stuck pigs.

Jack's stunned eyes locked with Zet.

"They served their purpose," Zet said coolly. "There is no reason for them to interfere."

Jack swallowed his disgust. Even though they had been sent here to kill his family, he didn't think they deserved to be betrayed by who they thought was their leader. But Zet had done him a favor. He wouldn't need to waste precious seconds killing them himself. Now, all he had to focus on was separating Zet from the Orvtu.

And he already had a plan for that.

Jack glanced behind Zet where his mahnku—a transparent, smoky-blue monkey-like creature—slowly materialized from the Domustiar. It crouched, hiding behind a fallen tree. Jack would be foolish to think that he could deal with Zet in a direct confrontation, even while burning his aura this way. In a battle of attrition, he'd lose. Instead, the purpose of burning his life force like this was to give himself enough time to execute his plan. Now, he just needed to be patient and create the opening he needed.

I was not known just for my power, Zet... Here I will show you precisely why I was to be named Archmage.

Jack teleported away as tendrils of light shot out of the Orvtu, grasping desperately at the open air where Jack once stood. Zet stood confidently back and, as he raised his free hand, the ground split open wide, lava exploding out to the surface.

Jack pulled at the mana around him, commanding an ocean's worth of water to be borne from it. Water suddenly fell from the sky in a thick blanket as Jack flooded the landscape. Hot steam coated the air in a thick blanket of heat as the water rapidly cooled the magma, leaving behind brittle obsidian in its place.

Zet growled in frustration as he hurled a fireball at Jack, who split it in half with a torrent of his own flames, sending the two halves crackling into the dirt. Two stone slabs shot up on either side of Jack and rushed toward him. Jack thrust his hands out to his sides, swirling blue runes hovering just above his palms, the stone walls grinding to a halt as Jack's hands touched them. The walls pulled away from him, the rune that was in his hands now engraved into the stone. The rune flashed blue before launching after Zet, spinning end-over-end through the air.

Zet batted the walls away from him with a flick of his wrist as he commanded the wind to cast the walls aside. The runes on the walls glowed brighter as they got further away from each other. The walls stopped midair and shot back toward Zet as if connected to each other by rubber. Zet teleported out of the way as the stones smashed into each other.

Jack appeared behind Zet, water rushing in all around them. Ice shot out of the water, showering Zet in a volley of arrow-like projectiles. Blue fire erupted around Zet, evaporating the water and melting the ice, thick steam momentarily coating the area. It was almost impossible to see.

Now.

Illusions of Jack began littering the battlefield, completely surrounding where Zet had been standing before. As his illusions appeared, their shadows shot into the mist, hunting for Zet's. Jack felt soft thuds in his mind as his shadow stitches found their marks and locked onto Zet. The mist was suddenly pushed away by a tempest that almost took Jack off his feet. Zet looked around, eyeing Jack's illusions with distaste.

"This again?" Zet said, sounding almost disappointed. "This shadow stitching cannot stop me."

As he raised the Orvtu, Jack could feel his stitching beginning to strain against the pressure.

Just a little more...

Zet extended the Orvtu out toward Jack, tendrils of light thrashing against the ground as he did.

Jack smiled as he brought his hands together, his illusions following suit. The black, uneven lines from the shadow stitching glowed blue as a giant rune under Zet was activated. A crystalline dome appeared around Zet, trapping him inside, with just his hand exposed.

Zet tugged hard at his arm, his usual stoic appearance broken by shock. The mahnku appeared beneath Zet's hand, snatching the Orvtu from his grasp and bounding over to Jack.

"*NO!*" Zet's roar was muffled by the dome.

A giant portal opened beneath the crystal structure, swallowing it and Zet along with Jack's illusions.

Jack felt his legs buckle beneath him as his aura began to flicker and dim. He wiped the back of his hand across his nose, smearing it with a thin layer of blood.

The mahnku approached Jack slowly, its head cocked to one side.

"I'm all right." Jack smiled at it, and the mahnku dropped the Orvtu in Jack's outstretched hand.

"Thank you, mahnku. Go home and get some rest. You deserve it."

The mahnku's lips curled in its version of a smile before it howled and disappeared in a blue mist.

Jack gripped the Orvtu tightly as he began to tremble and shake. That dome wouldn't hold Zet for long and, when he returned, Jack would have to end things quickly.

His time was running out.

He could feel it.

The Orvtu was like the sun, heavy and scorchingly hot, in the palm of his hand. There was a weight and intensity with the Ortvu that he hadn't noticed before, and one that Jack had never seen in all of his years studying artifacts. What's more, there was now an odd pulling sensation that tugged at the center of his being, as if it were sucking him into an unseen void.

Something was wrong with the Orvtu. He could feel a deep instability at its center. There was a power there that was growing exponentially as it continued to feed off its surroundings.

It was activated by aura magic...

Jack's aura flickered again, and the Orvtu glowed brighter.

It feeds off aura.

Not only that, but it stores *it...*

This artifact was never meant to be used as a weapon.

No, this was meant to kill not only the user but, judging based on the energy Jack felt within it, also kill anyone within the same *kingdom* as the user.

It was a trap.

The Orvtu glowed brighter as Jack's aura continued to dim. He felt something deep within the Orvtu crack as the light became blinding.

"Its next use will be its last..." Jack whispered.

Zet appeared opposite Jack, his reptilian eyes bearing down on him in rage. White tendrils slammed the ground haphazardly as they sought Zet, who teleported quickly out of the way, but Jack followed closely after him.

Jack appeared ahead of Zet, cutting him off as he tried to outrun the Orvtu. The Orvtu's tendrils wrapped around Zet, almost crushing him beneath its grasp. Zet thrashed about, his body quickly aging as his life was drained from him.

Jack felt another crack form in the Orvtu.

It was going to explode soon in a catastrophic display of power. It would kill most of Klantra.

Jack could feel it.

He couldn't stop it. Not completely.

But he could contain it.

Jack clutched the Orvtu tightly, the orb smoking against his skin as it burned in his palm.

Jack looked toward the hilltop where what remained of his family stood watching in silent awe. He scanned the crowd and found Alison and Isaac.

Take care of each other.

He flashed another beaming, wide smile at them as he felt the heat of the Orvtu engulf his right side. The light from the Orvtu was expanding now, swallowing everything around it. Zet had completely disappeared in the blinding white light.

Jack reached deeper into the mana that coursed through him and pulled on it hard. His aura flared brighter, and so too did the Orvtu. A shimmering green barrier rose around the Orvtu's building light, stopping its growth as Jack encased himself and the Orvtu inside his bolstered abjuration magic.

I'm sorry I couldn't keep my promise. I hope you can guide him from here... wherever you are. Jack thought, glancing up at the sky.

Jack felt the Orvtu disintegrate in his palm. He stumbled backwards as the Orvtu tried to explode outwards, his aura flickering.

Goodbye, everyone. Jack pulled harder once more at the mana within him, his green barrier blazing a brilliant emerald around the white light of the Orvtu.

Jack felt the Orvtu's power attempt once more to explode outwards. A thunderous boom shook him as the energy from the Orvtu roared inside the cage Jack had created. Jack felt the heat from the raw power of the Orvtu overtake his senses as he felt himself slip away back into darkness.

END OF PART 3

PART 4

THE ONES WE LEFT BEHIND

CHAPTER THIRTY

Something cracked inside Isaac.

Something deep in the recesses of his mind, something bent and snapped under an unseen pressure.

He doubled over onto his hands and knees as he watched Jack's barrier creep up along the light of the Orvtu. A shockwave rattled the air, sending everyone to their knees. There was another boom accompanied by a blinding flash of green light.

Then everything was quiet.

Nobody moved.

Everyone just stared down into the giant pit where Jack and the gray-skinned man once stood. There was no Orvtu, no reptile man.

No Jack.

Everything around where Jack was had been completely vaporized, leaving not even a speck of dirt behind.

Isaac felt Alison place a tender hand on his back as he felt his stomach churn. What were they supposed to do now?

What was *he* supposed to do now?

What sense of control could he grasp onto now to feel like his entire life hadn't just been ripped to shreds right before his eyes? Just like the Temple and the Trials, he found himself feeling helpless.

He kept waiting for Jack to appear, battered and bruised sure, but still appear alive and well with his giant grin to tell everyone everything was going to be fine. But the longer Isaac stared, the more disheartened he became. Jack wasn't coming back.

Isaac's breathing became shallow and rapid, his hands tingling as if they had lost circulation, and his vision filled with tiny black stars.

What was he going to do? He wasn't anywhere near ready to face the world on his own. His recent adventures had shown him that.

What were any of them going to do? If Jack couldn't survive, what hope did the rest of them have?

What were—

"Isaac, are you okay?" Alison's face suddenly filled his vision as she gently pushed him up so he was sitting back on his calves, his vision clearing.

He opened his mouth to speak, but no words came out. His throat was tight as if someone were choking him. He felt cold, as if he had fallen into a frozen lake, but he was drenched in sweat. Each thundering heartbeat hammered in his skull, amplifying his unease and vertigo.

Then he broke down in tears. He fell against Alison and shuddered through sobbing fits as tears streamed down his face. He felt her shake as she wept too, her tears running down and plopping silently onto his hair. They sat there wrapped around each other for some time.

"We should go look for survivors..." someone said finally, breaking the silence that hung over them like a thick blanket.

"We need to bury our dead," added another.

"We need to gather our things and go to the Order. They'll take us in."

"We can do all of that," Alison sniffled, addressing everyone. "A group of us will go down and search for any survivors while another group digs the graves. Once all of that is done, we'll retrieve what we can and head to the Order."

Murmurs of agreement spread throughout the group.

Alison stood and helped Isaac to his feet as she did so.

"We should get moving. Let's go, everyone." Alison waved her hand, beckoning the Greys to follow. Isaac watched as Alison marched forward, tears still streaming down her cheeks in thick pools, but still leading everyone down the hill toward the Manor.

What does it take to be like her? Isaac wondered.

Isaac paused as he broke through the tree line while the other Greys rushed off to their chosen duties. Being on the Manor grounds was even worse than seeing it from above and, without the chaos of battle, he could take everything in more clearly. The once vibrant green grass was reduced mostly to cinders, leaving what remained of the ground blackened and desolate. The pungent stench of death and the metallic sting of blood were like a punch to Isaac's nose that would've made him incredibly nauseous if he weren't already. All around him, he could see dismembered limbs and mangled bodies that covered the ground like the rose and lilac bushes once did. The grounds were completely terra-formed, with giant fissures separating entire sections of the property.

Oddly, above it all, the thing that unsettled Isaac the most was how quiet it was. He used to be able to hear the owls chattering as dusk approached or animals rushing through the woods, crushing leaves and branches as they went. But now, it was all so silent that Isaac could hear his heart thumping in his ears.

Is this what death sounds like?

Smoke was still streaming up from portions of the Manor. No longer thick enough to block out the sky, but enough to leave a dark line across the rising moons. Isaac shook his head incredulously. Was this really the same day they had reunited Cela and Thomas? Isaac walked slowly to the rightmost side of the Manor, where he had seen a large hole in the side of it from the hilltop. He jumped carefully across the newly created ravines, minding his footing as sections of dirt often fell away from him, tumbling into the chasms below.

As he approached the hole, Isaac could barely make out the shallow grooves in the dirt where it looked like a whip had been thrashing about. The outside walls on this side were both scorched and ice-kissed. Isaac peered through the giant opening, looking directly into the Manor. Strangely, opposite him there was a perfectly square hole in the middle of the Manor, as if someone had cut one of the rooms out.

Isaac stopped as he was stepping into the Manor, a black mass catching his attention from the corner of his eye. He glanced over at it, then stared at the charred body. Before he could even begin to wonder who it was, he saw the blackened razor-whip just a few feet away.

"There you are!" Alison called, catching up to him. "I was looking all over for—" She stopped, her eyes locked on the body. "Is that—"

"Jane," Isaac finished, wiping his eyes and feeling numb again.

Is all of this real?

That couldn't *really* be Jane, could it?

The same lady who would always steal him more sweets when he was a kid?

Not possible.

Alison sniffled and knelt beside Jane, resting her hand gently on her face. She sat there for a moment before standing.

"C'mon." She turned and headed toward the Manor. "Let's check the rest of the house."

They searched the Manor and, unsurprisingly, they found no survivors inside. Isaac was shocked to learn, though, that some people *were* found outside, buried beneath rubble or mounds of dirt.

One person no one could find was Margaret. Already there was speculation that perhaps Margaret helped Adara and they fled together. Clearly, they didn't know Margaret as well as Isaac did. She couldn't stand Adara, and she would never betray them and side with her.

Then again, he thought he knew Adara well enough to think she'd never betray them either.

Isaac got pulled to help with healing the injured with what remained of the Healing Arcanists, in addition to digging graves. With him being the last Omnis Arcanist in the family, everyone was relying on him more now because he could do almost everything. For now, he worked with the healers to mend the wounded enough to where they could make the journey to the Order. That was all they could do for now. Everyone was exhausted.

And they had family to bury.

With the help of the others, it was quick work to construct graves and headstones for everyone. Though it was a miserable business finding something to cover the bodies with. Isaac and Alison saw to Jane's body personally, shrouding her in her favorite blanket—a red and green knitted fleece she made herself—and laid her weapon on top of her, her hand clutching the handle of her trick cane.

They worked until the sun came up the next morning. There was only one grave left to dig: Jack's.

Everyone knew it had to be done, but no one wanted to make the move to do it first. Isaac understood their hesitation. Making that headstone would make everything more real.

Isaac walked to the outer crest of the crater that was left behind from the orb's explosion. He put his hand on the ground and raised it slowly. A thick, smooth rock followed his motion, and stopped after it was a few feet tall. Another Grey came over and pushed his thumb into the stone, hot flame smoldering on the end of the digit. Everyone watched as he carefully burned Jack's epitaph.

JACK GREY

A DEAR FRIEND

&

BELOVED FATHER

Isaac felt more tears streak down his cheeks, but he didn't feel the same anguish he had felt on top of the hill. No, now he just felt hollow inside, as if some part of him had been removed.

Isaac sat staring unblinkingly at Jack's headstone. All of a long, accomplished life of a cherished man reduced down to a simple rock and a sentence.

Was all of this supposed to give the ones left behind some sense of closure?

How could he feel good about that?

Alison sat down beside him, taking his hand in hers.

"He's still with us, you know," Alison said, running her thumb along the back of his hand comfortingly. "All of them are, in a way. They live on through us, through our memories, through our actions..."

Alison's eyes were red and tired-looking, and her cheeks were puffy. It looked like she had been crying nonstop for quite some time. Isaac could only assume he looked the same.

Isaac nodded numbly as she spoke. He understood, on some level, what she was saying. That their spirits live on through them and that they were never truly without them.

But that didn't take the sting away now. He didn't want their memory with him; he wanted *them* here *now*.

It wasn't fair.

Then again, Isaac was learning that nothing was ever really fair. Like Jack had said, you just have to make the most of what you are given. What he was supposed to focus on here though, to give him some sense of autonomy back, he hadn't the slightest clue. Jack was dead. Sigmund was dead. Jane was dead.

Where was his choice in all of that?

They sat in silence together, holding each other tightly. There was a fear in their embrace, a fear that if they didn't hold on hard enough, the other might disappear in the breeze. Eventually, another Grey came over and asked them to gather their belongings, if they could find them. Everyone was eager to get to the Order. Without Margaret, it was going to be a long journey.

Alison and Isaac shuffled through the Manor at a snail's pace, each step echoing eerily. Despite some of the torches lighting their way, everything seemed darker. There was a lifelessness to the Manor now.

"Will you be okay?" Alison asked him as they stopped at her room.

Isaac peered down the hallway hesitantly. "Yeah... I'm good. I'll meet you back here."

Alison nodded, took a deep breath, and slowly entered her room.

Isaac waited until the door was mostly closed behind her. He could hear her muffled weeping on the other side, the sound tugged at whatever remained of his shattered heart.

He dully walked down to his room, an ornate 'I' neatly carved into the door that Jack had done himself.

He fingered the smooth grooves of the 'I', his fingers tracing over the sanded surface. After a few moments, he pushed the door open. It swung silently before knocking into the wall behind it with a soft thud. Part of his ceiling had collapsed, and one wall had been destroyed, leaving shattered wood everywhere. A fallen beam had crushed his bed, and the debris covered part of the trunk that he had at the foot of it. The small desk he had in the corner was completely obliterated, as if it had been smashed by a giant's club. His armoire was split in half by Creator knows what, his clothes flung all about.

He crouched down and carefully looked under his bed and reached for the extra backpack he had underneath it. It had been just far enough away from the center of the bed that it wasn't trapped by the fallen beam. He quickly threw whatever clothes were intact into his pack before he turned his attention to his trunk.

His trunk was the place where he kept all his most prized possessions for safekeeping. Isaac summoned up a slight wind to, very carefully, push some of the debris off the chest so he could get to the trunk.

He popped the latch and opened the chest with a loud creak. Tucked in one corner was the first Grey cloak Jack had ever given him. Much too small for him now, but he had hoped to give it to a son or a daughter someday. Beside it were his first sets of training swords, wooden for his safety as Sigmund insisted. The grips were worn and blackened from sweat, and the wood cracked and dented. Next to that was the sleek, black hexagonal case with a heavy, intricate padlock that dangled in front of it that housed the dragon egg. It seemed to exude heat, even with it locked safely inside the container. He stashed all of these in his pack, along with a couple of other items he collected over the years, and slung the heavy, oblong bag over his shoulders.

He stood and walked sluggishly over to the half-open door. Isaac turned and looked around his room once more. Memories flashed through his mind. He could see Jack and Jane reading him stories as a child in here, sitting at the foot of the bed and Isaac clinging to every word. He could see Margaret hiding in Isaac's closet and jumping out when he didn't expect it. He could see Sigmund's disgruntled face, with a much shorter beard back then, as he waited impatiently for Isaac to get ready so he could begin his training for the day.

All of that was gone.

He closed the door firmly behind him.

Isaac met Alison in the hallway, who was sporting her own over-stuffed backpack.

"There was too much stuff to try to decide what to take." She attempted a smile. "But we can come back for more later, maybe."

Isaac glanced back toward his room. "Yeah, maybe."

She grabbed his hand, interlocking her fingers with his. "Ready?"

"As ever," Isaac said as he walked down the Manor halls one last time.

* * * * *

The trek to the Order was long and exhausting. The weather had not been on their side since the moment they left the Manor. Rain and hail assaulted them for most of the two-day journey. Their clothes were muddy and damp. Even with them using magic to keep some of the rain off of them, the cold and the wet still stuck to them through the cracks in their defenses.

They must've been quite the sight when they finally arrived at the front door of the Order, judging by how quickly the doors were opened and they were swarmed by people asking if they needed help and wrapping blankets around them. All of them asking questions and getting everyone's answers all at once.

"Creator..." Isaac heard one of the Mages say as they streamed into the Order's Keep. "Someone alert Aephes. Immediately."

Isaac and Alison, like most other Greys, were shuffled into the infirmary for a Healer Mage to take a look at them. They sat on the same bed together; their only injuries were from the fight with the vampires a few days earlier. Isaac had grown so accustomed to having a rib out of place that, after the Healer Mage put it back, it felt wrong and unnatural. It was a foreign sensation to be able to breathe easier after days of tight-chested wheezing. It wasn't long after the Healer Mage had seen them that Olfen, Olyen, Fraunt, and Meri showed up and flung themselves on them. Fraunt kept his distance, preferring to stand awkwardly in the corner while staring at them with what Isaac assumed to be Fraunt's version of sympathy.

Olfen clapped Isaac on the back gently, as if he were fragile and didn't want to break him. "I'm sorry, Isaac. I—we—truly are. We can only imagine what you're going through." Olfen grabbed Isaac in a big bear hug, and Isaac feebly wrapped one arm around his back.

"I am sorry for your loss," Olyen whispered, even lower than normal.

"We're here if you need us." Meri's voice cracked, releasing Alison from a hug that Isaac could tell was a bit too tight for her liking at the moment.

"Thank you," Isaac said, attempting a half-smile.

"Isaac." Aephes' voice boomed from behind Olfen, making him jump. "And you must be Alison." Aephes offered a small smile. "Welcome to the Order, though I am sorry that your first visit is under these circumstances."

Aephes turned to Olfen. "Would you excuse us for a moment, please?"

Olfen nodded. "We'll be here for you guys if you need us. Find us when you can, but get some rest too."

"We will," Alison responded with a light smile.

Olfen took Meri's hand and grabbed Olyen lightly by the shoulder. Fraunt was the last one to leave, begrudgingly as always. He continued his staring until at last he said:

"Grey men, do not be sad." And then turned and joined the rest of them.

Isaac didn't know what he'd do without Fraunt's words of timeless wisdom.

"I heard everything from the others... I am terribly sorry, you two," Aephes began slowly, sitting down on the cot opposite him, his long flowing cloak folding underneath him.

"Did you find them?" Isaac asked hopefully.

Aephes hesitated, then shook his head. "We haven't been able to locate Margaret. And without her to give us the location of the artifact room, it will be nearly impossible for us to find it."

"So does this mean Margaret was helping Adara…?" Alison asked, her jaw set.

Aephes shook his head again. "No, not necessarily. I don't want to make assumptions until I know for sure. It's possible that Adara killed Margaret and took the room herself. We won't know for sure until something happens. However, we're going to continue to look for that room. It's imperative that those artifacts be kept tightly guarded."

"And Sigmund?" Isaac dreaded asking that question. Even though he and Alison knew with a high level of certainty that he was dead, he didn't want the confirmation. He didn't want to know what state Sigmund was found in. But they had to know for sure.

Aephes leaned back on the cot uncomfortably. It was weird how small he looked now, as if he had shrunk right before Isaac's eyes.

"Yes… We found Sigmund. In Beignknost, as you said. We followed the destruction his battle with Laydin the Butcher had left and found his body sitting peacefully facing the sunrise close to the Butcher's body. He had been dead for quite some time. I'm deeply sorry."

"Thank you for telling us," Alison said shakily. Isaac felt the soft plop of her tears hitting the back of his hand as she nestled her head against his shoulder. Isaac just stared at the floor, feeling too numb to cry anymore.

Aephes cleared his throat uncomfortably. "We have rooms for both of you, next to each other, and you're more than welcome to stay here as long as you like. However, if you plan on leaving, I ask that you stay at least until tomorrow. We will be having a ceremony for Jack, and the Elder Mages will be there to tell us the future of the Order in light of recent events. If you would be so kind as to join us tomorrow morning, I'd really appreciate it."

They both nodded.

"Now, if you would, please follow me to your quarters."

Aephes led them down a series of winding halls decorated with pictures of Arcanists in long-forgotten battles and stained glass windows that sent colorful beams of light sparkling along the floor and walls.

Aephes stopped in front of two surprisingly unremarkable-looking wooden doors. He opened both of them to reveal two identical rooms. They both had the same porcelain, sleek white walls and floors with a comfortable-enough looking bed, a desk, and an armoire neatly placed in the corner of the room. The Order of Dormiri's symbol was carved into the marble above the bed.

"I apologize for the lack of furnishings. These rooms are typically reserved for new students until we find them a permanent home. You'll find clean clothes in the dressers if you need them. If there is anything you wish to have cleaned, place it outside your door. Please let me know if there is anything we can get you."

They nodded their thanks to him, and he hesitated before slowly walking off to tend to the other Grey members streaming in.

Alison gazed into her blank, cookie-cutter room.

"Well, it's not a home yet, but..." Her voice trailed off. "Do you want some company tonight, or would you prefer some space?"

Isaac was silent for a moment. "I think I'd like some time alone for a bit."

Alison nodded. "Of course. I'll be on the other side of the wall if you need anything." She gave him a tight hug before shuffling tiredly into her room and closing the door.

Isaac followed suit, closing the door behind him and taking in the small expanse of white that surrounded him. He made his way over to the dresser. He knew he was in desperate need of fresh clothes and, judging by the smell that seemed to follow him everywhere, a bath. Isaac slid open one of the drawers and examined the clothes inside: a silky white long-sleeved shirt, a matching pair of white pants, and a swirling rainbow-colored robe reserved for Omnis Arcanists. He closed the drawer, ignoring them.

Isaac slowly lowered his backpack to the floor, careful not to break or crush anything he had inside. He unclipped the gray cloak from around his shoulders and held it in his hands. His muscles felt stiff and tired, and his shoulders clicked as he swung his arms around his body. The cloak was spattered with dirt and hardened blood. The Grey family crest was the only thing left untouched, free of any sign of wear. He ran his fingers over the carefully sewn symbol, feeling the slight ridges from the threads.

He folded the cloak as neatly as he could and placed it on his desk. Hopefully, a good wash would restore it to at least some of its former glory.

Isaac carefully lowered himself onto the bed, letting the soft, feathery mattress envelop him as he lay down and stared at the ceiling. He hadn't realized how tired he was until his head hit the pillow. Everything suddenly ached with the stress of days' worth of exertion with no breaks. His stiff muscles became painfully hot and started to throb. Despite the mattress being comfortable, Isaac couldn't find a way to settle himself. His mind was too active and his body too alive with pain.

What am I supposed to do now?

That was the question all of them were probably wondering. Where do they go from here? Without Jack, the Grey family as they know it would most likely dissolve. Sure, the Order would gladly take them all in, but the family Jack had worked so hard to cultivate would be gone forever.

All because of Adara.

Isaac gritted his teeth. No one seemed entirely sure what she had done but, between Sigmund's warning and his conversation with other Greys, she had played a major role in getting that gray-skinned man inside the barrier that protected the Manor. He wished he were strong enough to track her down somehow and repay her for all the damage she had done...

But she was gone. She had disappeared sometime after the fighting started. That goal would have to wait for another time.

For now, though, he was uncertain as to what he should be doing. Rather, there was a clash between what he *wanted* and what he *should* do. He knew Alison wouldn't let any of this slow her down. She'd mourn, sure, as Isaac was sure she was doing now. After that, though, she'd be training and doing whatever she could to push herself forward. Never letting anything stop her.

But not Isaac. Not now, anyway. Not after everything that's happened. The last time he felt he had truly pushed himself was after the Temple, where he tried *desperately* to reclaim some semblance of control. To not feel so fucking useless.

He hasn't gotten over that feeling yet, and he wasn't sure when he would. Especially when life did everything it could to push him down. He no longer had any desire to push himself or to take contracts like he once had. Like Jack had encouraged him to do.

Now, he felt cold and broken. Like cracked glass that hasn't quite shattered yet. To make matters worse, the insidious whispering thoughts had returned, beating his already damaged confidence bloody.

What's the point of continuing?

It'd be so much easier if you just quit.

No more fear. No more pain...

Isaac wiped his hand across his cheek and was surprised to find tears there. He didn't want to abandon everything he had longed for. For his entire life, he had this dream of being a great Arcanist who could make a difference in the world. To go out on these grand adventures like he and Alison had always talked about.

To be like Jack.

He didn't want to quit. Isaac had promised Jack that he would keep trying, no matter how long it took. He made a promise that he fully intended to keep. But these thoughts were so paralyzing...

Isaac took in a shaky breath. He was too tired to fight back against the whispers swirling around his skull, chattering to him like unseen ghosts, luring him to his demise. He was too tired to try to push himself forward *again* and hope things would be better. He wasn't like Alison. He wasn't like Sigmund.

Isaac balled his fists up in the blanket.

He wasn't like Jack.

For now, he'd train at the Order, and he'd go back out again once he was ready. Once he felt strong enough to never feel helpless again.

Once all the whispers stopped.

He just needed time, that's all.

Isaac rolled onto his side, curling up into a tight ball as he drifted in and out of a restless sleep.

CHAPTER THIRTY-ONE

T HEY WERE PACKED INTO THE MAIN COURTYARD like fish in a barrel. It seemed like every Arcanist across all of Eutrox and, hell, maybe even some from Aesus, had shown up to pay their respects. Isaac would've felt more flattered by everyone's attendance if he wasn't forced to sit so close to them.

It's too early in the morning to be stuck next to so many people.

Like everything else about the Order, the courtyard was grand and otherworldly. The floors and walls continued the color scheme of 'nothing exists but marble white', with thick columns lining the walkways and shrubs nestled between them. Twinkling, rainbow-colored light inched lazily up and down the branches of every plant that lined the path. Red sheer curtains hung from the columns. Still images, as if their likeness had been frozen in time, of deceased Arcanists appeared ethereally on the curtains.

Alison squeezed his hand lightly and smiled reassuringly at him. He smiled back. She hadn't left his side since they got to the Courtyard. Which he didn't mind. He wanted her as close to him as possible right now.

The crowd around him started to murmur as Aephes strolled to the elevated marble platform that he had created in the middle of the Courtyard, followed closely behind by a group of men carrying a large, rectangular-shaped object covered in a thick black cloth.

"What do you think that is?" Alison whispered.

Isaac shrugged. "Perhaps it's a plaque we can all share for surviving."

She elbowed him in the ribs.

"Are you still coming with me to talk with the rest of the family?" she asked.

Isaac nodded. "Of course. I'm interested in seeing what everyone wants to do."

Alison frowned. "From what I've heard, many of them are staying here. Others are heading off on their own. I don't know many who want to rebuild..."

Isaac opened his mouth to speak, but was cut off by Aephes.

"Good morning, everyone," Aephes's voice boomed, a sad, soft smile spread across his face. "While it brings me great pleasure to see all of you today, I wish it were under different circumstances. We have gathered here to celebrate the life of an esteemed Arcanist, and dear friend, Jack Grey. Jack did a great many things during his six hundred years' time here. Jack and his family took it upon themselves to heal the relationship between the Arcanists and the Vaccars, something the Order did not think would be possible for several thousand more years. In addition, the Grey family was our line of defense against the artifacts the Ancient Ones left behind, safeguarding and studying them for our protection. They kept not only unsuspecting Arcanists, but also Vaccars, safe from the Ancient One's cruel machinations. In light of his passing, the Elder Mages called a meeting with the members of the High Council to discuss how the Order could best honor Jack, and we came up with three solutions."

Aephes held his hand out before him, and a white-gold circular stone rose from the platform. A grand tree with thousands of branches and grasping roots was carved deeply into the rock, with the sun rising on the right side of the tree and two descending crescent moons on the left.

"That's—" Isaac began.

"That's us. Our family..." Alison breathed.

"First, this symbol of the Grey family will be displayed here, in the Courtyard of Ages, to honor Jack and his family's legacy. Further, those who lost their lives will be immortalized here in the Curtains of Yesterday, allowing family members to see their loved ones until the end of time. One needs only to look at the curtains and the person whom you are thinking of will appear."

Isaac turned as Alison gasped in disbelief, her eyes locked on a curtain.

"It's Sigmund," she choked out.

Isaac looked to the curtain too, holding Sigmund's name in his mind. Slowly, the old man's visage appeared clear as day and grumpy as ever on the crimson cloth. The image was uncanny, almost as if Sigmund himself were standing right there, just a few feet away.

A twinge of pain shot through his heart. For all the grief he probably gave Sigmund, Isaac couldn't imagine a world where Sigmund wasn't there begrudgingly guiding him along.

And yet, here he was, living in that world.

"Second..." Aephes continued.

He motioned to the men who walked up with him. They slowly pulled the cloth away, revealing a detailed portrait of Jack. Isaac felt his heart skip a beat and his throat grow tight at the sight of Jack's beaming grin. Like Sigmund, the details of the painting were so vivid that it felt like Jack was there in the flesh.

"Second, as many of you are aware, Jack was offered the position of Archmage a few hundred years ago. A position that, at the time, he declined so he could focus all his efforts on the Grey family and his missions there. Since then, the Archmage seat has been left empty by the Elder Mages, as they saw no other Arcanist as being fit for the role. To honor him, the Elder Mages have decided to give Jack the title of Archmage posthumously, and enshrine him forever in the Hall of the Archmages, where he belongs. With that being said, the Elder Mages would like to pay their respects and announce the last dedication."

Fervent whispers erupted throughout the crowd.

"The Elder Mages? Here?" he heard someone ask.

Admittedly, Isaac knew very little about the Elder Mages. He only knew that they were the heads and the founders of the Order of Dormiri. They were so old their age practically didn't matter anymore. They mostly kept to their tower, so for anyone to see them that wasn't a High Council member was a rarity.

Aephes stepped to the side just as two men and two women appeared in a flash of purple and black light.

One woman was extremely tall, reminding Isaac of Sasha from the Trials, but with blazing blonde hair and swirling purple eyes. Like the rest of them, she wore a white coat with the Order of Dormiri's symbol emblazoned in red on the cuffs.

The other woman was remarkably short compared to the first, her appearance akin to a doll. She had long, dark red hair like blackened blood. A gray cloth with a single, large black eye painted at the center covered her real eyes. Beneath her white cloak, she wore a long, dark blue dress that shimmered like ocean waves against her body. She cast a soft, sweet smile out at the crowd.

The man to the right of the doll-woman was missing his left arm, the coat sleeve tucked back into itself. His hair was fiery red and in wild tufts, just like Margaret's. His eyes were a burning amber that, unlike the other Elder Mages so far, pierced Isaac with harsh indifference and contempt.

All of them stood around and slightly behind the last man. Tall with copper skin, short brown hair, and a lean physique that made him look like a bronze statue of a soldier come to life. He had kind hazel eyes that seemed to pull you in the longer you stared.

"It is my pleasure to introduce to you the Elder Mages: Alycca, Ailith, Gideon, and Tor," Aephes announced.

All the Elders except for Gideon—who stared out at everyone with an icy glare—bowed their heads.

"Thanks, Aephes," Tor said. His accent was strange, unlike anything Isaac had ever heard before. It was... old, perhaps almost Elvish.

"Welcome, everyone. I want to address the Grey family directly—Gideon, stop glaring or you're going back," Tor paused. Gideon growled and turned his head away from the crowd, refusing to look at them without the intent to kill.

"Thank you. I'm sorry. As I was saying... To the Grey family, we are truly sorry for your loss. Jack was a remarkable man who, especially in his younger years, certainly kept us on our toes with his antics. I had the distinct pleasure of training him and was lucky enough to call him my friend. There are few people who could hold such raw potential as Jack and still remain pure of heart. He was nothing short of incredible. I know no one here will soon forget Jack Grey."

Tor paused again to walk over to Jack's portrait. He looked over it for a few moments and smiled back at it.

"To truly honor Jack's spirit, the Elders have decided to make some drastic changes to how the Order functions. When we first founded the Order, it was to honor our teacher, Dormiri—a Primis who risked his life to teach the Luminares how to use magic. To honor him, the Order was constructed as a sanctuary for all Arcanists to learn. To grow. To seek shelter from the ire of the Vaccars. During those thousands of years, the Order has been largely neutral. Never moving or wishing to draw any more attention toward it than it already had. We did so because we thought we were doing the best for our Arcanists. By staying away, the Vaccars left us alone. We always hoped that one day the sins of our forefathers might be forgiven.

"Then Jack Grey came, and he dared to confront the problem directly by showing the Vaccars that we are not the monsters who ruled over mortalkind in the past. He slowly whittled away at the wall the Vaccars had built between us. To our surprise, it was working. For the first time in thousands of years, Vaccars and Arcanists started to talk. But Jack did more than just begin to mend our relationship with the world. Jack took it upon himself, and his family, to protect everyone from the Ancient One's artifacts. Dangerous magical technologies designed with one purpose in mind: to kill. These missions are too important to let die with Jack Grey."

Tor paused to gaze over the crowd, looking at each person. Isaac felt a chill go down his spine as his gaze passed over him.

"It is for that reason that the Order will be taking a more proactive role," Tor continued. "The Order will no longer be a passive entity. From this moment forward, the Order will be putting together teams of powerful, capable Arcanists to hunt down, collect, and study the remaining artifacts left behind by the Ancient Ones. Further, the Order will be communicating with the Seven Kingdoms of Man and letting every king, queen, lord, and lady know that we are here for them in Jack Grey's stead. We will foster the world Jack dreamed of, where the sins of the Ancient Ones are forgotten and the world can be made anew."

Applause erupted all around him in thunderous waves. Even Alison had joined in, her gaze locked onto Jack's picture, tears streaming down her face.

For the first time in days, Isaac genuinely smiled. He clapped his hands together, applauding as loudly as he could. The portrait and everything was nice, but to see that Jack and his family had made such a profound difference that even the Elders took notice and decided to take action…

It felt good.

It almost felt like everyone wasn't really gone.

Isaac locked eyes with Tor again. He stared at Isaac with a patient, silent understanding that reminded him of how Jack would look at him.

"All members of the Grey family are more than welcome to stay here for as long as they like," Tor said once the applause had subsided. "We will house, feed, and train you indefinitely. We would be honored to share in your experience and knowledge. Anything you would like to add, Aephes?"

Aephes shook his head and bowed. "No, Elder."

Tor nodded. "Thank you all for coming. Please, find a Grey and show them some kindness in these dark times. It was a pleasure to see you all."

The Elders—besides Gideon—bowed their heads once more and disappeared in the blink of an eye. The platform Aephes created lowered until the Grey symbol monument was at ground level. The portrait was wrapped up again and carried off, with Aephes trailing behind.

"C'mon, we're supposed to meet everyone at the garden," Alison said, dragging him through the dispersing crowd.

* * * * *

The discussion with the family was lengthy but, in the end, reached the conclusion Alison had been alluding to earlier. Most of them had decided to stay with the Order, while others were going to strike out on their own.

No one wanted to rebuild.

With the Order taking up Jack's primary duties that the Greys used to oversee, they saw no reason to resurrect the family he had created. They thought the Order taking over would have been what Jack wanted.

"We're doing what we always did, but now it's with the Order. We're still helping realize his dream," they argued.

The meeting ended, with most people going their separate ways, leaving only Alison and Isaac in the garden.

"I don't understand why they wouldn't want to rebuild..." Alison said defeatedly. The pain on her face was like a knife in Isaac's stomach.

"Well, it was as they said: the Order is now committed to carrying out Jack's mission. It makes sense for most to just stay here."

"It's not just about what Jack did. It's about what the family stood for. What it did for other people—people like us. Didn't that mean anything to them?" Alison frowned at Isaac's indifferent expression. "Didn't it mean anything to you?"

Isaac leaned back on his palms, blades of grass pushing their way between his fingers. He looked up and closed his eyes as a cool spring breeze washed over him, bringing the fresh scent of flowers into his nose.

"Of course it meant something to me," Isaac said finally. "Without Jack, without the Greys, I would have nothing."

"So why not fight harder for this?"

Isaac sighed, his finger unconsciously playing with a blade of grass. "I'm just not ready to restart yet. Maybe someday, but... not now. Not yet. I need to take some time for myself, I think, before jumping into something of that magnitude."

Alison brought her knees up to her chest and wrapped her arms tightly around them, resting her chin on her knees.

"I would love nothing more than to rebuild the Grey family to be exactly how I remembered it. To give people the same opportunity that I had. I want to live out my days with you and go on adventures together. That's all I want out of life," she said, then smiled as Isaac fumbled for a response.

"Don't worry, I understand that my goal of creating a new Grey family is unrealistic, at least right now. I need more experience first. I also know that you've been going through a lot, so that'd be a lot for me to demand of you."

Isaac smiled. "Thank you."

She was silent for a while before speaking again. "I think I'm going to take Mikael up on his offer and do more contracts with him. I think the Venatores would be a good place to get the experience I'm looking for. Would you want to come with me? I'll still be living and training here, obviously, but... I really want to do this."

Isaac stared into her eyes, unrelenting determination twinkling in them. It wasn't hard to tell that she yearned for adventure. At one point, Isaac was the same way. Always looking forward to the next mission. But now...

Isaac felt a chill run down his spine at the thought of facing the vampires again. Even if he faced them down with Mikael and Alison again, there was no guarantee that they'd survive.

"I think I need to focus on training first, but... I'd like to at least go with you sometimes. Maybe wait in a town nearby when you go on these missions. Wouldn't be good for me to stay locked up in the Order all the time."

Alison smiled amusedly. "No, I don't think they are in need of any more lifeless statues lurking around the halls."

"I'll rejoin you someday, I promise, I just..." Isaac paused as he felt the tightness growing in his chest again. The feeling from the Temple, the Trials, and the vampire contract welling up inside him at the mere thought of going out again.

"I just need time."

Alison scooted herself closer and wrapped her arms around him. Isaac returned the hug, nuzzling against her neck, letting the warmth of her body wash over him. He took a deep breath, taking in her berry-scented skin, and felt his entire body relax as if every inch of him had been holding its breath. His thoughts, for the moment, stopped.

If only we could be this way forever.

"Oi! Isaac! Alison!"

They pulled away from each other just enough to see Olfen and Meri running down the steps into the garden with Olyen and Fraunt trailing closely behind.

"How're you two holding up?" Meri asked, sitting down next to Alison.

"We're doing better, I think." Alison glanced quickly at Isaac and smiled.

"Best as I can be right now," Isaac said, watching Fraunt as he circled him like a predator stalking its prey.

"And have you two decided what you're doing?" Olfen asked warily, standing with Olyen in front of them.

Alison nodded. "Yes, we'll be staying here at the Order, at least for the time being."

Olfen's face broke into a huge grin as he wrapped his arms around both of them and lifted them into the air. "Ahh, I'm relieved to hear that."

"Maybe I should've left," Isaac coughed out, feeling as if his ribs were about to crack again.

Olfen laughed and set them down.

"I am glad you are staying," Olyen whispered.

"Sorry if we interrupted anything, but a group of us are meeting in the dining hall in a few minutes for a welcome feast for you Grey folk. Would you care to join?" Olfen asked.

"We'd love to." Alison grabbed Isaac's hand.

"Fantastic." Olfen clapped Isaac on the back, and led them toward the dining hall.

CHAPTER THIRTY-TWO

Adara's footsteps fell silently in the dirt as she navigated her way through the thick underbrush of the forest. A small magelight hung over her shoulder, her only means of seeing clearly since the large, dark clouds had blocked out the moons for most of the night.

"Another meeting..." A chill went down Adara's spine. It wasn't that she didn't mind talking to the master. It was just the two of them she couldn't stand.

Especially in the months since Jack Grey's death, they have been particularly nasty about her unsuccessful attempts at locating the artifact room. It certainly wasn't because of lack of trying on her part. Jack had so carefully protected the room that it was nearly impossible to find through magical means.

Which left Adara no choice but to search the hard way: scouring every inch of Eutrox and Aesus to find where Margaret could've moved the damn room to. If they asked for a status update now, she wouldn't have a satisfactory answer.

Again.

She toyed with different theories as to why this meeting had been called. Something important must have come to the master's attention. He wasn't too keen on meeting frequently. Coming out too often could lead to unwanted attention. He was, after all, Creation's most hunted being. He had to be careful.

Adara cursed as she stumbled, her foot catching on a root. After several minutes, her magelight finally illuminated the deceptively small pitch-black tent. From the outside, it could be interpreted as any other traveler's camp for the night.

But she knew better.

She ran her hands over her clothes to smooth them before lowering her head and stepping through the flaps of the tent.

The inside was a large, cozy space that smelled like a bakery. The soft, dark carpet beneath her felt as if she were walking on a cloud. Swaths of colorful cloth and banners hung from the ceiling, each representing one of the seven Archangels of Heaven or the six Raigurs of Hell.

A long bookcase covered most of the back wall, with aged leather-bound books with spines too faded to read. To her right was a long wooden table with equally long benches. The table was littered with newly baked sweets and fresh fruit. A roaring fire lapped at the fireplace walls on the left side of the room, warming the chairs and their occupants that gathered around it.

Eyes like fire—a fierce, beautiful amber color—pulled her attention to them. The gaze warmed her from her center, as if she were being wrapped in a blanket. The eyes were like beacons of light against his dark skin. His brown hair was pulled back into a tight knot behind his head, making his scarred face look long and narrow.

Her heart skipped a beat when she saw the sword sitting in his lap. One of his hands lay half on the dark leather hilt and half on the silver cross-guard, and his other hand rested on the white scabbard. The sword was removed slightly from its housing, just enough so that she could see the beginning of the dazzling gold blade.

Lux. The sword that embodies light itself. It was breathtaking. And it belonged to *him.*

Adara smoothed out her clothes again, making sure she looked as presentable as possible.

"Xyteres." Adara bowed at the waist.

"Nevermind any of that." The kindness in his voice always startled her, even after all this time. "Come. Sit."

"Sit. Stay. Good dog," Devlin mocked. He had one arm slung over the back of the chair and one leg kicked up on the arm.

Adara locked eyes with Devlin and snarled as she took a seat beside Xyteres. He flashed a cheeky grin back.

"You call me a dog, yet I was not the one discarded by my family like a puppy they didn't want," Adara snapped back.

Devlin sat up, his smile disappearing from his face.

"Are you two done?" The man sitting next to Devlin interjected, stopping Devlin before he could respond. His long white hair hung down into his boyish face, making his crystal blue eyes look like gems nestled in snow.

Adara didn't care much for Nyx either, but, at the very least, he seemed to reign Devlin in.

Sometimes.

"Thank you all for coming," a voice hummed out from the sword, filled with a patience and kindness that could come only from another world. Adara felt a jolt of electricity run down her spine, her body tingling and warm.

Ranatrael. She thought, enamored.

"Not like we had much of a choice, eh?" Devlin said.

Ran chuckled—oh, what a divine sound!—"No, I suppose not," Ran said. "I suppose you are all aware as to what this may be about."

They all nodded.

"The kid," Nyx offered, leaning forward, clasping his hands together.

"Yes." His voice was so light and soft, Adara felt like she was floating down an easy stream.

"Since Jack's death, we know he went to the Order, effectively making it impossible for us to attack directly without drawing too much attention. With Zet gone, if we send anyone to the Order, it will surely draw the immediate attention of the Dogmata. They claim not to observe too much of what happens down here, but their eyes are always looking outward... Especially anything that might involve me."

"I have heard that he and the girl leave the Order sporadically," Nyx added. "Adara, have you been able to ascertain a pattern to their departures?"

She shook her head. "No. I've devoted much of my time to trying to locate Jack's artifact room—"

"More excuses," Devlin scoffed.

Adara felt her blood boil. "Would you like to hunt down the most powerfully guarded room in the entire world, save for the one you're sitting in?"

"I'm sure I would've found it by now."

"Enough. Both of you," Nyx snapped.

Devlin began to speak, but waved his hand at Adara and closed his mouth.

"Who's a good doggie?" Adara mocked in a baby-like tone.

"My friends," Ranatrael interrupted as Devlin was about to retort. "I do not wish for us to fight amongst ourselves. We cannot do anything together if we aren't united. While the missing room does set us back, it is nothing we cannot overcome. We clearly underestimated our adversaries. We thought sending Laydin after Isaac would've been enough. It wasn't. We thought that Adara going after the artifact room alone would've been enough. It wasn't. No plan ever executes the way you hope it will. It is for that reason that we must adapt and proceed with what has been left for us to use. Understood?"

They all nodded. Adara let out a sigh of relief. Ranatrael was an honest man. Fair. Sensible. She appreciated his tact.

Especially when it came to shutting Devlin up.

"Now, yes, it has been difficult to locate Isaac—and the room—but Xyteres might have a solution at least to the former."

"Yes." Xyteres cleared his throat. "There is talk that a Grey—a woman—has been assisting a Venatores named Mikael Gilano in interfering with a Pure Blood's operation..."

"Vladimyr, eh? They're pissing him off?" Devlin asked.

"Indeed," Xyteres said.

"This woman must be Alison Grey, yes?" Nyx asked. "Would explain their departures from the Order if she's working with the Venatores."

"Yes," Xyteres confirmed.

"So… what are we going to do with that, then?" Devlin questioned. "We're asking him for help, aren't we?"

Ranatrael let out a heavy sigh. "Yes… unfortunately."

"You really want Isaac that badly that you'd work with a fucking *vampire*?" Devlin spat on the floor. "We don't *need* my brother. We haven't so far. Why would we need him now? Are you that afraid of Heaven and Aethaniel, hm?"

The room was silent for a moment. Adara held her breath, anxious to see how Ranatrael—or Xyteres—would respond. She had never known Ranatrael to be aggressive, but she had also never heard someone challenge his decision so brazenly.

"I'm glad you asked, Devlin," Ran answered calmly. "I am not afraid of Heaven, or my brother, but I do know what both are capable of. And I do not know what kind of state I will be in once I am freed from this… prison… that my siblings put me in. Since it has taken me this long to recover enough strength to speak through my weapon, I imagine I will not be in a good place when I return. It is for that reason that I need as much protection and as much time as possible to recover. I anticipate that my power will return quickly once I am released, but in those first few minutes where I am like a fledgling again, I will need help.

"What's more, I desire nothing more than to settle this conflict with as few deaths as possible, though I have not been successful in that regard. Perhaps with a Xyar on our side, Heaven will back down and not bother with fighting. I have never—*ever*—wished for the battle that Heaven brought to me. I did not want to fight my siblings. I did not want to kill Jack Grey. Doing so pained me greatly because I knew how much he meant to Isaac. But, at the same time, I knew Jack Grey had to be removed or else he would pose a serious problem. I make these kinds of decisions every day. It is the price I must pay to advance what I know in my heart to be right, even if all of Creation refuses to see it."

"You truly think that there is no other way to win, then?" Devlin pressed.

"I think there are multiple paths to victory, but I prefer the one that's *not* paved by blood and bone. I would at least like to offer Isaac the chance to side with me, and show him where I am coming from."

"And if he refuses you, Lord of Light?" Devlin interrogated.

"Then I will do what I must. I cannot allow Heaven to gain a Xyar."

Devlin rolled his eyes, throwing his hands up in the air. "We'll see. So, what does Vladimyr propose?"

"We spoke with Vladimyr after it became clear that our interests aligned, even if superficially: we both want to find the ones attacking his operation. If we can find Alison and Mikael, we can find Isaac. Vladimyr has already begun an extensive hunt for them and has assigned his second in command to find them. Vladimyr's actions are not of any interest to the Dogmata, and Aethaniel will not step in to interfere with Isaac's life due to the pact he made with the Dogmata. So, we have arranged for Vladimyr to help us locate Isaac and help convince him to join our side."

"What does he want in return?" Nyx asked.

"He has asked that, once we have completed our battles against Heaven, we supplement his forces with Demons," Xyteres answered.

Devlin scratched his chin. "Vladimyr is fine with him only getting Mikael, and not Isaac's bitch as well? Doesn't seem like he'd be willing to part with half a prize."

"The terms of the agreement are conditional," Xyteres said. "If Isaac refuses to join Ranatrael, then he, Alison, and Mikael are given to Vladimyr. However, if Isaac sides with us, Vladimyr has agreed to back down."

"If Isaac does refuse, what then? Wasn't he a vital part of your plan?" Adara asked, giddy at being able to speak with him directly.

"He could be," Ranatrael admitted. "But, he can just as easily be a terrible enemy, so, if he doesn't join, or won't at least hear me out, I cannot risk him Ascending... We'd make other preparations."

"Are you sure you want to work with this vampire?" Nyx spat out the word *vampire* with disgust.

"I do not want to work with him," Ranatrael confessed. "But currently our interests align, and we have to use what we can to avoid drawing the Dogmata's attention."

"Fine." Nyx leaned back in his chair.

"How do we plan on 'convincing' Isaac to join us? What makes you think he'll side with us? With you?" Devlin questioned.

"Another good question, Devlin. You will be playing a major role in that endeavor. Once Isaac is discovered, you will meet with him as soon as possible and work to show him why what we're doing is right."

"You've got to be shitting me." Devlin stood from his chair. "I'm not doing it."

"Devlin—"

"*NO!*" Devlin roared. "You're out of your *fucking* mind. Perhaps all that time locked away has made you delirious. Find someone else." Devlin turned and began to storm off.

"Devlin. It can be no one else." Ranatrael's voice stopped Devlin. "Once Isaac remembers that you're his brother, he will listen to you. What happened between you two wasn't fair, but it also wasn't his fault."

"I do not want to see him..." Devlin said slowly.

"I know you don't." Adara could almost hear Ranatrael smile patiently through the sword. "But we need you, Devlin. The hatred that Heaven harbors towards Hell and the indifference they have towards mortals must end. Help me end it and make sure that what happened to your mother never happens again."

Devlin's shoulders slumped forward. A defeated position that Adara had never seen Devlin take before.

"Fine..." Devlin sighed, "Just tell me what to do."

"Everyone will receive final instructions shortly. Thank you, Devlin. This means a great deal to me."

Devlin threw a hand in the air. "Yeah, yeah..."

"Does anyone have any further questions or objections?" Ranatrael asked.

The room was silent.

"Nyx and Devlin, I will be in contact with you shortly," Xyteres said, his fingers drumming silently along the scabbard. "Adara, continue your search for the artifact room. We cannot free Ranatrael without it."

"Understood," Adara said, while the other two nodded.

I won't let you down. She thought, her eyes fixated on Ranatrael. As she stared at Lux, she was filled with a sense of hope that made her skin tingle with renewed optimism.

"You are all dismissed. Thank you again for granting me an audience," Ranatrael said.

Adara stood and bowed to Xyteres and Ranatrael, while Devlin and Nyx walked out of the tent.

* * * * *

"They're a rowdy bunch, aren't they?" Ranatrael said once they had all left.

"Indeed. But nothing I have not dealt with before," Xyteres said, watching the flames in the fire.

Ranatrael chuckled. "You're quite right about that."

"How are you feeling with everything?"

"I've been wondering the same thing," Ranatrael mused, Lux vibrating as he hummed. "To be honest, I'm still uneasy. I know what I must do, and I am taking the steps to do it, but..."

"It's difficult, isn't it?"

"Yes. Very. I never wanted any of this, Xyteres. This has all been thrust upon me. I no longer see myself as an arbiter of my own fate, but more as an observer to the events being played before me, already predestined, like a play."

"You have shit taste in plays," Xyteres chuckled.

Ranatrael laughed. "Apparently so. I hope that, at the end of it all, the peace I envision will be worth the weight of the blood I have spilled to build it."

Xyteres nodded solemnly. "Are you beginning to regret your decisions?"

"No, no... No regrets, just an old being's wish for things to have gone differently."

"Don't we all?"

Ranatrael chuckled again. "Quite. I am going to retire for now, Xyteres. I need to rest and build up more of my strength to whittle away at these seals. I entrust myself to you, as always."

"Do not worry, Ran, I have you." Xyteres pushed Lux completely into the scabbard and, as he did, Ranatrael's presence left the room.

They had spent too much time here. Any longer and it'd give the Dogmata's scouts enough time to pick up on Ranatrael's presence, even as meager as it is now.

Xyteres waved a hand, and the tent around him dissolved, leaving him alone in a dark forest. He paused and looked down at Lux.

I hope this is worth it in the end, too, my friend.

Xyteres stepped forward and left the forest, and entered a place that both chilled him to the bone, and made his flesh feel like it were boiling from the heat simultaneously. The only place that Heaven was hesitant to enter in their search for Ranatrael.

The place Xyteres called home.

CHAPTER THIRTY-THREE

Isaac pulled his cloak tighter around his body as a cold breeze washed over him. He continued to meander down the path back toward Ritka, a small town near the border of Efona, the furthest south that Isaac had ever been. Which he assumed would've meant warmer weather despite the leaves beginning to change color, but he was wrong.

He looked up at the trees that canopied the well-worn path to Ritka, watching as the afternoon sun made the orange and yellow leaves seem to glow. Another breeze made the leaves rustle, bringing with it the crisp smell of encroaching autumn.

Isaac shuffled back through the town, watching as people uneasily skirted away from him back into their patchwork wooden huts. He unconsciously rubbed at the Grey symbol on his cloak. The people in the last few towns they had been to weren't too keen on having Arcanists around but, at the very least, they left them alone.

Though Isaac did think he was pressing his luck a bit after doing the same loop around town for the fourth or fifth time. Pretty soon they might start thinking he's putting some kind of curse on it.

But he had to do something to pass the time while Alison and Mikael finished their contract. After Jack's funeral, Alison had been quick to reach out to Mikael and start taking up whatever missions she could. Mikael was happy to oblige. After the contract they had done to find Cela, the Venatores became particularly interested in other missing person's reports. That had become Alison and Mikael's singular focus for the past year: taking contracts to find missing people to see if they were somehow connected to the "bigger hunt."

Most of the time, they were.

Whatever operation this Pure Blood vampire was running, Mikael and Alison were doing their best to interrupt it. Something that Isaac had warned against after they found a rather large nest of vampires. But they both reassured him that they had the Venatores backing them so, if anything happened, they could go to them.

Isaac felt an old, almost unrecognizable yearning for adventure, for helping people. The faces of the people they helped return to their families when they went after Cela were burned into his memory. Perhaps he could...

No. He shook his head, his hands beginning to tremble, the hunger for taking up contracts again vanishing as quickly as it came.

I'm not ready yet. Isaac thought, plopping himself down under a tree just outside of the town. He placed his backpack behind him and leaned into it, using it as a pillow.

Perhaps I'd be better suited to doing what Olfen, Olyen, and Meri are doing now? He mused, watching the leaves dance in the wind. Those three had volunteered to help the Order work with some of the Kingdoms, as Jack had done, to build relationships with the Vaccars. Like him and Alison, they left the Order periodically because of it. From what he gathered, they quite enjoyed it, and they seemed excited to be helping to make a difference.

But... the thought of having to deal with the kings and queens of the Seven Kingdoms didn't exactly intrigue him. Sure, it might be interesting for a time, but how long would it take until Isaac slipped up and suddenly he was marked for death?

Given his mouth and luck, he guessed not very long at all.

Isaac watched a few of the townspeople huddle behind one of the huts nearby, failing in their mission of being stealthy, if that was at all their goal. They pointed at him and whispered in a hushed, hurried tone.

Isaac sighed, not eager to move from his spot.

Hopefully, Alison and Mikael would return soon.

*   *   *   *

Alison winced as she turned her back on Trovst. A humble farming town just over an hour's walk away from Ritka, with fields that stretched impossibly far out into the horizon. The farms weren't big enough to supply any kingdom, but it was enough to hold the community together. Under different circumstances, she might've enjoyed her trip to the quaint village with its crude huts and equally gruff residents.

Their contract was originally for a missing person in Ritka. Another isolated town in the middle of nowhere that made an easy target for Vladimyr. However, their mission in Ritka led them to Trovst, where they learned that two young boys had gone missing as well. Farmhands. But in a town this small, anyone who was a farmhand was also family.

Alison glanced over her shoulder, doing her best to ignore the townspeople's icy glares as they watched her and Mikael leave defeatedly.

They hadn't been able to save anyone this time.

It was a first for them. In the forty-odd contracts she had done with Mikael, they had always managed to save *somebody*. But not this time. They had been able to find where they had been held captive easily enough, in a cramped cavern in the foothills that lined the west side of Trovst. But by the time they got there, there was no one around. From what Mikael could tell, they had left maybe only an hour before they had gotten there.

She glanced over at Mikael, who was rubbing his chin absently in thought.

"I can't believe we were too late," Alison said, her shoulders slumped forward, her sword—a gift from the Venatores at her initiation—slapped sadly against her thigh.

"Hmm..." Mikael hummed, his jaw set. "While I am upset that we could not help them, I'm afraid I am more troubled by something else."

"Care to share?"

"Well, for starters, vampires should not be moving during the day. Even if they moved them with horses, most wouldn't dare expose themselves in the sunlight when they are much weaker. And..."

Mikael paused, drumming his fingers against the pommel of his sword.

"And..." He continued, "They left too suddenly. Why? If they planned to move, why not move them the night prior? Or even tonight? It's as if they expected us to arrive."

He has a good point. She thought. Vampires should *not* be moving during the day. While it doesn't hurt them, being exposed for too long can sap them completely of their inhuman abilities. They could always hide in the shadows to regain some of their strength, but they wouldn't dare risk setting out during the day unless they had absolutely no choice.

"Perhaps Vladimyr is getting desperate and is moving his cattle during the day now to throw us off?" Alison offered.

Mikael shook his head. "I would be wary about calling him desperate. He may be irritated with our meddling, sure. But Vladimyr, according to our records, is one of the *oldest* vampires in existence with an army of vampires in the tens of thousands, if not more. Even after centuries of hunting, we do not know where he is located because he is so skilled at remaining concealed, just like his other Pure Blood brethren. No, if this is indeed his doing, it's because it is purposeful. He's doing it with a plan."

Alison shivered, suddenly feeling cold. There was an undertone of worry that she hadn't heard before in Mikael's voice that emphasized just how scary these Pure Bloods really were. Even the Lycans in the Venatores had only trace encounters with them over the millennia and, so far, the Pure Bloods had won every time.

Alison knocked into Mikael's shoulder as he stopped on the path suddenly, his eyes calm but alert.

"What is it?" she whispered, her hand racing to her sword as she focused on the sounds around her.

"We're being followed," Mikael whispered back, turning around in a circle.

All Alison could hear was the gentle rustle of the near-autumn leaves. The sound of small animals diving in and out of the underbrush. Birds chirping melodically together.

But beneath it all, very faintly, she could hear something else, a high-pitched scream like a banshee wailing in the night.

And it was coming from every direction.

The wind whipped around them and, in an instant, they were encircled by hooded figures in long dark cloaks that brushed against the ground. A mountainous hooded figure emerged from the trees in front of them, his hands raised. The rest of the hooded men dropped to one knee, their heads bowed.

"Wait." His voice was pleading and soft. The man slowly pulled back his hood as he approached them, revealing a tuft of curly, dirty-blonde hair and baby blue eyes.

And deathly pale skin.

Alison gripped the hilt of her sword and drew it slightly from its scabbard, the Rune of Fire glowing as it sensed her intention. She could feel the heat beginning to waft off the sword in slow, intense waves.

"I mean you no harm, truly," the man said, placing a hand over his heart. "You may know me. I am Staev."

"You know him?" Alison asked Mikael, noticing his hesitation to draw his blade.

He nodded slowly. "Aye, Vladimyr's second in command. Oh, the things we've heard about you…"

Staev's face seemed to turn red—if vampire's faces could do such a thing—and waved his hand dismissively. "I did what I had to do to survive. But I am not here to talk about my checkered past. I am here with a proposition… and a warning."

Alison and Mikael exchanged looks.

"What is it?" Mikael asked.

"Vladimyr is coming for you. Both of you," Staev said flatly. "I was personally charged with overseeing your discovery and capture. Something I had never intended to do. In truth, my scouts discovered you leaving the Order months ago, but I have been able to delay reporting their findings to Vladimyr. You no longer have that luxury. A scout who is not loyal to me was given the orders to hunt for you, and he found you. As we speak, Vladimyr is sending a division to Ritka with plans to ambush you once you arrive. They plan to take you two and Isaac captive but, if you hurry, you may be able to flee before they arrive. Or, at the very least, get a decent distance away."

Alison felt her chest tighten and could hear her heart pounding in her ears.

Isaac... They had left him completely alone back in Ritka. If those vampires got there before they were able to get him out...

"We have to get back. Now!" Alison started to leave, but Mikael grabbed her shoulder, stopping her.

"Why should we trust you? Why help us?" Mikael questioned calmly.

"Vladimyr must be killed," Staev said matter-of-factly. "None of us asked for this... *life*. We were forced into it. Condemned to it..." Staev's eyes grew distant and cold momentarily before speaking again. "For centuries my followers and I have been biding our time, gathering strength, waiting for the right moment to strike against him. When I heard that the Venatores, and now a Grey, were taking more aggressive action—enough to draw Vladimyr's attention—I knew our time had come. This is the chance that we have been waiting for. But I understand that trust is not given. It is earned."

Staev reached slowly into his cloak and retrieved a thick stack of wrapped parchment and tossed it to Mikael, who caught it against his chest.

"Inside that parchment you will find directions to Vladimyr's fortress, the Sanguine Keep. However, I will reserve the instructions for how to navigate through the cursed forest that surrounds it to myself until an agreement has been made between the two of us. I hope you understand.

"Now, I suggest that you move quickly to collect Isaac and head to Ahntwen to deliver that information. I have arranged for an associate of mine, a Pure Blood, to meet you in Vurt two weeks after you arrive in Ahntwen. He will wait there for an additional week for you, or another Venatores representative, to arrive. After that time, if we have received no word from you, then we go our separate ways forever."

A Pure Blood? Another one? Alison could tell by Mikael's expression that he was wondering the same thing, but decided not to press for any answers.

"I do not know if we can trust you yet, Staev, but you have taken a good step in the right direction," Mikael said, bowing his head slightly out of respect.

To Alison's surprise, Staev returned the gesture. "I will have a few scouts following the division coming after you to keep me updated. Unfortunately, these updates will be passed along to Vladimyr. I hope you understand. Please know that my men cannot aid you, no matter how much I may want them to. I cannot risk putting their lives in danger. I'm sorry."

Staev bowed his head again, his eyes downcast this time as if he couldn't meet their eyes, his face a hard mask of sorrow. Alison eyed him carefully. She was wary about trusting him, but if what he said was true, then they were all in danger, and they had to get moving. Quickly.

"Thank you, Staev... We'll be in touch." Mikael turned, starting back down the trail leading back to Ritka. "Come on, we don't have much time."

Alison nodded, taking off in a sprint down the path, her pack thumping almost as hard and heavy on her back as her pulse in her skull.

Please, Creator, let us make it back before they arrive.

* * * * *

Isaac threw open the tavern door and rushed outside, just as another knife flew by his head. He skidded across the dirt as he cut sharply to the right, sprinting toward the tree line. He stopped running once he was a few hundred feet into the woods, far enough back that he couldn't be seen from the road. Isaac looked down at his cloak, which was partially covered in thin, slimy gruel. He tried his best to wipe it off with his hands, but it just seemed to spread it around more. He should've known better than to try to break bread with the townspeople. Especially with how skittish they had been already about him.

Isaac's stomach growled loudly. He'd have to settle for the bread they had brought with them. Disappointed, he sat down and began rummaging through his pack.

A high-pitched howl made Isaac freeze. He closed his eyes and tilted his head, focusing as hard as he could. Perhaps he was just hearing things. Maybe it—

Isaac's eyes snapped open. The howl, while still almost imperceptible, was growing slightly louder and coming closer very quickly.

Isaac rolled forward, narrowly missing being tackled from the side as a black blur sped by where he had been sitting. Isaac turned around and locked eyes with the pale-faced creature that had almost carried him away like a toddler.

Vampire. Isaac shuddered. He hadn't seen one in over a year, but the sound they made when they moved was something that was hard to forget. The vampire rushed him again, slashing madly at him with its nails so long and sharp, they could've been talons. Isaac tried ducking out of the way, but was too slow, and found himself quickly cut in several places. How was he supposed to fight them again? Judging by the vampire's speed, he was a very low Generation. Even so, Isaac felt too out of practice to be able to keep up.

And he could hear another one closing in on him.

Isaac fell backwards as the vampire lunged at him, following him to the ground. His breaths became shallow, rapid, desperate fits to get air, his hands shaking as if he had just been struck by lightning. He had to get away somehow and get help. He had to get this *fucking* creature away from him.

Fire. Isaac thought, remembering back to the contract.

"Get off of me!" Isaac roared, flames erupting in front of him, guided by his still-shaking hands. The vampire tried to leap away, but had been too close to Isaac to avoid the torrent of flame. The creature stumbled backwards, its undead body quickly becoming engulfed in fire. It took one last shambling step forward before falling to the ground.

Isaac's heart pounded in his ears, almost drowning out the sound of the vampire that rushed him from behind. Isaac turned, fire spraying from his hands in a thick line, catching the vampire as it tried to strafe around it. The fire raged up the vampire's body, consuming it in seconds.

I have to get out of this forest. Isaac thought, extinguishing the small fires he had accidentally started. He wasn't equipped to handle them in this setting. But he'd have to do *something* until Mikael and Alison returned. But what could he do? What if a high Generation vampire showed up?

The hair on the back of Isaac's neck stood on end as he felt something looming over him. He spun around as another vampire appeared directly above him.

It must've used the trees to hide from me. Isaac thought as he rushed to bring his hands up. He was moving too slowly, and the vampire was coming too quickly. He wouldn't be able to kill it in time.

Isaac closed his eyes tightly, waiting for the vampire to strike. Instead, he felt an intense wave of heat rush by his head and heard the vampire scream. Isaac opened his eyes in time to see a stream of black fire push the vampire out of the way and reduce it to ashes.

Black fire? He had never seen, or even heard of, fire that burned like that. Whatever it was, it had to burn hot enough to incinerate the vampire in seconds.

"Are you alright?" someone asked from his side.

Isaac turned and saw a familiar-looking man, though he couldn't quite place where he knew him from. He had short, curly black hair and dark brown eyes that seemed to glare at the world with a predatory intensity. He was about Isaac's height and had the same caramel-colored skin as most mortals of the Seven Kingdoms.

Behind him, a white-haired man decapitated another vampire with what looked like a short knife.

"Are you alright?" the man repeated, taking a step closer.

Isaac shook his head free of its stupor. "Uh... yes, thank you. I'm fine."

Isaac's head began to ache, but not like he had been struck. It was a throbbing ache that sat deep in the depths of his mind. An ache that got stronger the longer he looked at the stranger.

Or maybe he wasn't a stranger. He looked so familiar… But from where?

"C'mon, we have to get to the village and protect them," he said, walking past him, his friend following closely behind. "More will be coming, and even though you are the target, it wouldn't be beneath them to attack other people if it meant getting to you."

The man paused. "Your friends should be here… where are they?"

How does he know about Alison and Mikael?

"Hold on a second, what're you talking about? Who are you?" Isaac asked, following after him.

Why am I following him? Despite Isaac not knowing who this person was, he instinctively wanted to trust him.

The pulsating in his head intensified.

"You could say Nyx and I are freelance hunters. We've been hunting vampires for years, snuffing them out where we can. Just a few days ago, we learned from a nest we wiped out that another division of vampires was being sent out here to capture a Venatores hunter and two Greys. We couldn't let that happen, so we set out immediately. I'd say we got here just in time."

Isaac felt his blood run cold. *Does this have something to do with what Alison and Mikael are doing? Are they in danger right now too?*

Isaac's head swam as the throbbing in his head grew to be almost unbearable. Isaac clutched at his skull, his fingers digging painfully into his scalp.

He knew this man from somewhere…

"I shouldn't be surprised that you don't recognize me."

Isaac locked eyes with him as he spoke again.

"After all, it's been many years since you've seen your brother."

Isaac's head erupted in pain as flashes of images exploded across his vision. They were grainy and hard to make out. He felt as if a dam in his mind had cracked, letting out only a trickle of information at a time.

He fell to his knees, doubling over. His head felt like someone had smashed it open with a hammer. More scenes played in his mind, slowly forming a fuzzy, cohesive whole. There were still parts missing, but he could see some of it...

He could see a boy, much younger than he was now, who matched the man's features exactly.

... And he was his brother.

Isaac looked up, tears streaming down his cheeks.

"Devlin?"

END OF BOOK 1